*For Ms. Connie*

The one who sits beside me

The one who said to me "Write."

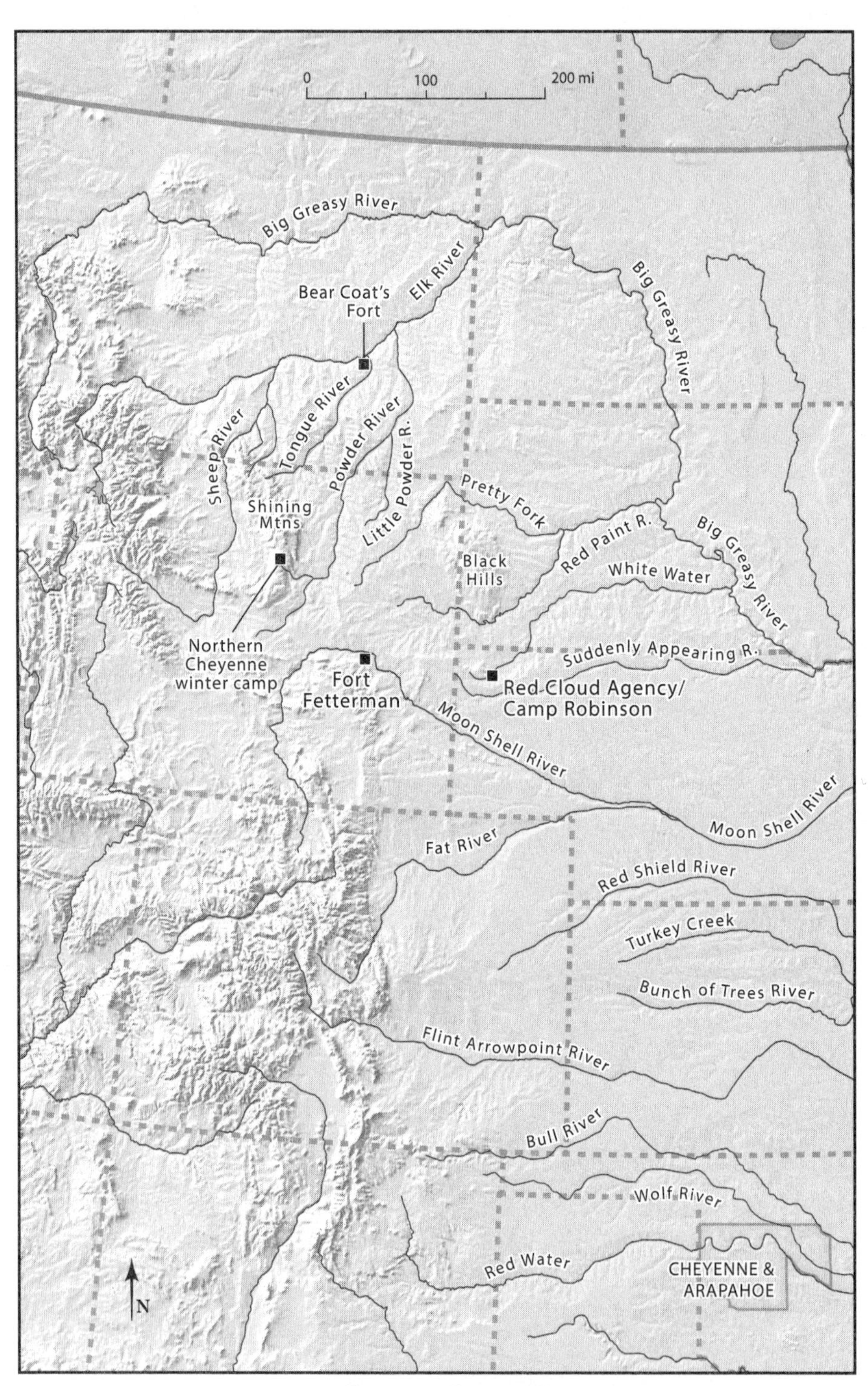


Cheyenne Country

# Table of Contents

# Preface

AT SOME POINT, EARLY IN THEIR LIVES, EVERY CHILD ON THE Northern Cheyenne Indian Reservation hears a rendition of the tale about "Our ancestors, long time ago." The story is always told with great pride, but often with little detail and few facts. Some are lucky and are born into a family where oral tradition is practiced as diligently as it was in the old days while the rest, a large majority in fact, are not quite so lucky. I was one of the not so lucky. I am the product of three generations of Indian boarding schools where civility was often beaten into us as the Indian was beaten out.

I recall visiting an old family cemetery with my father one summer when I was quite young. While there, I asked Dad if we had any famous relatives who were involved in Cheyenne history around the time of the fight at the Little Bighorn. He said that he wasn't sure but had heard that, "Your Grampa Rowland was supposed to have been a scout or something." That was it, my one and only Cheyenne history lesson from my father.

I did have the benefit of hearing many of the old Cheyenne stories from friends and other relatives as I grew up, but the same story would often change based on who told it. A hundred years had gone by and it seemed that everyone had a grandparent who told them a different version of it based on what their own grandparents, the ones who lived through it, shared with them. Some stories were changed, or possibly never were told, out of fear of retribution. Those that were told often came from each individual's unique perspective based on where they were during certain events and how involved they were. Because of this, I realized that any cohesive familial rendering of Cheyenne history was, like Cheyenne tradition and Cheyenne language, at risk of going the way of the buffalo.

The good news is that others have realized the dilemma as well, and changes have started to take place. Early ethnographers and modern academics have provided the Cheyenne a great service by recording many different aspects of their remarkable history. In addition, in 1999, the legislature of Montana, the state within which the Northern Cheyenne Reservation is located, passed Article X, Section 1(2), commonly known as the Indian Education for All act which states that the state recognizes the distinct and unique cultural heritage of American Indians and is committed in its educational goals to the preservation of their cultural heritage.

Traditional tribal societies have seen growth in their numbers, and the tribal government has made historical preservation a priority. The tribal community college, Chief Dull Knife College, has collected and preserved documents, recorded oral histories, and has committed substantial time, effort, and resources into a language preservation program at the school. Many, such as this author, have begun to research our history and write our own understanding and unique Cheyenne perspective of our ancestors, their stories, and the complex interpersonal relationships that many outside the tribe aren't raised with. If nothing else, we Cheyenne are a resilient people.

In addition to writing this three volume historical novel series, *The Cheyenne Story*, I have written non-fiction historical articles and, lately, been fortunate enough to have become involved in a project called *The Cheyenne Healing Trail*, which is an effort to memorialize the path traversed by a group of Cheyenne when they escaped the confines of a barracks prison at Fort Robinson in northwest Nebraska. Our work on this trail, along with the time and effort put forth to build the existing commemorative monument at the site (by those who were involved before me), represent the growing passion behind the determined effort of the Cheyenne people to honor their ancestors, recognize their history and to reclaim both as their own. We are all healing through our learning, re-framing, and sharing of our own rich tribal history.

This book, and those that follow, are dedicated to that healing movement. I am honored to be able to participate in any project that brings an awareness of our ancestor's efforts to secure our homeland for each new generation.

I acknowledge those who have helped this book become a reality in the back pages, but one organization that I must recognize forthwith is the Mari Sandoz Heritage Society. It was very important to Sandoz while she was alive to support the writers of Plains history. I have often said that I feel I write in the spirit of Sandoz, and whether others agree or not, there can be no argument about the fact that the Mari Sandoz Heritage Society operates in her spirit. After providing me with a generous endowment to research their Sandoz collection at Chadron State College in Chadron, Nebraska, they also helped with publication costs. *Nea'eše* my friends, I am deeply honored and gratified by your generosity.

In light of historical information made available since 1953, when Sandoz published her often-cited book, *Cheyenne Autumn*, and out of respect for her desire to portray the Cheyenne story accurately, I feel I must mention a departure from her writings in my depiction of Little Wolf's family.

In *Cheyenne Autumn*, Sandoz presents five members of Little Wolf's family: his wives, Feather on Head and Quiet One; two sons, Wooden Thigh and Pawnee; and one daughter, Pretty Walker. In her research she notes that Pretty Walker is but a nickname, and in the book she states that she had been called that for so long her real name had been forgotten. Indian census rolls for the Tongue River Agency, beginning in 1885 and going forward consistently, show the following: Little Wolf's wives' names were Lightning and Two Woman and no sons are shown in the household; however, there are three daughters, Chopping Woman, White Voice (Pretty Walker's age), and Medicine Woman. (The rolls also indicate a few younger children in the household, which I address in the end notes.)

Medicine Woman received the anglicized name of Lydia and grew up to marry Wild Hog's youngest son, Bird, thus becoming Lydia Wild Hog. In telling her personal story, she mentioned that her childhood name was Day Woman. I have taken that to mean her childhood prior to at least 1885 when she was known as Medicine Woman.

These are the names that I use to portray the family. Although the sons are not included on the census rolls, I do include Wooden Thigh and Pawnee, as they are in fact recorded elsewhere in the census material.

This is a story about the Cheyenne people. I'm proud to say that my great-great grandfather played a role in many of the events that took place, but the story is, as it should be, about the people. Over the years much has been written about events experienced by the tribe but, with a few generalized exceptions, very little has been written about what took place in their hearts during those events, and that's a major oversight. We Cheyenne are more often led through this world by our hearts.

In general, most histories describe that our leaders were troubled, angered, or confused, and that our women and children were terrified, taken, or killed. That's it. That's pretty much what the books say about the Cheyenne capacity for emotion. My own personal experience of growing up, quite literally, in the middle of the tribe is quite different. I will attempt in this three-volume account to explore as much of the Cheyenne capacity for human emotion as I can, in particular their capacities for humor and familial love, especially for their children.

Some may regard this story as a tragedy, or a litany of wrongs wreaked upon an undeserving people. The fact is it is much more complex than that. It is a story about good people who are trying their best to do the right thing as they understand it. It also presents, the "fools on both sides," as the Lakota leader Red Cloud described them, who do little more than serve their own self interests. In reality, on any given day, we are all capable of being both good person and fool. We all have our failings, regardless of the culture we were raised in. In the face of those shortcomings, we hope that history will look back on us with an understanding if not forgiving eye. In the end, I hope the story will show that in addition to being resilient and passionate, the Cheyenne are also a forgiving people who understand that we are all human and all trying to do our best as we travel through this journey called life.

# List of Characters

THIS LIST OF SEVENTY-FOUR CHARACTERS IS BY NO MEANS COMPLETE but it does capture those primary and secondary characters considered more pertinent to the story. Some of the family members listed are not mentioned in this part of the story, but will be as the story unfolds in volumes two and three. In writing a story about any tribe one must remember that an entire tribe is involved and not just a representative sample or a few token figureheads. That approach has been taken far too often with indigenous people and overlooks the fact that each member is raised to consider the greater whole. This means the list also includes those who outside cultures might consider as being inanimate or mythical.

**Spiritual Entities**

- Sacred Buffalo Hat
- Sacred Arrows
- Winter Man
- Bear Butte
- Sweet Medicine
- Sun
- Wind

**Little Wolf Family**

- Little Wolf
- Lightning (wife)
- Two Woman (wife)
- Wooden Thigh
- Chopping Woman
- Walking Whirlwind

- White Voice
- Pawnee
- Day Woman

**Morning Star Family**

- Morning Star, a.k.a. Dull Knife
- Pawnee Woman (wife)
- Short One (wife)
- Medicine Club
- Hump
- Pure Woman
- Little Hump
- Standing Bull
- Trail Woman
- Broken Foot Woman
- Holding Woman
- Young Bird
- Going In First Woman
- Princess

**Bill Rowland Family**

- Bill Rowland,
- Sis Frog (wife)
- William Jr.
- James
- Alice Jane
- Willis
- Benjamin
- Zachary
- Jack
- Patrick
- Edward

**Brothers-in-law**

- Roan Bear
- Hard Robe
- Little Fish

**Wild Hog Family**

- Wild Hog
- Stands In The Lodge (wife)
- Blanche
- Bird

**Red Pipe Family**

- Red Pipe
- Iron Tooth Woman (wife)
- Gathering His Medicine
- Stands In The Clouds Woman
- Morning Woman

**Military Officers & Government Officials**

- Gen. George R. Crook
- Col. Ranald S. Mackenzie
- Lt. William P. Clark
- Lt. Hayden DeLany
- Lt. Henry W. Lawton
- John J. Saville, early Red Cloud Agent
- George W. Manypenny, 1876 Commission Chairman

**Councilmen, Society Members & Tribal Members**

- Antelope
- Bear Sitting Down
- Black Coyote
- Bobtail Horse
- Box Elder
- Bridge
- Gathering His Medicine
- Hail
- Last Bull
- Living Bear
- Medicine Top
- Necklace
- Old Crow
- Plenty Bears

- Plenty Camps
- Split Nose
- Starving Elk
- Turtle's Road
- Two Moons
- Vanishing Wolf Heart
- Walks Different
- Whetstone
- Wolf Tooth
- Young Two Moons

**Lakota**

- Crazy Horse
- Sitting Bull
- Carries The Drum
- Billy Garnett

# Winter Man's Warning

*EŠE'HE* HAD CLIMBED ABOVE THE EASTERN RIM OF THE VALLEY AND was well started on his daily walk across the sky when Little Wolf started his walk to the home of his friend, Split Nose. The Elk Soldier headman's lodge was on the other side of the camp, near where the warm spring fed into the creek. A skin of light frost had covered the ground during the night, so Little Wolf kept to where the grass had been trampled down during the prior day's activity, trying to keep his leggings dry.

This was their first morning in the new camp location; the lodges around him had all been raised just the day before. The people were still in the process of settling into their new home. Mounds of dirt and rocks were piled outside some of the lodges. The more industrious women had dug out the center of their lodge floors, and some had already staked their covers down to prepare their homes for a long, comfortable stay at the new campsite.

Others, mostly the younger women, had merely placed rocks around the edges of their lodge covers in the old way, choosing not to struggle with the difficult chores of digging or staking in the hard, rock-filled ground. Little Wolf made note of the better-prepared lodges to help him decide which invitations to dinner he might accept later in the cold winter.

A handful of women were leaving to collect firewood along the creek. They were chatting and joking with each other. Each carried a coil of rope on her shoulder to bundle the wood she would carry on their return. All looked eager to explore the creek's provisions. One of them, Walks Different, gave a smile and nod as she passed. The Sweet Medicine Chief gave a nod of his head and returned her friendly greeting.

Five moons earlier, at the first few camps after the big fight at the Little Sheep River, the chief's walks through camp had not been as warmly received. He had arrived at the large camp just shortly after the soldiers had all been killed on the hill above camp. Many thought, by his late arrival, that he might have actually helped the soldiers to find them.

It had taken much explaining by the middle-aged leader and those he had traveled with to assure the Cheyenne and Lakota doubters that they had only discovered the soldiers the day before and had followed them at a safe distance to see where they were going. People were just now beginning to trust him again, and Little Wolf was grateful, though he still wrestled with the guilt of not having been present when so many brave men had given up their lives.

A cutting wind suddenly gusted down the side of the mountain, as if someone had called for it to give the newly pitched lodges their first test of stability. The morning was already chilly, but this rogue wind carried an even colder bite, causing the short but stocky man to pull his buffalo robe up higher around his neck.

"*Vo'keme*, Winter Man, I hear you," he muttered into his robe. "You say you will be coming for your long visit with us soon. *Epeva'e*, I think you should come now. We are ready for you, and you will make the soldiers stay away."

The chief looked to the upper reaches of the tall, mountainous ridge to the west, but the only snow falling there was that which had blown from the branches of trees standing near the top. Winter Man had made his claim on these higher places during the last moon. The bad-tempered wind this morning was but a warning of his intent to eventually extend that claim.

"Ah! You never listen!" Little Wolf grumbled as he buried his face deeper into his robe and continued on his way, the wind pestering his leggings with each step.

The pile outside told the chief that the floor of Split Nose's lodge had been dug out; however, the cover had yet to be staked down. Other than light smoke coming from the lodge fire and a paint horse picketed nearby, there was little to indicate that anyone was home. He cleared his throat as he drew near the door, but he heard no response from inside. He gave a loud cough. Still no answer.

The sound of heavy footsteps and a sudden movement to his right caught his eye. He spun around to the sight of a huge naked man covered in frost and running toward him. The giant's eyes were wild and frantic. His long, unbraided hair was frosted white, giving him the appearance of a giant icicled porcupine. His frozen locks rattled against each other, and small chunks of ice sprinkled down around him as he ran straight at Little Wolf. "Aaahhh! *Hosovo'ne'eohtse*, step back!" the large man bellowed as he pounded past the chief and ducked inside the lodge. Little Wolf watched open-mouthed as the door flopped closed behind the shivering hulk.

"You missed a good swim, my friend!" a friendly voice called from behind him. Split Nose and three others, all bundled in robes, came trotting from the same direction as the frosted man. All were clearly feeling the chill of their frosty morning swim, which had been cut short because of the frigid wind. Their loose hair had stiffened with ice and clattered like gourd rattles as they jogged. Split Nose carried an extra robe in his arms.

"Wild Hog's robe was under mine, but he was too cold to look for it." He pointed with his chin. "Get in there with him. We are coming."

Little Wolf ducked into the lodge as the others hurried behind him, puffing away the cold that gripped them. Inside, the large man had already stacked more branches on the fire and was busy stirring the coals. Little Wolf moved over next to him and smiled as the entire group huddled around the revived flames. Each man held open his robe to capture as much heat as he could from the growing fire.

"*Nea'ěše, nea'ěše.*" A chorus of thank-yous chattered from around the circle. Had this been a larger group, with men from other warrior societies, they all would have made more of an effort to appear unaffected by the cold. However, given that it was just Elk Horn Scrapers here, they allowed themselves the luxury of shivering uncontrollably. The men laughed and visited as they began to warm, rubbing the heat into their limbs and stripping ice from their hair.

Little Wolf leaned toward Wild Hog. "Too bad I had to pray this morning, or I could have enjoyed the swim as much as the rest of you."

"I prayed from the creek all the way here." The large man joked back, "*Ma'heo'o*, do not let me freeze to death!"

"A smoke, a smoke," cried Bobtail Horse, one of the younger men. He pointed to his pipe bag with his chin. "That is always a good end to a swim."

Little Wolf passed the long beaded pouch to its owner, who had wrapped his robe now around his waist, having been sufficiently warmed by the fire. Bobtail Horse took the bag and began to slide the stem out. As he did so the faint sound of a howling wolf rose above the uneven whack, whack, whack of the wind slapping the lodge skin against its supporting poles. Shouts were heard from outside the lodge, then came the sound of running. Little Wolf listened for a moment and then rose and crawled behind those sitting to his right, moving toward the door.

"Get yourselves ready. I will go see what this is," he said.

Outside the lodge, people were running toward a low pass on the southwest side of camp. Four riders were descending the slope there, each howling like a lonely wolf. They drove three horses ahead of them. Even in the cold temperatures, the red soil in the valley remained loose and light, and the dust stirred up by the hooves of all seven animals was swept into a long plume that poured through camp.

The chief turned quickly to his left and walked against the stream of people making his way to the large Council Lodge that stood in the clearing at the center of camp.

Split Nose caught up with him, wearing only leggings and his buffalo robe. "Are they back?"

"Yes," Little Wolf replied, "our wolves have returned from spying on the soldier's camp."

They walked to the clearing in the center of the camp crescent to find Morning Star approaching from the far side. The older man was wrapped tightly in a painted robe, but his loose hair tossed wildly in the red-tinged wind. The men nodded their greetings as they arrived together at the east-facing door of the large Council Lodge.

The four wolves drove the loose horses to the camp herd on the north side of the creek and were then escorted to the center of camp by the noisy crowd. They circled the clearing the traditional four times at a slow lope before approaching a mound of rocks and dirt that had been built up in front of the Council Lodge. Little Wolf and Morning Star waited on the lodge side of the mound with three others: Old Bear, Black Hairy Dog, and Coal Bear, all chosen leaders of the tribe.

Little Wolf removed a long-stemmed, decorated pipe from the ornate pipe bag hanging at his waist and filled it as the riders dismounted. Split Nose and others took the men by the arms, and, one by one and in ceremonial fashion, sat them on the ground facing the tribal leaders. Each had taken the time before arriving at the camp to paint themselves in anticipation of this moment.

The chief lit his pipe, made four symbolic circles over the mound with it, then handed it across the mound to Hail, the leader of the four wolves, who was painted in white dots resembling his namesake. Hail accepted the pipe, made his offerings to the four directions, the sky, and the earth, and then took four draws of smoke. As he exhaled, the wind snatched the smoke from his lips and swept it behind him. He passed the pipe to the next scout. After all four had smoked, he began his report.

"May the Arrows hear what I am about to say." He had to shout to be heard above the wind. "We return with word about the soldiers traveling across the flat land to the east of here." He paused briefly, choosing only truthful words to tell his story. "We watched them for some time and saw that there are many soldiers in their camp. More than two soldiers for every person in this camp here, even the women and children. They also had many *xamaevo'ėstaneo'o*, native people riding along with them as soldier wolves to help them—three, four hundred maybe. I think they are moving north toward Tongue River. I don't know if they are looking for us, but they look ready to fight anyone they find."

A murmur of concern rolled through the crowd as Hail continued.

"We talked about things and decided that we should see if we could learn more about what they are up to, so we decided that with that many native people in camp, we could go in there and look around and not be discovered. Young Two Moons and Necklace were the two who went. I will let Young Two Moons tell you what they found."

With that, the lean young man sitting next to Hail with a large white crescent smeared across his face cleared his throat and began to speak.

"Arrows hear me," he started. "It is true, what Hail has said. Necklace and I pretended we were with these soldier wolves and walked into their camp to learn more. We heard four different tongues spoken in this camp. There are many of the Wolf People and Snakes that ride with them."

"*Hiiii!*" the crowd cried in unison, their shock dissolving into mutters as they cursed the mention of their traditional enemies: the Pawnee and Shoshoni.

"There are Lakota there."

Several gasps came from the crowd at the news that even their old allies rode with the soldiers.

"And *Tsitsistas.*"

The crowd erupted with protests and denials. "No, it can't be!" one hollered. "What Cheyenne would do such a thing?" another shouted. "Who? How can that be? Tell us!" An insistent chant started up from the throng of people that surrounded the men.

"I speak to the Arrows on this!" Young Two Moon raised his voice, reminding the crowd that he had sworn his honesty to the Arrows.

The Arrows were one of the Cheyenne's two holiest covenants between the people and *Ma'heo'o*, the Holy One. These four Arrows were given to them through the cultural prophet Sweet Medicine in the old times. To lie when speaking to them would damage the Arrows, create untold miseries for the one who dared to deceive, and bring about hard times for the tribe as a whole.

"I speak true words with a good heart now. I say I heard our own tongue spoken there, and I saw Cheyenne in that camp."

Black Hairy Dog was the young Keeper of the Sacred Arrows who had recently inherited his position when his father, Stone Forehead, was killed in a fight with soldiers in the far south. He raised his hand to quiet the crowd so he could ask the tired man his own question.

"Who did you see there?"

"It was night, and there was a hand game being played at one of the fires. I heard a Cheyenne voice in the crowd, and when I looked across the circle to see where it was coming from, I saw our friends Old Crow and Roan Bear standing among some Lakota. They were cheering the game and didn't see us."

Little Wolf was stunned. How it could be that Old Crow, a member of the Cheyenne Council of Forty-Four, was in a white soldier's war camp? He wanted to end the fighting with the whites as much as anyone.

"Necklace and I took those three horses you saw us bring in from their herd to prove that we were there." Young Two Moons paused as if telling this bad story had tired him. He glanced around at the crowd, making sure that he had their ears before finishing. "I think these soldiers are going north, maybe after the Oglala and the other Lakota camped with Crazy Horse. But if they come here instead, I think it will be a big fight if they reach this camp. *Hena'haanehe.* Now I am done talking."

For several moments, the only clear sound heard was an unsecured lodge door slapping open and closed in the persistent wind.

The five leaders across the mound stood in silent consideration of the information they had just received. Finally, Black Hairy Dog cleared his throat. It was his place to speak first as he was the Arrows Keeper, and it was to the Arrows that the wolves had given their report.

"I have not been the Arrows Keeper for long. I brought them to the north because of the troubles you have had with the soldiers. It worries me though that they have *Tsitsistas*, Cheyenne, with them, maybe even to bring them here against their own people. It would hurt the Arrows if they did, but we should not wait here to see if that will happen. We need to leave this place."

The Arrows Keeper raised his voice to be heard above the wind. "I say we must break camp. We must leave these mountains and travel along their edge to the north to find Crazy Horse and the Oglala and join their camp. We will be safer in a larger camp."

As abruptly as it had arrived, the wind suddenly stopped. Its roar diminished as it traveled eastward out of the valley, leaving an eerie silence behind it.

At that very moment, a tall, burly man stepped out of the crowd standing behind the wolves. His voice boomed into the sudden quiet, sounding like one of the soldier's wagon guns.

"*Hova'ăhane*, no!"

Like a flock of sparrows in flight, all heads turned in unison toward this man who dared to speak over the Arrows Keeper. It was Last Bull, the young head chief of the Kit Fox warriors.

"We should not run like cowards!" the disrespectful man continued. "We should stay here and fight them if they come, just as we did with the ones who charged on us at the Little Sheep River."

A look of irritation briefly crossed the faces of Black Hairy Dog and the other leaders. The tension was immediate and had an almost audible quality, like a bowstring being stretched taut. Then, as a true leader must, the Arrows Keeper took a deep breath to quiet his emotions. He turned away from Last Bull to speak to the crowd in a calm voice.

"My friends, we should not be fighting against each other now. We only harm the Arrows when we do that. This man says we should stay here. Maybe he is right, but maybe we should leave instead. Now, we have a little time to decide this. Let us smoke on this for a day and decide tomorrow what we will do. If the soldiers are coming for us, they will need to find us first, but we have only a short time."

Black Hairy Dog thanked the wolves for their service. He released them to their families, and the crowd began to disperse.

Little Wolf watched Last Bull walk away with several of his men from the Kit Fox Society. The man's hands cut and punched through the air in front of them as he spoke. The chief knew this would not end well.

# A Scout and a Spy

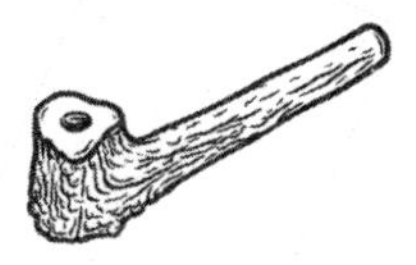

Bear Sitting Down was no liar. I had known the man since he was a young'un, during the early years at Fort Laramie. He was in it for the money, sure, and a chance to be a "big Indin," but I knew he mainly wanted to keep any more of his kin from getting killed, and he spoke with a good heart.

The Cheyenne called him a soldier wolf, on account of he'd taken up scouting for the white soldiers. He'd just rode down out of Tongue River country and now sat by the Sibley stove at the back of General Crook's wall tent, telling us what he seen up north. As he spoke, his hands carved through the air, showing me rivers, mountains, and bands of Indians moving around the country in all different directions.

Little Beaver Dam sat across the stove from Bear Sitting Down. He was still a few winters shy of twenty by my guess and looked mighty scared. He was a prisoner of the soldiers, which was for sure enough reason for him to be spooked, but he had also just seen and heard the older Cheyenne tell me, straight out, that most of what he, himself, had told me the day before was bullshit.

I told the boy "*Hetomestötse*, tell the truth." I signed the words, in case his folk said it any different. You never knew with some of them far northern bands, they kept to themselves a lot.

The boy nodded, cleared his throat, and admitted that Bear Sitting Down's words were true. His hands trembled as he signed back to me. I eyeballed him for a bit and felt a shiver slide down my backbone. This weren't good news.

I turned to the bearded man behind me at the same moment a hard, cold wind blew aside the door of the wall tent. The crowd of soldiers gathered inside with us did little to slow it down, and it deepened the chill that I already felt in my marrow. The cone-shaped Sibley stove, now at my back, seemed to be making a puny effort at best.

The general spoke over the sound of the wind. "What did they say, Rowland?"

General Crook didn't look like a soldier of any sorts. He wore as much buffler and buckskin as any Indian or trader did this time of year. The only thing on him that would make you think he was a soldier, let alone a general, was his worn-out slouch hat. Even that was in such poor shape you'd swear he'd found it rolling out on the prairie somewhere. His blue-gray eyes stayed stuck on me while his aide-de-camp, Lieutenant Clark, scurried about trying to tie the tent flap shut to stop the wind.

"Well, sir, it appears that right after your scouts captured Little Beaver Dam, his family found out, got spooked, and run off north. Seems they caught up with Crazy Horse's bunch and let him know that we're out here looking for him. The whole band headed up toward the Elk—uh, what you call the Yellowstone River—to try and join back up with Sitting Bull."

Crook's brow pinched as he considered the news. The tent was silent for a moment until a voice from the front of the tent cut through the crowd.

"What did he say about the Cheyenne?"

It was Lieutenant Clark. He was still tugging on the door flap, fighting a losing battle against the stiff wind that threatened to yank the canvas from his hands.

"Yes, sir." I raised my voice to be heard above the sound of the wind-rattled tent. I had to take a moment to gather my thoughts. It appeared that Clark had understood some of what Bear Sitting Down had just told me.

"So, Bear Sitting Down says that the Cheyenne ain't clean over to the other side of the mountains like we figgered. He says they're up in one a them canyons on this side, not too godawful far from here."

Crook turned to watch the lieutenant finish his fight with the stubborn door flap then pulled his robe up to his chin, cleared his throat, and turned back to me. "How far off are they, Rowland?"

"Crazy Horse or the Cheyenne, sir?"

"Cheyenne."

I turned back to ask Bear Sitting Down. "A day's ride, maybe two," I translated.

General Crook eyed me a moment. He glanced to the two Cheyenne then back to me. His fingers tugged his heavy, gray-brown beard into two separate tufts, as if he were separating true from false in what he'd just been told. He turned, quick-like, to the younger soldiers clustered behind him. There weren't but a few in this crowd who was near as old as the general or me.

"Gentlemen, given this new bit of information, I believe we shall forgo our pursuit of the Sioux, and Colonel Mackenzie should proceed without delay to the Cheyenne camp in the Bighorns."

The officers went all abuzz as I looked back at the two Cheyenne. They both had questions in their eyes about Crook's words, but I couldn't tell them anything just then. Best I could do was to shoot a mean glance down at the Sibley stove and give my head a small shake, letting them know that things weren't looking so good.

I had signed on with the expedition with the understanding that we were riding out after the Sioux, or Lakota as they called themselves, in particular Crazy Horse and his northern band of Oglala. Bear Sitting Down, and the few other Cheyenne riding with us, had thought the same thing. The army said that it was Crazy Horse who led the attacks on both Crook and Custer that past summer, and Crook was hot to get his payback. I sure didn't think he'd change course all-a-sudden like he did.

For a man who was supposedly out attacking columns of soldiers, Crazy Horse generally kept his folk far to the north, closer to Sitting Bull and his Hunkpapa, and away from the forts and agencies. I never had dealings with either man, so it weren't hard for me to consider helping to bring them in.

After the Custer fight, most all the agency Indians run off from the Red Cloud Agency out of fear that the soldiers at Camp Robinson, just across the river, might come after them in revenge. With scarce few Indians hanging around Red Cloud, there really weren't much interpreting work to be had there, and a man had to feed his family. My wife, Sis, and our nine children were back there, and the scout wages I'd make on this ride-along would help keep them fed, at least through this winter.

So, Crook changed his plans right then and there, and things began moving pretty damned fast. Lieutenant Clark had to quickly untie the door damn near as soon as he got it cinched up. Most of the young officers left the tent on the jump, like they was running out to fight that blasted wind that was still snapping at the walls of the tent. Weren't long after, and the bugle was squawking out "Boots and Saddles" over the top of the thousand or better dog tents scattered among the sage and greasewood crowding the banks of the Crazy Woman's Fork of the Powder River.

Little Beaver Dam was led back to the makeshift guardhouse by a pair of soldiers. He was a full head shorter than his escorts, but he still managed to muster up a stubborn look as he walked from the tent. He wasn't about to let any of the other Indians in camp see his fear.

I showed Bear Sitting Down where the Cheyenne scouts and I were camped, just a short walk from the general's tent. He left me then to go get his horse.

Eight Cheyenne were riding with the column, and Bear Sitting Down would make nine. When I arrived at the fire, four of the boys were curled up out of the wind under crude willow shelters the Cheyenne called *ho-tashko*, or war lodges. The other four sat at a fire on the lee side of a tall stand of big sage. What little smoke came from the low flames was quickly whipped out across the prairie.

Three of the boys stood up when they saw me coming: Roan Bear, Hard Robe, and Little Fish, all younger brothers of my wife, Sis. The oldest of the bunch, Roan Bear, called to me. "*Maešehe*, my brother-in-law, I think *Vo'keme*, Winter Man, comes to fight with us today. Come up to the fire. You look like you are troubled by more than the cold. Tell us what bothers you?"

The fella who had stayed sitting at the fire was Old Crow. He was near my age, mid-forties, and a member of the Cheyenne Council of Forty-Four. He gave me a hallo nod as I squatted next to him behind the sagebrush.

I told the boys about the talk with the general. I signed as I spoke, like I always did, to make sure I was fully understood.

"Bad talk!" I began. "Bear Sitting Down told Three Stars Crook that Crazy Horse is taking his people up beyond Elk River where we can't find them. Little Beaver Dam's family ran to him and told him that we were out here looking for him."

"So, we go back?" Old Crow asked as he pressed the tip of a small stick against a knot of sagebrush in the coals of the fire. He fixed his gaze on me, seemingly unaware of the cold gusts swirling around us.

"No, friend, he also told them about a big camp of Cheyenne in the mountains over there." I tossed my chin toward the west. "He said there are many lodges there, like timber in the canyons. Three Stars says that we should now go there and attack them instead."

All-a-sudden, the others come scrambling outta their war lodges to join Roan Bear and his brothers in their protest. "No! We were only going after Crazy Horse" they hollered. "How can we fight our own people? We cannot do this! Go tell them we cannot do this!"

I knew this was coming and tried to shout 'em down the best I could. "I cannot change this! No one can change this."

They didn't quiet down until Old Crow spoke. Being older and a Council member, he held some influence. He raised the smoking tip of his stick, intending to ask me a question, and the others quieted down to listen.

"Five sleeps ago, when Three Stars held council with all the scouts, he said that he did not want to fight anyone. He said that he wanted to talk with the northern bands and get them to go into the agencies. Do you still think this is true? Do we go to talk with them and not to fight?"

"It could be that way." I had to raise my voice when the grumbling started in again. "I think Three Stars is an honest man, and he speaks with a good heart, but I don't know—no one knows—what might happen if we find them up there. Many people will be frightened and angry on both sides. Things can happen fast at times like that. It does not matter, though." I stood up to make my point, still signing my words. "We all gave Three Stars our promise that we would help him bring the northern bands in to the agencies. We all need to remember our words. So, go now, get ready. We are leaving right away."

Nobody budged.

Old Crow pushed the knots of sage apart and off of the coals, slowly razing the fire without creating a spray of embers. As each twist was nudged to the side, he shared a thought. "Many of our enemies, the Wolf People and the Snakes, are in this soldier camp with us. They have sworn their friendship to us because we all ride with the white man now, but they still see those in the mountain camp as their enemies. If we do not ride into the mountains with them, then I think there will be fighting up there for sure. If we do go, then maybe there will be a chance for talking first."

The boys took a moment to consider Old Crow's words before each one drifted away to his war lodge to collect his belongings. When they were gone, Old Crow stood and spoke his mind while he took a pair of stiff steps toward me.

"All these other Indians will be hot to go in after the camp up there, but these soldiers worry me just as much. Too many here are ready to kill any Indian to get a payback for the big fight last summer."

The wind picked up, getting downright obnoxious as Old Crow leaned closer. "Winter Man sends us this warning that hard times are coming to us very soon. We should be ready."

My friend headed for his war lodge, and I turned to see what was taking Bear Sitting Down so long to get his horse. I spied him off behind the general's tent, talking to a Lakota scout. I was trying to read their signs when I caught sight of Lieutenant Clark peeking from the flap of the general's tent then snapping it closed. Apparently, he had been watching my little council with Old Crow and the boys. The man clearly didn't trust me. Here I am, rousing these boys to go riding in against their own kin, and he's in there suspecting me. That little son of a bitch.

I turned toward the Bighorns in the west to try and imagine where the Cheyenne might be holed up there. The wind was damned cold, though, and my eyes watered to the point I couldn't see a blasted thing. I left Bear Sitting Down to fend for himself and headed off to my tent to gather my kit. I snugged the army-issue sealskin cap down tight on my head and pushed my buffler robe up around my neck best I could. I turned my back on the bothersome gusts and cursed, giving as much disrespect to Winter Man as he was giving to me. "Goddam wind," I muttered.

# A Chief's Counsel

LITTLE WOLF STARED INTO THE FIRE AND GROWLED, "LAST BULL!" like a wary camp dog guarding his meal from the rest of the pack. *Eše'he* had just started his downward walk to the western horizon on the day of the big wind when Morning Star's wife, Short One, chased the family out of the lodge. She used the excuse of going to her daughter-in-law's to sharpen knives to allow the two leaders a chance to speak privately.

"He had no right to speak as he did!" Little Wolf kept his voice low to avoid being heard outside the lodge skin. Dissent, in the Cheyenne way, was typically expressed through one's silence on a matter, but Little Wolf felt that Last Bull's brazen words raised a bigger concern. "Society chiefs have never been allowed to speak at Council. He was given the chance at the Lakota Councils this summer, and now he thinks that he can talk over the Arrows Keeper to have his way!"

Morning Star quietly listened to the younger man's complaint. The lines on his face, like his old body, were straight, long, and relaxed. A Cheyenne leader for well over thirty winters, he had struggled with similar political dilemmas himself; none, however, had such potential for dire consequences. He also had shared many of those struggles in private, like this, away from the eyes and ears of the people. It was not the way of a chief to allow his anger or frustration to be seen in the larger circle of camp.

The older man nodded as he pulled a three-fingered pinch of sugar from the bag in his hand and tossed into a cup of coffee that sat on the flat stone between him and the fire. "He is young and sees a chance to have his name spoken around lodge fires." He carefully brushed the last few grains from his fingers into his drink. The small cup was delicate and ornate with a broken handle. It was part of a gift from a younger man in the tribe, plunder from one of his first daring raids given as an offering of respect to the old chief. He stirred the coffee with a twig, then cradled the rim between his thumb and middle finger and carefully lifted the cup with a slight tremor in both hands. He took a sip and frowned, placed the cup back on the stone, and reached for more sugar.

"There was a time in our own lives when we would have done the same thing," he continued as he reached into the near-empty sack. "A time when we would have wanted all the people to hear what it was that we had to say about what they should do."

Little Wolf leaned forward to make his point. "But we would never have spoken over the Keeper of the Arrows." He thrust his right hand forward, palm up, as if it held evidence that supported his words.

"No, that is true," Morning Star shook his head. "We would not have been that disrespectful, but these are different times, difficult times. The people are fighting among themselves as often as they fight the white soldiers. We must be careful. We can cause harm to the Arrows by fighting among ourselves."

Morning Star tossed another pinch of sugar in his coffee and stirred it as he went on. "It is good that Black Hairy Dog has brought the Arrows up from the south to be with us. We will need their protection if the soldiers come after us. You have always respected the Arrows and the Sacred Hat, even though I know you do not believe they protect us as they do. Your way was always to trust a man based on his acts, not his medicine. You care more about strategy and planning than tradition, but you have been an Old Man Chief for some time now, and you understand how important it is for our people that you put their needs before your own."

Little Wolf cradled a tin cup of coffee in his hands and inhaled the brew's heady scent. He knew that what his friend said was true. He had indeed been brash and arrogant in his younger days, respectful only of true warriors like Morning Star, who feared no one and fought with fury and tenacity.

The liner of Morning Star's opulent lodge was painted with depictions of many of his brave deeds over the years. One image showed how he captured his second wife, Pawnee Woman, during a raid of the Wolf People's camp, while another showed the time that he saved his brother-in-law from being captured by the Snakes, and yet another, the day he killed a grizzly bear with nothing but his knife. The pictures went on, circling the lodge, showing all who entered that there was not a man in the tribe more deserving of respect than this now, soft-spoken elder.

Little Wolf was called Two Tails in those earlier times. He idolized Morning Star and so joined the Dog Soldiers Society. His old friend was right; Little Wolf had fought more for personal gain and the love of fighting then and less for the protection of the people. He later sought political power and privilege and switched his allegiance to the Elk Soldiers. He understood little about the true qualities of leadership then, but he watched closely when Morning Star became an Old Man Chief. His changed behavior taught Little Wolf that the traditional position of chief was more about being a servant to the people than being one who directs them. Still, the younger man struggled with accepting cumbersome tradition.

Tradition told Little Wolf that, if properly respected, *Maahotse*, the Sacred Arrows, brought success during war and the hunt, and that *Esevone*, the Sacred Buffalo Hat, was a source of health and spiritual protection for the tribe. It ensured the return of the buffalo and provided for the overall well-being of the tribe.

Experience, on the other hand, told him that the people were better protected by the blood of their warriors and that their bellies were kept full by the perseverance and skill of their hunters. He had no quarrel with those who stood by tradition—that is, until it got in the way of keeping people alive.

The lodge had gone quiet. A large ember crumbled in the fire pit, and the wood shifted. The flames crackled loudly then faded. Little Wolf reached for a short branch and prodded the logs until the flames reappeared. He tossed the branch on top of the revived fire, added a second for good measure, and sat back.

He noticed that his friend's hair had been rebraided. This meant that he was done mourning the death of his eldest son, Medicine Club, who had been killed in the fight at Little Sheep River. His sorrow was ongoing, but this matter with the soldiers required his full attention, and the people needed him more than he needed to continue to grieve.

Morning Star sipped his coffee and nodded his approval. "This change in you started after you left the Dog Men and joined the Elk Soldiers. I thought that you were thinking only of yourself then, but you began to show more concern for the people. Perhaps it will be that way with Last Bull."

"Many things have changed since that time," Little Wolf replied. "I walk a different road today. We both do, my friend. Ever since we traveled east to the white man's country and saw how many they are and how big their villages are, I am afraid for our people. Last Bull has not seen these things. He thinks we can always beat their soldiers and continue living in this good way." He reached for another branch and adjusted the now crackling fire to a slower burn. "He has learned nothing from being headman of the Kit Fox. He has only made them act like he does. We both know what people call those men of his, the Wife Stealers Society, the Beating Up Warriors. Split Nose joked about him yesterday, and he is not the only one."

Morning Star knew the reputation of the men of the Kit Fox Society, but he wouldn't allow any resentment toward them to affect his judgment. "What you say is true friend," he replied, "but we separated from the big camp last summer because it is not easy to feed a camp that big in the winter. If we joined Crazy Horse now, it would be hard to find enough meat for everyone. It is better that we stay apart from them, even though we are not as strong to fight this way."

Little Wolf nursed his coffee. His old friend was right, which allowed him a bit of selfish comfort. "Yes," he nodded, "if the soldiers are out after him, it would be foolish of us to try to go there now. And you know my heart when it comes to Crazy Horse. There would be problems if we were in the same camp together for too long."

Both men sat quietly for a moment, pondering their dilemma as the fire crackled between them.

Little Wolf broke their silence with the question neither man wanted to ask. "What if the soldiers come after us instead? We should be ready to leave this place before they get here. We should go now, before Winter Man comes and deep snow makes it difficult to travel. My way would be to go straight to the Red Cloud Agency. We are promised by treaty to be allowed to live there in peace."

"Much has happened this summer," Morning Star said. "The soldiers were embarrassed in the fight at Roseberry River, then returned and lost many in the fight at Little Sheep River. Standing Elk told me the soldier chief killed there was Long Hair. He was one of their favorites, so they are angry now and will always come after us. I am also afraid that Last Bull is convinced that, whenever they do come, we will always win."

The silence resumed until a soft cough sounded outside the door.

"Come inside!" Morning Star raised his voice to be heard beyond the lodge skin.

The door opened, and a handsome young man leaned into the lodge, his long hair reaching almost to the ground as he did. It was Standing Bull, one of Morning Star's four remaining sons. All of Morning Star's children were handsome and carried themselves with a natural poise, so much so that the family had come to be known among the Cheyenne and their allies as "the Beautiful People."

"My mother says to tell you that if she is not allowed to come back to her lodge fire to cook, we will all starve," he reported. "She said to tell you her knives are sharp, and she's ready."

"*Shaa!*" Morning Star exclaimed as he leaned into his backrest. "Is she ready for a fight or for cooking?"

The young man smiled, glanced back over his shoulder, then joked to his father, "I think both. You should be careful."

"Well, you better not make her wait. Go to your brother's lodge and get her. Tell her I've been waiting here all this time. She's late."

Standing Bull laughed and left for his older brother's lodge to retrieve his mother.

"Will you remind her about the Arrows when she gets here?" Little Wolf asked as a smile crept across his face.

"I may not have time. She can be quick." Morning Star replied, staring at the closed door, his face set for war.

Little Wolf admired how his older friend could so easily work humor into difficult times. It had helped the people through many troubles—almost as often as his war club had.

Morning Star posed a final thought as they waited for Short One to arrive. "You and I remember the stories our elders told us about the old ways of planting corn, before the horses came to us. It is not so hard for those of us who remember those stories to think about going to the agencies and trying to follow that road again. But these younger ones, who have only known chasing buffalo . . ." The chief stared into his coffee and shook his head. "They do not like to think of such a thing. They will fight anyone, maybe even another Cheyenne, if they are told it will be taken from them. They care nothing for the old stories, but they must remember the Arrows."

Short One pushed through the door like a sudden spring squall. Without a word, the round but stout-looking woman laid her bundle of knives down and reached for her cooking pot. She filled it with water from a skin by the door and placed it by the fire, then turned and pulled roots and seasonings from various containers to begin the night's meal.

Morning Star watched for a while then smiled. "Ah, here's my good-looking wife coming to take care of me now. Did I ever tell you what a good cook she is?"

Little Wolf grinned. His friend's teasing was too intimate for those outside the lodge to witness, but Short One showed no embarrassment whatsoever

"*Noohe*, you better start treating me good," she said. "I heard what you told your son. You're lucky I came back here at all."

The old chief reached for the nearly depleted sugar sack near his cup and held it up, ignoring his wife's protest. "Next spring, when the box elder trees start pushing leaves, you will need to take some of their sweet-water. We are almost out of the white man's sand."

Short One's eyes narrowed, and Little Wolf decided that it was a good time to excuse himself.

The chief's heart was lighter as he made his way home. Though he had often struggled with the reasons behind the old ways, he had come to respect their purpose. Perhaps Last Bull could be persuaded to do so as well. The sound of laughter drew him to a group of boys who had struck up an evening game called Coyote. He knew most of the children who were playing and smiled as he spied one of his favorites, a young boy named Gathering His Medicine, the son of Red Pipe and Iron Tooth Woman. The boy was about twelve winters old and was playing the role of Protector.

The youth stood at the front of a line of boys standing oldest to youngest. Each was clinging tightly to the shoulders of the boy in front of him. Another boy, Young Bird, the youngest son of Morning Star and Quiet One, was playing the role of Coyote. He was trying to duck and dodge his way around Gathering His Medicine, reaching as he did to try and touch as many of those in the line behind him to take them out of the game. The boys went rambling through camp as the Protector hustled to match the Coyote move for move and keep the line safe. As the line flung itself back and forth, trying to avoid the lunges of the Coyote, a little one on the end of the line who was unable to keep up with the rapid whipping motion was tossed, tumbling and laughing, into the grass, while the Coyote raced to gobble him up.

Gathering His Medicine scowled as the taken one trotted off to the side to watch the remainder of the game. He took his job seriously and showed good focus and agility as he countered the efforts of Young Bird. Still, one after another, those at the end of the line would go rolling away to get pounced on by the Coyote while everyone laughed.

Protector was a difficult position to play, and Gathering His Medicine was getting frustrated. Little Wolf understood the feeling, having played the game himself many times in his own youth. He had found, early on, that he preferred to be the Coyote.

Leaving the boys to their fun, the chief walked on toward his lodge. Each cone-shaped home cast a soft amber glow into the evening light, illuminating his path. He smiled as the elated shrieks of another small boy being eaten alive echoed off the canyon walls behind him.

He pushed aside the door flap to his home and was surprised to find only Lightning, his first wife, the one he sat beside, and his two younger daughters.

The girls were finishing their last chores for the day. Day Woman, his youngest, was stacking firewood to the left of the door. Little Wolf picked up two pieces of wood that had tumbled in front of him and placed them on the stack. He gave the eleven-year-old a quick wink and grinned, which brought a beaming smile to her chubby face.

"*Nea'eše*," she puffed as she turned back to finish her work.

Little Wolf stepped to his right, moving carefully around the fire and White Voice, who was about to hang a bladder of fat near the door. She was his only child with his second wife, Two Woman, and at sixteen winters, his oldest child still living in his lodge.

Lightning had moved toward the fire when her husband appeared at the lodge door. She pulled a piece of boiled meat from the brass kettle warming beside the fire to prepare a dish for him.

Little Wolf reached his robes and gave a small groan as he leaned against his backrest. "Where is Two Woman?" he asked.

Lightning placed the food in front of her husband and replied as she wiped a bead of sweat off her forehead with the back of her wrist. "At the moon lodge. We were staking down the cover of Walking Whirlwind and Chopping Woman's lodge when she had to leave."

The moon lodges had been raised across the creek from the main camp. These were the tepees where married women went to stay during their bleeding time to avoid bringing harm to their husbands. He questioned many of these older customs, which he thought did little more than stand in the way of getting things done. The belief was that a woman's medicine was very powerful at this time, and if she had anything to do with a man's belongings or ceremonies, his medicine would be weakened, and he would be at risk for being wounded or killed in battle. After many years of marriage, and serving many years on the Council of Forty-Four, Little Wolf had slowly, sometimes painfully, learned to allow others to believe what they wanted; a significant change for this once hard-driving, young warrior of the people.

Night settled in, and so did the girls and their mother. Lightning cleaned up the remains of the meal and pulled out a pair of moccasins that she was beading. White Voice leaned against her backrest and immersed herself in measuring and cutting a piece of buckskin for a belt she was making, while Day Woman played idly with a doeskin doll her sister had given her years ago.

The stillness of evening made the lodge feel empty. As she often did, Day Woman gave a voice to the obvious conditions around her. "I miss Pawnee. *Neho'e*, Father, when will he be done hunting with Wooden Thigh?" she asked.

"They said they wanted to make plenty of meat for winter, *Katse'e*, little girl. They might be out another day or two," Little Wolf answered, sliding down lower on his backrest.

Pawnee and Wooden Thigh were Little Wolf's adopted sons. Wooden Thigh had married a few winters back and had left the lodge, while Pawnee, at fourteen winters, still lived with the family. He was maturing, though, and left with the men more often these days. Whenever he was gone, Day Woman would often cast little sighs over his empty sleeping robes, which were next to hers. Like any child, she went from missing her old playmate to anticipating the arrival of her new one in a heartbeat.

"Chopping Woman's belly is getting so big!" she exclaimed unexpectedly. "The baby inside was busy today, and she let me feel it. She thinks it's going to be a girl. I think it is too."

Chopping Woman was the eldest of Little Wolf's and Listening Stand's daughters. She had married last spring at the Red Cloud Agency and moved her braids behind her shoulders, in the manner of a good wife. She and her husband, Walking Whirlwind, were expecting their first child in about two moons. The young couple's small, canvas lodge was pitched close behind the larger, smoke-charred hide lodge of her parents. There were still nights, like this one, when her old place by the lodge fire seemed empty to the entire family.

Little Wolf smiled. In addition to stirring and feeding the fire, Day Woman had, ever since she could talk, placed herself in charge of stirring and feeding the conversation in the lodge. She never failed at either job and proceeded with both as she reached for a branch to poke the coals.

"That boy Looking Back has been coming around and talking to White Voice a lot lately. Maybe they'll get married next and have a baby."

White Voice's head snapped up from the buckskin in her hand, her eyes wide with surprise. She and Lightning both admonished the talkative little girl with a quick "Hsssst!"

Little Wolf settled further into his robes. His smile faded as his thoughts moved from his chatty daughter to the empty spaces across the lodge, then wandered down the creek through the narrow gap on the east end and far out onto the sagebrush-covered plains below, to a large camp of soldiers.

# Alone Among Friends

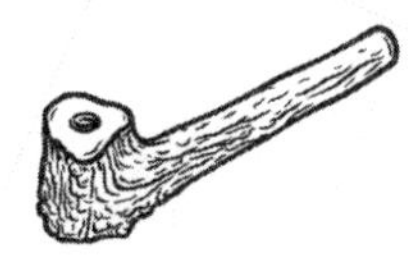

WHAT I THOUGHT WAS GOING TO BE AN ALL-OUT BLUE NORTHER ended near quick as it started. Winter Man's warning, as Old Crow called it, went on warning whatever sorry souls it caught wandering out on the miles of treeless prairie to the east of us.

It was well into Nebraska by the time I reached down to finish saddling Ulysses. I pulled the latigo through the cinch ring and give it a good tug. The big buckskin was getting better about not swelling up when the cinch tightened, so I was able to saddle him quickly and get moving.

My brother-in-law, Little Wolf, had given me the horse as thanks for interpreting for him and the other Council chiefs back in seventy-three when we all traveled to Washington DC to talk with President Grant. The chiefs went there to tell him that they intended to stay put with their Lakota friends in the Powder River country. Grant wanted them to move south to Indian Territory to live on an agency with their relatives, the Southern Cheyenne. From where I sat during their talks, Grant acted like a bit of a horse's ass, talking down to the chiefs like they was children. So, when Little Wolf gave me the horse with the big hindquarters, well, the name just seemed to fit.

Ulysses was the most sure-footed animal I had, and knowing the terrain of the mountains we were headed for now, I was glad I had decided to bring him along. I figured I'd use an army mount if the trail started to wear the buckskin down. Most of the other scouts and interpreters on the expedition were using their own stock as well. Some brought a string of horses in order to keep a fresh mount along the way.

I flipped the reins over Ulysses' head, slid them down along his neck, and talked soft while giving the champing horse a few reassuring pats.

"Well, boy, I don't think our old friend's gonna be too happy to see us coming over the hill this time, now is he, eh? What do you think, huh? Nope, I reckon not. I hope to hell we can get some talking done 'fore people start shooting at each other. That'd be good, eh? Yup, yup, well, by god, we'll just try to get that done then won't we, eh? For sure we will, boy. Ho, now. Ho."

I swung up into the saddle, and Ulysses minced a few steps sideways before I turned him toward the growing column of riders west of camp. Soon as I got started, hoofbeats sounded to my right. Billy Garnett came trotting up alongside on a short, muscular sorrel and slowed to a walk.

"Morning, Bill. Sounds like we got us a change a plans here."

"Peers that way, Billy."

Billy Garnett was a smooth-faced, twenty-two-year-old half-breed serving as a Lakota interpreter on the ride. I first met the youngster when he was a quiet, respectable boy growing up around Fort Laramie. He was close to the same age as William Jr., my oldest boy, and went by Billy Hunter back then, using his step-father, John Hunter's name. Hunter was a no-account who ran a so-called hog farm down near Fort Laramie where he whored out Billy's mother and other girls, until he was shot and killed back in sixty-eight. Afterward, Billy hooked up with a fella named Bat Pourier, who also happened to be on the ride with us. Bat ran with a rough crowd of mixed-breed toughs, and Billy had been a bit of a snapper-head ever since they got together. We both hired on at the Red Cloud Agency back in seventy-three, about the time that Billy discovered he was the bastard son of Major Richard Garnett. Garnett was a past commander of Fort Laramie who later died a Confederate hero at Gettysburg. The boy had since put that relationship to considerable use among officers who had known his father and were now stationed throughout the chain of military forts in the northern plains. It wasn't long before Billy changed his last name to Garnett and developed a sense of entitlement. He started putting on airs and expecting considerations from others that he hadn't earned. Doc Saville, the old Red Cloud agent, fired Billy once for being disrespectful. The boy threatened to use his old man's name with the higher-ups and forced the

Doc to hire him back. These days I tolerated the youngster, but it took some doing.

"Who all do ya think is up there in that camp?" Billy asked.

I couldn't tell if he was interested in their welfare or if he was just digging up dirt to use later. You couldn't give him any information and expect him to keep it dry.

I dropped the reins over the saddle horn, letting Ulysses keep a slow walk toward the column while I reached for my fixings. We were ten days out from Fort Fetterman, and my tobacco had started to dry out. I kept it greased to help it hold some moisture and pack into my deer horn pipe better. There would be no smoking once I was in formation, so I scratched a lucifer to light it quickly. The white-tipped stick sparked and flared, and when the sulfur cleared, I sucked the flames down into the bowl. A good smoke always relaxed me, and I decided to humor the boy.

"Well, Billy, it's likely their main winter camp. I reckon there could be at least a couple of the Old Man Chiefs, and likely most of the Council. Maybe Coal Bear, the Sacred Hat Keeper. I heard Black Hairy Dog brought the Sacred Arrows up from the south recently, so he might be up there too."

"They probly know we're out here." Billy tried to sound reassuring. "They'll likely skedaddle once they see us coming. I tried to tell the general that we should've sent troops out to push their scouts back so they couldn't tell that we're headed up there. I doubt we'll see more'n sign now. I keep trying to tell him, but he just don't listen."

That wasn't his idea, but that didn't stop him from laying claim to it. Truth was, the Lakota scouts had been talking for some time about jumping the Cheyenne and "using them up" before going after Crazy Horse. From a fighting standpoint, this made sense; I just didn't figure the general, who seemed all hell-bent on catching Crazy Horse, would have made that call. But he did.

Old Crow and the others were waiting for me when we reached the column. Billy moved on to join the Lakota scouts. I finished my smoke as the rest of the formation fell into place and the bugler blew "Forward."

Our detachment numbered over a thousand riders with more than a third being Indian scouts. Along with our little party of nine Cheyenne, a hundred or so of the others were Lakota and Arapaho, who were Cheyenne allies. Problem was, the other two hundred were Pawnee and Shoshone, both traditional enemies of the Cheyenne. I figured there was a good chance that, even if we didn't find anyone to attack, we might easily have a good fight kick up within our own ranks.

Colonel Ranald Mackenzie was a brilliant young officer, but he was a moody cuss. He had earned the rank of brevet major general during the Civil War. He'd lost a couple fingers from his right hand during the siege of Petersburg, which earned him the name of Bad Hand from the Cheyenne and Lakota. Two years ago, troops under his command had wiped out the combined winter camp of the Southern Cheyenne, Kiowa, and Comanche at Palo Duro Canyon in the Texas Panhandle. I was afraid that this ride might result in a sad repeat of that ambuscade.

We made ten miles across frozen ground that afternoon before Mackenzie had us bivouac for the night. We kept a low ridge to the west to shield our campfires from the sight of anyone in the mountains. We had orders to leave our tents behind so we could move faster. We were in for some chilly nights. The way the Cheyenne deal with this is to build one big war lodge and have everybody crawl in together. Not the most ideal sleeping arrangements, but it beats the hell out of freezing to death.

The following morning was for sure less miserable without an icy wind pouring down on us. We continued southwest, moving closer to the Bighorns. The Cheyenne called this range the Shining Mountains, and on mornings like this one, the name fit perfectly. The first rays of the morning sun struck their entire vertical expanse. They practically glowed in contrast to the gray morning shadow that still covered the surrounding prairie. They were pretty as a shawl dancer in firelight.

Long, winding drifts of snow snaked along the shaded slopes at the higher elevations. The Cheyenne say that Winter Man lives up there and that only the brave men, or the crazy ones, climb up that high, and when they do, they put themselves at risk of becoming bewitched or dying in some pitiful way.

Dawn soon lit the prairie, and a sparse flurry of crystallized snow drifting from a cloudless sky added flashes of iridescent color to the morning ride. The flakes drifted lazily over us as we snaked our way around dense masses of greasewood and big sage, some near tall as a horse. We continued to draw closer to the foothills, often crossing over crude dikes gouged across the narrow but deep-walled creeks by an advance detail of soldiers.

I hadn't spent a lot of time in the mountains ahead of us, but I knew what we were up against. Before long the prairie would rise, becoming long slopes and swells, low ridges that would soon grow to rugged knolls and buttes, each towering higher than the last, creating a maze of creeks and gullies that laced between them. It was a devilish place that would demand a world of sweat and suffering from any traveler unfamiliar with its passages. The prairie grass would dwindle, giving way to gritty red clay and sandstone. The greasewood and big sage would change over to cedar and thorn-infested scrub mahogany. It appeared as if the terrain had been built by demons who were looking to take a man apart, first by tearing at his body, then ripping away his spirit.

We were moving due west now, toward the east face the range that rose nearly straight up from the foothills in front of us. Scouts had been sent ahead to try to locate the camp and find a suitable way to approach it. The column would trail along the foot of the range, doing our best to stay hidden until they returned.

The flurries came to an end about the time Lieutenant Clark separated himself from the front of the column. He rode off to the right and sat there, watching the riders moving past him. I figured he was doing a nose count, until he fell in alongside as I rode past. By my guess the officer was in his early thirties. He had only been with the command a couple-three months, but from what I'd seen, he was pretty quick at picking up on the way things were done. The general must have noticed it too, seeing as how he placed the young officer in charge of all the scouts except for the Pawnee, who were led by a pair of brothers, Frank and Luther North.

"Colder'n hell today, isn't it, Rowland?" Clark tugged his white, wide-brimmed Stetson closer to his exposed ears.

"Could be colder," I answered, "Probly will be soon, from the looks of them sundogs up there."

Clark turned in his saddle to glance into the southeastern sky at the small rainbow-like bands that cradled the rising sun. "You're probably right." He sighed. "I hope we can get up in there and pull those Indians out without it turning into any long-winded affair. I sure wouldn't want to be up there when a storm hits."

"You and me both," I replied.

Clark rode around a large stand of greasewood and revived the conversation. "So, Rowland, this has got to be a bit of a difficult undertaking for you, riding after the same people you've lived with for so many years. How's all this sitting with you? I can't imagine it's an easy thing."

"Well, sir, to be honest, it ain't."

The column bottlenecked at a narrow dike crossing a deep streambed that was crowded on one side by a dense wall of sagebrush. Clark rode around the knot of people and horses and barked a few orders, setting priorities for who crossed first. The muddle soon trickled, single file, across the dirt ramp that had been torn from the banks on either side of the creek.

The lieutenant waited for me on the other side while Ulysses sniffed uncertainly at the musty odors coming from the large clods cluttering the edges of the fresh causeway. After I crossed, the lieutenant continued as if our conversation had not been interrupted.

"So, Rowland, I couldn't help but notice when you briefed your scouts about the general's decision yesterday. There were a couple of signs you made that I didn't understand. For instance, what does this mean?"

Clark grabbed his left index finger with his right hand before pointing to the sky and to the ground with it. I watched Clark's clumsy signs then eyed the man who had just admitted to having spied on me. A chilly silence rode between us for a few strides.

"I told them to keep their promise." I dropped the reins and signed the words as I spoke them, but I kept my eyes glued on Clark. Ulysses sensed I was upset and tossed his head. "They ain't exactly happy about this change a plans either, you see." I reached up and collected the reins that had slid up around Ulysses' ears. "They'd just as soon we'd kept on for Crazy Horse, seeing's how that's what we was setting out to do at the beginning of this parade." I tried damned hard to keep my voice at a respectful tone. "I told them that we each signed on to help the general bring all the Indians in, not just Crazy Horse. Ain't a one of us liking it, 'Tenant, but we said we'd help out, so we're keeping our word."

Clark pursed his lips and gave a sympathetic look. "I believe that, Rowland."

"Then why you keeping such a close eye on us?" I studied the high country, giving him a moment to explain.

"It's not that I don't trust you," he said. "I just happened to notice the conversation as I was tending to the general's tent. Just so you know, I honestly think it's a difficult but very honorable thing that both you and your scouts are doing, if that helps at all."

I gave the reins a snap to let Ulysses know that I was still in control of both him and my emotions. The buckskin quieted down and returned to watching the slick ground in front of him. "I ain't too sure about the honorable part of that, 'Tenant," I replied. "But it is for sure a bugger of a thing to be caught up in. I just hope we can talk 'em down outta there 'fore anybody gets killed."

"I can only imagine," Clark said. "How long have you lived with the Cheyenne?"

I was still leery of where this was going, but the man appeared to be making his best effort to be considerate, so I decided to follow suit. I never had been much for telling stories about myself, and it took some doing to reach back that far.

"Well, I first came to Fort Laramie just a week after the government took it over, back in forty-nine. I was riding with Capt'n Stansbury and his outfit, on our way to survey the Great Salt Lake Valley. We stopped at the fort again on our way back the next year. That time, there was some big doings going on, with folks getting ready for the Horse Creek Treaty.

"I tell ya, there was Indians coming in from every which way, all wanting to talk about all them gold miners running across their land to the mines in California. I decided to stay when the survey outfit headed back to Kansas. I figured I'd try my hand at doing some trading with the different tribes and took a liking to being in the Cheyenne camp. Well, one thing led to another, 'n I met Sis, my wife, and, well, that was that, as they say. We got hitched and a course there ain't no way I'm a taking her anywhere, seeing's how, in the Cheyenne way, the husband moves in with the wife's people, so here I stayed."

I surprised myself with all the gab, but I always talked easier in the saddle. Being cooped up in a room, eyeball to eyeball, was uncomfortable for me.

"That would be a good twenty-six years." Clark grinned. "Why that's longer than many of these soldiers here have been alive. I was all of six about then."

I was amazed at the amount of time that had passed. Well over half my life. "Reckon so. Sometimes I'm a bit surprised I been able to keep what little hair I have left through that time. Been a lot that's happened."

Clark's horse slipped on the slick ground and stumbled a few steps. The surprised officer leaned far back in the saddle, giving the small bay mare her head as she struggled to get her feet back under her. As he regained his seat, he chuckled.

"I imagine so. Why, that goes back past the Fetterman fight and Sand Creek. Hell, that was even before Solomon's Fork and the Grattan incident, wasn't it?"

I'd been at the last two run-ins that he mentioned and had seen the fallout from the others. Sand Creek was especially bloody. I had heard that Chivington's troops had butchered many of their victims and later paraded through Denver City with scalps, hands, even women's private parts on display for all to see. It only takes being in but one of those bloody affairs to change a person. Clark had rattled them off like they were nothing more than scenes from one of his favorite stage plays. What did this greenhorn know? I was fast losing interest with the conversation and stared off toward the mountains that kept getting taller in front of us.

"Yeh, been a while," was all I could muster in response.

Clark must have realized his mistake and changed the subject. "Rowland, you may have noticed that I am trying to learn that sign language you use with the Indians. I've picked up quite a bit since I arrived in August, but I'm still not grasping it as fast as I would like. The reason I dropped back to talk with you is that I'm hoping I might arrange to have you give me lessons."

I turned to gawk at him in surprise.

"I'd compensate you, of course," he said.

"Compensate me? So, you been spying on me to try to learn sign talk, and now you want to pay me to teach you?"

"Well, I wouldn't call it spying, but yes. I'm a quick study, and I think that with your help, I could be conversant in short order."

"Conversant? You do know that they'll need to understand you too?"

The lieutenant chuckled and dropped his reins. "I'm sure I could say that differently."

He flicked his right index finger near his mouth then quickly tapped the fingers of his right hand on top of the fingers of his left hand, then tapped his left fingers on his right, and repeated the flick near his mouth. He was sloppy, but the signs were close enough to tell he meant "speak sign talk."

It was about then that it occurred to me that this young officer might actually give a half a damn about understanding these Indins instead of being hell-bent to wipe 'em out like all the others I'd known.

"So, what else did you catch from my talk with Old Crow and the others yesterday?"

Clark smiled. "Well, our orders are to try to talk the Cheyenne into surrendering. I saw you sign to your scouts that we would be attacking the village, but that's not our plan." He showed the sign for attack: both fists starting near his right shoulder then moving, palms down, down and to the left while he spread his fingers.

"I know the plan, 'Tenant, and they know it too. It just seems that plans have a way of, well, of not working out sometimes. Lieutenant Grattan had himself a plan, so did Captain Fetterman. Custer had a plan a few months back too, and that sure as hell didn't work out too godawful well for him, now did it? I'm afraid there's quite a few on this ride with us who are looking to get payback for all of them. My guess is that we'll be hitting that camp full chisel when we find it."

Clark opened his mouth to reply just as handful of Indians appeared on a hill in front of us. I recognized them as some of the scouts that had been sent out earlier. Their sudden appearance caused a huge stir in those scouts who had remained with the column and frightened the soldiers who thought they were under attack.

"Come with me!" Clark hollered as he spurred his horse toward the front of the column in anticipation of Colonel Mackenzie's call.

I gave a quick glance toward Old Crow and the Cheyenne scouts. Old Crow stared back at me. His face lacked expression, but his eyes were full of questions.

"Git!" I gave Ulysses a quick dig with my heels and leaned forward as the big horse lunged underneath me.

CHAPTER FIVE

# Distracted till Dark

THE ARAPAHO SCOUTS THAT HAD APPEARED ON THE HILLSIDE earlier in the day brought with them the exact news that I had not wanted to hear. The Cheyenne camp had been found, and it was close. The scouts reported that they had seen a few lodges, but because of the difficult terrain, they were unable to get into a position to see the whole village. They were certain it was the main camp, though, because they could see the large horse herd to the north. "Heap ponies, heap ponies, heap, heap!" They barked their news at Colonel Mackenzie the way camp dogs greet a stranger.

I knew they had all been promised a share of the horses captured by the expedition as a part of their compensation. I found myself getting angry at the scouts for their mindless greed. I was also angry at Mackenzie and the army for their dogged push to break the lives of the people I had lived with for the last twenty-six years, and I was angry at the Cheyenne for their stubborn fight to keep that life, even though they knew that it had to come to an end. Most of all, I was angry at myself for being caught up in the middle of it all and for having the stupid, useless idea that I could somehow make a difference.

We were at the very foot of the Bighorns now, where a solid wall of earth and rock rose straight to the sky. Colonel Mackenzie had ordered us into a fireless camp to wait for nightfall, at which time we would resume our ride up to the Indian camp.

We bivouacked in a protected basin created by the hollow between a pair of adjacent ridges that abutted the mountain wall. The southern ridge had an overhang of red sandstone along the length of it, and the northern one had a gentler slope. There was good water and grass for the horses, but only raw salt pork and hardtack for the troops.

I was sitting near the bottom of the northern ridge, still gnawing on a piece of hardtack, when Lieutenant Clark showed up. He nodded his head in a polite greeting to Old Crow and the others then gave me a cheery hallo.

"My lord, what interesting country we're headed into, eh Rowland? Say, are you about done with your meal?"

I eyed the officer in mid-gnaw. I could tell this wasn't an official visit. The lieutenant never made such small talk when it came to army matters. He'd just show up, bark out his orders, and be done with it. We were close to finding the camp, I had little stomach for chitchat, and I was getting mighty upset.

"'Tenant, meaning no disrespect sir, you're a likable fella and all, and I appreciate company as much as the next, but I don't see why you're so godawful interested in my affairs of late. Not calling you nosy, mind you, just not sure what it is you're wanting from me."

Clark looked surprised. "I—I'm sorry, Rowland. I had no idea I was annoying you. I have no intention of being a bother here. It's just that, it may be a while before we leave here, and I thought I'd see about a lesson in sign language while we wait. That's all."

"A lesson? You want a lesson now? We're fixing to run up into these mountains and jump a whole tribe of Indins, and you wanna learn sign talk?"

"I'm sorry, Rowland." The lieutenant drew back, surprised at my response. "Perhaps afterward, when we get back to the main column? My apologies." Clark turned to leave, looking a bit embarrassed for his poor timing.

When the lieutenant retreated, I felt an odd thing happen. It was like a small flicker of hope turned away with him. I realized it might be my only chance, so I went after it.

"'Tenant."

Clark turned back, a bit red-faced but hopeful.

"I probly should be apologizing to you. I'm just a bit on edge here, sir. To tell the truth, I could use a good distraction right about now. What say we make a quick go of it and see if we can't each help the other here?

"Honestly? I don't want to be a bother."

"Naw, it ain't no bother, 'Tenant, for sure. It would be good for me to think about sumthin other'n what we'll be heading off to do come dark. Pull up a rock."

Clark gave a smile and sat down on a flat-topped boulder next to me, and I started.

"Well, let's see here. So, I know you savvy the sign for Cheyenne." I drew my right index finger across my left forearm three times. "What say we start there?"

"I think that would be just fine," he said.

"And the sign for Pawnee is also the sign for wolf," I continued.

Lieutenant Clark copied the sign I just made: his right hand tipped forward from the wrist with the first two fingers split into a fork.

"Careful to keep your hand in front of your shoulder, though, not your eyes. That means *see*." I reached over to lower the officer's hand. "They're called the Wolf People by most tribes. The Shoshone are called Snakes, like this." I snaked my right hand forward from my side.

"I learned that one this summer," Clark replied, imitating the smooth weaving motion. "What fascinates me is that these gestures used in sign language are so universal. They allow all the different tribes, even adversaries, to communicate with each another."

I nodded. "I've even seen where different bands from the same tribe might argue over how to say a word, especially if they ain't seen one another for a while. Sign talk uses some pretty common words and phrases that help 'em get past that."

Clark tucked his hands under his arms to warm them. "So, you mean that they actually develop different dialects when they separate for a time?"

"If that ten-dollar word means they speak in a little different tongue, then yeah, that's right. It's the same as me having a Missouri drawl and you a bit of Yankee twang, but we both know what a head nod means."

Clark nodded and smiled as I continued.

"You can't put every word you say into your signs, though, or you'd just start adding your own . . . What's that word again, dialect? And you'd be forever and a day trying to get something said."

Clark nodded again, then stared at me for a couple seconds. I could almost see his thoughts becoming words before he changed the subject. "Just so you know, Rowland, it's not lost on me that you've probably got family up in that camp."

I exhaled a long cloud of smoke. This is what I had been waiting for. I looked back toward Old Crow and the others who were wrapped in their blankets and staying just out of reach of the creeping shadow above us. I turned back and looked Clark in the eye.

"We all do, sir."

Clark's brow furrowed as he considered the dilemma the Cheyenne scouts and I were in.

"Tell me about the Cheyenne, Rowland."

There it was. The tinder had caught. I took a long draw on my pipe and commenced adding wood to the small flame of concern that seemed to be growing in the officer. I knew there would be no way to stop the column from striking the Cheyenne camp, so my only hope was to try and find some way to rein in the eagerness for a fight, and I knew Clark had Mackenzie's ear.

"Well, they're good folk, 'Tenant, friendly as all get out if you give 'em a chance. Not to say I haven't had my squabbles with different ones from time to time." I leaned forward and lifted the flap of my sealskin cap to show him a scar behind my right ear where I had a silver plate stuck in my head.

"What's that from?" he asked.

"A little hooch-induced run-in with Roan Bear and my other brothers-in-law over there. It was back in fifty-nine, during the early days of Denver City. We settled it since, but I make a point of staying away from whiskey these days."

Clark nodded. "I've been told that you killed a Cheyenne just last year."

I was surprised at the turn in the conversation. "Where'd you catch wind of that?"

"Billy Garnett. Is it not true?"

Billy and that blasted mouth of his. "Yeah, it's true. A man name of Water Walker. He ran with them northern bands. He was fixing to kill me first though."

Clark looked intrigued, so I gave him the whole load of hay as I had my smoke.

"Doc Saville was the agent at the Red Cloud Agency back then. He was the one who patched my busted head at Denver City. He hired me on as soon as he took over at the agency from Agent Daniels back in seventy-three. Daniels had run me and a few others off when the old agency was down on the Platte. It was just before he moved it north to the White River country, where it stands today. He said we was selling 'em whiskey, but the real story was he didn't like that we told them they'd be better off staying put on the Platte and not moving to White River like he wanted. There's a lot more trade that takes place there on account of the Oregon Trail.

"Anyway, I owed the Doc plenty for patching me up in Denver City and hiring me on at Red Cloud. Well, it happened that his nephew, Frank, got killed when them northern bands come in to the agency and started raising hell back in seventy-four. The Doc needed somebody to go for help, so I took a ride to Fort Laramie that night to tell General Smith to send some troops up there to help settle things down. Thing is, once they got there, they never left. That's how Camp Robinson got its start. The soldiers camped next to the agency for a spell then moved over to where the post now stands.

"Well, my bringing the soldiers didn't sit too well with Water Walker and them others in the northern bands. After a few threats about doing so, he busted into my cabin and pulled his gun on me and my family. I just barely managed to get him first."

"Frightening," Clark interrupted.

"Oh, for sure it was. I run Sis and the kids up to the agency stockade afterward and left them with the Doc. I knew that Water Walker's friends and kin would be coming for me, so I hightailed it the mile and a half to Camp Robinson where Major Mason give me the honor of being the first resident in his new guardhouse—for my own protection, of course. After that, all they could do was burn my cabin and kill my stock before they headed back north to avoid the soldier's getting after them.

"So, you see, it ain't all the Lakota and Cheyenne who are causing the problems. It's them northern bands from both tribes that don't want nothing to do with the white man. The other, more peaceable, ones are just getting caught in the middle.

"Look, I was in that camp near Fort Laramie way back when Lieutenant Grattan got hisself and all them others killed, and I seen what happened to Capt'n Fetterman and his bunch. Now Custer and most of the Seventh are gone. It don't take but one or two hotheads out looking for a fight, on either side, to end up getting a whole bunch of other good folks killed.

"The Cheyenne up there ain't looking for a fight, 'Tenant, they're trying to avoid one. There might be a few ornery ones in the bunch, but I know for a fact that most of them left the agency last summer because they was afraid they was going to catch hell for what happened at the Little Bighorn."

Clark listened to me going on, and the look in his eye told me he understood, so I kept talking.

"They're a pretty decent bunch a folk. And I can tell you, I ain't never been anywhere else where a soul can feel so welcomed, if you know what I mean. It seems like everybody's related to each other in one way or another, and if they ain't, they'll most likely adopt one another as uncles or aunties or such.

"They got real close ties, sir, everywhere you look. Why, a soul can't go anywhere in their camp and not get offered something to eat, even if yer off visiting a widow, or a grampa and gramma. Most likely they got the food from somebody else in the tribe, but that don't mean nothing. In their way, they ain't doing it right if they ain't feeding you."

Clark gave a chuckle. His gaze drifted up the mountainside, and a smile crept onto his face. "I remember Mrs. Agonito, my friend Anthony's mother, back in Deer River. She always had something cooking when I'd go to their house to play as a child. Mmm, I remember the smell of her tomatoes stewing. Filled the entire neighborhood." He sniffed the air like he expected the scent to come drifting, ever so lightly, into the chilly mountain shadow.

I figured I'd push it just a bit further.

"These are real people, 'Tenant. They got their young'uns and little babies up there."

It was like the man was there in the camp for just a bit when, all-a-sudden, the soldier in him reared up. He blinked hard, shook his head, and gave me a hard look.

"How is it they can be so savage though, Rowland? The stories I've heard are incredible—mutilations, torture, just horrible, devilish things."

"I can't explain a lot of that, sir, but I heard the Lakota Chief, Red Cloud, say once that there are fools on both sides of this thing, and I tend to agree. I think when you deal with any group of folks, you gotta allow for the fools. You can't explain 'em, and you sure as hell can't excuse them, but you know they're there, and if a person don't allow for 'em, I'd say they're fools themselves."

I tried to get him back to focusing on their dilemma. "Like I said, there's good ones and bad ones, just the same as everywhere else, sir. All in all, though, these people are just trying to hang on to their ways best they can. Now they're out here on the dodge, holed up in these mountains, trying to last out the winter so they can hunt up some buffler next summer, but that ain't gonna happen. You know it, I know it, and they're about to."

Clark rubbed the short growth of soft blond hair on his chin. I couldn't tell if he was warming his face or considering my words.

"I'm sure we can talk them out of there, Rowland. If we can get a quick surround of the camp, like we did with Red Cloud and Red Leaf's camps last month, we just need to convince their chief, Dull Knife, that it's pointless to resist."

"No, that's . . .'Tenant, that won't do. It just won't do."

"Why not? I don't see why it wouldn't."

A few months earlier, Red Cloud and Red Leaf had moved their bands away from the agency, protesting the terms of a new treaty that forced them to give up the Black Hills, sacred land to Lakota and Cheyenne alike. Many of these same troops that were with us on this ride were able to do a surprise surround of their camps and force them back onto the agency without any shooting whatsoever. I couldn't see that happening here, though.

"First off, yer gonna want to call him by his Cheyenne name, Morning Star. Dull Knife's what his Lakota kin call him. He'd listen to you, but in front of his own people, he'd just as soon answer to Morning Star. Next thing is, he's not the only one yer needing to convince. A Cheyenne camp the size they say this one is means you got all sorts of Council chiefs and Society chiefs, not to mention two or three other Old Man Chiefs. You just ain't gonna ride in there and get one man to lead all them others out. It just don't work that way with them. It ain't like there's just one big toad in that puddle."

"How do you sign that? Morning Star?"

I showed him the sign. "He's a good man. One of the best fighting men they ever had. He's getting up in years now, but he's still as respected as he's ever been. Everyone loves him and listens to him, but you'd still need to talk with them others, sir."

The officer seemed fascinated. "So, what's the difference between them? You called them Old Man Chiefs, and what were the others?" he asked.

"Council chiefs and society chiefs," I answered. "You also have the Keepers of the sacred bundles. In terms that you would use, society chiefs are the military leaders, like generals, you might say. Councilmen are just what you'd think they are. They're like senators who speak for the different bands when they all come together."

"And Old Man Chiefs?" Clark asked.

"Well, maybe you'd understand better if I called them by their other name, the Peace chiefs. They act like a counterweight to the bickering of the Council and the hotheaded nature of the society chiefs. Their job is to keep things calm in the middle of tough times. You'd think they'd be the ones you needed to convince, but all them others have just as much say."

"And who are these other key men, Rowland? Perhaps if we got enough of them to see the folly of fighting, they could convince others?"

I gave a big sigh. "Off the top of my head, sir, you probly got the Keepers, Black Hairy Dog and Coal Bear, and the other three Old Man Chiefs, Little Wolf, Black Moccasin, and Old Bear. There's some councilmen, Standing Elk, Ice, and Two Moons, and some society chiefs, Last Bull and Tangle Hair. I can go on, sir."

I counted all my fingers, hoping he'd see the folly in his sketchy plan. I watched him when I stopped at ten names, but he didn't look a bit concerned. He wasn't about to give up on the idea that a forced parley was going to work.

"Who would stand with Morning Star if we convinced him?" he asked.

I stuffed my hands back in my mittens. He seemed more set on figuring out some way to change their minds than trying to change Mackenzie's, but I had to work whatever angle I had.

"Little Wolf would be one for sure. It's really his camp up there. Course, even he can only do so much on account of all them others."

"Little Wolf?" Clark dropped his open hand, palm down, as if patting a small boy on the head, then signed wolf again. "Why is it his camp? You say he's an Old Man Chief like Dull—er, Morning Star?"

"Close enough," I said, regarding his signs. "But he's also what's called Sweet Medicine Chief, kind of a spiritual leader, more like a pope than a preacher, though. He's also still an unofficial head man in one of their warrior societies. The Cheyenne ain't ever allowed a man to be all them things at once before. He's a different sorta fella. He'd have some pull for sure, but it just depends on if he can get through to the others. I can tell you this much: I took that trip to Washington with him, Morning Star, and all them other Council chiefs a few years back, and ever since, he and Morning Star are probly the ones most convinced that there ain't no sense in fighting. Well, other'n Old Crow over there. He went along with us."

I nodded toward Old Crow and the others, who had ended their walk at a safe distance from the top of the ridge. No one was allowed to go all the way to the top and risk being seen, so the Cheyenne were walking slowly back toward us. The mountain's shadow now covered the entire valley and stretched out into the plains. It would soon completely engulf them, dragging nightfall like a blanket close behind.

"Old Bear, Black Moccasin, Coal Bear, and Black Hairy Dog will all more'n likely throw in with Morning Star and Little Wolf. Most of 'em are older and got cooler heads. I'm telling ya, though, there's some of them younger Council and Society chiefs that have been just hell-bent on staying out, and after whipping up on Custer, they'll probly think they can handle us too.

"Little Wolf left the agency just before the Custer fight. He said he was going to try to talk 'em outta fighting, but it's hard saying where he stands now, after that mare's nest. I'm sure most of the others got their dander up pretty damned good, though. Surround or no surround, they ain't about to just give up. Little Wolf might be able to convince some of them if he's given any time to work on 'em."

Clark had been studying the seams of his mittens as he listened. He nodded through my whole rant, and I could see his concern grow as I explained the situation to him. My hope had grown with it.

A young soldier came climbing up the draw in our direction, obviously on the hunt for something, or someone.

"Lieutenant Clark! Anyone seen Clark!" The soldier tried to keep his voice from carrying too far while still being heard among the troops.

"Here, soldier! Up here!" Clark replied, using the same muffled bark.

I recognized Colonel Mackenzie's orderly, Private Smith, and knew before he uttered a word what his message was going to be.

"General says he's wanting to see you, sir. Says we're mounting up soon."

"Thank you, Private. Tell him I'm on my way."

"Yes, sir." The young man turned and trotted back down the draw.

"The boy won't call McKenzie by anything but his brevet," laughed Clark as he stood stretching his legs and back, trying to get some blood moving. "We'll have another chance to visit, Bill. I'm glad we had this talk. I'm not sure if there's anything I can do about it, but I understand your situation better now, and I truly appreciate your insight."

"Thank you, sir. I 'preciate your taking the time to listen. Maybe things'll turn out all right after all. A fella can always hope, eh?"

"That's right. I'll see you soon, and thank you for the lesson." Clark slipped his right mitten off and touched his fingertips to his lips before extending his hand, palm up, toward me.

I nodded, you're welcome, and he headed off after the orderly.

Old Crow appeared behind me with a look that said he knew something was up. "Where is White Hat going?" he asked, using the name all the scouts had started to call the friendly little soldier chief.

"Off to do his job, my friend. Now we need to get ready to do ours."

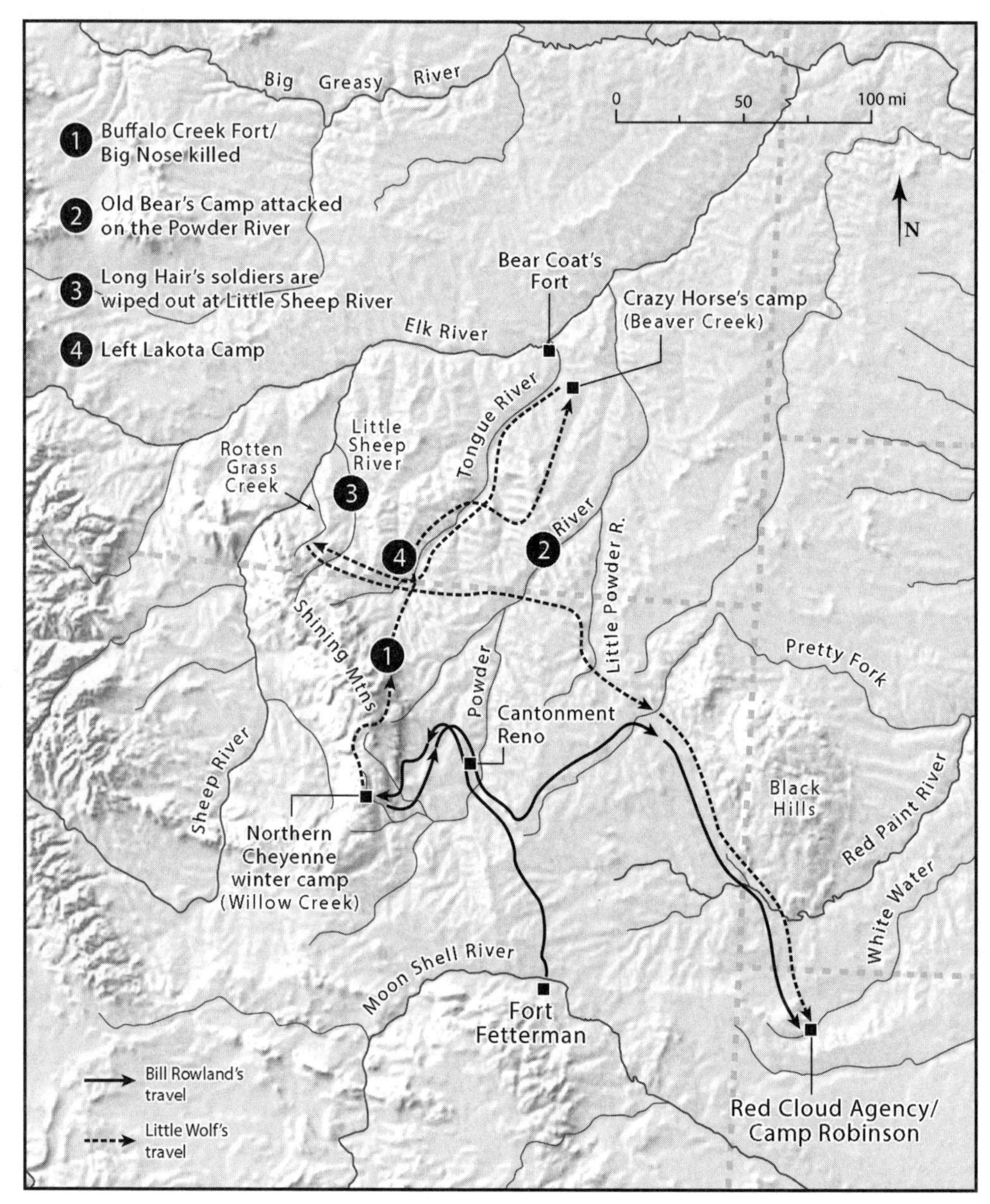


Big Slope Country

# An Insolent Indian

COLD AIR HAD SETTLED INTO THE VALLEY OVERNIGHT, BUT THE amber glow of over a hundred and fifty lodges gathered in the valley below him warmed Little Wolf's heart. He stood on a red sand hillside behind camp singing softly and smoking as he waited for *Ešeʼhe* to cast his first rays over the eastern horizon.

Every pole in each of the cone-shaped lodges below had been raised leaning into the others next to it. Together, they created the familiar dwelling circle below. These circles were where the Cheyenne lived and raised their young, teaching them how, like the lodge poles, they needed to rely on each other to create a larger circle where they all could live as a tribe, ultimately becoming part of the greater circle created by all of life leaning on Grandmother Earth and the Creator.

It had been his custom since becoming Sweet Medicine Chief to climb a hill overlooking camp at daybreak and pray. Though he often scoffed at many traditions as being a waste of time, he felt that this morning ritual of his served a worthwhile purpose. The presence of their chosen man watching over them at the start of each day gave reassurance to the women and children in camp that all was well. It made for a happy camp.

He recalled from his own childhood when High Backed Wolf, who was Sweet Medicine Chief at that time, would do the same. His mother would look to find where he stood and sing an honor song when she saw him each morning.

"*Motseʼeoeve hėstaneheono*, we are Sweet Medicine's People," she would sing. "There is our chosen man."

*Ešeʼheʼs* light first struck the western peaks behind him, and he waited until it crept down past where he stood. When it touched the tips of the lodges, he climbed on his horse and started back down the hill toward his lodge. Lightning would have his morning meal waiting for him.

He had crossed the creek and was approaching the backside of the village when a camp crier appeared, riding his morning circle around the lodges. The man's deep, resonant voice droned the camp news into the morning air, but the noisy stream behind Little Wolf made it difficult to catch his words. He heard something about the Council meeting to be held that evening, but the rest was lost in the sound of rushing water.

A young man walked out from between two lodges and hailed the crier. Little Wolf recognized the young man as Medicine Top, the son of his old friend Box Elder. Medicine Top handed the crier a little bundle, no doubt a gift of tobacco, to add his bit of news to the morning's report. As the young man walked away, the crier resumed his ride, but at a faster pace.

The chief trotted forward to distance himself from the noisy creek. He fell in behind the crier and heard the reason for the man's quickened step. "Our friend Box Elder says he has had an important vision given to him early this morning! He saw the white man's soldiers coming into our camp! Now, elders, women, and children! Elders, women, and children! Our friend says you should pack your belongings and be ready to go into the hills behind camp! Elders, women, and children! Make yourselves ready to leave the camp!"

People poured from their lodges to stare dumbfounded at the crier as if he carried a white soldier on his back as he gave the news. The man continued his ride around camp, eventually disappearing behind the lodges near the creek. The sound of his voice lessened as he moved away, but his words were echoed in a murmur that quickly rose into shouts of concern.

"The Council will be meeting earlier than we thought today," Little Wolf mused out loud as he turned and rode through camp. He had to get home as quickly as possible to help Lightning calm their daughters.

He had passed just a few lodges when a mounted man named Whetstone loped past him to the edge of camp and began trotting his horse back and forth, shouting loudly.

"Hear me! Hear me! No one should leave! We will not run into the hills because an old man has had a dream! Go home! Stay in camp! Last Bull says anyone who tries to leave will be whipped back to camp!"

A group of Kit Fox men hustled between the lodges, brandishing their quirts and telling people, "Stay home. Do not pack. Wait until the Council meeting." Some ignored the threats and continued their preparations to leave. Whetstone's older brother, a small, wiry Kit Fox named Black Coyote, jumped off his horse, and without a word slammed the butt of his leaded quirt against one man's head, knocking him to the ground. He pulled his knife and cut the cinch of a pack strapped to the horse the man had been leading, sending its contents crashing to the ground. He turned and raised his quirt again, causing the man's family to step back in fear.

"No one is leaving camp," he shouted, "We are *Tsitsistats*. We do not run like cowards."

The belligerent man suddenly noticed Little Wolf watching him from atop his horse. His first reaction was concern for being caught, but a sneer soon crossed his lips when he realized the chief would do nothing to stop him. There had been a time in his life when Little Wolf might have confronted Black Coyote, demanding that those who wanted to leave be allowed to do so, and another time when he might actually have been the one yielding the quirt holding them back. Today, however, his place was to do neither. A chief was required to walk with a quiet heart and calm demeanor in difficult situations such as this.

Little Wolf restrained his anger behind a small but confident smile then turned, keeping Black Coyote in sight until the last moment, and left for his lodge, ignoring the stares of those around him.

He approached his lodge from the rear and saw his son-in-law, Walking Whirlwind. He called to the young man. "Go find Plenty Bears, the Elk Soldiers' crier. Tell him to go out and announce that all Council members should go to the Council Lodge as soon as they can. We cannot wait until tonight to settle this. I will make myself ready and be there soon myself."

Walking Whirlwind nodded, swung up on his horse, and rode away.

The chief arrived at the Council Lodge a short time later, having changed into clothes more suitable for a formal Council meeting. As soon as he was spotted, the crowd pressed in around him, demanding that something be decided. He pushed past them and entered the lodge, only to reappear moments later with a bundle of short, colored sticks in his hands. He called two older boys over and told them, "Go to each Council member's lodge and give them one of these. We will call them to Council in the old way if they cannot hear the crier."

Alone and in pairs, the councilmen pressed their way through the crowd of people. Once inside, each man took his customary position in the inner circle. The members of the warrior societies took their usual places in a second row behind them. Tradition held that these society men could attend the gathering but were not allowed to speak unless they were first acknowledged by a Council member.

Despite the sudden call and all the upheaval in camp, the Cheyenne Council was slow to gather. Little Wolf was aware that not all forty-four members of the body would be there. *Some are gone, but many do not think this is that important*, he thought. *They see it as just another power struggle between the Kit Fox and the Elk Horn Scrapers. They think the white soldiers will continue north looking for Crazy Horse.*

The pipe was passed, binding each man who smoked to speak the truth. After the customary greetings were given, Standing Elk, a Council member with strong political aspirations, rose to lodge a complaint.

"Friends, I want to say before we begin that it is not right that we come together so quickly. There are many who have not arrived yet. They planned to be here later when we first said to meet. I say we should wait for them."

Little Wolf recognized Standing Elk's usual effort to obtain as many political allies as he could to support him on any issues he might have concerns about. The chief was glad to hear Black Hairy Dog urge the Council to proceed.

"I know my friend Standing Elk wants to be sure everyone's thoughts are considered," Black Hairy Dog responded, "but we cannot wait for everyone to be here. We must hear what Box Elder has seen and decide what to do about it. This is not a decision to just move the camp. Our families may be in danger now, and we must decide quickly." The Arrows Keeper turned to the frail-looking elder sitting next to him. "Tell us what you have seen, my friend," he said.

Box Elder had long sat in the inner circle as a member of the Council. At well past seventy winters, everyone in the lodge knew that beneath his simple robe, his slight frame was seamed with the scars from wounds gained both in battle and prayer as he sacrificed his body in service to his people. Time and the elements had weathered the old man's face much like they made the deep creases and crevices in the land around them. He had given his eyes to *Ešeʼhe* many years ago so he might attain the gift of prophecy. That sacrifice was evident in the milky white sheath that now covered each of his pupils. His reward for that exchange was considerable, and he had helped the people on many occasions with his gift. His son, Medicine Top, though not a Council member, was allowed to sit next to him to help him with the pipe and other responsibilities.

The old prophet cleared his throat and shared the scene that had played out in front of his sightless eyes while he prayed in his lodge that morning. It was as simple as the story the crier had shared.

"I felt heaviness in my heart when I prayed this morning. I knew *Maʼheoʼo* wanted to show me something, but I was afraid to look. It took me a long time to be ready, but when I was, I saw soldiers coming into our camp. There were many of them, and they were all shooting at us and burning our lodges. There was nothing we could do to stop them, and many people were killed. I told my son to go tell the crier about this and to tell him to warn everyone that the weak ones should get themselves ready to leave this place. I am ready to go. We all should be away from here already. That is what I saw, and that is all I have to say. *Henaʼhaanehe*, I am done talking now."

There were two men Little Wolf had known in his life who had convinced him that, if there was ever such a thing as true medicine, they possessed it. Box Elder, with his gift of prophecy, was one. Bridge, the old Ree medicine man who cared for the people with his power to heal, was the other. Both had proven time and again that their abilities went far above mere guesswork or showmanship, and both used their gifts to serve in a humble way. Little Wolf admired that, and when either man spoke, he listened closely.

A reverent silence followed Box Elder's story until Last Bull rose to his feet in the second row and again spoke beyond his position.

"Where are these soldiers that our women must run from? Where are the brave *Tsitsistas* who should run toward them? We fought the soldiers and beat them at Little Sheep River, and we drove them back before that at the fight on Roseberry River. Are you afraid to fight without Crazy Horse? Do you forget that the Kit Fox men wiped out an entire Snake camp since then? We are not afraid, why are you?"

He referred to a recent fight on the west side of the mountains where his men had found and destroyed a Shoshone village whose men must have been off hunting. They killed all its inhabitants, taking many scalps and other trophies in the process.

Last Bull's audacity reminded Little Wolf of his own in his younger days. Physically, the young Kit Fox head man resembled Morning Star in his youth. He was tall, stocky, and had an imposing presence, that of a man who could hold his own in any fight. He had taken the time today to come dressed in his finest buckskin, dyed and beaded in great detail. On his head sat the wide-brimmed hat taken from a soldier he had killed at Little Sheep River.

"Look! Look at this place!" The confident man waved his arm as if everyone might suddenly be able to see through the lodge skin cover. "How can they hurt us here? Will they stand on top of the mountains and roll stones at us? If they follow our trail here from the south, we will see them coming long before they get here, and they would have to string out single file like sheep if they come by the steep trails to the east. We can shoot them down one by one."

The Council was quiet after Last Bull's harangue, though Little Wolf could see Split Nose, in his own position in the second row, struggling to hold his tongue. *He will have his talk with this man later*, the chief thought. *He will not speak out of place and dishonor this lodge.*

Last Bull's brash attitude was not wise for the welfare of the camp, and someone needed to say something. Little Wolf placed his hand on his chest where the chief's bundle hung under his shirt, seeking the strength and wisdom it offered to those who wore it, then stood to gain everyone's attention. He took a moment and cleared his throat to indicate that his words came from a good heart.

"My friends, it is true the soldiers have failed in their last attacks. Maybe if they come they will fail again. But it could end like the fight on the Powder River last spring when they came into our camp and destroyed it. Just as Box Elder saw in his vision today. I think our men will fight well if they have to, but I do not think it would be wise to have our women and children here during that fight. They are too many to take to the mountain quickly if fighting starts, so let us have them go there now and pile stones for protection. Then, if any fighting happens, we will not need to worry about them."

Little Wolf removed his hand from the chief's bundle and reached for a silver medallion that hung on the outside of his shirt. "If they come, the white soldier chiefs might want to talk peace if they see that we have only our men here and that we are ready for them."

The medallion was the peace medal he had received from the White Father on his trip to the east three winters earlier. He had also received a holster with a set of pearl-handled revolvers, which were now slung around his hips. They looked as out of place there as Last Bull's wide-brimmed hat did on the taller man's head. The ornately tooled holster had a silver plate on it with what Bill Rowland said were the white man words for the chief's name carved into it.

Last Bull stepped between two Council members and moved brazenly out into the center of the circle where he again demanded to be heard.

"Talk? They will here come to kill us, and you would talk? Where is the brave man Little Wolf, who I have heard so many stories about? You ran to the agency after that early fight at Powder River, and you were not even with us during the other two fights this summer. Ah! I remember. You came just after the last one. Some say you came with the soldiers. Maybe you have talked to these soldiers too much already. I say you should put your peace medal away and put your hands on the guns they gave you. They will help us more."

The young head man's words were impertinent. Never had such

disrespect been shown during a Council meeting. The entire assembly sat in slack-jawed silence as the scene played out in front of them.

After the attack at Powder River, Little Wolf had been conflicted. Most of the camp had been destroyed, and Old Bear and the other leaders had decided to set out to find Crazy Horse. Though Little Wolf was at odds with the Lakota leader, he traveled with them to ensure the safety of the weak ones. However, once they found the Lakota camp and everyone was safe, he wasted no time in racing back to gather his family, who he had left at the Red Cloud Agency. He feared there might be retaliation for the fight, even though the Cheyenne were not the aggressors. When he arrived, he found plans had been made for his eldest daughter, Chopping Woman, to marry Walking Whirlwind, and yet again, tradition would interfere with his desire to act quickly. Weddings took time. The ceremony itself was nothing, but a lodge must be prepared for the new couple, and gifts must be made and exchanged. Unless the soldiers were to come shooting, there would be no hasty departure. The soldiers had appeared nervous, and rumors were being spread about plans for a big attack, but there had been no effort made to harass any of the bands staying at the agency. The soldiers were focused more on the large gathering that had developed as a result of the Powder River fight. Little Wolf felt an obligation to return to the large camp to warn them as well as try to convince the Cheyenne at least to come in to the agency for their own safety. His timing was poor, and he had arrived on the heels of the soldiers immediately after the main part of the fight had finished.

Little Wolf felt his teeth grinding at Last Bull's disrespectful behavior. The Cheyenne way was that only after a man had insulted him five times was a chief allowed to retaliate or show anger against him in any way. It was after the fight at Little Sheep River that Last Bull had first suggested that Little Wolf might have come with those soldiers, making this the second time he had slandered him in this way. Both men knew the count.

The chief knew his late arrival at that fight would haunt him for a long time to come. His explanations would do little to convince anyone who still questioned his allegiance. He glanced down at

Morning Star, who stared respectfully toward the center of the lodge, appearing unmoved by either man's words, as was fitting of a chief. Little Wolf's friend and all the older, more traditional leaders in camp would never weaken the Arrows by getting involved in a power struggle with the insolent society chief.

*This cannot be settled in Council,* Little Wolf thought, *but something must be done soon.*

Last Bull stepped toward the lodge door. "If these soldiers are coming for us, then the Kit Fox will fight them by ourselves if you are all afraid. The camp will not move. Now, my boys and I will have a scalp dance to celebrate our victory over the Snakes. You can all wait here. Maybe the soldiers will come talk to you."

With that, he ducked out the door, and all the Kit Fox men stood up and followed him. Once outside, he hollered for everyone to hear, "Start gathering wood, my friends! We will have a big dance tonight!"

The canyon echoed with yelps and hollering as they left the clearing to gather wood. Inside the Council Lodge, all was quiet, until Split Nose gave a small cough from his place in the second row. Black Hairy Dog nodded to the Elk Soldier's head man.

The society chief stood and addressed the Council in a manner more fitting of someone who spoke from the back row.

"My friends, this is a hard time for us to be fighting with each other. I believe the words of our friend Box Elder, and I think his vision might be the truth. Let the Kit Fox have their dance. We don't need to fight with them about that, but we must still have our loved ones leave this place. Now, I think we should all go from here to help them get ready to go up on the mountainside. By the time the Kit Fox have their fire built, everyone will be ready to go. We men can stay here and have this dance with them, but the weak ones must go away. *Hena'haanehe.*"

Murmurs of approval came from around the lodge. A few others spoke in support of his plan, and the Council ended.

The packing was done inside lodges to avoid a confrontation with the Kit Fox. Little Wolf and Walking Whirlwind kept watch while the women and girls worked together to pack what they needed to stay away from camp for a few days. Robes, food, camp tools—enough to keep them comfortable if this turned into an extended stay but still light enough so they could travel quickly. Some belongings would be carried up the mountainside on their backs while the rest would be strapped to horses. They would leave their lodges standing.

Day Woman gathered items as her mother called for them. Two Woman had left the moon lodge early, and she and White Voice helped the pregnant Chopping Woman gather and pack the supplies from her lodge. If Box Elder's vision was true, they had much to do even after they reached the safety of the hills behind camp.

When the time came, Little Wolf and Walking Whirlwind each heaved a pack up on a horse as Lightning and Two Woman quickly strapped it to the animal. The two men planned to escort their family to the western edge of camp where they would disappear into the high hillside behind camp. As they walked past the last lodges, they could see a knot of people on the flat behind camp, about halfway to the hill that Little Wolf had prayed on that morning. Black Coyote, Whetstone, and a few others were again chastising the crowd with quirts in hand.

"Go back! We are all dancing tonight! No one is going to the hills. Go back and unpack. The fire is ready to be lit." Some retreated immediately, while others tried to push their way past the cordon of men. Black Coyote brandished his knife again, this time cutting both the pack cinch and the horse it encircled. The horse squealed in pain and charged toward the creek, sending the pack crashing to the ground.

"Where is Last Bull?" Little Wolf raised his voice to be heard above the quarreling.

Black Coyote's head snapped around as he tracked the familiar voice calling to him. "He waits for everyone at the fire!" The small man snarled before going back to harassing the people in front of him.

Little Wolf turned to Lightning. "Return to the lodges with Walking Whirlwind. Keep everyone together, and I'll be there after I have talked with Last Bull."

Little Wolf left his family and rode toward the center of camp. He dismounted behind the Council Lodge and tethered his horse to some deer sage. He then walked toward the large stack of wood in the middle of the clearing. Two men were busy lighting the tinder at the base of the pyre. Flames appeared, and their brightness soon revealed how dim the evening had already become. On the far side of the growing fire, Last Bull and Split Nose were engaged in a heated discussion.

Several Elk Soldiers stood behind Split Nose, who was finally speaking his mind to Last Bull. "The Elks are camp guard now. Why do you think the Kit Fox can just decide that no one will leave? You are becoming too proud, I think. You disrespect the Arrows and the Council, and now you put the lives of our women and children at risk."

"You worry too much, my friend." Last Bull dismissed the man's concerns while glancing around to make sure there were enough Kit Fox men available should they be needed. "This is a time to celebrate! We have won many fights this summer. We should be celebrating those victories, not running in fear."

"This is no victory dance," Split Nose said. "You want only to remind us that we did not have the ears to hear your warning about the soldiers coming to attack Old Bear's camp on Powder River last spring. No one listened to you, and the soldiers destroyed that camp. Now you will listen to no one, and the same thing will happen here if we do not leave."

Last Bull had always denied he was resentful for being ignored, but it was abundantly clear that the insult played a part in his determination to be heard now.

A large drum, captured during the defeat of the Snake village, was brought out and set in place. The Kit Fox men began to gather around it, testing its tone with light drumming while warming up their voices. The deep, resonating thumps sent a palpable energy into the air, the way a heart pushes life into the body. The drummers soon found a rhythm and were raising their voices when a rider galloped into the clearing from the east.

"*Otahe! Otahe!* Listen to me!" he called. "*Otahe!* My horses! Someone stole my horses!" He saw Little Wolf standing with the two society headmen and rode over. A circle of people gathered around.

The man, Sits in the Night, struggled to catch his breath. "I went downstream to check on my horses," he gasped. "When I came near where they should have been, I saw riders driving them away. I could hear them whipping them as they ran, and I heard a rumbling from farther down the creek. I think the white soldiers might be down there."

Split Nose turned to Last Bull. "Will you listen now? This man has seen these things with his own eyes! You cannot keep saying there is nothing to worry about."

"Let him go chase his horses if he worries about them," Last Bull retorted. "The Crows who stole from the herd two camps ago are probably back. The man said they ran away, so no one is attacking us. If it makes you less afraid, I will have a man go watch, and he will let us know if anyone comes to steal more horses. But we will still dance tonight." He signaled for the drummers to resume. "What are you so afraid of?" he goaded Split Nose, his voice rising above the drumbeats. "You will not be the only man killed if we are attacked by the white soldiers. Don't be so afraid!"

A few men started dancing right away, seemingly unconcerned by the most recent warning. Little Wolf glanced around and could see others being prodded and poked by the Kit Fox until they, too, were inside the circle.

Split Nose had to shout now as the drummers began to sing. "I don't care for myself. I am thinking of the women and children! I want them to go to the hills where they will be safe! Then we can fight and not worry about them!"

Last Bull was unmoved. His lips curled in a mocking sneer.

The frustrated Elk Soldier threw his arms forward, while he shouted as if throwing his last argument at him the Kit Fox leader. "You will know in the morning how wrong you are! Wait until morning!"

# Climbing to Conflict

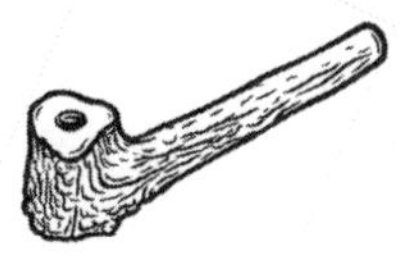

The horse in front of me had stopped. "What's the hold-up?" I asked in a hushed voice.

The only reply was the sound of hooves pounding the ground and the shadowy image of the horse's hindquarters dropping out of sight. "God damn …" was all I could get out before being knocked off my feet by a thrashing leg of the falling animal. Ulysses snorted and drew back, snapping the reins out of my hand as the buckskin tried to keep his own feet underneath him.

I landed on my back with a grunt and skittered down the slope to my left. I quick flattened out to keep from sliding over the edge, but a layer of loose gravel rolled underneath me, and off into the gully I went. My right knee slammed into a rock on the way down, pitching me to the left and away from the horse. I landed in a heap on an icy crust of snow at the bottom of the narrow, twisting ravine.

We had been climbing a steep incline with the ravine on our left. The trail was so narrow and slick that the entire company had to dismount and creep, single file, along its edge. The horse had fallen headfirst into the deep gully, taking myself and the poor private who had foolishly held on to the reins with him.

Once the shower of pebbles stopped, I collected myself and turned to check on the horse and the young private. My eyes adjusted to the darkness, and I could see the horse lying on its left side with its left rear leg extending back toward him. The cannon bone had snapped and protruded through the skin, its grisly whiteness visible even in the dark gully. The right leg was thrust forward and disappeared behind a hard corner in the trench.

Muted calls floated down from the soldiers above. "You awright, soldier? What the hell happened?"

"I'm okay," I called back in a hoarse whisper.

I peeked around the crumbling corner and made out the dark shape of the young private, half covered by the neck and front quarters of the horse. He was just beginning to regain his bearings and trying to sit up, but he was pinned by the weight of the horse. The animal wasn't moving and gave only small, rhythmic groans, obviously dazed and in great pain.

"Ah, ahhh!" the private began to wail as he came to and realized his predicament.

Our orders were to maintain complete silence, and the boy's cries were irritating to boot.

"Shush! You be quiet, now!" I snapped.

I tried to step onto the saddle to avoid stepping on the horse then hopped to the front end of the broken animal. The poor critter still gave a short grunt and a squeal at the unavoidable pressure on its shattered ribcage. I clamped one hand on the boy's mouth to quiet him then slid my other under an arm and began tugging to pull him out from under the dying animal. He didn't budge, so I repeated myself. "You be quiet, hear?"

I took my hand from the soldier's mouth, slid it under his other arm, and pulled with all I had, moving the boy just enough that he could start kicking himself clear. He tumbled away from the animal and stood on wobbly legs. He reached to the wall of the trench to steady himself with one arm, then reached down to rub his sore legs with his other.

"You okay?" I asked.

"Y—yeah, just bruised up, I reckon," he stammered.

I pulled my knife from its sheath and knelt on the horse's head. The long blade slid easily into the horse's neck, severing the windpipe and jugular in two quick thrusts.

"Go run in the tall grass, friend," I whispered.

The animal started to bleed out. Its last breaths rasped from its slashed throat as I wiped my blade on its neck and turned to the soldier.

"Grab your kit, and let's get outta this grave," I said as I stood. I then called to those on the trail above us, "We're both okay! Send down a rope!"

There wasn't enough blood on me to spook Ulysses when I got to the top, but the suspicious horse still gave me a good sniffing. I took his reins from the soldier holding them, patted his neck to settle him a bit, then limped up the trail to give the others room to help their friend out of the trench. I found a wide spot in the trail and decided to trust Ulysses's four good legs instead of my two sore ones. I spoke to him as I climbed aboard.

"So why didn't you catch me? I know, I know, it was my own damned fault for not paying attention, yer right. All right, boy, let's get on with it, eh. Just keep a better eye out for me, will ya? This is some tough country we're in."

I first laid eyes on these hills from a distance back in forty-nine. I would sit at the campfire with Captain Stansbury, listening to his stories about something he called geology. He made sure to use words that I could understand when he explained how country like this had been worn down by water for centuries, creating twisting gullies and eventually becoming the hellish maze we were now traipsing through.

The column had covered nearly twenty miles since we had started that evening. The waxing half-moon that lit the trail earlier had slipped behind the mountains, and starlight was all we traveled by now. We were heading up the side of a ridge that was gouged and torn by narrow, twisting crevices, making tough going for man and horse alike. The rocky slopes were spotted with a spiny scrub mahogany that ripped at any flesh or flannel that wandered into it.

I continued complaining to Ulysses as we tried to catch up with the others ahead of us. "I tell ya, if it don't beat you to a pulp, it'll cut you to shreds, eh boy? All-bally-which-way like it is, some of the meanest damned country I ever come across, that's for sure. It's tough enough for a soul to have to pick their way through it in the daylight, but to go charging through it in the wee hours like this is damn near suicide if ya ask me."

I neared the top of the ridge, where I found Old Crow and the other Cheyenne scouts waiting for me.

"We thought you got lost. We left a good trail." My friend's somber expression did not match his smartass remark.

"I stopped to help one of the boys find his way out of a little hole he fell into," I replied.

"Some of these young soldiers are just pitiful to watch when they get away from camp," he said. "I think if they did not have another soldier's horse to follow, they would all fall off a cliff."

I chuckled and reached to rub my sore knee. "And if you aren't careful, they'll take you with them."

We started into the canyon on the other side of the ridge. Halfway down, Old Crow turned in his saddle and tilted his head as if he'd heard something. I slowed Ulysses and tried to listen.

I caught Old Crow's eye.

"Drum" was all he said.

"How far away?" I asked.

"Up this canyon a short way, very close."

The front of the column had stopped at the bottom of the hill and waited for everyone to catch up. I continued to listen closely and finally heard the recurring thumps. I noted the quick rhythm, "*Ea'o'tseo'o*. Scalp dance," I said.

Old Crow nodded. I looked back at Roan Bear and the others. Their heads were all turned, listening to the soft but rapid thuds bouncing through the night air.

Lieutenant Clark appeared, riding back along the ranks with another soldier at his side. He caught sight of us and rode over.

"Bill, this is Second Lieutenant DeLany. He'll be riding with you and the Cheyenne from here on. I'll be moving between different units, and he will act as my point of contact with you."

DeLany nodded at me and gave the Cheyenne a cursory glance.

"Yes, sir," I answered and gave DeLany a nod back. "Whatever you say."

"I'm going to have the lieutenant show your men to their place in the column, and I'd like to have a word with you alone."

"Yes, sir."

I told Old Crow and the rest to go with DeLany then followed Clark off the trail to let others pass.

The officer wasted no time. "Bill, I've been talking with the colonel, and here's the best I could do for you and your scouts. He's a little put out right now because of all the delays in getting here, but when we advance on the village, which should be just a couple miles ahead of us here, he wants the scouts involved in making the surround. He'll have the Pawnee and Shoshone take the lead into the village, and after them will come the Arapaho and the Sioux. Your Cheyenne will bring up the rear of the initial maneuver. This will keep you close to him in the event that we are able to start a parlay with those in camp after the surround is complete."

I tried to sound grateful. "Thank you, 'Tenant. It's not the best arrangement for sure. Those damn Pawnee and Snakes are going to be hard to control when they get close to camp. I'd just as soon have them at the back of the whole damned parade, but at least me and the boys won't have to go in there and do any shooting."

"I understand you have mixed feelings about this," Clark said, "but you're right, at least you won't have to worry about being in the thick of the fighting should any break out. Here comes Garnett and the Lakota. I need to speak with him."

Clark left, and I rode down to join the others. The eastern sky was just starting to show the dark horizon below it. The stars would soon all fade from view, eventually leaving the morning star to stand alone in the east in that brief moment before dawn.

I found the boys waiting at our spot in the formation. They seemed edgy. The Lakota were still descending the ridge, so there was an empty space between them and the Pawnee. When I got there, we watched the twitchy little bastards strip off their military uniforms down to only a breechcloth and begin painting themselves for war. Some had replaced their military headgear with traditional porcupine and deer tail roaches; others donned bear claw necklaces and bone breastplates. Most had changed their mounts and now rode their war horses. They were clearly getting more excited by the minute.

My gut started to ache.

The soft, steady whump, whump, whump of the Cheyenne drum now throbbed like a heartbeat, adding to the predawn tension and keeping everyone on edge.

"How ya doing, Bill?" Billy Garnett appeared from the darkness as he and the Lakota assumed their place behind the Pawnee. The boy had already changed his mount and now straddled a tall, nervous, dun that worried at his bit.

I was startled at first, then replied, "Oh, just all chirked up and excited, Billy. You'd best be getting up to your place now, son. We're fixing to leave here in a bit."

He caught my sarcasm and puzzled a bit. "Uh, reckon so," he said then turned the dun away. Any concern he had for my grouch disappeared when a couple of his friends caught up with him. He slapped them each on the shoulder and began sharing his excitement with them.

Mackenzie and Clark had moved to the front, and the company soon started to move again. The strict orders for silence in the ranks remained, and everyone was admonished to stay in formation until orders were given to do otherwise. The sound of the drum grew louder as we rode along the narrow canyon floor toward a slight crest about a half-mile west of us.

Lieutenant Clark again worked his way back through the scouts when we drew closer, taking a moment to speak with each interpreter on his way. He finished with the Lakota then headed for me. We kept a slow pace as Clark spoke.

"Bill, there's been a change of plans. We will stage at the bend ahead of us here. Our reconnaissance tells us that the camp is about a mile and a half past that point and is primarily on the south side of the stream that cuts through a long valley. The horse herd is on the north side. What the colonel wants now is for the Pawnee and Shoshone to take the left flank while four companies under Major Gordon will take the right, cutting the village off from the horse herd. The Arapaho, Sioux, and your Cheyenne will ride with me. We'll move quickly through the village to its opposite side to complete the surround. It's his hope that familiar friends and allies riding through the camp and encouraging them to surrender will ease some of the panic that's sure to result."

I felt like a green-broke horse hunkering down and strangling itself against the rope tightening around its neck. It was all I could do to choke out a few words.

"I can't do any shooting, 'Tenant."

Ulysses pawed at the ground, sensing my discomfort.

"I know, Bill, I know. Just don't do anything to make it obvious to those around you. I'll try not to put you or your men in any tight spots, but I can't guarantee anything."

We stared at each other a moment as if making some sort of silent pact between us. Best I could do was nod my agreement.

A question appeared in Clark's eyes. "If we happen to get separated, I was wondering, what's the sign for friend?" he asked.

There were two ways of signing that word, but I decided to show him only one. I dropped the reins and held both my hands up, index fingers together in front of my throat. I raised them together about head high, pushing them slightly away and said, "*Hoovehe*." Clark dropped his reins and repeated both the sign and the word.

"Remember," I said, "you'll need to put your gun down to say it."

Clark grinned just as the drum beats stopped. The once unnoticed sounds of horses coughing, bridles rattling, and hooves clicking on rocks now seemed to echo through the canyon. Clark hissed, "Be ready, Bill!" then spun and rode back toward Mackenzie.

The column covered the last half-mile quickly as the eastern sky continued to lighten, casting bright rays of pink and gold into the sparse clouds above our heads. We assembled behind a low ridge jutting into the narrow canyon that was the eastern end of a long valley that appeared to broaden out the farther west it went.

Mackenzie gathered the interpreters at the front to give us his final instructions to share with the scouts. When I arrived there, I could see that a few horses had wandered to the eastern tip of the valley and were visible through the fog that shrouded the creek below us. I could smell the campfires as Mackenzie gave his talk.

"Tell your men I want every man here to remember his promise to General Crook and to be a good Indian today. Our main goals are to surround the village and capture the horses. There is to be no shooting unless the Cheyenne fire upon us first." As he spoke, Mackenzie tracked the eyes of a few of the men who were watching something happening behind him.

A Lakota scout was already making his way downhill toward the Cheyenne horses.

"What is that man doing down there?" Mackenzie barked at Billy Garnett. "Go get him and bring him back here!"

"Yes, sir!" Billy spurred his horse over the side of the ridge and down after the man. Another rider raced over the edge behind him. It was Billy's friend, Bat Pourier.

I stood in my stirrups to watch Billy and Bat approach the scout. The three men were talking when a fourth appeared and rode right past them without even a hallo. The first scout clearly wasn't about to miss out on claiming any horses and chased after the man. Billy and Bat gave a short glance up toward Mackenzie then turned and hustled after the others. All four now seemed hell-bent for horses.

"Son of a bitch!" Mackenzie spat in anger then turned and barked at Lieutenant Clark and Frank North, "Go! Get them all in there!"

I nudged Ulysses off to the side to wait for the Cheyenne while the Pawnee and Shoshone all headed over the ridge and the first hard rays of sunlight struck the high peaks to the west.

# Riding to Ruination

Little Wolf stumbled slightly on his way back to his lodge. He was tired. He had sent a message to his wives early in the night that he would be staying at the scalp dance to ensure that Last Bull and his Kit Fox did not try to take even more advantage of the people they had already forced to attend. Some of the women had gone so far as to tie their daughters together with rawhide thongs before they allowed them to dance to keep the rowdy Kit Fox men from grabbing one and carrying her off.

After a time, Black Coyote appeared at the dance carrying a brightly painted parfleche. Throughout the night the sinister little man would pull one of several scalps he had taken during the attack on the Snakes camp and dance to tell the story of how he took it from its previous owner. But he spent most of his time walking among his fellow Kit Fox, encouraging them to inspect the rest of the contents of the parfleche and laughing gleefully when they would turn their heads and quickly shove it back to him. Little Wolf had no interest in finding out what he was showing them.

*Ešeʼhe* was about to step into the sky when the dance finally ended. Little Wolf studied the ground now to avoid another stumble. He wouldn't go to the hill to pray this morning. He needed to get some rest. Afterward, whether Morning Star and the others thought it would harm the Arrows or not, they must get the people to the hills.

As if the chief's thoughts had summoned him, Black Hairy Dog walked from behind a lodge leading two horses loaded with belongings. Little Wolf had missed the passing of the man's wife as he stumbled toward home. She now walked several steps in front of him with a securely wrapped bundle on her back. The young Arrows Keeper startled when he noticed Little Wolf. Their eyes met for a moment before the Keeper turned without a word and resumed walking toward the rear of the camp. Little Wolf knew what the man was doing but continued on his own way, acting as if he had seen nothing.

He arrived home and checked the picket ropes of his large paint stallion and a couple other horses before he went inside. As he expected, Lightning and his daughters were all awake. They sat quietly around the fire, and each had a pack nearby with the loaded horse packs waiting by the door, ready to go when it was time. Two Woman was in the small lodge with Chopping Woman, helping her to stay ready. The chief slipped off his fringed scalp shirt, stretched out on his robes, and did his best to reassure his family.

"It's over for now. After I rest we can load the horses again and take you all up on the hillside. The Kit Fox men are as tired as the rest of us. I don't think they will put up a fight."

Lightning and the girls didn't move. They had waited all night, so a short time longer would not be difficult.

The tired man finally let his eyes close. He relaxed and sank heavily into the soft grass bunched inside his buffalo robe mattress.

The stampede of scouts came to a sudden stop, and I felt hope. The Pawnee had bottlenecked on the narrow trail running between the base of the steep, rugged hillside and the creek. The Snakes came behind them and tried to climb up the steep slope to get past, and the whole bunch stacked up like cordwood.

I was back on the ridge and had gotten a better view of the triangular valley in front of us. It widened out from a couple hundred yards across where we stood at it its eastern tip to being about a mile wide at the western end, a couple miles away. The winding creek split it almost right down the middle with some nice, flat bottomland on the south side. An elevated bench littered with small, red hills was on the north side. The large horse herd sprawled all across the bench and all the way down into the creek bottom below us. I could see smoke rising from where the camp lay behind a thick stand of willows and box elder trees on the south side at the far end. We still had a long ride before we got there.

The most striking feature of the canyon, however, was the contrast between the southern wall—a deep-red sedimentary rock formation that had probably been there since the dawn of time—and the northern wall, a towering, rugged cliff of white limestone that dominated the landscape.

Below me, Mackenzie had already crossed over to the north side of the creek and now sat watching the crippling congestion on our side. He finally pointed in the direction of the Pawnee and barked out an order. Private Smith raced down to the creek, waving his arms to get the attention of Frank North. Smith stayed on his side of the creek as he and North had a very animated exchange. Smith didn't know sign talk, but his arms still sliced the air as he tried to communicate without shouting. North eventually got the message and gave his reins a hard yank. He spun his horse around and raced back to his men. He growled out a few words in Skidi, the Pawnee language, and signed that they should all cross the creek. The scouts all turned right and started to slog their way across. With the Pawnee out of the way, the Snakes were now able to move along the hillside toward the village.

Any hope I had vanished as I descended into the shroud of fog below me. I felt a hardness growing inside, as if a wall were being built. We moved into the thick stand of box elder trees that lined the winding creek at the bottom of the hill and weaved our way through. I snapped the reins to get Ulysses to lift his head.

"Pay attention now," I muttered under my breath.

Lieutenant Clark took the lead as we moved onto the valley floor. We emerged from the first stand of trees into a long meadow, where several of the Cheyenne horses looked up from their peaceful grazing.

Once past the large hill on the left, the southern wall changed over to a series of lower points and knobs that ran along the south side of the valley. West of these smaller knobs stood another high, red hill with a steep north-facing cliff. Below this cliff rose the smoke from scores of lodges blending lazily into the still, early-morning air above the trees.

We caught up with Billy and the other three breakaways in a large clearing about halfway to the camp. They had come to a stop on the far side and were all staring up at the knolls to their left. I followed their gaze and made out a small figure perched on top of one with a sharp-pointed tip. Just as it occurred to me that I was looking at a man, a puff of smoke burst from the rifle that he held. He was shooting at Billy's bunch. Half a heartbeat later, the sound from the man's rifle crackled through the creek bottom.

For a moment no one moved. Then I heard Billy shout excitedly.

"He shot first! Now fire!"

An icy dagger slid into my heart.

The meadow erupted in an explosion of sound and motion. Billy and his boys opened up on the already fleeing watchman as he ducked behind the pointy knoll. The cloud of smoke created from their four rifles all firing at once shot up like a flag, signaling to everyone following behind them to surge forward into a headlong charge toward the sleepy village on the other end of the valley.

The Cheyenne horse herd spooked from the gunshots and the clatter of our ensuing charge. They scattered chaotically in front of us. Many of the animals wore buffalo shoes, heavy wraps of buffalo hide tied around their hooves to protect them from all the rocks in the valley. This made it difficult for them to get started as they frantically lunged to escape the clamor.

Lieutenant Clark ordered us to a gallop, and the cold air rushed against my face, causing my eyes to water. Icy tears streamed along my temples and into the earflaps of my sealskin cap, becoming frozen runnels of ice that stung my exposed skin.

Ulysses easily kept pace with the other horses as they ran. Even with my blurry eyes, I could see Lieutenant Clark out in front, his large white Stetson pulled tightly down to his ears as he led the charge toward the village.

I eventually had to turn my head to the left, away from the breeze, as we raced across the meadow. I rubbed the ice from my eyes and saw the Snakes, now well beyond the pointed knoll and galloping past the others. Those in front were already heading up the first slope of the large hill that rose to the south of the still hidden village.

When I looked forward again, I saw that Garnett and his bunch had swerved to their right and crossed to the north side of the creek, no doubt afraid to enter the camp by themselves. They were headed for the vantage point of a large red knoll that rose above the trees there. This left only a few frightened horses and a small stand of trees between our group and the main village of the Northern Cheyenne.

Little Wolf's mind was drifting when he heard what sounded like a pitch-filled pine knot exploding in the fire. An echo rattled along the canyon walls, seeming to crack against each stone it met on its journey. The sound faded in the distance and was soon followed by an even louder series of pops. It took Little Wolf's tired mind a moment to recognize the sound of gunfire.

Fighting past his slumber, Little Wolf sat up and listened for the next sound to help him decide whether or not he had been dreaming. It came when Split Nose hollered from the east side of the camp.

"Soldiers have charged the camp! Soldiers have charged the camp!"

Immediately afterward, Black Hairy Dog cried out from somewhere near the rear of the camp. "Get your guns ready! The camp is charged on! They are coming!"

Little Wolf shouted as he shrugged back into his shirt and reached for his holster. "Grab your packs and run to the hills—now!"

He lunged out the door and untied the first horse. He leaned down and hoisted Day Woman onto the horse's back. He tied a quick set of reins from the lead rope and pushed them into the girl's hands. He slapped the horse on the rump to start it moving. White Voice had run toward the small lodge behind them. Lightning had already grabbed the tether of the next horse and was struggling to mount the frightened animal with her heavy pack. Little

Wolf gave her a boost up, and she turned to give him a fearful look. He gave the horse a sharp smack, shouting "Heya!" and the horse lurched forward.

The chief grabbed his rifle from its stand outside his lodge and swung onto the back of his paint stallion. Glancing over his shoulder, he saw Two Woman, White Voice, and Inside Woman all heading off toward the rear of the camp. Walking Whirlwind had pushed Inside Woman up on his warhorse, taking no chances with getting her to safety.

"Get them to the edge of the camp then come back!" the chief hollered to his son-in-law.

He urged the paint horse forward, thinking only of getting to someplace visible where he could get the attention of the soldiers. He had to see if they would talk before any more shooting took place. He saw the top of the red knoll jutting above the treetops on the north side of the creek and raced toward it.

He weaved his way through the oncoming stampede of fleeing women and children. He saw Standing Bull, Morning Star's son, run past as he neared the creek. The young man was trying to get to the horse herd east of camp. He wore only a blanket around his waist and carried his rifle in one hand and a coiled rope in the other. His long, unbraided hair flew wildly behind him.

*He did not picket a horse last night!* Little Wolf thought.

He rode past the lodges, splashed across the creek, and crashed through the underbrush on its north side. He emerged to a small open flat at the foot of the knoll and was surprised to see four men were already crouched at the top.

*I am too late*, he thought. *Someone is already there!* Two of the men on the knoll suddenly raised their rifles and fired, and Little Wolf's charging horse collapsed underneath him.

He hit the ground hard then struggled to his knees. Dazed and groggy, he fumbled about, trying to remove the bridle from his dead horse with his right hand while patting the ground with his left, searching for his lost rifle. He had no luck with either and never heard the shot that sent the bullet that struck his head.

We crashed through the last stand of trees and galloped into the long clearing where the camp was located. Ulysses sported streaks of foamed sweat where the reins had rubbed along his neck and another streak along the fringe of his saddle blanket. His breathing kept time with the rapid rhythm of his hooves clattering over the rock-strewn ground. The center of camp was empty ahead of us, but people were running between the lodges on either side of us. Most had been woken from a dead sleep, and some wore little more than a blanket as they ran. Several wore nothing. All were frightened.

I caught a movement to my right and turned to see a man racing for the trees along the creek. Standing Bull, one of Morning Star's sons, stopped in his tracks and stared back. His lips moved, but I couldn't hear what he said. I could read his eyes, however, and they asked but one damning word.

"*Tsehehamooneto*? Uncle?"

Shame hit me like a brick in the chest. "Aw, shit," was all I could say as I turned to keep up with the charging scouts.

Old Crow and the other scouts began crying out to their fleeing relatives. "We are *Tsitsistats!* Do not shoot! Do not fight with us! There are too many soldiers here with us! You cannot win!" I joined in shouting, "*Hoovėhe, nėstseeševe'ponenene!* Friend, do not shoot! Friend, do not shoot!" We were moving so blasted fast, I doubted if anyone heard us until we were right on top of them.

We were halfway through the central clearing when a rider came charging from between the three ceremonial lodges on the far side. I recognized Necklace as he cleared the lodges and saw that his rifle was aimed at Lieutenant Clark. Before he could shoot, Lieutenant DeLany fired twice with his pistol, knocking the man off his horse. He landed in a heap on the ground as his horse veered to our left and disappeared behind the lodges.

We followed the horse between the lodges on the south side of the camp and ourselves, and raced toward the back of the camp.

We reached the west end and gathered together on the slope at the very base of the red cliff. We had gained a bit of elevation, which gave us a good view of the camp and most of the valley, though I hated what I saw.

A heavy cloud of red dust had been kicked up, partially obscuring several hundred women, children, and elders, all running for their lives into one of the large draws behind camp. Others could be seen dashing around inside the cover of the trees and bushes along the creek. Large groups of panicked horses raced in erratic circles everywhere, adding to the dust and the danger of everyone's flight.

My throat tightened, and breathing came hard. An old feeling came flooding into me, and my head started to hurt. Almost twenty years earlier, Roan Bear had clubbed me from behind in a drunken brawl. I came to with blood in my eyes and saw him and his brothers taking Sis and our babies away. They had set fire to our cabin and everything else I had and left me for dead. Everything that meant anything to me was gone. And I was to blame.

Lieutenant DeLany's voice came from what seemed like a half-mile away.

"Are we going after 'em, sir?"

I was overwhelmed with dread until Lieutenant Clark replied.

"No, Lieutenant. Our orders are to secure the back side of this village. We have done that, so now we hold our position."

I looked up, and Clark quickly switched his gaze from me to the junior officer.

"Yes, sir," DeLany replied.

People continued to dash between the lodges behind us, desperate to get out of camp. Many changed course and headed for the creek after seeing us on the slope above them. A few fired hasty shots at us as they ran, making for some tense moments, as we had very little cover. The Lakota scouts fired back while we waited for the rest of the column to carry out their responsibilities. It didn't take long.

A noise like hail striking the lodges and the ground sounded around us. Then came the distinctive crack of Spencer rifles above us. This told me that the Snake scouts had reached the top of the red cliff and had started to pelt the camp with their rifle fire. The occasional boom of a Springfield breechloader mixed in among the repeaters. It wasn't too long before the ground around us started to jump.

Clark realized the danger and hollered, "Take cover! Be quick! They don't know who we are from up there!"

I made the translation in both Cheyenne and Lakota, since Billy was gone, and the scouts scattered. Some jumped from their horses and scurried for the north side of the lodges, while I raced with others up the slope and out of sight from those on the hilltop.

Clark held his ground, yelling and waving his hat to signal to them. The shower of bullets soon found other targets.

As soon as the bullets stopped, a high-pitched noise started in the trees at the east end of camp, quickly rising to a disturbing, eerie screech. It came from the Pawnee, who were blowing on eagle bone whistles as they began to enter the Cheyenne camp.

1 East Gap staging area
2 Standing Bull killed
3 Necklace killed
4 Little Wolf shot from his horse
5 Red Pipe killed
6 Gathering at the back of camp
7 Split Nose killed
8 Mckinney's charge stopped by Cheyenne
9 Cheyenne burials
10 Little Wolf's stand/Walks Different killed
11 Bill & Morning Star parley
12 First warming fire

N
North Fork Willow Creek
South Fork Willow Creek
McKinney's charge
Cavalry advance
Pawnee
Lakota & Cheyenne
Willow Creek
Shoshone scouts
0 0.25 0.5 mi

WILLOW CREEK CAMP

# Courage and Consternation

A PAINFUL SHRIEK STABBED INSIDE LITTLE WOLF'S HEAD, PRODDING him toward consciousness. The shrill sound pierced deeper into his skull with each throb of his heart. He gathered that he lay on his side and fought to open his eyes. His left one parted—a blurry slit that he tried to focus through as a wave of nausea swept through him. He retched. His empty stomach brought nothing forward. His head throbbed even worse, and the incessant screech continued.

*Move*, his mind told him. *Move, get away!* His right eye opened, and he found himself staring at the back of his now-dead horse. After a moment, he realized that the painful noise was coming from the other side of the rock-still animal. He lifted his head slowly, despite feeling as if he were being repeatedly clubbed.

He glanced over the horse's body and saw a line of mounted Wolf People charging from behind a hill. Each was stripped and painted for war. Many were howling like their namesake, but most were blowing relentlessly on their eagle bone whistles. They streamed through the trees in front of him and crossed a creek. *The creek!* He remembered now. *Move!* his head told him again, and this time his body responded.

He shot a glance toward the top of the knoll and was relieved to see that the men who had fired on him were gone. He pushed himself up and staggered to the bushes behind him. His pipe bag snagged on the branch of a fallen log and was torn from his belt. He tumbled behind the log, rose to his knees, and pulled a pistol from his holster, waiting for anyone who might come chasing after him. No one did.

He reached to the back of his pounding head and felt a large welt with a nasty gash where a bullet had brushed his skull. He lowered his arm and realized that his right shoulder had also been grazed. It hurt, but his head wound made him dizzy and nauseous.

There would be no chance to talk now. When the Wolf People attacked, the choice was only to fight or run. He knew that in his condition, he could not fight, not even to delay this many of them. Screams echoed from across the creek. The sound of the women and children running for their lives told him what he must do next. But how could he reach them? "*Ma'heo'o.*" He breathed the name of the Holy One, a one-word prayer of desperation.

The column of Wolf men had crossed the creek but suddenly stopped. They were now bunched together under the trees east of camp. Several of them were staring and pointing toward the top of the red cliff south of camp. Following their gaze, Little Wolf saw a long line of men perched near the edge of the cliff in various positions, some standing, some kneeling, and some lying down. All of them were firing their rifles into the camp.

Here was his chance. The charge of the Wolf People had been delayed by the rifle fire from above. This meant there would be enough time to help the women and children get to the safety of the hills if he were quick about it. With his head still pounding, he rose and ran through the brush in a crouch until he could stand without being seen by the Wolf men.

He crossed to the south side of the creek and moved slowly through the dense brush there. His responsibility as an Old Man Chief was to help the weak ones get to safety while the younger men fought the enemy. He was looking among the lodges on the north side of camp and searching for stragglers when he saw his friend Red Pipe walking near Split Nose's lodge on his way to fire on the Wolf men. He had heard their whistles and was trying to give his family time to escape.

A bullet from the rifles on the hilltop ripped through his friend's neck. As his body hit the ground, Little Wolf heard a stifled scream. Iron Tooth Woman, Red Pipe's wife, and their children were standing behind a nearby lodge. They watched helplessly as Red Pipe died.

Gathering His Medicine raced into the clearing to try to save his father. Little Wolf ran from the opposite direction past Red Pipe's body to grab the sobbing boy and wrestle him back behind the cover of a nearby lodge.

"*Otahe! He'kotoo'estse,*" he shouted at the youngster. "Listen to me! Sit still, calm down!" He grabbed the boy's shirt and stared hard into his eyes. "You can't help him. He is killed. *Otahe!* Listen to me. Your family needs you. You are their man now. They need your help, your protection!"

The sight of the blood smeared across the face of the Sweet Medicine Chief brought the youngster to his senses. His eyes found Little Wolf's eyes, and he heard his words.

Iron Tooth Woman had wisely stayed behind the lodge with a younger son and daughter. She stood there in shock as bullets continued to fall like rain from the sky around her husband.

Little Wolf instructed the stunned boy, "Get ready to run to the creek when I tell you."

He signed to Iron Tooth Woman, telling her to run for the cover of the trees along the creek. He then stepped out from behind the lodge to draw the attention of the men on the hill. The first few bullets struck the ground at his feet, and he shouted to the boy, "Now! Run to your family!"

When Gathering His Medicine raced away, Little Wolf turned and ran quickly back to Red Pipe's body. He grabbed the dead man's weapon and started for the trees himself. A bullet slammed into the old muzzle-loader, knocking it from his grasp. The broken gun stock tore a gash across his left forearm, and he instinctively cradled it to his chest with his right. Regaining his stride, he bolted for the cover of the trees.

He ducked behind one of the few large cottonwoods and checked his wound. A portion of the gun's wooden ramrod was embedded under the skin, creating a finger-long bulge. Without hesitating, the chief leaned hard against the tree and extracted the large splinter as if he were pulling a knife from its sheath. He tore a piece of fringe from his shirt and tied it around the wound using his good hand and his teeth.

He joined the distraught family under the canopy of leafless trees and directed them immediately across the stream. Iron Tooth Woman carried her daughter, and Gathering His Medicine held his younger brother's hand as they waded through the low but fast-moving stream. Little Wolf knew they weren't safe yet, but he took a moment to reflect on how grateful he was that the shooters on the hill had kept the Wolf men from advancing into camp, or they could have all been killed.

Women and children began peeking out from their hiding places in the underbrush on the far side of the stream. They had been uncertain of where to go until they saw their chief helping Iron Tooth Woman and her children through the moving water.

"*Nestsėhe'ooestse!* Come here quickly!" the chief called out as he climbed onto the bank and hid behind a large chokecherry bush. About twenty panicked women and children soon huddled close to him behind the dense stand of brush. He urged them all north to a line of trees that extended toward a dry ravine on the west side of the large red knoll.

The ravine was the largest of several trenches that twisted their way from the steep north wall across the elevated flat to the creek. It was deep and wide enough that two men could ride abreast through much of it without being seen by anyone unless the observers were standing near its edge on the flat above.

Before they reached the safety of the ravine, the sounds of many feet running hard coming from behind them. Little Wolf spun around as three Cheyenne men came sprinting through the brush. Their breathing was ragged with desperation as they approached. Bull Hump, Morning Star's oldest remaining son, led the way. He was followed closely by a man named Yellow Eagle, and behind him ran Walking Whirlwind. Young Two Moon rode up behind the three men on his horse and passed them all just before they got to the washout.

Little Wolf said nothing to the men as they passed. He knew where they were going and did not want to delay them. From where he now stood, he could see the heads of several more warriors farther inside the ravine who were waiting for the others to join them. They were creating a line of defense there and intending to keep the soldiers from charging across the northern flat and completely surrounding the camp. This would also allow the weak ones with him a secure channel to run through to get to the safety of the north wall.

The wounded chief led the women and children into the ravine and past the line of warriors. He gave Walking Whirlwind a quick, questioning look as he passed by.

"*Emanėstsenovo.* They are safe," was all his son-in-law said.

Iron Tooth Woman began singing a strong heart song along with Walks Different, one of the wood gatherers Little Wolf had greeted that first morning in the new camp. Other women joined in as the group hustled up the winding trench. Each sang loudly, encouraging their men to be brave and to fight off the invaders.

A few of the men fell in to help Little Wolf escort the women and children. After several twists and turns, they neared the top of the ravine where the ground became steeper as it approached the north wall. Here their pace slowed a bit. A frightening rumble began behind them that was enhanced by the sound of many iron-clad hooves hitting stones. Glancing back toward the red knoll, Little Wolf watched as a line of soldiers mounted on bay horses charged the lower gulch where their warriors lay in wait. For a moment, it looked as if the horsemen intended to jump the trench, but they abruptly veered to their right, clearly surprised at the chasm that suddenly appeared in front of them. They were even more surprised when the men hidden in its sandy bottom rose up and released a volley of gunfire into their ranks.

Several horses fell before the sound of the gunfire reached Little Wolf's ears, making it appear as if nothing more than the burst of smoke from the Cheyenne rifles had knocked them over. The riders sprawled onto the ground. Some scrambled back behind their fallen mounts, while others stayed where they fell.

The women around Little Wolf broke into a high-pitched tremolo, praising their brave men for stopping the charge. Two or three Cheyenne leaped up onto the flat and raced to count coup and to collect the rifles of the fallen soldiers. Some close-quarter shooting broke out over the top of the fallen horses until another wave of soldiers on gray horses charged up from the rear to protect their fallen comrades.

The Cheyenne men scrambled back into the ravine and out of sight just before the second surge of horsemen arrived to blast a fiery barrage down into it. A few of the Cheyenne appeared and scrambled through the zigzag turns before stopping to make another stand as the soldiers advanced on them.

The women's celebratory trill choked to a pitiful end and was replaced by a low keening that made Little Wolf suddenly aware that his party had stopped moving when the first charge occurred. The soldiers were now moving up the slope in their direction.

"*Amaxėstse!* Run away now!" he cried. "*No'hovaoohe'tome!* Run to the hills!"

The group turned in unison and again hustled up the sandy-bottomed wash. They reached a place where the trench branched in several different directions at the base of the north wall. No one noticed when Walks Different ran into an early branch that extended farther toward the west.

Little Wolf peered up at the towering height of the rugged wall. It looked completely different now that he stood at its base. He knew what he was looking for, however. There was one large chute among the many that had been gouged through the sandstone cliffs by the annual spring runoff. It would lead to a high bench about halfway up the slope. If they could reach that after a steep initial climb through the chute, everyone would be safe. If necessary, they could then travel west along the bench all the way to the top of the wall.

It took a moment, but he found the chute. To get there, they would need to climb out of the trench and travel over open ground. A quick glance back at the advancing soldiers told him there was no time to consider doing anything else.

He took off his gun belt and handed it to a man named Bull Head, one of the few remaining Dog Soldiers among the Northern Cheyenne.

"Take this. You are the rear guard for these weak ones now."

He pulled one pistol from its holster for himself, checked to make sure its cylinder was full, then turned to the rest and hollered, "You must all run up to that hole in the rocks there. Wait here, and I will tell each of you when to go."

He gripped Gathering His Medicine by the shoulders for the second time that day. "When I tell you to, you must tell your family and other small groups of these people to run up behind that small ridge. They will be safe from the bullets there."

The boy was clearly frightened, but he nodded without hesitation. "I will," he replied.

With that, Little Wolf climbed quickly out of the end of the trench and ran thirty paces or so across an open area before he was able to duck behind a slope that tapered gradually up to his left. He was soon out of sight from the approaching soldiers, but he could still see those waiting in the ravine. Once behind this protective slope, the people would be safe until they had to make a short climb from there to the base of the chute. Then they would be briefly visible to the soldiers.

The slope Little Wolf stood behind was one of several sandy, red slopes and hillocks that stood near the base of the towering wall. Some had the appearance of leaning against the much taller ridge, resembling stubby, red fingers all trying to hold the white behemoth in its place. The slope that he stood on curved, creating a small basin behind it where runoff from the high wall converged in the spring before flowing down the long ravine they had just come up.

He signaled for everyone in the gulch to wait while he climbed up the slope to survey the valley below. From here he could see all the way down the length of the crooked trench and across the valley to the high, red cliff on the south side of the camp. What had once been their comfortable mountain valley home was now a battlefield littered with the bodies of dead and dying men and horses.

A cloud of red dust that had been churned into the air by the charging soldiers and frightened horse herd now hung above the chaotic scene. The first direct beams of *Eše'he's* light reached through the upper half of the dust cloud, painting it bright crimson and making it appear as if the blood that had been spilled on the ground had somehow also been splashed into the sky.

The ground around Little Wolf suddenly started to jump as if covered with *Hahkota*, the grasshopper. He had been noticed, and the soldiers' bullets now tore at the ground around him. At this distance, he knew that if he kept moving, he would be difficult to hit. He fired a shot at the soldiers to keep their attention then signaled Gathering His Medicine to send the first group of women and children. As he turned back to the battle, he noticed a solitary woman peering at him from out of the ditch that ran to the west of him.

"*Onetȧhevo'hȧ'ehnėstse!* Walks Different!" he hollered her name when he recognized her.

"Little Wolf!" she cried. "Where is everyone? I thought they followed me this way. Help me get out of here!" The frightened woman climbed up the side of the trench and started toward him.

"Wait! No! Do not come up here!" Little Wolf yelled as he waved her back.

Walks Different paused for a moment. Confusion crossed her face as the ground started to jump in front of her, and a bullet tore through the lower part of her chest. Blood poured down her stomach as she took a step forward to keep from falling, then she pitched backward in a somersault, her limp arms and legs flailing as her body tumbled into the trench behind her.

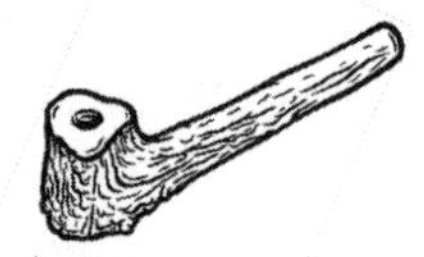

The Pawnee whistles had gone silent. Clark called me over to talk with him and Lieutenant DeLany.

"I'm not sure what's going on here, Bill. The Pawnee whistles aren't sounding, which I assume means they've stopped their advance. I don't see any sign of them, so I'm heading back in that direction to see what the holdup is. I want you all to hold this position until the Pawnee show up to relieve you."

Clark seemed confident that the Snakes on the hilltop wouldn't fire on him and trotted off down the slope, quickly disappearing between the lodges. Between the Cheyenne stampeding out, us stampeding in, and the Snakes blasting the place all to hell, every animal that remained in camp was scared to death. Horses, dogs, chickens, and even a couple hogs all ran in confused circles. Each animal bawled in fear until it sounded like their cries all joined together in one constant, unearthly howl that hung in the air, carried on a thick curtain of red dust.

I caught a glimpse of Clark riding through the surrounding chaos completely undisturbed and realized that his big, white Stetson was the first thing anyone would see. As long as that stayed on his head and he stayed on this side of the creek, he was safe as a baby in a cradle.

I heard the charge on the other side of the creek begin before I saw it. The rumble of hooves sounded on the north side of the red knob. A line of bay horses galloped along the flat there only to be waylaid by a group of Cheyenne who were waiting for them in the long ravine.

There was some back and forth for a while, until the soldiers got the upper hand. It wasn't long before the Cheyenne were on the run up the ravine and the flat behind them swarmed with soldiers and scouts.

At the far end of the ravine, a good half-mile away from my position, people were crawling out of the main ravine and running up into hills at the base of the north wall. I looked closer and saw what appeared to be a woman crawl out up of a side gully to the left of the others and stand up like a prairie dog at its burrow. Puffs of dust quickly kicked up around her, and she all-a-sudden pitched backward into the gully. My heart sank as quickly as the woman fell. It was right there that I felt something close up around me, as if I had fallen into that unexpected grave with her.

# Loss and Lamentation

Little Wolf stared at the spot where Walks Different had disappeared. *I should not have called her name*, he thought. *I should have just said go back.* During the moment that he took to second-guess himself, a bullet creased the back of his right thigh, spinning him around and sending him crashing to the ground behind the crest of the ridge.

The coarse, red sand scraped his face when he landed. He writhed and groaned as he clutched at the pain in his leg. The people from the first group had arrived, and several rushed to his side. He lay still a moment and caught his breath, waiting for the pain to subside. He sat up and squeezed his leg. He looked the wound over as best he could and saw that the bullet had passed through the fleshy part of his upper thigh, just below his rump. If he could keep it from bleeding and could still walk, he would be okay. A woman named Stands in the Wind handed him a strip of cloth torn from her shawl and helped him tie it tightly around his leg.

"Walks Different?" he asked her.

Stands in the Wind looked over the rise and shook her head. Tears filled her eyes. "I think she is killed."

Little Wolf stared at his feet for a moment, grieving the loss of the friendly woman. They couldn't do it now, but they had to retrieve her body, likely after dark when they could slip back into the ravine undetected.

He rolled onto his knees and used his good leg to stand. He would limp, and it would hurt, but he could walk. Ignoring the pain in both his leg and his heart as best he could, he hobbled to the top of the slope again and took a couple more shots at the soldiers to draw their attention back to him. He limped back and forth to avoid being an easy target as he studied the scene below.

The shooters on the cliff above the camp had stopped firing, and several were now riding back down the long slope they had used to climb up there earlier. The Wolf People had swarmed through the village and were now gathered at the back side of the camp.

He waved a few more people to the safe spot behind the ridge and stared angrily at the invaders at the west end of his camp. Blue-tinged plumes of smoke suddenly puffed from several of their rifles. Shots were being fired at what was left of the horse herd, which had gathered in the southwest part of the valley.

A closer look showed that a lone mounted Cheyenne was galloping around the anxious herd, trying to drive it back into the canyon to the west. The man suddenly slid to his left, giving the appearance that he was avoiding the bullets, until his arms lost their grip on the horse's mane and he tumbled to the ground. The soft crackle from the rifles that killed him eventually rattled across the distance to reach Little Wolf's ears.

The boom of closer gunshots sounded to his left. Bull Hump and the others came into view as they fired from a bend in the twisting washout then disappeared as they moved behind a higher bend. They fired again, slowing the attackers as best they could. The soldiers continued to advance along the ravine toward the women and children despite the efforts of their brave men to stop them. Little Wolf raised the pistol and fired one more shot just as a soldier's bullet came buzzing through the air like an angry bee and clipped his left shoulder.

"Ahhh!" the chief groaned as he recoiled in pain and limped several feet to his right. It stung, but he knew the wound was minor, similar to the one on his right shoulder. With the bullets from the advancing soldiers gaining in accuracy, Little Wolf knew he needed to get the last of the people out of the ravine. *I am wasting time*, he thought. *These people must go up into the rocks before the soldiers get here.*

He signed for the last of his group to leave the ravine. About twenty people climbed out of the trench, and all scrambled for the safe area behind the slope that their chief stood upon. A group of women lagged behind the larger bunch, clinging to each other as they cautiously inched forward. They were afraid to advance too far into the clearing lest they need to run back to the safety of the washout. Bull Head, who remained in the ditch to guard the rear, hollered at them "*He'nevo'àheotse! Amaxèstse!* Scatter quickly! Run away now!" As the frightened stragglers turned to run, three of them tumbled to the ground.

Stands in the Wind and her daughter, Little Sage Standing, both landed hard when they fell. The third, Wet Face Woman, tumbled then struggled back to her feet. She reached to try and pull the other two up, but neither responded to her desperate pleas.

Bull Head rushed from the trench where he and others had stayed to help when the fighting got closer. He gave Wet Face Woman a gentle nudge toward the safe area then lifted Little Sage Standing in his arms. The young woman stirred as she was raised, her left arm suddenly flailing at an unseen assailant. He placed the wounded girl over his shoulder as two other men, Wolf Tooth and White Frog, appeared from the trench to scoop up the body of Stands in the Wind and carry her behind the ridge.

Little Wolf fired a final shot then shoved the pistol in his belt, knowing he had but one bullet left. He limped down the backside of the ridge to where the final group was preparing to climb up into the chute in the tall rocks behind them. Once there, they could all climb to the high ledge where he knew soldiers would not dare to follow.

Everyone started crawling up the steep rocks toward the ledge. Wolf Tooth and White Frog wrestled Stands in the Wind's body up the steep incline as well. Their intent was to get her up to the high ledge and slide her into a suitable rock crevice where only the most determined grave robber could find her. Little Sage Standing had returned to her senses. She had been shot in the right shoulder and had been knocked unconscious when she hit the ground. Bull Head turned her over to her relatives and started back toward the trench.

He reached the end of the slope, where he thrust his Dog Soldier's stake into the ground. This signaled that until another Cheyenne pulled the stake and released him from the spot, he intended to stay there and stop the soldiers or die trying. He held Little Wolf's other pistol in his hand, ready to fire at the first soldier to show himself around the end of the slope.

The last of the warriors soon fought their way out of the trench and came around the end of the slope. They raced past Bull Head on their way to the chute. Little Wolf noticed immediately that Walking Whirlwind was not among them.

The bottom of the chute was now visible to the soldiers who had advanced within firing range. Their bullets zipped into the ground at feet of the men and ricocheted off of the rock walls around them. Little Wolf started down toward Bull Head, intending to release him from his position, but had made only two limping steps when he saw the first soldier come around the end of the slope.

Bull Head raised the pistol at the white man, whose eyes opened wide in fright. The soldier had been focused on the men higher up near the chute and was surprised to find the Dog Soldier waiting for him as he came around the corner. Bull Head fired. The sound of the pistol filled the depression between the ridge and the tall north wall. A moment passed where everyone, including the trembling soldier, waited for the bullet to send him crashing to the ground. At this moment, Little Wolf recalled how his first few shots with the pistols had all sailed high over his intended target because of the gun's unexpected kick. The soldier thrust his rifle forward and shot Bull Head through the chest.

More soldiers hustled around the slope as the first man urinated himself and sank to his knees, shaken by his brush with death. The fresh arrivals swarmed past their comrade, firing steadily at the few Cheyenne who remained at the mouth of the chute.

A bullet caught Little Wolf in the upper left chest, driving him backward. He felt himself losing consciousness again. When the darkness came this time, he felt a pair of large hands grabbing him.

The young Pawnee reached for Old Crow's gun, but my friend drew it back. I stepped forward and raised my hand to let the youngster know that he should rethink his attempt to disarm the man. The Pawnee's eyes flashed, and he took a quick step backward himself. He'd started to raise his own rifle when Frank North rode forward and barked something at him in Skidi. The man's head snapped around to look up at North and, after a moment to consider his leader's words, he cast a scowl at Old Crow and moved away.

I nodded at North. "Obliged, Frank."

"I'd be keeping your boys close together until the shooting settles down, Rowland," North advised. "There's likely still a few of their folk hiding inside these lodges here that they might get mistook for."

"That'd be my aim," I assured him.

North was a decent enough fellow, but I had a powerful suspicion of anyone who was that friendly with the Pawnee, let alone one acting as their leader.

Shortly after Lieutenant Clark had ridden back through camp when the Pawnee whistles had stopped, the whistles started up again. On came the Wolf People, moving through the camp like their namesake in a swarming pack and hunting for something to kill.

Several had fanned out along the back side of camp, eying the horse heard that had gathered on the flat there. But most of the greedy sons a bitches raced back and forth among the lodges. An occasional rifle shot was heard, which told me that a Cheyenne, most likely too old or weak to run to the hills, had been found and killed. The entire camp had been taken.

I could still see stragglers hustling up the creek and moving through the ravines, desperate to reunite with their kinsmen. It weren't long before a few rounds came zipping over the top of a portion of the horse herd on the flat. It was more of a harassing fire than any kind of counterattack.

The Pawnee studied the hills, trying to figure out just where the shooters were located so they could return fire. About that time, a single rider came galloping around the southern side of the herd, waving a blanket and trying to drive them back to the western hills. The Pawnee took great sport in trying to bring the man down. When the first volley was fired at him, the rider slipped behind the neck of his horse and continued around the herd.

Old Crow recognized the target of the Pawnee rifles before the rider ducked out of sight. He leaned toward me and breathed his name: "Split Nose!"

I knew the man well. "He's a little old to be making a ride like that," I muttered back.

Old Crow kept his voice low. "They need those horses."

Split Nose was apparently a bit slow in sliding behind his horse's neck. A Pawnee bullet must have caught him as he went over the side. His arms lost their grip, and he tried to hold to his horse with his legs until they too went limp. He slipped from the running horse.

"*Shaa!*" Old Crow's growl was lost in the lusty roar that came from the Pawnee as Split Nose rolled dead on the ground.

A couple of younger Pawnee tried to run out to count coup on the body, but they were turned back by a rash of hot fire that surprised them from the southwest hills. The Pawnee were returning fire toward the hills as several more riders galloped out of the trees at the far end of the valley. These riders paid no mind to the herd and rode only to claim the body of their lost friend. They were all driven back as the Pawnee threw a wall of bullets at them. One man got close enough to throw a blanket over the body before he too was forced back to the cover of the trees.

A few more volleys were exchanged, and another group of riders appeared from behind the trees. They split into two smaller groups, and with the gunfire being divided between them, a couple riders were finally able to reach the body. One jumped from his horse and lifted the dead man up to the other rider, who galloped back to the trees as his friend remounted and followed close on his heels.

I recognized one. "Dog Speaking," I said. "But I didn't see who the other was."

I turned to Old Crow to see if he knew, but my friend just stared mournfully at the place where the riders had disappeared into the trees.

With their sport finished, the Pawnee turned to helping their friends ransack the lodges. They ran from one to the other, crying "*Ki-de-de-de!*" as they celebrated their victory.

I figured we'd all had about enough, so I approached Lieutenant DeLany.

"'Tenant, seeing's how the Pawnee are all present and accounted for, we'd appreciate it if we could be leaving 'bout now?"

DeLany shot a glance toward the center of camp, where the Pawnee had become increasingly more engrossed in their plunder. "I think that would be a good idea, Rowland. No sense in putting your men through . . ."

I didn't hear him finish. I'd already swung up on Ulysses and was off to find Lieutenant Clark. The Cheyenne scouts all mounted and followed. It took him a while, but DeLany came trotting alongside us as we passed by the first few lodges. The red knoll to the northeast and across the creek seemed the likeliest place to find Clark. I could see soldiers sprawled along its ridge, firing at targets across the upper flat.

The Pawnee continued to dash in and out of the lodges around us, so DeLany moved to the front of our party, and I rode near the middle to help avoid a run-in. It helped, but I still found myself looking for the owner of a home we approached only to have a Pawnee suddenly pop out of it holding the prized pipe or shield of someone I knew. I kept my hand tight around the handle of my Spencer but rode on in silence.

Several of the lodges had long slits in the back where their occupants had cut through it to avoid the risk of getting shot by going out the front. The slashed hide draped into the lodge, creating a gaping hole. It weren't long before—between the actual thieving by the Pawnee and the feeling that I was taking something just by glancing inside the lodges—I eventually couldn't bring myself to look at any of them. Best I could do was chew my upper lip and keep my eyes to the front. I noticed that the rest of the boys were keeping their eyes averted as well.

We approached the north side of the camp near the creek, where I recognized the lodge of Split Nose. DeLany and those in front of me came to a stop as they rounded the lodge. I rode forward and saw they had found a body in a bloody heap on the ground. I gave Ulysses a squeeze with my legs and trotted toward the dead man. I dismounted, dropped to a knee, rolled the corpse over, and immediately closed my eyes.

"*Shaa!*" the Cheyenne behind me cried in unison when they recognized the man.

Red Pipe had been scalped, and his arms and legs were mutilated, which told me that the Pawnee had found him before we did. I wrapped him in a blanket that had been tossed out of the lodge and whispered, "Come with us, brother."

I hoisted Red Pipe's body up to where Old Crow could grab the blanket and help me lay him over Ulysses's saddle. I turned to DeLany and, without asking the question, waited for his answer. DeLany studied my eyes for a bit and nodded.

Our party had now become a funeral march. We changed our direction and moved toward the center of camp to where the body of Necklace lay. We entered the clearing and found Lieutenant Clark coming from the east on his way back through camp.

He saw the body draped over my saddle and sighed. He knew it wasn't one of the scouts. "Did you know him, Rowland?" he asked.

"Name's Red Pipe. He had a wife and a few young-uns."

Clark squinted down at his saddle horn. The fact that it bothered him so much helped.

"We're fixing to bury him, sir," I said.

The officer searched the trampled grass and rounded stones in front of his horse as he considered his response then looked me square in the eye.

"I think you should, Bill. In fact, there's another fellow lying just across the creek behind me here that you should tend to as well. I think that would be a good detail for you and your men to take on." He hesitated a moment then continued, "And I'm sorry to have to tell you, but I also know where there are several others that you'll need to gather up. It will have to be later, though, when things cool down a bit."

"What do you mean, several others?" I asked.

"Well, there was quite a skirmish on the other side of this knoll here. Things got pretty hot for a while, but we secured the large ravine that several Cheyenne were using as a breastwork. Most of them got away up into the north wall there, but . . ." Clark looked at me and shook his head. ". . . some didn't."

"How many you figger?" I asked.

"Half-dozen or so."

My insides puckered, but I looked Clark in the eye and thanked him. "We'll get these men taken care of here. Just let us know when to head up there."

"Right," Clark answered. "I'll also let the colonel know what you're up to, Bill. He's here in the camp somewhere. I was just going to look for him. Lieutenant DeLany, you stay with them."

"Sir!" DeLany saluted.

Clark rode off to find the colonel, and I turned to tell the others about the ravine.

# *Ehoometatsesta* (He Felt Guilty about It)

We found Necklace, and I was happy to see that the man still had his hair. The Pawnee must have missed his body lying in the tall grass of the large clearing when they raced through camp. The scouts celebrated their brave friend's intact scalp as they lifted him onto the back of a horse. I noticed DeLany breathe a sigh of relief. We moved on to find the body that Clark had mentioned.

The body turned out to be Standing Bull. The young man had forded the creek after I saw him that morning and ran for the horse herd, but he never made it. He lay half-hidden in a thicket of skunk brush. He had been scalped, and his blood-crusted skull was an obscene knob that jutted from what remained of his now-matted long hair.

His body was laid over a horse like the others, and we carried them all up behind the ridge of knolls to the south. The southern incline there had a crumbling rim of red sandstone with numerous crevices where the bodies, and any more after them, could be placed. DeLany kept watch from one of the points. He stayed back out of respect and as a deterrent, lest any Snakes coming off of the red cliff mistook the burial detail for hostiles. Short prayers were said and a song sung for each man. Anything longer would have to wait until after all the grim work ahead was completed. It was nearing midday when we rode single file down from the burial area and back into the creek bottom.

DeLany pointed out where a field hospital had been set up between the large red knoll and the creek. The slow-traveling pack train had also arrived, and soldiers were busy unloading supplies just east of the hospital. The terrain dropped from the higher flat down to a narrow strip of bottomland that ran along the north side of the creek here. This kept everyone tucked safely out of sight of some Cheyenne sharpshooters who had climbed the north wall and now stubbornly refused to allow the soldiers any free movement across the flat.

I knew there would be food somewhere in the vicinity. I figured it best to leave Old Crow and the others in a sharp bend on the south side of the creek. They weren't in any mood to mingle with soldiers right then, so DeLany and I started over to see if we could round up a meal for us all.

We crossed the creek and entered the whirl of orderly activity. Tents were being pitched, supplies stacked, and fires started. Mules were being led back and forth—upstream to be relieved of their burdens, then downstream as they were taken to picket. The first fire we saw had a cooking pot on it, and we were headed toward it when I heard a familiar laugh floating above the sound of the creek behind us.

All the activity around us blurred when I saw Billy Garnett wading across the creek. He was on his way back from the Cheyenne camp, smiling and talking with his friend Bat Pourier. The older scout was leading a horse burdened with an overloaded sawbuck. Garnett reached down for a drink of water as they crossed the creek. When he stepped up on to the creek's bank, he raised an ornate china cup with a broken handle to his mouth.

The youngster caught me staring at him when he threw back his drink. He did a quick turn to Pourier, acting as if he hadn't noticed me at all, and casually dropped his arm to his side. The cup slipped from his hand, shattering into a hundred pieces on the round stones at his feet. Big Bat gave me a quick glance and moved off to his left. Garnett followed. The loose pack shifted side to side as the horse trailed behind them.

"Awful big-balled for a shoat." I heard my father's voice slip from my own mouth before I knew what I was saying.

"What was that, Rowland?" DeLany asked.

"Nothing. Just . . . nothing."

I turned back to stare at the remnants of the cup on the water's edge.

"Looks like mess is getting started over there," Delay said.

The officer's excitement over finding a meal reminded me of our task at hand. A few soldiers were lining up at the fire to get fed, and a large kettle of coffee had been started nearby.

I brought a tin of beans back, but Old Crow and the boys refused to eat. They said they couldn't until they had found who else of their friends and family had been killed. They needed to get them buried. Lieutenant Clark was nowhere to be found, so I told DeLany that based on what I saw of the skirmish, the bodies couldn't be too far up the gully and he decided we could go.

We skirted the hospital, riding through the brush along the creek toward the opening of the ravine on the other side. Our horses all started to fidget near the body of a dead horse that had been dragged from the clearing to make room for the hospital. My heart dropped when I recognized the large paint stallion that belonged to Little Wolf. What a loss this would be if he had been killed.

"His body is not here," Old Crow said as he glanced around the area.

A spot of color in the brush caught my eye, and I stepped down off Ulysses. I lifted an ornately beaded pipe bag from the branch of a small log. I recognized it and started speaking in both Cheyenne and English, trying to reassure myself along with the others.

"He could have gone up the gully here and gotten away. Come on now, *nonotoveohtse*, hurry. We must hurry in there. He ain't dead if we don't find him dead."

The others dismounted, and we all led our horses into the ravine. DeLany took the lead again to reassure anyone we met that the Cheyenne with us were allies. He moved right along while I hung back with the others. The bottom of the trench had been churned to fine dust by many desperate feet, but it was not the loose soil that slowed our step.

The ravine ran straight for a hundred yards then twisted to the right. A smaller trench opened to the left at the bend, and it was there we found the first six bodies stacked against a red cutbank like cordwood to keep them out from underfoot. None of the men had on much for clothing, which made sense, what with their rush to get out of camp, but it was pretty clear that the soldiers had grabbed themselves some quick souvenirs as well. I knew it was the soldiers on account of the ragged swatches torn from each man's scalp. The Pawnee weren't that sloppy when they took a topknot.

We stepped toward the bodies with lead in our legs.

The first man off the pile was Walking Calf, a young fella who usually camped with the northern bands. He had a gaping bullet wound in his neck and appeared to have been trampled by more than one horse. Bear Sitting Down gasped as the second body was rolled over. It was High Bull, his cousin. Roan Bear helped him lift his relative carefully onto the back of his horse, where Bear Sitting Down stayed cleaning his cousin's hair. We turned over the third man and saw that it was Walking Whirlwind, Little Wolf's new son-in-law. His eyes were open and full of dirt.

Those same eyes had been shining when he and Inside Woman were married at the agency early last spring. In fact, he smiled that whole day, and there had been rumors that Inside Woman had become pregnant right after the wedding and just before they left with Little Wolf to join Sitting Bull's big camp last summer.

All the crippling guilt that I had felt over the last day and a half had finally been given a face, and it was staring right at me through dirt-filled eyes. In that moment, everything that had been "up in those mountains" suddenly reached out and grabbed me by the throat. I had to turn away. I found myself staring at a clump of deer sage that jutted out from the sandy red wall of the trench. "This ain't right," I growled at it.

The others had joined Bear Sitting Down in singing the honor song as they tended to the bodies. I placed my hand on Hard Robe's shoulder.

"Put him on my horse," I told him.

Everything was too close now—the small trench, the bodies, the scouts, DeLany, fear, guilt—everything was just too damned close. I stepped around DeLany and out into the main branch of the ravine. I stood there trembling and in a cold sweat. Everything I had been walling off inside of me came busting out.

"This ain't right, god damn it! Son of a bitch!"

I didn't know who I was hollering at—the soldiers, the Cheyenne, myself, God? It really didn't matter, because the Cheyenne kept singing behind me, a bugle sounded on the other side of the knoll calling soldiers to mess, and the shooting continued up at the head of the ravine. My hollering didn't even make a damned echo to show I'd been heard.

I did hear the hoofbeats of a horse coming down the ravine toward me at an easy lope. I looked up, and it took me a moment to recognize Lieutenant Clark. He clutched his white Stetson against his chest to avoid making himself an easy target for the Cheyenne marksmen on the mountainside behind him.

"There you are, Bill. I was just coming to look for you."

The lieutenant dismounted, making sure to keep his horse between him and any bullets that might reach that far. A fine layer of red dust now covered his greatcoat.

He saw my scowl and looked behind me to the scouts still sorting through the bodies in the trench. He glanced away for a moment, searching for words.

"I see you've started." His tone was solemn. It helped that he understood this was some rough going for us, but it made nothing easier, and I was still hot.

"The boys were itching to get up here. I tried to find you."

"That's fine, Bill. I would have said to go ahead anyway."

"I reckoned as much."

The scouts pulled out the last three bodies. Hawks Visit, followed by Burns Red in the Sun, then Old Bull. I knew them all.

The scouts tended to the last three while Clark filled me in on why he came back for us. "Bill, I think we have a chance to discuss surrender with the Cheyenne at the head of this gully here. I'd like you to come up and give us a hand with the translation."

"You had words with 'em?"

"No, not yet, but they've been trying to wave a white flag for a while now," he said. "We've had some trouble getting the orders out to everyone to stop firing on it, but they've continued to raise it anyway. I think they're serious."

"Ain't much about this blow up that ain't serious, far as I see it," I groused.

Clark's head snapped toward me. "Bill, that's uncalled for."

"I know, I . . . Dammit, sir, I apologize. This just ain't no place ever I wanted to be. We just chased these people from their homes, killed their kin, and now you're asking me to go parley with them."

Clark waited while I struggled with his request. We both knew it would be an order if he repeated it.

I looked down the trench toward the abandoned camp and realized we had not found Little Wolf.

"Bill."

"I'll do it," I snapped. "Let's get these fellas on their way first." I couldn't bear the answer, so I spoke to the sage again. "We got any bodies between here and there?"

"A couple," Clark replied. "There may be more up farther. I don't know for sure."

I reached for Ulysses' reins then realized that Walking Whirlwind was across his back.

"I'll take him." Bear Sitting Down moved the body to another horse.

"Old Crow, Roan Bear, Hard Robe, and Little Fish, come with us," I called. "Everyone else, take these brave men up to the rocks."

Bear Sitting Down and the others went back to singing as they resumed preparing their friends and family to be carried to their graves. DeLany stayed with them to ensure their safety while we started up the ravine with Clark.

We hustled up the twisting curves of the trench. An occasional bullet would spray red dust as it hit the banks above us. A Cheyenne sniper somewhere high on the white ridge was trying to make our ride a bit more difficult. We galloped through the straight parts where we were more exposed, but we were otherwise well protected by the high walls of the ditch.

Clark and I rounded one bend together and nearly trampled another Cheyenne body.

"I forgot he was there," Clark said.

"*Vo'aa'e*," I spoke his name.

"Antelope?" Clark repeated the name in English. "That's his name, Antelope?"

Old Crow and the others came around the corner as I knelt at the dead man's side.

"*Noma'keso, Hestaneha.* Little Fish, take him." I called my youngest brother-in-law to help me lift the battered body out of the trail. Little Fish slid off his horse and helped me place our friend over his saddle.

Antelope had been scalped, and the cuts were cleaner, more practiced than those on the others. His limbs had also been gashed, so he could not run or hunt in the afterlife.

"Looks like a Pawnee found his way in with the boys working up higher here," I told Clark.

"There's another body just a couple bends up from here," Clark replied. "You may want to send them back together."

I held my hand out, palm down, to Little Fish, letting him know to wait there while we went to collect the next man.

Clark didn't ask me the next man's name, but I told him anyway.

"*Ma'heono*, Sacred Powers," I said as we laid the body over the saddle. "I'm surprised to find him up here at the front of things. He was a pretty easygoing sort."

Our friend was also cleanly scalped and was just as butchered as Antelope. He also had been run over several times by horses charging up the now quite narrow trench. A feather slipped from his hair and fluttered to the ground. Clark reached for it, trying to help. The scouts immediately stopped what they were doing and turned to stare as Clark froze in mid-reach and gave me a questioning look.

"Cheyenne way is to leave any feather what fell on the ground there."

"Why is that, Bill?"

"Bad medicine, sir. There's a ceremony for it, but we don't have the time."

"Sorry," Clark said as he stepped back toward his horse, nodding at the Cheyenne men to continue.

Old Crow finished wrapping the man's hacked and disjointed body in canvas and tied it to the back of a horse. He cinched the last knot, and Roan Bear turned the horse around, heading back to where Little Fish waited for him.

"Okay," I asked. "Where do we go from here?"

"Up there." Clark jerked his thumb over his shoulder toward the top of a red slope that appeared to lean against the base of the north wall.

A short time later, we were crouched close together behind the ridge of the slope. The soldiers that were scattered on the red hills around us were ordered to cease firing to allow us a chance to have our parley.

"Right up there is where we've seen a white flag being waved every now and again." Clark pointed to a spot high inside a deep crevice.

I looked things over a bit then shouted, "*Neneeva'eve*? Who are you?"

Things was quiet for quite some time until a thin voice finally floated down from the rocks. "Who are you down there? *Netonėšenohtovetsėhesenestse*? How do you know how to talk Cheyenne?"

"*Haahpe'e'haestse!* Holler loudly!" I replied. "It is a long way between us. I am your good friend, *To'ėsemotšėške*, Long Knife."

A longer silence followed after I shouted the name most Cheyenne knew me by.

After a bit, Lieutenant Clark leaned toward me. "What's going on, Bill? What did you say? Why are they so quiet?"

"I just introduced myself is all," I told him. "No doubt they're busy trying to round up someone important enough to speak for them."

"*To'ėsemotšėške*." A deep voice groaned my Cheyenne name from the rocks above us, sounding like the Almighty himself. "Why do you fight with the soldiers against us?"

"*Vooheheve*," Old Crow whispered.

I let loose a sigh and couldn't help but grin when I turned to Clark.

"And that would be Morning Star."

# A Parley before Parting

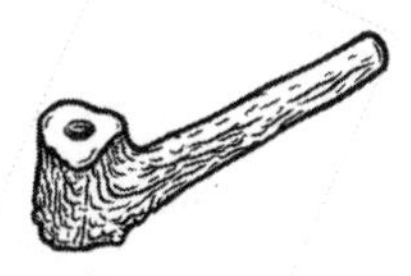

I SEARCHED THE ROCKS ABOVE THE RUGGED CREASE WHERE THE RED slope met the white wall for some sign of my friend. He had asked why I was there, so I took a deep breath and was about to explain when Clark leaned in.

"What did he say?"

I held my finger up to let him know I'd answer his question. I shouted in Cheyenne toward the rocks above us, "*Vooheheve*, it is good to hear your voice, my friend. When we started, we were going to have a talk with Crazy Horse. I did not know we would come here."

I turned back to Clark. "He wanted to know why I'm here fighting against them with you all. I just told him that we were out looking for Crazy Horse at first."

"We need to try to get them to surrender, Bill. See if you can get them to come down out of there."

"I'll give it a try, sir, but I'm figuring that'll be tougher than pulling turnips from August hardpan."

I looked up over the top of the slope just as a bullet struck the ground near Hard Robe, spraying red sand into his face. He quick spun away and curled up, grabbing at his eyes. Old Crow jumped on him and dragged him out of harm's way, checking him over for any serious wound as they slid down the hill together.

This wouldn't do. "*To'ha'ovenano!*" I hollered. "Stop them! It is time for us to talk about making peace. We do not want any more to get killed. Too many people are already killed."

I had to get his attention and that of the others in earshot. I knew what would work, but I felt like a heel for using it.

"*Vooheheve, hoovehe*, Morning Star, my friend, my heart is on the ground today. Your son, Standing Bull, has been killed in this fight. I saw this myself."

I gave my friend time to absorb the news of his son's death. Below me, Old Crow was spitting into Hard Robe's eyes and trying to wash the sand out of them as the man writhed underneath him.

"What did you tell him?" Clark asked as he also watched Old Crow tend to Hard Robe.

"I just told him his son was killed. Hopefully, it helps him and the rest think a bit harder 'bout giving up."

A frail silence stretched between the red slope and the north wall.

Clark got antsy. "What's going on? Why won't he answer?"

"He just got told his son's dead, 'Tenant. He might need a minute to chew on that."

Clark realized his thoughtless impatience and closed his eyes. He gave his head a small shake and muttered to himself, "Of course."

A few moments passed before Morning Star's deep voice again rose from behind the rocks. It was clear the news of his son's death weighed heavy on the old man's heart.

"Now, I have lost two sons. Young Bird has also been killed by the soldier's guns today. Many families are crying here because of all those they have lost."

Young Bird was only ten or twelve years old, close to my son Ben's age. Now I felt like a real ass for using Standing Bull's death to stoke his emotions. Even worse, I now had to use both those losses to try to get him to surrender.

"We both knew this day might come after we traveled to the White Father's lodge in the east. We have seen how many they are and how strong they are. The others must understand that it makes no sense to fight. There are even more soldiers out on the prairie below us waiting to come behind these. More Cheyenne could be killed."

"I am ready to come in now," Morning Star replied, "but these others with me, they will not talk peace. I cannot tell them not to be angry or afraid. Too many have been killed here."

"Who are the other Old Man Chiefs here with you?" I wanted to get an idea of who "they" might be. "I know Little Wolf will come talk peace with us."

There was another long pause.

"The soldiers have shot him. He has no words for peace or war now."

A younger voice interrupted us before I could ask more about my friend. "Let the other soldiers come!" The man's words were quick, cutting through the air like a striking snake. "We have sent out runners to find Crazy Horse! He will be coming soon to help us make these white soldiers cry, like those we killed last summer!"

"Who is that?" Clark asked. "He sounded angry, more defiant."

"I'm not sure who it is," I said. "It sounds a bit like a fella named Gray Head, a Council chief. He says they sent for Crazy Horse, and that he's on his way here. Most likely pulling our leg. Bear Sitting Down said the Lakota hightailed it way north of here."

"*Ma'haokohtše*, Old Crow!" Still another voice cried out. "I see you there! What are you doing here? You should leave this place. We can beat these *Ve'ho'e*, these white men, if they fight by themselves, but we should not have to fight you too!"

"Old Bear," I whispered to Clark, "another Old Man Chief."

Before I could translate Old Bear's words, Old Crow hollered back, "I am sorry that I must fight against you!" I was surprised to hear his voice coming from above us on the slope. He had left Hard Robe below and had climbed along the backside of the ridge to a small point above us. "I have left many bullets here on this point for you!" he cried out. "You will need them when you leave here!"

Clark was furious. "What's he doing up there?" he snapped. "Tell him to get back here now! What did he say to them?"

"*Ma'haokohtše, ne'anòhevonehnèstse!* Old Crow, you climb down from there!" I called to my friend, waving him back to us. I had to grit my teeth for a moment before turning back to Clark. "He was just trying to help, sir. He told them he didn't want to fight with them and that, uh, that they should just give up and come down outta there."

Clark glared at Old Crow as he slid back down the slope toward Hard Robe, who now was squinting and picking at his eyes. The officer turned and barked at two soldiers who held horses below us. "I want a man posted with those two until we leave this place."

One of the men immediately climbed up to Hard Robe and led him back to the horses. He waved for Old Crow to follow.

"What's been said so far, Bill?" Clark groused. "Tell me where things stand."

I filled him in on everything except Old Crow leaving the ammunition. I felt bad about that, but I knew that what Old Crow said was true. The fighting was all but over, and the Cheyenne would dearly need it when they left this place. I finished with a bit of advice for the lieutenant.

"I honestly don't see any sense in trying to get them to come crawling down outta there, sir. They're hunkered down like a badger under the porch. The only way they'll be coming outta there is looking to take as many of us with them before they all get killed."

Clark quieted down and spoke with a bit of compassion. "Give it one more good try, Bill. We have all of their belongings and horses, they're hurting right now, and we all know things are going to get worse come nightfall. Tell them we'll take care of their wounded."

I studied the concern in Clark's eyes for a moment then took a moment to gather my words. "*Vooheheve*, it will be very cold soon! *Vo'keme* will be reaching down the mountain tonight. You have little ones and old ones with you who have no blankets. There are many wounded among you. Everyone will suffer in the cold night that is coming! Send your weak ones out. We will take care of them."

Morning Star answered right away. "We will not give the white soldiers any more than they have already taken from us today. Tell them to go away. We will take care of our weak ones."

I looked at Clark and shook my head.

"*To'ėsemotšėške!*" Morning Star called me by name.

"*Henova'e?* What is it?

"Did my son die well?"

"He was very brave, *hoovehe*. He died at the front of the fight. We buried him in those hills to the south."

A long silence followed by a soft moan of wind signaled that our talk was finished.

"What did he say at the end there, Bill?" Clark asked as we turned to leave.

"Just asking 'bout his boy, sir."

"I see."

We started back down the trench. I walked alongside Old Crow, who had the body of Walks Different slung over his horse. I had known the woman. She was friendly, a little shy at first, but she loved to tease once she got to know a person. We found her and another man in short side ditches near the base of the north wall. The man had been tore up so bad that no one could figure out who he was. I had him strapped to Ulysses and wrapped in my slicker to try to keep his body intact and to keep his blood off of my saddle.

I caught Old Crow's eye and pursed my lips to point at the sky to the west. Old Crow looked up at the clouds coming over the horizon faster than the sun was sinking toward it. Old Crow shook his head. He knew what the oncoming storm meant for his devastated kinfolk.

We were halfway down the ravine when a dark cloud began to rise from the camp below. The teepees were being burned, and the black smoke quickly replaced the red dust in the late afternoon air.

"Aw, shit!" was all I could say.

Cries of anguish coming from the north wall echoed my emotion. A fresh round of bullets pelted the ground above our heads.

Two Tails listened as *Naměšeme*, grandfather, sang a healing song. The old man's voice kept time with the rhythm of the rain that rattled against the lodge skin. Thunder boomed loudly, and he heard weeping. *Someone important must be dying*, he thought. *Even the sky is crying.*

The young boy heard his own voice ask, "*Nevaahe tseneveohtaoo'ėstse?* Grandfather, who is on the scaffold?"

Bridge gave his gourd rattle a few final shakes and finished his song. The old Arikara medicine man leaned closer and answered, causing his patient's eyes to flutter. "Not you, nesene. Not today."

Another gunshot boomed from the nearby rocks and startled the patient, who opened his eyes. The loud weeping persisted, and despite a sharp pain, Little Wolf turned his head to see the blurry shapes of a handful of women crouching over a prone female and preparing her for burial.

*I was dreaming.*

The realization surprised him.

A groan escaped his throat as he rolled back to the buffalo robe he had been placed on. For the second time that day, the chief struggled back to consciousness, recalling the bitter reality of the camp being charged, the ensuing gun battle, and the bloody stampede to safety.

The diminutive healer kneeling over him placed a slender hand on the buffalo hide bandage tied hair-in around Little Wolf's chest where the last bullet had struck him.

"You will not cross the four rivers today, my friend," Bridge said, his reedy voice sounded scarcely above a whisper.

Little Wolf nodded in gratitude and struggled to focus on the bloodshot yet reassuring eyes of the healer who was *he'emane'e*, one who walks as both man and woman.

When the chief's eyes became steady, Bridge smiled softly and instructed the wounded leader, "*Ne'ešehosotomoo'ėstse*, you must rest now." Then he stood and carefully gathered his own robe about him. After one final look he shuffled off to tend to the other injured scattered along the high, protected ledge on the north wall.

A shift in the light drew Little Wolf's attention upward. *Ešė'he* had just slipped behind some encroaching clouds, inviting a surge of cold air into the valley. The chief grimaced as he again raised himself on an elbow and looked to the west. There in the evening sky above the departing medicine man, large curtains of goose down clouds shrouded the mountain tops.

"*Vo'keme*, why must you decide to come for your visit now?" The Sweet Medicine Chief chided Winter Man's poor timing. He shook his aching head and struggled to sit up. The people were in need.

I shrugged my robe up higher on my shoulders and waited for Lieutenant Clark to return from his briefing with Mackenzie and the other officers. They were meeting upstream in the smoldering Cheyenne camp.

The Cheyenne scouts and I were camped in the creek bend, near the ridge where we had spent most of our day burying family and friends. The boys had built their war lodges and crawled under their robes, trying to insulate themselves from both the cold and from the reality of their part in the gruesome activities of the day.

I had taken first watch. I sat by the fire with my eyes on the red hills to the south but with my heart roaming high up on the white ridge behind me. I couldn't help but feel I should be doing something to help all the wounded there. The pungent odor of burned lodges stunk up the air, adding to my sour mood.

Clark emerged from the darkness and stepped into the wavering halo of campfire light. "It sounds like we'll be leaving in the morning, Bill." He searched for a place to sit. "The colonel wants to withdraw before midday. He has no intention of leaving the Cheyenne anything to subsist on."

"I figured as much," I said. I slid a few feet to my left, making room on the log I sat on. "You'll be less of a target on this side of the fire, sir." I pulled my pipe out and reached for my fixings as the lieutenant walked around the flames.

"Thank you, Bill. You been taking any rounds this evening?"

"Naw, sir, not a one." I pulled the loaded deer horn pipe from my pouch, packed the tobacco with my thumb, and rerolled the buckskin bag with my other hand. "I've heard the fella touching off that big Sharps from time to time, though. I reckon he has some targets up-crick he's been pestering." I lifted a stick from the fire to light my smoke.

"You're right about that," Clark chuckled. "Captain North said he had a cup of coffee shot off of a log right next to him shortly after dark. Honestly, between you and me, Bill, it wouldn't have bothered me a bit if it had been in his hand. He's getting pretty full of himself. Acts like his Pawnee won this fight all by themselves."

I started my smoke with the brand and listened to the lieutenant unload. The officer had disliked North since early in the expedition when the Pawnee leader insisted that he and his scouts answer only to Mackenzie and no one else, bypassing Clark completely.

The Pawnee and Snakes had commandeered the drum we'd listened to on our ride in and started in giving it a few whacks after the officers' meeting finished. It didn't take long before they were raising holy hell on it, celebrating their big victory.

"I wish the colonel hadn't let them camp over there," I said. North and the Pawnee scouts had been assigned to camp in what remained of the sacked village. "I know there's bodies scattered all around in there. It would be tough enough to go back in there to gather 'em up, but we sure as hell ain't going anywhere near that place with all them screaming bastards running around."

Clark nodded. A slight smile crossed his face after hearing me bitch. He tapped the flat of the fingers of his right hand on top of his left hand and repeated the sign with the hands reversed. He then raised his right hand to his mouth and flicked his index finger out like it was a snake's tongue.

He was asking me how to sign a word.

"What, bastard?" I smiled back at him.

Clark winked.

The stick in my hand had gone out as we talked, so I poked it back into the fire and raised my right hand like a fist with my thumb inserted between my index and middle finger. I gave it an angry shake for emphasis. I grinned as Clark mimicked the sign with equal enthusiasm.

I lifted the stick, puffed my pipe back to life, and exhaled. The smoke seemed a little more satisfying for some reason. "It's been a while since we heard that fella with the Sharps. My guess is he'll be saving what rounds he's got left for food instead of fighting."

"Let's hope so," Clark said. "I really don't think they've got much fight left in them anyway." Despite the cold, Clark slipped his hat off and gave it a quick but careful inspection before he continued. "Word is they lost their chief, Bill."

I knew who he meant, but asked anyway. "Which one?"

"Little Wolf. It seems we have two men who each claim they killed him. Billy Garnett is telling everyone that he shot him right away at the beginning of the fight, knocked right off his horse, he said."

"Billy said that?"

"Yes, across the creek there, where the hospital is now. Pourier backs him up on it. Did you find a body there?"

"No, sir. Little Wolf's horse was there, though. Billy might have clipped him, but I think the boy's telling tales about him being dead. No doubt just trying to make a name for himself."

"Could be. I can see that. Here's where it gets interesting, though. At our meeting, Sergeant McClellan claimed that he shot him near the top of the ravine. It was in the vicinity of where we found that poor soul at the end there, the one who was so cut up."

The gruesome image of the man's unrecognizable features flashed in my head. This seemed more likely. I stared at the fire while Morning Star's words from that afternoon came back to me: *Your soldiers have shot him. He has no words for peace or war now.*

"How does he know it was him?" I asked.

"He showed us a holster he had taken off of him that had a silver plate with his name scribed on it. Can't imagine where he might have gotten his hands on something that nice, but it said Little Wolf. I read it myself."

My mind raced back three years and across many miles to the day my friend accepted the gift from President Grant during our trip to Washington. He had just finished brushing his fingertips across the strange signs scratched into the shiny gun belt and looked at me with a question in his eyes.

# Leaving a Life

LARGE FLAKES OF SNOW FLOATED FROM THE NIGHT SKY. A FEW HAD collected in Morning Star's recently unbraided hair as the old chief explained the plan to depart. "There must be no fires until we get up over the ridge," he directed. "We do not want the soldiers to have anything to shoot at. Once you get over the top, out of sight, you should build the first fire so people can find their way to it. Then build the next one not too far away, so they can see it, then the next one, and so on."

The tall Elk Soldier Wild Hog stepped up to share information that he had. "Word has been passed along to those who wait in the hills at the far end of the valley. Everyone will move up the mountain. They have some horses down there that will be brought up a few at a time."

Many in the crowd were relieved. They didn't know if their loved ones were among the survivors, but having horses would be critical during the struggles that lay ahead of them. Without horses, many more lives would surely be lost.

The tall man continued with some disturbing news. "Black Hairy Dog is leaving us," he said. "He is taking the Arrows and traveling back to our southern relatives. He said that if our own people are helping these soldiers to fight us, the Arrows are not safe here. Their power is weakened by Old Crow and those others who are with him."

A groan moved through the crowd. They had lost so much on this day. Many had family members killed; their homes, with all of their family's belongings, had all been overrun; most of the horse herd was captured; and now one of the two sacred bundles was leaving them.

Little Wolf stood off to one side, leaning against a boulder and slouched under the warm but heavy robe given to him by Bridge. Morning Star had sought him out, and after a brief talk, they agreed that due to Little Wolf's condition, the older man should do the talking. Both men agreed that because the valley below now swarmed with Wolf People, it was impossible to consider surrendering. Several white soldiers had also been killed, and revenge for those deaths was likely.

They had to leave this place.

Morning Star's plan was set in motion. Everyone started walking up the long crease along the north wall to where it crested at the far west end of the valley. It would be there where many would find out whether or not their family members had survived.

Little Wolf limped up the trail, which had been made slick by the melting snowfall and the many feet traveling it ahead of him. He had heard the story of Walking Whirlwind's brave death in the ravine from Bull Hump, Morning Star's oldest son. He worried as he walked if anyone would be waiting at the top of this trail to hear that story.

The wounded man tired quickly and was limping badly when Wild Hog caught up with him.

"How bad are your wounds?" the big man asked.

"*Esaahova'ėhevėheo'o*. They are nothing." Little Wolf puffed as he labored up the slope. He tried to speed up a bit to prove his point but quickly resumed his awkward gait.

"Put your hand on my shoulder," Wild Hog said. Little Wolf glanced up at the tall man. He tried to act insulted by the suggestion that he needed help to walk, but he knew he would only slow everyone down if he were too proud to accept the offer. He slid his right hand up onto Wild Hog's left shoulder, and the two men continued up the rugged slope, looking from a distance like two old friends out for an evening stroll. Little Wolf questioned his friend as they walked.

"You said that Old Crow and others were here with the soldiers?"

"Yes, they came with Long Knife, Rowland, to the base of the hill. He said they thought they were going to fight Crazy Horse. I believe him. Old Crow was kind and left us some bullets."

"I know many here will say bad things about them," Little Wolf replied, "but I have known both men a long time. Neither of them would want this for any of their relatives. They did not want to come here and have this happen."

The men came to a place where the downhill side of the ledge lowered, allowing them to look into the valley. They had smelled the lodges burning earlier, but only now could they see what was happening below. The camp crescent was nothing more than a semicircle of embers glowing through a thick layer of dark smoke. The entire village had been burned to the ground. Little Wolf heard Wild Hog take several gulps of air.

"We have lost everything," his friend groaned.

Little Wolf was stunned. He shared Wild Hog's despair but reminded him, "We have people who are waiting for us." He squeezed Wild Hog's shoulder, and they resumed their slow climb.

Snow covered the ground by the time they neared the top of the trail on the west end of the ridge. A fire had been started in a low swale, despite Morning Star's warning against it. But it wasn't visible from below, and the weak light gave them a point to move toward.

They drew close, and people began appearing from the darkness around them. Most had on little if any clothing. Many had bloody wounds on their legs and arms from climbing through the thorny brush that blanketed the high mountain wall. Several were wounded, some severely.

"When we get to the fire, you should leave me and go look for your own family," Little Wolf told Wild Hog. "I am better now."

The young warrior's already protruding brow lowered as his friend and mentor labored up the slope. The older man's pace quickened as they neared the fire, but his limp had gotten worse. "*Haaahe, nȧhtanėheševe*. Yes, I will do that," Wild Hog agreed, "but first we will find someone to walk with you."

The shadowy figures in front of the flames obscured the faces of those on the other side, making it difficult for Little Wolf to recognize anyone. Cries of delight mixed with weeping could be heard as friends and family were reunited. A familiar young voice caught Little Wolf's ear.

"*Neho'e! Neho'e!* Father! Father!"

Day Woman raced from around the fire, prompting Wild Hog

to step forward and lift his hand to keep the girl from injuring her wounded father in her enthusiasm.

The rest of the chief's family followed their youngest to his side, and the reunion was comforting. It was the first time Little Wolf understood their relief when he returned from a war party. They were alive! They had survived the invasion, scaled the snow-slickened mountain in the dark, and were now in his arms.

"Where is White Voice?" he asked.

"She is safe," Two Woman replied. "She is helping some old ones walk to the next fire."

"The horses?"

"Day Woman's fell with her crossing the stream, and a man said he needed the others to try to catch some of the loose ones."

Wild Hog caught Little Wolf's eye and nodded before he left. His friend was safely in the arms of his loved ones. It was time for him to begin looking for his own wife, Stands in the Lodge, and their two children.

Unlike many around them, Little Wolf's family had been prepared to travel. They were dressed for the weather, with the exception of Day Woman, who had lost her robe when her horse fell.

Little Wolf shrugged off the heavy cape that Bridge had given him. His arms were still too weak to toss the heavy hide the way he wanted to, so he called to the closest man walking past them and handed him his knife.

"*Taesetove e'evo'äxeha*. Cut this in half," he said.

Lightning and Two Woman held the robe up for the man while he worked the knife down the center, splitting it in two. Little Wolf thanked him and gave him one of the pieces before he left. The chief then wrapped the other half gingerly around his shivering daughter.

"*Nėstsevovohponeexoveestsehena*, you must wear a warm coat," he said. "Are you hurt from your fall?"

"*Hova'åhane*, no, the dirt was made soft by all those who ran ahead of me."

Little Wolf rose, and Chopping Woman stepped forward. Her eyes held a question that her mouth dared not ask. He first met her eyes. She glanced away then returned his gaze, which held only his deep sadness. The young woman choked out a sob as her body followed her heart to the ground.

Two Woman reached down and spoke softly to her between sobs. She allowed her a moment to grieve then struggled to get the child-heavy woman back to her feet. The family had reunited as best it could, and it was now time to move. A second fire had been built near the top of the ridge behind them, and it was time to make room at this one for those still coming up the mountain.

Lightning squatted down in front of Day Woman and gripped her by the shoulders. "*Katse'e*, little girl, you should walk with your father. He needs your help now. Watch him as we walk between these fires. Make sure he keeps moving when others are not around the two of you."

Day Woman nodded. There was no time to be afraid. They had to leave this place.

Lightning hurried to help Two Woman with their eldest while Little Wolf and Day Woman kept a slower pace. The snow was getting deeper, and the wound in Little Wolf's leg ached from the effort of trying to avoid slipping. His buckskin shirt and leggings were now soaked and heavy and did little to fend off the cold wind.

They arrived at the second fire and stepped inside the ring of people where they found several parents holding their children's bare feet to the flames. Those with robes and blankets invited anyone without one to share what warmth their bodies could muster together.

Tears welled in Little Wolf's eyes. He leaned down to Day Woman and whispered, "*Noheto*. Let us go. We should leave room for those who need to warm themselves."

The pair made their way out of the crowd and pushed north, crossing over the crest of the ridge. His leg felt like it was on fire now, and he was using the rest of his body to compensate. They had started down to the larger blaze on that side when a muffled and irregular thudding sounded behind them. It grew louder, and he paused to peer back through the darkness.

"*Otahe, mo'ehno'hame*. Listen, horses," he whispered to Day Woman.

The young girl stifled a cry and stepped closer to her father, uncertain whether to run or try to help him get away.

A cluster of large, dark shapes entered the edge of the clearing behind them. Little Wolf could hear others crying out in fear as they started to run in the opposite direction.

"*Noxa'e!* Wait!" he called out into the darkness. "*Noxa'e!*"

This was not the thundering clamor of hundreds of iron-clad hooves but the irregular rhythm of a small herd of unshod horses at a trot. They were Cheyenne horses being herded by their own men. The small herd swept past them as they were driven with purpose toward the fire ahead.

Father and daughter arrived at the blaze just as one of the horses was wrestled to the ground. Starving Elk, a friend of the family, knelt on the animal's head and thrust his knife into its throat. Two other men held fast to ropes they had tossed around the rear legs and waited for the old mare to stop her thrashing. The horse stopped struggling and was rolled onto its back. Starving Elk moved quickly to its exposed belly and skillfully sliced through the stomach muscles, opening the abdomen as a cloud of steam rose around him. He moved aside, and Box Elder was carried from the surrounding crowd by Medicine Top and another man. The blind elder was helped to place his bare feet into the animal's warm intestines. The small man cried out in pain as steam billowed around him and his feet absorbed the sudden warmth. An elderly woman was also helped to stand in the animal's viscera; she too groaned pitifully at the abrupt temperature change.

The two elders were lifted from the horse's belly and their feet carefully dried with grass. Starving Elk had been busy removing strips of hide that he wrapped around their feet as makeshift moccasins. While he worked, two more elders were helped into the still-steaming cavity.

A second horse was brought down and killed. The entrails of this animal were pulled from its abdominal cavity, and a call went out for infants to be brought forward. A young mother handed her child over, and it was slipped from its blanket and laid inside the abdominal cavity. A second soon joined it, then a third.

While the body heat of the two animals was being scavenged, some of the women went to work slicing hunks of flesh off of them. Lacking their usual cooking utensils, they placed the meat directly onto the coals of the fire to cook it as quickly as possible. It had been a long day, and the climb up the mountainside had everyone hungry and tired.

"When did you eat last?" Little Wolf asked his daughter.

"Mmm. We had some dried meat early this morning before the soldiers came."

"Go up there and get something." Little Wolf nodded toward the fire.

Day Woman stepped up, and one of the women handed her a piece of rare meat. Day Woman thanked her and returned to her father's side.

"We should go," the chief said as he turned to leave. "We will rest awhile at the next fire."

Day Woman touched his arm before they started. He turned to see what she wanted, and she held up the horse meat.

"You take a bite before we go," she said.

"Come." Little Wolf ignored the offer.

"No."

The girl held the meat out to her father, refusing to move.

Little Wolf smiled and held both her hands in his as he took a small bite.

"Mmmm. Now, come."

The chief chewed the spongy flesh and turned to limp away. He made it to the edge of the crowd huddled around the fire when he saw Last Bull berating one of the Kit Fox men holding the horse herd.

"*Nenomahtse'heoneve!* You are a thief!" Last Bull hollered as he struck the man in the chest with the handle of his quirt, knocking him off his horse.

The man, named Two Twists, stumbled to his feet and turned to face Last Bull, who caused his horse to bump against him, knocking him over again as he continued to scold him.

"That is my bowstring. I saw you take it from my stand outside my lodge during the fight."

Two Twists was stunned at the man's anger. "The Wolf men were in our camp! You had your rifle to fight with, and mine was gone. What would you have me do?"

"Give it to me." Last Bull raised his arm to strike the man with his quirt again, but Young Two Moons rode between them.

"*Neve'nėheševe!* Stop doing that!" Young Two Moons barked. "People are watching us." He tried to speak quietly to Last Bull, but his words carried in the still evening air. "You are embarrassing yourself and the Kit Fox."

Last Bull glanced over his shoulder to where Little Wolf and nearly everyone else in the crowd stood watching the argument.

"*Neve'nėheševe!*" Young Two Moons repeated himself then rode past the man as if he were just passing by.

Last Bull weighed Young Two Moon's words then glared at Two Twists. "I give it to you," he growled. Then he urged his horse forward and rode off into the darkness toward the next fire.

The storm continued to add to the ankle-deep blanket of snow as Little Wolf turned toward the fourth fire. Day Woman held her father's hand as a strong wind moved across the high plateau. They had traveled a good distance when she noticed that her father was laboring heavily. His face was ashen, but it was his eyes that captured her attention. There was fierceness in them that she had never seen before, a grim determination that both frightened and astonished her. It was as if he were pushing back death itself to make it to the next fire. Tears blurred her vision as she wrestled with the conflicting feelings of fear and pride.

Despite his exertion, he held her hand with a gentle grip. "*Neve'ea'xaame, katse'e, he'konetanȯhtse.* Don't cry, little girl, be strong."

She heard him speaking softly from the other side of her tears. She wiped her eyes with the back of her free hand. If he could walk without falling, she would walk without crying.

# All Our Taking Ways

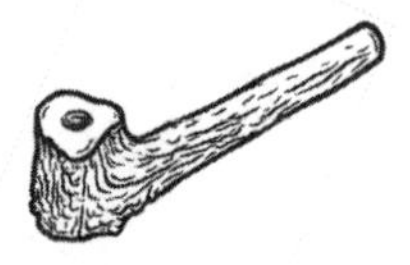

We woke that next morning to a couple inches of fresh snow with more coming down. The fires had smoldered through the night and pushed a dark layer of smoke up against the low ceiling of clouds that had settled into the canyon. The sour smell of burned lodges hung in the air. It was as if the Almighty himself decided He'd rather not look at what had happened the day before and had spread out a clean, white blanket to keep the sight and stench of it all from reaching Him. Problem was, we mortals can't absolve ourselves so easily, and we each had to carry a bit of that stench with us when we left.I held my finger up to let him know I'd answer his question. I shothers in earshot. I knew what would work, but I felt like a heel for using it.

Snow fell off and on throughout the day. There was no need to cover ground quickly, so Mackenzie decided to bypass the slippery trail over the ridge where the young soldier and I had taken our tumble. Instead, we followed the long canyon east, down to where it merged with another drainage to create a small valley.

Everyone was exhausted when we arrived, and we pitched camp under a revived shower of snow. The alternate trail we used had not been an easier one by any means. Footing was still bad and several more horses died as the result of tumbles in the fresh-fallen snow. The possibility that the Cheyenne might somehow regroup and mount an ambush at any moment kept us all on edge throughout the day.

I slipped my saddle off of Ulysses, laid it on a spot I had cleared, and tossed my rubber ground cover over the top of it. The buckskin wouldn't need the hobbles that the other soldiers were putting on their mounts, but I reached down to clean his hooves and check each for cuts or bruising. I patted him on the rump and poured out a small portion of oats that I had squirreled away in a saddlebag. Ulysses nickered as the snow cooled his weary back and the feedbag slipped over his muzzle.

"*Netaexo'ȧsenȧhnemane.* Let us build a fire," I grunted to Old Crow and nodded toward a couple small dead cedars standing in a nearby draw. Once it was started, we would see to our evening rations of salt pork and hardtack.

Hard Robe and the others began scouring the area for enough wood and sagebrush to keep the fire going through the evening. Little Fish was struggling with one of the cedars when the sound of several rifle shots boomed in rapid succession from somewhere just up the creek. Everyone dove for cover.

The sound of several hundred rifles being grabbed and aimed created a soft rattle that ended in a tense silence. The quiet was soon broken by the voices of officers calling out to one another as they checked for casualties and tried to decide what to do next.

I dove behind a snowbank and trained my rifle sights on a barren slope about a hundred yards up-creek. It sounded like the shots came from there, but I wasn't sure. The cold from the ground crept into my body, but I lay still, waiting for the first wave of warriors to come screaming over the top of the slope toward us.

Old Crow lay on his back beside me. He was doing nothing to ready his rifle or even pretend that he was going to use it. I took a quick double-take. I understood that the man would likely not fire at his own people, but there was something else.

"You don't think it's them?"

"They are weak. They would not make an attack like this now."

A voice cried out from behind the barren slope, "Shit, don't shoot. We're friendlies. Friendlies!"

I looked over the top of my rifle sights and through the early twilight. A man with his rifle raised high overhead appeared on the top of the slope.

"Garnett." I scowled. "Blasted kid! What the hell's he done now?"

A collective groan went through the company as rifles were lowered, and everyone in the company took a collective breath to calm down.

"*Tatanka!* Buffalo!" Garnett hollered for everyone to hear. "We shot some buffalo. That's what the shooting was about. No call to get all worked up."

Many of the soldiers started hustling toward the promise of fresh meat for their campfires. I stood up and brushed the snow off, muttering as I tried to beat the cold out of my arms and legs. "Goddam kid. Captain's son or not, I don't see how he gets away with shit like that." I looked up to catch both Clark and DeLany riding at a trot toward the slope Garnett had disappeared back behind. They clearly shared my dissatisfaction with the careless gunfire.

"There you go, now. Those two are apt to be taking a pound of flesh off of him, that's for sure. Goddam fool kid."

Old Crow smiled at my grumbling. Hard Robe and the others knew the Lakota word for buffalo and started off toward the slope themselves.

The snow tapered off later that evening. After a dinner of fresh meat for the lucky scouts and soldiers who were able to get to the carcasses fast enough, the Pawnee started up a scalp dance. I had some of the meat with the boys, but none of us was in the mood for the carrying on.

The drumming and singing grew louder as the dance progressed. From where we camped, I could see down into the dance area. It was mostly Pawnee who were dancing, but I did catch a glimpse of Billy Garnett and a few of the Lakota moving in there among them.

Lieutenant Clark appeared at the edge of our fire a bit after dark. I was having a smoke and sitting cross-legged with my back to the festivities, so I didn't see him coming.

"Evening, Bill."

I looked to my right and was surprised to see a pair of soldiers standing next to the lieutenant.

"What's this?" I asked.

"The colonel would like a word with you."

"What about?"

"He said he'd like to review some of the material that was found in the lodges yesterday."

I sighed. This wasn't going to be easy duty. "You want Old Crow to come and help? He'd know their belongings better'n I would."

"I don't think that will be necessary, Bill. I'm not sure he would be familiar with most of these items."

Now I was curious. "All right. I wanted to have a word with you and the colonel about some of the shit Billy's been pulling anyway."

"That was a foolish stunt that he pulled earlier." Clark smirked." Let's talk while we're walking.

I tapped my spent pipe on a rock then turned to the scouts and told them, "*Noxa'e, hetsėhoehe nėšeešėhoo'e*. Wait, stay here."

"Let them know that these men will be staying here until you get back."

"What? Why's that?"

"I'll explain on the way. We'd best get on the jump here."

I explained about the soldiers staying then left with the lieutenant.

"Garnett's lucky he and his boys had a decent aim," Clark said as he found a quick pace. "There would have been more consequences if they hadn't at least had meat to show for their stupidity."

"Makin' meat don't make it right in my book," I grumbled.

Clark grunted. "You sure seem to have taken a dislike for the man all of a sudden, Bill. What's that about?"

"He's a boy. He's got some growing up to do, that's all."

We skirted one campfire then another as we trudged through the trampled snow toward Mackenzie's fire.

"It sounds like more than that. It's about that first shot, isn't it? The one he took at the beginning of the fight."

The lieutenant kept a pretty quick gait. It was dark, so I fell in behind him and did my best to keep up while I continued to grouse. "You know, I knew his father at Fort Laramie, back in the day. If Capt'n Garnett knew his boy was doing shit like that, he'd a brought him up short in front of all of us. Wouldn't put up with it for a minute, that's for sure."

"Watch it!" a voice growled from the sagebrush in front of us.

The lieutenant two-stepped around a tent pitched on a rare flat spot between two large clusters of brush.

"Sorry, soldier," he apologized and kept moving. "If it makes any difference, Bill, I've reprimanded Garnett for the scare he gave us this afternoon, and the colonel has already informed him that he will not receive any of the horses that were promised to the scouts, as punishment for disobeying his orders on the morning of the attack."

It made a difference, but not a big one.

"Kid's damned lucky," I noted. "I've seen Mackenzie go a helluva lot harder on others for less."

"That's true," Clark replied, "but aside from his father's name, Garnett is a bright, resourceful fella in his own right. He could prove to be very helpful as things move forward."

"Helpful? Ha!" I snorted. "I'm sorry, sir, but I don't see how disobeying orders and nearly getting himself blasted to hell is being any kinda helpful."

"He has connections to the Lakota that will give us a lot of leverage when the time comes to take advantage of them. We can't just toss someone like him aside because he's taken a couple missteps."

I saw I wasn't getting anywhere with this, so I dropped it and raised another concern. "So, why do you have guards posted on my men?"

Clark paused at the change in topic and, instead of answering, simply motioned that we were close to Mackenzie's fire. "We're here. Let's let the colonel fill you in on that."

When Ranald Mackenzie had first arrived at Camp Robinson, three months earlier in August, he looked every bit the dapper young military officer. However, when the lieutenant and I found him on this night, he resembled any one of the several hundred other tired and grubby soldiers we had just walked past. Just like them he sat huddled in his blanket, staring at a small fire and trying to stay warm.

"Evening, Rowland. Lieutenant." He stood and greeted us as we approached.

"Evening, sir," Clark and I replied together.

The colonel grabbed a bough of sagebrush and swept the light dusting of fresh snow off of a log by the fire.

"So, Rowland, tell me, how are you dealing with the events of yesterday?" He indicated that we should sit as he spoke.

Mackenzie didn't appear to be in a very celebratory mood, despite the decisive victory. He seemed to be waiting for me to share my woes about the fight so he could, in turn, tell me his.

"Well, I ain't happy, if that's what yer asking, sir."

"I imagine not." Mackenzie settled back on his log. "I overheard some of your conversation as you approached, and I understand your concern about the guards watching your Cheyenne friends."

"Well, yes, sir." I was surprised he had heard me but was relieved that the subject had been broached.

"Truth is, it's necessary for their own protection."

"Necessary, sir?" I studied Mackenzie's expression, which seemed to grow darker by the minute.

"Rowland, you should know that there were more than just Cheyenne belongings taken out of those lodges up there." Mackenzie reached into his greatcoat, carefully removing what looked to be a folded American flag. "They found a large amount of personal effects belonging to the 7th Cavalry, which means, of course, that it came from the engagement at the Little Bighorn."

As he spoke, the colonel unfolded the colorful piece of silk and held it forward in the campfire light to show me a small American flag that had been folded and stitched into what was now, evidently, a pillowcase.

"We've seen this guidon, gauntlets, a watch, and more. We've even recovered the Company G guard roster."

I must have looked a bit unconcerned.

"You don't appear too bothered to hear about these discoveries, Rowland."

"Oh, meaning no disrespect, sir," I replied. "Believe me, I'm plenty bothered that you found those things and that Custer and his boys were all laid low like they were. It's just that, well, I wasn't there to see it, and I really only knew a few of them in passing, and most of that's military issue you're describing.

"See, I've lived with these people in camps like the one we just destroyed for some time now, and I've been walking around here seeing these boys waving family heirlooms and belongings that been with the Cheyenne for fifty, sixty, a hunnert years or better. It just seems like everybody's carrying a satchel or two just chock-full of the spoils of war these days."

"Well," Mackenzie sighed, "I'm sorry to say that there's more to it than that. It's actually the reason I called you here this evening and why I've left guards with your scouts. I don't know if you've noticed, but the Shoshone aren't taking part in the scalp dance up there. That's because they're all pretty distraught right now. It seems that this parfleche was found in one of the lodges, and it has them pretty upset."

I reached for the brightly dyed leather bag that the colonel had given Clark to hand me. I undid the elk antler button and opened it, tilting it toward the firelight so I could see inside. I knew the hair was human as soon as I saw it. Scalps, several of them, all adorned with small totems and charms. I saw by the designs that they were Shoshone. The bag seemed heavier than what several scalps should weigh, so I reached in and pushed them aside. My fingers brushed against some smaller ones.

I jerked my arm back and looked back at the colonel.

"Hands?"

The officers sat stock-still as I looked from one to the other. Fine snow started to filter down from the black sky and drifted between us.

"Over a dozen, all are barely more than infants if you look close," Mackenzie said. "Some of the Shoshone recognized the trinkets on a few of the scalps, and they're fairly certain that they're from relatives in their own camp. Needless to say, they want to leave and get back there as soon as possible, but I can't release them until we're back with the main column.

"Now, I've spoken with Tom Cosgrove, their interpreter, and he's assured me that he doesn't think that they'll be looking for any trouble with your Cheyenne, but I think it would be wise if you let them know that they should be on guard tonight. Perhaps just to be mindful of the situation and to keep a respectful distance during the rest of our ride back."

I kept staring at the parfleche and gave a couple of absentminded nods. I heard what the colonel was saying, but my mind was on the move, drifting on its own accord back to my home at the Red Cloud Agency near Camp Robinson and the small hands that had waved goodbye to me when I left there, what now seemed like a very, very long time ago.

Of the ten children Sis and I had, four were under the age of six. I was riding away on Ulysses when I last laid eyes on them. Jack, Patrick, and Frank were all clinging to their mother's skirt, and each had given me an uncertain wave goodbye. Alice Jane, our only daughter, was fifteen this year. She held Frank, her one-year-old brother, and was coaxing him into flexing his chubby fingers in farewell.

"You look shocked, Rowland. Are you that surprised your friends were capable of doing something like this?"

I struggled to come back to the campfire and focus on what the colonel was asking me. "No, sir, I ain't surprised. There ain't many of them that would do something like this, though."

I had to clear the emotion from my throat before I could continue. "Um, likely some of those from the northern bands—Last Bull or Black Coyote, maybe. Black Coyote also has a brother Whetstone, and a brother-in-law, Vanishing Wolf Heart. Any one of them could have done something like this. I don't know, sir. With that many hands in there, it could be that they all got together for a raid somewhere."

I shook my head and looked up at Mackenzie. "But there's a rotten tater or two in every cellar, sir. A feller can't go throwing the whole pile out just on account a them."

Mackenzie nodded. "You're right, and I'm aware of that. All I need to do is look around at all the scouts here, and I can see many men of exceptional character. I dare say they've handled themselves better than most of the regulars here. Truth be told, as sad and as gruesome as this discovery is, I doubt many—other than possibly the Shoshone—would really try to hold the whole tribe accountable for this."

I sat staring at the bag, still shaking my head, amazed at how my bellyaching for a fight had just been knocked right out of me. I still would never trust Billy Garnett any more than I would a green-broke stud-horse, but the contents of the satchel in front of me left me speechless. I looked at Mackenzie and understood the sadness in his eyes a little better now.

"There's one more thing," Mackenzie said. "I thought you might be interested in knowing that we had a few of the Pawnee come in late this afternoon and inform us that earlier this morning, they had about eighty head of horses taken from them by a large force of Cheyenne, about six miles north of here."

I took a quick breath. It was good to hear they still had some fight in them but also realized what that bit of news might mean. "So, we headed up after 'em in the morning?"

"No, no, we won't." Mackenzie shook his head. "We've got dead and wounded of our own, and I can't justify chasing off into the mountains after an enemy who is on the move and is watching for us. I think we've hurt them pretty bad already. They're sure to have many wounded with them, and from what I saw, hardly any were dressed for the weather. No, I think that in their condition, the mountains will be hard enough on them as it is."

I was dismissed. I walked back to my own fire. I glanced over at the revelry taking place at the dance. I saw a young Pawnee in the middle of the gathering spinning like a Kansas dust devil. He had one arm raised high in the air and was holding a scalp with hair so long it nearly reached the ground.

# Fear and Freezing

Going In Woman tied a sprig of white sage against the palm of her daughter's hand. She wrapped a scrap of blanket around the gray-tinged infant and handed the tiny bundle up to her brother, Standing Bear, who crouched on a lower branch of a mature pine. He nestled his niece's body securely in the crook of a branch high on the tree then lowered himself to the ground. The young man said a quiet prayer then dug a hole in the snow at the base of the tree and tucked a small piece of horse meat there—sustenance for the child's spirit in the next world. Going In Woman pressed her back against the tree and slid down until she was squatting at its base, weeping. She had also lost her husband in the attack, but his body was not recovered. There had been no such ceremony for him. Her sister, Little Hill, removed her red scarf and tore off strips for friends and family members to wrap and tie whatever small offerings of tobacco they could scrounge up to the lower branches of the tree, completing the humble burial site.

Red Earth Woman had frozen to death, despite her mother's desperate attempt to hold her tight against her own shivering body. Going In Woman had carried the body most of the morning until her tears and stifled sobs revealed the tragic situation to her family. Her child was the eleventh infant to die during the night.

The ceremony had finished, and Little Wolf nodded to Lightning so they could start back to the fires on the trail below. The snow had returned just before sunrise and was now as deep as a man's footprint was long. From their elevated position near the small copse of trees, they could see the crowds gathered around small fires that were scattered along the length of the open ledge below them.

Beyond the north-running ledge, the mountainside pitched down into a steep canyon, the floor of which rose to meet a saddle ridge to their left. Here, mountainside and canyon floor came together in a basin. Word had been passed along the fires that the intent was to cross this saddle and drop over the ridge into a larger, flat-bottomed canyon to the west. They would follow that canyon up to where Lodge Pole Creek started and descend along it to the plains. Once there, they would travel north to find the camp of Crazy Horse. The way would be very difficult, but they had to keep moving.

Some of the wounded and the elders unable to walk had been mounted on horses recovered from the battlefield. The best animals were used by the men who were building fires on the trail ahead or those out watching against another soldier attack. The only animals available to be killed for food, heat, and hide would be those that became too weak to be used any other way.

Light snow floated in the air as Little Wolf and Lightning walked through the crowds around the fires. They found Two Woman and the girls where they had left them, sitting together on a mat of fir boughs near the largest fire. Chopping Woman and Day Woman had fallen asleep with their heads wrapped in light scarves. Two Woman sat between them and had just pulled her robe over the top of all three of them to shield against the falling snow. The girls would be awakened soon so the family could move on to the next fire, allowing someone else to use the mat.

Three dogs were being cooked for those unable to chew the tough horse meat. Two had been laid directly on the coals of the fire, while the third was being boiled using a horse bladder to hold the water as heated stones were added to bring it to boil. Little Wolf was hungry but knew that he would also have to rest soon. He and his wives were wearing down. They had not slept for two nights now, and the combined effects of exhaustion, cold, and hunger could be as deadly as the soldier's bullets.

The cold had helped his injuries to heal. They were all flesh wounds, and the bleeding, swelling, and pain had been lessened by the frigid temperature. The large wound to his leg would keep him from being able to ride horseback for a while, but he still refused the offer of a seat on a travois. He needed to move among the people to hear as much as he could about the attack.

That morning, Dog Speaking had told him about Split Nose and his brave ride around the horse herd behind the camp. It saddened Little Wolf to realize that he had watched his friend die from across the valley without knowing it. He could see Medicine Top at the fire just behind them and decided to check on the condition of Box Elder. He left Lightning with the girls and hobbled off to talk to the young man. He was halfway to the fire when a series of rifle shots boomed up from the canyon.

He twisted around and loped awkwardly back toward his family. The screams and crying started immediately, and the crowd surged uphill, running away from the sound of the gunfire. Going In Woman looked up in surprise from the base of her child's burial tree to see the frightened crowd scrambling toward her.

The chief's wives and daughters waited for him at the fire, but he gave them a wave, indicating they should run uphill with the rest. Another volley of shots rumbled from the canyon and convinced them to run after the others.

Little Wolf reached for the pistol tucked in his belt. He opened the cylinder to make sure the one bullet was in position to be fired if needed. He flipped the gun closed and looked around to see who stood with him to fend off the charge.

Farther along the ledge, Wild Hog towered over a group of men standing near the basin. On the trail between stood a thin line of warriors, each man turning his head and listening, trying to gauge exactly where the attack would begin. The slope dropped off steeply below them, making it impossible for anyone to see for sure where the shots had come from.

A few more shots sounded, but these seemed farther away than the last volley. A silence settled in as even the frightened women and children higher up on the ridge grew quiet in anticipation.

A faint rumbling was heard—hoof beats, many of them, though still too far away to determine the source. The rumble was moving up the canyon to Little Wolf's left, toward Wild Hog and the others. The chief resumed his awkward lope as others around him started running in the same direction, hustling through the snow, desperately trying to come together to meet the oncoming assault.

Men raced past him carrying whatever they had for a weapon. A few had guns; some had either a bow or war club; others carried nothing more than a branch or rocks. It would be the end of everyone if the attackers got past them this time. The rumbling became louder.

A shout went up from Wild Hog and the others. The tall Cheyenne and those around him suddenly threw their arms in the air and cheered as if they were celebrating a winning bet on a horse race.

The rumbling grew louder as it moved up the canyon. Little Wolf still couldn't see the riders, but he slowed to a walk and watched Wild Hog and the others continue to rejoice at the sight of whatever, or whomever, was coming up from the canyon toward them.

The undulating backs of a herd of horses soon appeared just above the edge of the slope. They were barely visible through the falling snow, but as more appeared, it became clear that these were Cheyenne horses with Cheyenne riders driving them. The herd slowed to a stop in the basin near the ridge. The steep walls on all but the downhill side created a natural corral where close to a hundred animals soon milled around as people hurried forward to see them.

An impromptu Council meeting was called on a flat area beside the basin. Herders were posted, and the names of the wolves who brought the horses in were called out. The weary men were brought forward. Young Two Moon, Yellow Eagle, and Turtle's Road sat together in front of the chiefs this time.

Those of the Council who remained had been called, but there was no great Council Lodge to gather under. What came together that day was a simple circle of cold, weary people and the traditions that had guided them for generations. Black Hairy Dog was gone, but the presence of Coal Bear, Keeper of the Sacred Hat, was enough to remind everyone that, despite the calamity, the Cheyenne way was still intact.

The pipe was passed, and Young Two Moons was asked to tell the story of how they had come to capture the horses.

"I speak to the Arrows," he started, then paused, as if reflecting on their absence. "When we left, we were told to act as rear guard, so we went downhill to watch over the trail at the bottom of this canyon. We wanted to make sure the soldiers would not ride around from the other canyon and come here after us. We were about halfway down the slope when Yellow Eagle first saw a few of the Wolf People's warriors driving these horses up the canyon. I think they were lost." A few snickers floated through the crowd. "We waited in one of the side creeks until they came close, then we charged on them. We caught them by surprise, and they all started to run away. I think there were about five or six of them. One was so frightened he fell off his horse when he tried to turn and run. Another one took him up on his horse, and they rode together down the creek. Turtle's Road caught the man's horse, and his gun was still in the holster on the saddle."

The crowd cheered the story. The men gave a hearty "Hou! Hou! Hou!" and the women all trilled a high-pitched "Lu-lu-lu." Little Wolf watched the young man, Turtle's Road, as the crowd reacted. He was pleased but somewhat embarrassed by all the praise coming from the people for his actions.

"*Nepėhevehetaneve.* You are a good man," Coal Bear spoke after the crowd quieted. "You all are. You have brought more than just horses back to us. You have brought us hope."

The story was good to hear and the celebration good to see. Hope had indeed returned to the people, and Little Wolf knew that every bit of it would be needed to help them survive a very difficult journey ahead. He glanced around the crowd and enjoyed the smiles. A familiar face emerged from the throng, and the chief's mouth opened in surprise. It was Wooden Thigh, his eldest son.

The wolves were still finishing their report, so he could not leave just yet. He also wanted to propose afterward that they stay here for a while. The terrain provided them a good defensive position if an attack came from the canyon, and it would allow any stragglers time to find them. They could resume their trek over the rise to the next canyon in a day or two, and then travel along the high ridges and basins to the beginning of Lodge Pole Creek.

The Council agreed when he was able to speak, and Little Wolf was soon limping through the crowd, nodding greetings and giving encouragement to those who suffered. He walked toward where he had last seen Wooden Thigh and found him talking with friends. When Little Wolf approached, the younger men stepped away, and father and son stood face to face. At twenty-eight winters, Wooden Thigh was half a hand taller than his father and, like him, thick where it counted. He carried himself with the confidence of a chief's son and would certainly have been in the middle of the fight had he been in camp.

"It's good that you are here. We have had a hard fight and lost so much," Little Wolf said.

Wooden Thigh looked despondent. "We should have returned sooner. We were beyond the ridge and had no idea what was happening. We killed two elk and were getting ready to return when we saw the smoke in the sky late yesterday afternoon." The young man glanced around at the wounded and frostbitten people around him. "I knew something bad had happened with that much smoke. Starving Elk just told me about the attack. He said that many have been killed."

Little Wolf nodded. "More are dying around us as we travel. There are many wounded here. They suffer badly, along with the old and the young ones."

"We have meat," Wooden Thigh suddenly remembered. "We must let people know we have meat for them."

Gathering His Medicine was near, and Little Wolf called to him. "Find Plenty Bears and tell him I have work for him. I saw him over there during Council." The chief nodded toward a cluster of people. The boy nodded and headed off after the Elk Soldier's crier.

"Where is Pawnee?" Little Wolf asked about his younger son.

"He went to find his mother and sisters. He is very tired from the trip, but he did well. One of the elk is his."

"*Epeva'e*, we should go there ourselves. They will be happy to see you."

When Plenty Bears arrived, he was given a choice cut and asked to make a trip around the fires to quietly invite those who had wounded, elderly, or nursing mothers among them to send someone to Little Wolf's fire for elk meat.

A series of breastworks were built below the western rim of the canyon that afternoon. By evening, Little Wolf's family was nestled around a small fire behind a low wall of logs and stones. White Voice had returned for the night. She had been helping Starving Elk's elderly parents travel while he and his brother were out scouting. She would return there in the morning when it was time to travel again. It was a relief to have his family all gathered around the same fire again. Even with the heartbreaking loss of Walking Whirlwind and all their belongings, there were many around them who were worse off.

People came quickly looking for the meat and kept coming after it was gone. Lightning, Two Woman, and the girls had curled up together between the fresh elk hides when Wooden Thigh turned to his father.

"I will stay awake and tell any others who come for the meat that it is gone. I will not let them wake you."

The weary chief smiled. He knew he was politely being told to get some sleep.

# Drowning Ghosts

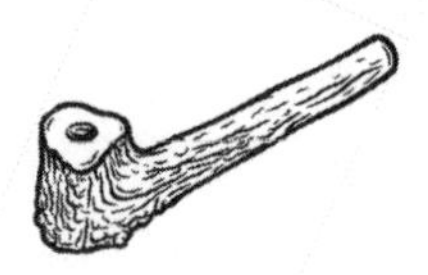

We rejoined Crook and the main column back on Crazy Woman Fork. The Shoshone scouts were immediately discharged so they might return to whatever was left of their families, and the general led us south, back to Cantonment Reno, for supplies.

Reno was the small, hastily built, and northernmost outpost in our supply chain. It stood along the west bank of the Powder River, about thirty miles due east of where the attack on the Cheyenne village had taken place. We had camped there a week earlier on our way north. A few of the buildings were constructed out of cottonwood logs, but most were odd tangles of log, adobe, and sod, and each had at least one piece of tarpaulin stretched across an unfinished opening. I had seen the early days of Fort Laramie in forty-nine, Fetterman in sixty-seven, and Camp Robinson in seventy-four. Reno was for sure the sorriest excuse for a military post I had ever come across in all that time.

Lieutenant Clark had asked for another sign talk lesson, so I walked over to his cabin after supper. The ten-day-old moon gave me just enough light to keep from stumbling on the uneven ground. I approached from the south and moved around to the east-facing front door. Greased paper windows, backed by canvas curtains, cast a soft, amber glow into the darkness. The door was canvas too, and I knew those inside didn't understand the Cheyenne way of standing to the side and coughing as a way of knocking, so I rapped on the wall and spoke up.

"'Tenant?"

"Enter." "Yes?" "Huh?" Three different voices answered together.

I raised the tarp aside and stepped inside.

Lieutenant Clark was on my right. He held a tallow lamp at eye level while he inspected the crumbling mud and straw bricks on that side of the cabin. Lieutenant DeLany lay on his bedroll near the rear log wall of the primitive structure. He gave a welcoming nod before returning to reading in the weak light of another lamp that was perched on an empty ammunition crate.

A third officer, Lieutenant Lawton, sat at a flat-topped steamer trunk that served as a table in the middle of the cabin. A third lamp and a half-gone bottle of whiskey sat in front of him. Lawton had been involved in the charge on the Cheyenne at the ravine and had seen the worst of what happened there. From the looks of him, I figured he had a few ghosts he was trying to drown.

Clark gave me a hallo. "Evening, Bill. Thanks for coming. I must say, this workmanship is deplorable. I don't see how these buildings can last more than a couple of years without some sort of major renovation. I'd tear them all down, frankly."

"Camp Robinson isn't much better," DeLany replied, looking up from his book. "I think the materials in this north country are quite inferior to the good adobe down south."

"The materials are fine," Lawton growled without looking up. "You Paddies just need to learn how to make adobe, that's all."

"Well, these weather conditions don't help anything, that's for sure," Clark replied.

"Fer shur! Ha!" Lawton guffawed. "I think you've had enough sign lessons, Nobby. You sound more and more like this old squaw man every day."

Clark shook his head and grinned as he walked to the steamer trunk. "Never mind Lawton here. He's a bit under the weather, as you can see."

The drunken officer grunted and stared at his bottle as if he wasn't sure how it had lost half its contents.

"I need to piss," he announced suddenly and rose to a pair of unsteady feet.

Lieutenant DeLany dropped his book and jumped to his friend's side. He helped the much taller man throw on a coat and stagger toward the door as I stepped out of the way.

During our stay at the cantonment a week earlier, a drunken enlisted man had wandered off during the night and froze to death. They had covered him with a pile of rocks down by the creek, a temporary grave until the ground thawed enough to bury him in the spring. That exact fate wouldn't await Lawton, though. Officers were treated differently when they died. A lieutenant named McKinney had been killed during the fight in the mountains, and his body was already crated up and ready to ship to Fort Laramie in the morning. DeLany was making sure that Lieutenant Lawton didn't make that trip with him.

"Come, sit." Clark motioned as he took Lawton's empty seat at the steamer and pushed another ammunition crate forward with his foot. He poured a splash of Lawton's whiskey in a tin cup and slid it across the top of the trunk toward me. I declined, so Clark pulled it back and took the shot himself.

"You'll have to forgive Lieutenant Lawton for his fuddled state. He's been having some difficulty dealing with Lieutenant McKinney's death. He issued the order for McKinney and his boys to circle the camp, No one was aware that the ravine was even there or that the Cheyenne were waiting inside it."

McKinney had been the first man killed when the Cheyenne rose up and surprised the charging soldiers.

"Oh, I understand, sir," I replied. "I been feeling the same about Little Wolf and those others. What was that he called you, though? Nobby?"

"Oh," Clark chuckled, "that's just a name I picked up during my time at West Point. I swear, Bill, I get Nobby from the officers, 'Tenant from you, White Hat from the scouts. I doubt that I'll know how to answer to Willy when I get back home."

"That's more names than most Indins I know." I smiled and started signing my words.

Clark pushed the tallow lamp to the side to see better, then signed, "Where do we start?"

I wasn't sure the officer could tell me, but asked anyway. "Well, rumor has it, we're heading north in a day or so. Any idea where?"

Clark answered immediately, hesitating only for help with a name. "Yes, that would be up the, uh …" Clark shook his opened hand to show he had a question. "How do you say Belle Fourche? What's the Cheyenne name for that river?"

I felt my shoulders relax a bit and showed the officer the sign for pretty, then fork, translating the French interpretation of the Cheyenne named river into sign language.

"Ah, of course!" Clark exclaimed. He practiced the signs a couple times then asked, "You seem relieved about the orders. Why is that?"

"Well, I was afraid we might be fixing to take another run at the Cheyenne."

"You think they might be out on the plains north of us by now?" Clark asked.

"Don't know for sure, sir. But I do know they can't be clear out on the Belle Fourche this soon. They would most likely head straight north—that's if they can make it out of them mountains at all."

"The general feels we hit them hard enough, and they'll likely all surrender before spring. He did send some scouts to look for any sign of them along the foothills to the north, but I'm thinking the old man has his sights set back on finding Crazy Horse."

I fixed a smoke while the lieutenant filled me in on Crook's plan. I peeled a sliver of wood from the crate I sat on and held it in the small flame of the tallow lamp until it flared to life. The lieutenant continued as I sucked the flame down into the tobacco.

"The general wants to head northeast, up the Belle Fourche, to keep us in grass. Seems the Indians burned a lot of the country along the Powder River north of us after the Custer fight last summer. He's also sent a couple men to muster up some replacement scouts from the Red Cloud Agency to replace the Shoshone. When they join up with us, we'll move to the Little Powder and follow it down along the eastern edge of the burned area to where it joins with the Powder. I'm not certain, but I'd say there's a fair chance we might continue north and pay a visit to General Miles at his new cantonment at the forks of the Tongue and Yellowstone Rivers."

That was far better news than what I was expecting. "I think he's right about the hurt we put on the Cheyenne," I replied. "They lost everything up there. Little Wolf getting killed is likely enough by itself to make them want to put as much country between us as they can."

"He really meant that much to them?"

"Yeah, to most of them. Though I imagine some would tell you different if you asked."

"How's that?"

I sat my pipe on the trunk so I could sign better. "Well, he was a good man, but he had his ways, like we all do. The meanest Indin you'd ever cross paths with if you had differences, but if he took a liking to you, he was one of the kindest sorts that anyone would care to meet. Smart too. Most Cheyenne saw him either one way or the other, but for sure they all wanted him on their side in a scrap. Count on that."

"Were you close, being his brother-in-law and all?"

"Not at first, but we became friendly over time. The first time I laid eyes on him was around the time of the Horse Crick Treaty, back in fifty-one. He rode in with the Dog Soldiers there and went by the name of Two Tails. Oh, he was a mean, nasty little shit back then."

"Two Tails?" Clark asked, practicing the sign.

"Yep, he changed it to Little Coyote, *O'komoxhaahketa*, when he left the Dog Soldiers and joined the Elk Horn Scrapers about fifteen years ago. Somewhere along the line, though, white folks got his name boogered up in translation and took to calling him *Ho'neheso*, Little Wolf. It's just stuck with him since.

"The two names sound nothing like one another," Clark mused. "How could there be any confusion?"

"Well, it weren't in the saying, but in the signing that it happened. See, you recall the sign for wolf?"

Clark nodded and put his right hand near his shoulder with the first two fingers extended, like wolf ears, then moved it forward and up.

"And small?" I asked.

Clark lowered his hand, palm down, to just a couple foot off the floor.

"So, that's small wolf that you just said, which is the same way you say coyote. You see, if all a person knows is sign language, he's bound to get em mixed up."

Clark nodded slowly. "So, I'd best be paying attention to their spoken word as well."

I nodded back and smiled. "Helps with some of those tricky details ."

"Anyway," I continued, "I kept a healthy distance from him back then. He weren't exactly what you'd call sociable. He'd just as soon shove a man outta his way than ask him to move. That's where a lot a people's hard feelings about him come from. He just said, did, and took whatever the hell he wanted without caring who he hurt."

"Well, how in the world did he ever become chief with that behavior?"

"That's the funny thing about a lot of these tribes. A man like that is a big help when it comes to fighting. Some men fight just for their own glory, but in the end, it still helps the tribe to stay safe and helps them get what they need. It's good to have a fighting man like that on your side. At first he was only after the honor it brought him, but once he was made a chief, I think he started to learn that there's a bit of give and take involved in staying one, y'know. You keep folks happy and safe, and they tend to want to keep you around."

"A few lessons in the importance of quid pro quo, eh? Seems no culture is safe from the necessary demands of politics, is it?"

"Not sure of that first squid crow thing, but I s'pose politics is a good name for the rest of it."

Clark chuckled. "Washington is rife with political tradeoffs. It's really is quite the mess. You wouldn't believe some of the goings on back there in the Capitol."

"Oh, I been there. Seen the elephant, as they say."

Clark looked surprised. "Really? When was this?"

"Late seventy-three," I said. "Little Wolf and Morning Star and a dozen or so of the Cheyenne Council of Forty-Four went to talk to President Grant. Doc Saville and a few others from Fort Laramie and the Red Cloud Agency came along with us. Grant wanted to strong-arm them into going south to Indin Territory."

"I wasn't aware of that, Bill. How did that go?"

"Not good. Little Wolf and Morning Star both reminded him that they signed a treaty back in sixty-eight at Laramie that said they could stay in the north."

"What did Grant say to that?"

I snorted. "You'd a thought one of them had pissed on his boots. He just give a sour look and acted like he didn't hear a word of it."

Clark grinned. "That's too bad. I know the president was convinced that separating the Indians from the settlers would help everyone. I do believe he had their best interests at heart."

"Well, one good thing did come out of that trip. It showed the Cheyenne what they was up against if they kept fighting. We saw all the cities—Philadelphia, New York, Washington. We saw the buildings, the bridges—they threw in everything from concert halls to slaughterhouses just for good measure. It worked too. After seeing what they was up against, Little Wolf and Morning Star realized real quick that they needed to find a new way to settle things without fighting."

"So, what were they doing out here with the hostiles?" Clark interrupted.

I had to think a second. "Well, let me ask you this: why did Lieutenant DeLany just go out into the cold with Lieutenant Lawton? I don't recall him saying he had to piss."

"Well, they're friends. He's just looking after him," Clark said. "Making sure he gets back safe."

"Same thing with Little Wolf," I said. "He went out to convince as many as he could to return to the agency before trouble started. Problem is, trouble came along before he could get to them."

The canvas door was flung aside, and Lieutenant DeLany ushered Lieutenant Lawton back into the cabin.

"All right, Hank, step up there," DeLany said. "Careful now, there's a step!"

The inebriated officer clung to the rough-hewn jamb while he struggled to raise his foot high enough to step over the sill log at the bottom of the door.

"Here we go." DeLany reached down and raised the man's leg, helping him clear the cottonwood log. The pair did an awkward, shuffling dance to Lawton's bedroll at the back of the cabin, where DeLany sat the big man down and wedged him into the corner. Lawton protested until DeLany grabbed the bottle off of the steamer trunk and wrapped the drunken man's fingers around it. He shook his head and gave us a wry smile before returning to his own bedroll and book.

I turned back to Clark. "See, there's a lot of good people out there who are just used to doing things a certain way. It ain't like they was all-out looking for trouble. They just weren't aware of how much trouble was out there looking for them. Little Wolf, Morning Star, and those others who made that trip to Washington, well, they seen it firsthand. They knew."

"So, you think Little Wolf was actually trying to convince the likes of Crazy Horse and the Lakota that they should give up the fight?"

"Well," it was my turn to chuckle, "no, I doubt he would have gone that far."

"What do you mean?"

"Them two fellas didn't exactly get along."

"Do tell, Bill." Clark looked completely captivated by the little-known rift between the two leaders.

I shook my hands out and rubbed them together, signaling that I was done signing for now. Clark nodded.

"It started after the Fetterman fight up on Buffalo Crick, when Little Wolf's brother, Big Nose, got killed."

"Big Nose?" Lawton chortled from behind his bottle.

I laughed at the soused officer. "It don't mean what you think, 'Tenant." I knew that Lawton was actually a very kind person when he wasn't drinking, which was likely the main reason why McKinney's death had hit him so hard.

"Man was a helluva tracker," I continued. "They said he could smell the enemy three ridges over."

"Where's this Buffalo Creek, Bill? Clark asked. "The Fetterman fight took place at Fort Phil Kearny on Big Piney Creek, just north of us."

"Same place," I explained. "Buffalo Crick's the Indin name for it. I forget to swap 'em sometimes. Anyway, Big Nose died in the fight there. Little Wolf told me afterward that his brother was the one who kept after them boys, teasing 'em, even running right through the middle of 'em till they got so damned pissed off that they come charging down that hill after him into their trap. He charged back into them then and ended up getting killed in the process.

"Well, the story started to spread later that it was Crazy Horse who brought them soldiers down instead of Big Nose. Now, you never heard Crazy Horse brag about it, but he has never set the record straight either, which, if you think about it, is pretty disrespectful to the man who died doing it. The story got so blamed big that the Lakota don't know that things coulda happened any other way now. Neither man spoke about it, but they never got along since that happened."

Clark tapped his finger on the steamer trunk, appearing deep in thought as he listened. "Seems like there isn't much of a united front here is there, Bill? It appears there are many of these rifts for either personal or political reasons."

"Well, sure. It's like you said, there ain't a nation anywhere that ain't got that kind of thing going on. There's plenty of bickering between different bands, and even inside 'em if somebody don't like how things are being done. Happens all the time."

Clark's finger gave the trunk a couple more solid thumps. "I think that just may come in handy, Bill. We need to find a way to make use of those internal schisms. I've seen General Crook use them to an advantage while working with the tribal leaders back at the agency."

I shook my head in warning. "I'd recommend staying outta their doings, sir. Things could turn ugly and come back to bite you."

Clark acted like he hadn't heard a word I said. His fingers sounded a steady rhythm on the steamer like a mantle clock ticking in a quiet room.

CHAPTER SEVENTEEN

# Looking for Lakota

LITTLE WOLF STUDIED THE ROLLING GRASSLAND SOUTH OF THE BIG lake, searching for any sign of the horse herd. He smiled when none of the animals could be found. The herders had been instructed to keep the herd bunched closely together in the bottom of a low swale south of the lake. This would prevent anyone who might be spying from the mountains behind them from finding their location. They would be allowed to graze freely only after dark, and that would not be long now as *Eše'he* had already stepped behind the mountains.

Had it had been six or seven sleeps since the fight? He couldn't recall. Most weren't actual sleeps anyway. The constant demands made of him by the mountains, the weather, and the people didn't allow for more than short naps.

Their wolves had recovered more horses during a trip back to the old camp to try and scavenge what they could from the charred and scattered remains. The horses were all they found that had any value, but those were enough to strengthen the hope that the people might survive until they found the Lakota.

Their torturous journey through the high country had been a deadly one for the people. Temperatures dropped, the snow deepened, and many more of the weak and wounded had died along the way. They came out of the mountains that morning and turned north as quickly as they could to put distance between themselves and the soldiers who they knew were somewhere to the south.

The Cheyenne called the body of water they camped beside the Big Lake. The whites called it De Smet, after their black-robe holy man. The Cheyenne arrived late in the afternoon and built their small fires in bottoms of the branching trenches that ran down a high slope overlooking the long body of frozen water from the southwest. This would keep them out of sight from the mountains rising behind them as well as provide them some protection from the chilly wind that always seemed to blow through this area.

He wore a poorly-fitting elk skin robe that Two Woman had worked diligently for several days to try and soften to the point that it was wearable. She was only somewhat successful, but it was far better than going without a robe at all. His wounds had healed enough that he had been able to ride for the first time today. He was sore now, but it felt good to stretch his legs after the ride through the foothills. He decided to take a walk to Morning Star's fire. It was time to visit his friend whose family had suffered so much loss.

Standing Bull and Young Bird were not their only family members killed during the fight. They had also lost Standing Hawk, the husband of Pure Woman, one of his daughters, and Walks in the Night, a granddaughter who had been trampled by horses during the stampede from camp. These recent deaths, along with that of Medicine Club, his son who was killed at the Little Sheep River fight, had left the old chief and his entire family despondent.

What remained of the Beautiful People now sat huddled around a fire of buffalo dung and sagebrush at the bottom of a narrow gully. The old Dog Soldier sat encircled by his wives, Pawnee Woman and Short One, and all their children and grandchildren. The women had just laid a slab of horse meat on the coals of the fire.

The old chief tossed his unbraided hair aside and looked up when his friend arrived. Little Wolf nodded a silent greeting. Morning Star acknowledged his visitor with a nod of his own which caused his hair to fall back over his brow.

Little Wolf inched down the embankment, and Pawnee Woman stood to give him her spot next to her husband. As she rose, her light blanket shifted, revealing that her legs and arms had been cut in the traditional Cheyenne woman's way of mourning. Though several days old, the wounds still oozed a bit when she stood. She stepped back and sat next to her daughter, Pure Woman, who had cut off much of her hair and had dried trails of blood showing on her exposed ankles.

"*Neá'eše*." Little Wolf nodded and thanked the woman before he sat down with a soft groan. He was polite and gave no indication of what he had just seen. Inside Woman and Two Woman wore the same type of cuts back at his fire.

Inside Woman was, of course, grieving the loss of the father of the child growing in her belly. Two Woman grieved the same loss, but she did so because she felt that she was responsible for it. She had helped raise the man's lodge when she should have been at the moon lodge. Little Wolf did not like the practice, even more so now that they were in such dire straits, making this desperate run for survival. It slowed their progress and put more than the women's lives at risk. He knew it would be pointless to say a word about it to any of them, though. It was just how things were done.

The two men sat next to each other silently, as if each were busy recounting the past several days and tracing in their minds the path that had brought them from that afternoon at the older man's fire to this cold and windy hillside.

Morning Star leaned toward Little Wolf. "How are your wounds? You seem to move better."

"Better. I think the cold has helped."

The older man thought for a moment. "I think that was the hardest fight we have been in for a long time."

"Yes, there are many who say it is because Long Knife, Old Crow, and the other Cheyenne rode with the soldiers."

Morning Star surprised him. "No, we should have moved the camp. Those Cheyenne did nothing to hurt our people. I believe Long Knife told the truth; they did not expect to be fighting against us. I think they did their best to keep things from being worse." The old man paused to brush a smudge of ash off his leggings. "They buried my son."

Little Wolf studied the ground in front of him before he spoke. "I heard they buried others."

Morning Star nodded, moved his hair aside, and looked up at the quarter moon in the early evening sky. "We should have moved the camp."

The silence returned for a moment as his eldest daughter, Trail

Woman, and Short One worked together to turn the horse meat and place a couple short branches beside it. The branches caught fire almost immediately, adding heat to the coals.

"Have we heard anything from our wolves?" the older man finally asked.

Little Wolf cleared his throat, heedful of the effect the information might have on those listening. "They are finding no one. The soldiers have scared everyone away from here, and much of the country to the north was burned after the big fight this summer, so no one is moving around out there. We may have a long way to go before we find anyone."

A gust of wind whistled across the hillside, sending a quick eddy down into the coulee, fanning Morning Star's hair and the campfire at the same time. Trail Woman busied herself banking the small bed of coals and adding more wood.

"Are the soldiers coming behind us?" Morning Star asked.

"No."

"Which society leads the way tomorrow?"

"The Elkhorn Scrapers. Wild Hog has stepped up to act as headman on his own, but they all follow him."

"*Epeva'e.* He will do well." Morning Star was quiet again for a moment then continued, "I think the best thing for us to do is to go down Crow Standing Off Creek to Tongue River, and when we come to Otter Creek, we should go across the hills to Powder River, below those burned places."

Little Wolf nodded. He had ridden that day with Wild Hog at the front of the people, and together they had already plotted the same course.

"*Epeva'e*," he said. "Should we wait for you in the morning before we start out?"

Morning Star gave his friend a brief smile. He knew he was being politely coaxed. "Another day, maybe two."

"*Epeva'e*."

Little Wolf accepted a portion of horse meat from Short One and groaned as he chewed his first mouthful, acting as if it were hump meat from a fat cow.

The next morning, Little Wolf led a buckskin mare next to a rock and struggled to slide his stiff leg over its back for the second time that morning. Wooden Thigh had given him the horse the day before when he decided it was time to ride again. His leg had stiffened from yesterday's ride, so he decided to walk a while to loosen it before he tried again. The mare was well trained and stood quietly while Little Wolf wiggled his way onto her back. Wooden Thigh waited until his father was mounted then urged him forward.

"I can see where Wild Hog and those at the front are nearing the pass that leads to Buffalo Creek," Wooden Thigh said. "We should be able to catch up with them soon."

They started away at a trot, moving toward the front of the procession of Cheyenne travelers. Little Wolf enjoyed being on a horse again with the ability to cover ground quickly. The mare had a fast stride and could easily make Wooden Thigh's plan a reality, but the chief's priorities changed quickly.

The long line of wind-battered people trudging along the frozen lake tore at his heart. The once-burgeoning caravan of travois laden with family belongings and historical treasures, which moved at the relaxed pace of a contented people, was gone. What he saw now was a disheveled string of partially clad fugitives bent into a cold and merciless wind, desperate to find anyone who might help them.

"Let us not ride past these people so quickly," he told his son. "It will help them to know that we are here with them."

Father and son slowed their pace and drew closer to the grim-looking procession. Many who they rode past had limbs that were still swollen and blackened from Winter Man's withering touch. Others who labored beside them strove to ignore the pain of unhealed battle wounds. Everyone who suffered so was urged forward by those who had little more than songs and fretful pleas with which to encourage them.

One consolation was that they had descended to the edge of the prairie. Here, the snow was only ankle-deep, not knee-deep as it had been in the mountains. The air still had a sharp bite, but the deadly cold of the higher elevations was mercifully behind them. The terrain was more accommodating, though still broken by ridges between mountain streams that would soon come together to form rivers.

They reined their horses to a stop on the southern ridge of Buffalo Creek, the northernmost tributary to Powder River. *Haa'havėhane*, Wind, had scoured the north side of the slope clear of any snow, and it continued to batter the amber grass on its way south across the foothills.

Those at the front of the line had followed the contours of the earth down into a wide valley. Off to the west, a smaller stream could be seen flowing into the larger Buffalo Creek from the higher slopes. Near this curving junction was the discordant image of rows of burned and decayed logs standing on end and arranged in a precise square.

Ten winters ago, soldiers had stuck these logs in the ground side by side as they erected a wall around a fort that they had just built. The buildings of the fort were no longer standing, however, because two years after they were built, Little Wolf and the Elk Soldiers had burned them to the ground.

The chief lifted his gaze north of the burned fort. His eyes could only show him the top of the ridge, but his heart carried him over to the other side, to the place where he once held his dying brother in his arms and told him what brave man he had been and what a great victory he had brought his people.

# The Expedition Ends

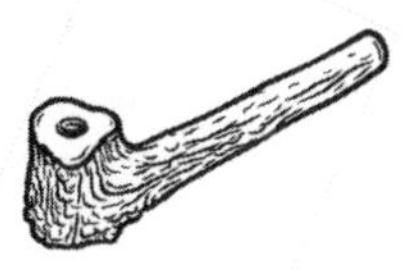

ULYSSES INCHED HIS WAY ONTO THE ICE-COVERED BELLE FOURCHE River. He wasn't sure if the few slippery steps to the watering hole, which had been chopped through the center of the frozen stream, were worth the trip. The buckskin inched forward and finally lowered his head, his nostrils snatching and purging the scent of the murky water flowing past. He raised his head and thrashed his hoof into the hole, trying to remove the small chunks of floating ice. I gave him a quick swat on the hindquarters with the halter rope.

"Here, now! Yer sure getting picky these days. A week ago, you was sucking snow from under sagebrush for your water, and now you're fussing over a little ice? Boy, I tell ya, some people."

In no response to my harangue, Ulysses finally lowered his muzzle and started to drink.

We had left Cantonment Reno and made a steady fifteen to twenty miles a day through the hundred miles of barren plains that stretched between the Bighorns and the Black Hills. Water was scarce here during the summer and froze solid all winter. The animals got by with eating snow, while the soldiers had to melt it. Problem was, the farther we traveled out on the prairie, the less snow we found.

We tramped northeast, moving along the dry bed of the upper Belle Fourche and watching expectantly as it gathered a little more water from each tributary we passed. Eventually, it started to show, first in small patches of frozen marsh, then in small pools that became a shallow but steady stream hidden under a thick sheet of ice.

After two weeks of hard trail, the upper branches of the Little Powder River now lay just beyond a ridge ten miles north of us. For the last week, we had moved camp only to find new grass for the animals while we waited for the replacement scouts to arrive from the

Red Cloud Agency. Once they arrived, we would move over the ridge and down the Little Powder.

Ulysses was drinking now, and I watched the muscular flex of his throat pull long draughts of water into his belly. A familiar laugh skittered into the chilly morning air a short way downstream. I stretched my neck to see around a low, sage-covered cut bank and spied Billy and another Lakota scout, each leading a couple horses to another watering hole that had been opened farther down the creek.

Billy was leading a wary piebald filly along with a bay mare with a yearling colt beside her, all nice-looking animals. He was caught up in his conversation with the scout. Neither one was paying any attention to their surroundings and didn't see me.

They were a ways off and speaking in Lakota, but I was fluent enough to understand. The scout spoke to Billy.

"The soldier with Little Wolf's holster still says that he is the one who killed him."

"He killed a man with Little Wolf's holster, that's all," Billy countered. "I knew Little Wolf from Red Cloud and Fort Laramie. That soldier didn't even know what he looked like. The fella he took that holster from likely found it on the ground near where I shot Little Wolf off his horse. Probably forgot which end of the ravine he was at."

"So, you have killed a man in battle, and you have taken these horses from the enemy as well. You are a warrior of the people now. Next, you need to take a scalp, and they will sing honor songs for you."

Billy laughed. "Not that long ago, I would have snuck into their camp at night and cut these loose from their owners' lodge. There is not much honor in just asking the general for them, but they are good horses anyway."

Needless to say, that last bit surprised me.

Cold water splashed on my face, and I raised my hand to block it. Ulysses was pawing at the murky water again. The horse lifted his head, opened his mouth wide, and coughed as if trying to rid himself of the taste of the brackish fluid.

"Yeah, I got a bad taste in my mouth too, fella. We can't always have spring water, though, can we?"

I led Ulysses up the bank behind us and made my way back to my tent, wading through the thick blanket of sagebrush that lined the narrow flat. The moisture on this portion of the river supported scattered stands of towering cottonwood trees whose bare winter branches scratched at the sky some sixty-odd feet above us.

Tents were raised in whatever order the trees and sagebrush allowed, meaning there was no order and little room to walk. As we approached our campsite, I saw that Lieutenant Clark had arrived and was involved in a discussion with Old Crow, practicing his now fair-to-middlin' sign talk. I slowed my step and watched their conversation.

Clark had just asked Old Crow how he was feeling about the fight. His two loose fists pummeled the air in front of his chest.

Old Crow raised his open hands, fingers forward, over his head and above his shoulders, then made the simple signs that stood for "no blood."

Clark shook his open hand and repeated the first sign, asking the Cheyenne what it meant. Old Crow stopped to think how to explain when I spoke up.

"He said the Holy One sees that my hands are clean, that I have no blood on them."

Both men turned as I stepped into their conversation.

"Ah, Bill, there you are. Old Crow said you wouldn't be gone long." The officer turned back to the Cheyenne and signed, "Good talk. Thank you."

Old Crow nodded and moved his right hand, palm down, forward from his heart then lifted it and flicked his index finger away from his mouth. "Good talk," he repeated to the officer.

Clark beamed and nodded, over-pronouncing one of the few spoken Cheyenne words that he knew: "*Eee-pee-va.*"

Old Crow smiled and agreed with the officer. "*Epeva'e*"

Clark spun on his heels to address me. "Bill, I have some news. Walk with me." He took a couple steps away and paused.

I handed Ulysses's halter rope to Old Crow and gave him an apologetic shrug, then turned and stepped toward the waiting officer. We headed back through the sagebrush and tents, weaving apart, then together, and apart again as we walked.

"'Tenant, I have a question about the hors—"

Clark cut me off. "Bill, General Crook just received word from General Sheridan that the expedition will be coming to an end."

"I'm sorry, sir, it sounded like you said—"

"You heard right. A courier just brought a letter in from Sheridan saying we've gone beyond our projected costs and we must leave the field as quickly as possible."

I came to a stop as I swallowed the news. "Seems awful sudden," I said.

Clark stopped and looked back at me. "I thought you'd be glad. I know it's been a tough ride for you."

"Oh, I'm damn glad, sir. It just caught me a bit off guard is all." I smiled as relief replaced my surprise.

Clark chuckled and resumed his quick pace. "Well, that's the military for you, Bill, hell-bent for a fight one day and taking itself apart at the seams the next. It does take some getting used to."

"So, we're headed back to Fetterman then? Is that the plan?" I had to do a quick-step to catch up with the fast-walking officer.

"Well, some of us are. That's why I'm talking with you on the run like this. See, we still have those scouts coming up from the Red Cloud Agency, so the general wants you and your men, along with Garnett and the Lakota, to leave right away to rendezvous and direct them to return to the agency. I'm to join you there in a couple of weeks."

I slowed my pace as the full meaning of his words hit me. "So, I'm leaving here . . . with Billy?"

Clark tossed "That's correct, Bill" over his shoulder and kept walking.

I stopped again and spoke to the back of the officer's white Stetson. "The hell you say."

Clark stopped, his chin dropped, and he heaved an exasperated sigh. He turned but didn't look at me. "Bill, I don't have time for this."

"I'm sorry, sir, I just don't know if I can—"

"You can and you will, Bill. This is not a request. These orders come from the general himself, and I will not be made to go back to him with your hurt feelings as an excuse for why they were not carried out." He gave me a look that said orders trumped friendship on this one and there would be no arguing.

There was one bone I just had to pick, though, and I got after it. "Well, if you're looking for Billy, I just saw him down by the creek watering those horses the general give him."

We had stopped near a cluster of tents where a group of soldiers had been getting quite an earful. Clark looked around and motioned for me to follow him to a small draw that rose to the flat above us where no tents were pitched. He leaned in close to avoid raising his voice this time.

"Bill, I advised the general to allow Garnett to select a couple horses out of the remainder of the herd after it had been picked over by the rest of the scouts. Now, I know you won't agree with my reasoning, but quite frankly, I don't need your approval. I have a feeling that the blow we just dealt to the Cheyenne is going to have a ripple effect on the resolve of many of the Lakota who hear about it. Because of that, we could start to see a lot of Sioux coming in who are willing to compromise and work with us to help bring in the others. A man like Billy will be of great use when that starts to happen. The horses are a cheap way of keeping him . . . cooperative."

"So, you're buying him off and ignoring how he flat disobeyed orders up in them mountains?"

"There's more to it than that, Bill."

"Not from where I'm standing."

"I figured that would be the case, but again, Bill, I'm sorry that it bothers you, but I don't need you to like it. This is nothing more than a tactical effort that will aid in bringing about a political resolution rather than a continuation of the hostilities, which are so damned costly to both sides—including, Bill, including all the lives that are lost in fights like the one we just had."

The lieutenant was pretty sure of himself and about how this was all going to come together for him. Nothing I was going to say would change his mind, that was clear, but it didn't mean I wouldn't try.

"I know it looks all good from your side of things, 'Tenant, but let me say my piece, and then I'll be done with it."

The officer waited quietly.

"All right, two things," I started. "The first is personal, I'll admit that. I don't like the idea that Billy is going to go on thinking he's all-a-sudden the cock of the walk here. The kid's got a lot of growing up to do yet, and you're setting him up like he's some kinda big Indin. He's gonna cause you more problems than anything once he gets it in his head that he's the linchpin in your plans. I'm afraid you're asking for a whole lotta trouble with that one.

"The second thing—and this is boogered from the start if you're relying on Billy to help you with it—the second thing is, I said before it ain't a smart idea to go messing with the way these Indins decide who's going to be the man in charge. You can't go around just making this man or that man chief and expect all the others to follow him. I seen that happen at different treaties, and it ain't never worked. All you end up with is a bunch of pissed-off Indins, a misunderstanding, and another fight on your hands. And 'Tenant, that ends up being blood on your hands." I wiggled my thumb and first two fingers down from my nose and mouth like they was blood flowing and showed him my hands, mimicking the last sign Old Crow had shown him.

"I appreciate your concern, Bill, I truly do. The strategy is to divide and conquer. It's an age-old and proven technique that, when done right, is very effective. As for Garnett, trust me, I'm aware of his desire to be, what do you call it, a big Indin? I assure you, Bill, that I am well aware that whether one is Indin or white man, pride is every man's ultimate weakness, the consequences of which will be his and his alone to deal with."

"Good words to mind, sir." Clark's eyes flashed briefly as he caught my meaning, but I was done. "I said my piece. How long before we head out?"

Clark looked me over for a bit then moved on himself. "The general wants to meet with all the scouts in an hour to explain the situation and to personally thank them for their service. You'll have the rest of today to prepare for your departure tomorrow morning."

"Well, fine then. Why don't I just head back to let Old Crow and the boys know while you go on and tell Billy and the others. You won't be needing me to help with that, will you?"

Clark gave me another look that lasted long enough to let me know that he could make me come if he wanted. After making his point, he released me. "I'll have them meet you at the quartermaster's in the morning to draw your supplies. Major Furey's already been informed and is making ready for your departure."

I studied the ground, searching for a way to end the spat on some sort of positive note. "That'll do" was all I could come up with.

I could tell the lieutenant was as surprised as I was at this rift in our friendship. I think we were both waiting for the other to say something to smooth it over, but neither of us did. We finally just turned and each went our own way.

# Making Meat

THE SUCCULENT FLAVOR OF FRESH BUFFALO MEAT FLOODED LITTLE Wolf's mouth. His eyes fluttered closed at the taste of the nourishing juices. There were a few pieces of ash from the meat lying on top of the live coals when it was cooked, but the flavor made up for the grit. It felt like he had just come up from the bottom of a deep river and was sucking in his first breath of precious air.

He glanced sideways at Lightning and chuckled. She sat motionless with her eyes closed and her finger nestled between her lips as if holding the flavor of her first bite there. She opened her eyes at his chuckle and gave a small laugh, her eyes welling with tears of joy.

The Cheyenne had crossed over the north ridge of Buffalo Creek and descended into the initial branches of Crow Standing Off Creek. There they heard the thunder of multiple rifle shots echo out of a draw ahead of them. After a period of anxious waiting, Starving Elk appeared on a ridge in front of them, spinning his horse in circles and using wolf sign to tell them that eleven buffalo had been killed. A high-pitched tremolo went up from all the women accompanied by a lusty cheer and singing from the men. The line surged forward with everyone wanting to hurry to the kill site.

When they arrived, many of the women had no butcher knives, so men's hunting knives were used to rend the carcasses. Each wolf-turned-hunter who had made more than one kill stood by his one chosen animal until his family members arrived to butcher it. The other carcasses were left for anyone to claim, though everyone was certain to receive a portion.

A thin line of ash trees hugged the frozen trickle of water in the main creek below them, and the people returned there with their meat to gather wood and build their fires. The women had been collecting whatever dry buffalo dung they could find on the windblown hills as they walked, but it was not enough, and the fires had to be spaced far apart along the creek to ensure that everyone had enough fuel to last the night. Making camp so far away from one another was a bit disconcerting for some. Nonetheless, all along the creek people could be heard singing songs of thanks to *Esevone*, the Sacred Buffalo Hat, who had provided by bringing these buffalo to them. For the moment all was right.

Starving Elk had given Little Wolf and his family some hump meat and tenderloin to thank White Voice for taking care of his parents on the trek. Before they ate, Little Wolf stepped to the fire and cut a small portion from the largest piece. His wives were puzzled. They knew he was making a food offering, but it was not his normal practice to perform such a ceremonial act. They watched as their husband carried the meat in his hand to a spot near the creek then raised it above his head and prayed quietly, turning to each of the four directions. He finished the small ceremony by burying the bite of meat as best he could in the frozen ground. He turned to walk back to the fire.

Day Woman whispered to her mother, "Why did he offer food to the ancestors? He has never done that before."

Lightning knew the child asked only out of curiosity. "He is saying that he is grateful for this gift, but he also offers it for his brother and others who were buried in these hills a long time ago."

"I had another uncle? What happened to him?"

Lightning steered he daughter away from talking about the dead, lest their spirits come back. "*Hsst*, now, we don't talk about those things."

Day Woman's eyes clouded with more questions about this uncle she had never heard about and confusion over why they couldn't talk about him.

Wooden Thigh and a couple others were each given a portion of the cooked meat to take with them. Little Wolf then sent them to watch the back trail in case anyone, friend or enemy, might be following behind them. They were told to stay out until dark.

Everyone had then enjoyed their first bites, placing the meat in their mouths and cutting off small chunks to chew. Little Wolf looked from Lightning's brimming eyes to where White Voice sat quietly enjoying her own meal. He smiled again then spoke out over the top of the fire.

"Hmm, this is good meat," he growled as he chewed. He cut off another bite, chewed it contentedly, and sighed. "We are lucky people to have others who think so well of us that they give us this good food when we need it, *Epeva'e*."

White Voice kept her head down but exchanged small smiles with Two Woman. This was great praise coming from her father.

When he had finished his first portion of meat, Little Wolf struggled to his feet. "Ahh, that meat was so good I am already full. I think I need to take a walk and rest my stomach. Pawnee, let us walk down the creek a ways and see how others are getting along."

Pawnee jumped obediently to his feet, grabbing the piece of meat handed to him by Two Woman. He started toward Little Wolf's side but felt his father's gaze bearing down upon him. When their eyes met, Little Wolf glanced down at Inside Woman, who was just finishing her first piece of buffalo. A slight tip of his head told Pawnee what was expected of him. Leaning down he placed the meat in his pregnant sister's hand, despite her protests, then trotted off to catch up with Little Wolf, who had already turned and was limping away.

The pair headed down the creek, staying out on the sagebrush flat to keep a polite distance from other people's fires. They moved past the first half-dozen fires despite receiving many offers to come and eat. Pawnee noticed that those waving at them to come over had either elderly or many children sitting among them.

His father politely declined each invitation, saying, "*Naešena'so'enohe*. Thank you, I am full already." He signed the words whenever they were too far away for him to speak without raising his voice to be heard. He would straighten the fingers of his right hand and push it away from his mouth, then with the same hand, he acted as if he were putting food in his mouth, and finally, he dropped it to his stomach and raised his horizontal index finger and vertical thumb to his throat.

They soon came to where the creek made a slow bend to the left around the base of a fairly high hill on the west side. Wolf Tooth, one of those who had helped him at the top of the ravine, was camped here. He was a young man who had married a pair of sisters. He, his wives, their parents, and one child were all that were at his fire. He was also one of the lucky wolves who had taken part in the kill, and he had plenty of meat to share. This time Little Wolf nodded at the invitation and stepped toward the fire.

"My friend, you should come help me eat some of this meat," the young man offered. "I would also ask you to smoke with me, but I lost my pipe in the mountains."

"You are kind, my friend. I lost many things up there myself, but it is good that we have generous people like you with us who share what they have. *Nea'ešе.*"

Little Wolf and Pawnee took the places that Wolf Tooth offered beside him. His wives were already busy scraping the hide of the buffalo their husband had killed. One stopped to cut each visitor a sizeable chunk off of the roasted meat.

"*Ho, nea'ešе!*" father and son repeated in turn as they were each handed their generous portions.

Wolf Tooth's mother-in-law held her grandchild and sat next to her husband across the fire from the visitors. Both of them wore decent robes, as did their daughters, and the child was well wrapped. Wolf Tooth, however, sat next to the fire in only a light buckskin shirt and leggings.

"Where are you going this evening?" the young man asked the chief.

Little Wolf had been watching the man's wives, who had gone back to working diligently on the hide, clearly trying to get it cleaned before nightfall. He turned back to his host. "To see my friend Morning Star. They have lost many at their fire. I like to make sure that they are looked after."

"Mmm, there are many people missing at our fires now. It is good that you look out for them. I think that it will not be long before we find the Lakota, though, and things will be better for all of us."

"I hope so," the chief replied. "We are more pitiful now than when we went to them last spring after the attack on the Powder River. At least some were able to save a few belongings from their lodges then."

Wolf Tooth nodded in agreement.

When they had finished their meal, Little Wolf turned to his host. "If the Lakota are as generous as you, we will all be very well taken care of. We are grateful to you and your family for letting us share your fire and your food, but I need to go now to check on my friend and his family." Little Wolf nodded to the couple across the fire, then stood and turned to Wolf Tooth, who had also risen to his feet.

"It is good that you stopped by to talk with us," Wolf Tooth said as he nodded to one of his wives. She then hurried and cut off another piece of meat for the departing visitors.

Pawnee accepted his, but Little Wolf smiled and, extending his finger and thumb, gave the sign for full.

As they started to walk away, Little Wolf turned back toward Wolf Tooth. "It looks like you will be getting a good robe soon."

Wolf Tooth smiled and placed his hand, palm down, in front of his heart and slid it forward, indicating that it would indeed be a good one.

Pawnee feasted on the roasted meat as he and his father started on their way to Morning Star's fire. He was oblivious to the additional offers of dinner as they proceeded or to the fact that his father's right hand completed the same motions again and again as they walked.

When they reached Morning Star's fire, Little Wolf found his friend in better spirits. It helped that Bull Hump, his eldest son, sat at the fire with him. Bull Hump was another of the wolves who had killed a buffalo and had plenty of meat to share with his family.

Their visit went well, and again Little Wolf and Pawnee had plenty to eat. The conversation was animated and lively, and Bull Hump even got his father to chuckle once with his teasing.

As they prepared to return to their own fire, Little Wolf mentioned in a casual way, "In a day or so, we will be coming to Tongue River where it begins to turn through the steep canyon walls. The Lakota might have wolves out watching to see who travels through there. I think that it won't be long now before we meet up with them. We should be ready."

Morning Star chewed thoughtfully then announced, "We will be ready together, friend. I think I will ride at the front with you tomorrow."

Little Wolf's heart lifted, but he responded as if he had been told only that the weather would be good the next day. "*Epeva'e*, I will look for you then," he replied, not wanting to embarrass his friend with a big reaction.

On their return, father and son again walked past Wolf Tooth's fire. They kept a respectful distance so as not to intrude upon them a second time, and this time the chief kept his eyes politely to the ground in front of him as they moved through the sagebrush. Being less tactful and young, Pawnee stole a quick glance toward the fire and noticed one of the man's wives adjusting the newly fleshed robe up onto his shoulders.

"*Shaa!*" he marveled out loud. "I have never seen a robe go from a buffalo's back to a man's back that fast in my life."

Little Wolf gave a quick look to see what his son was referring to, then grinned and scolded the youngster.

"*Oxėse tsėhetoo'ȯhtse. Neve'nėheševe!* Look away. Do not be doing that!"

The pair continued on their way to their own fire, where they found that the women and girls had been busy preparing grass and branch mats for beds. They had also piled enough wood and sagebrush nearby to keep the fire going all night. Wooden Thigh returned shortly after dark, and the family began to settle in for the night.

They slept near the fire in pairs to share body heat. White Voice had just knelt to take her usual place behind Two Woman when Inside Woman stepped over and spoke quietly to her. The younger girl nodded then stood and moved to the mat where Day Woman lay expecting Inside Woman to join her. Inside Woman instead took White Voice's place behind Two Woman, nestling her swollen belly against the small of her second mother's back. Two Woman looked back, surprised at first, then turned away and lay still. The young widow wrapped her arms around the older woman and spoke softly to her.

"Mother, let me sleep with you tonight. I need your help to keep this baby warm."

He couldn't hear her, but Little Wolf could see Two Woman's shoulders heave as she began to sob.

The following morning, just before sunrise, Little Wolf led the buckskin mare across the frozen stream then mounted and rode up the hill on the west side of the creek. It was the first time since the day before the attack that he felt good enough to resume his routine of early-morning prayer. He had considered starting again the previous morning, but the strong winds had discouraged him.

The combined inspiration of the buffalo kill, Morning Star's raised spirits, and Inside Woman's kindness gave him enough gratitude to push past his reluctance to climb the chilly hillside. Wooden Thigh gladly agreed to loan him the use of his pipe along with a pinch of greased agency tobacco and flint.

The eastern horizon began to lighten by the time he was half way up the hill. The chief dismounted and found a comfortable place to stand. He faced east, keeping his eyes lowered and anticipating the view that he would see before him when he looked up.

*Ešė'he's* approaching light was blocked by the thick blanket of clouds overhead, and a dark sea of shadow remained between Little Wolf and the horizon. Inside this shadow loomed light-blue bodies of snow broken into ghostly images created by the hills, trees, and stones casting their own darker shadows.

Missing from this mysterious scene were the glowing amber cones of Cheyenne lodges that should have been just below him. Instead, in their place, were beds of glowering coals, looking like festering red scabs scattered among the dark-blue, vein-like clusters of trees rooted beside the winding creek. Most still had an undisturbed layer of ash covering them as the exhausted people lying nearby still slept despite the coming dawn.

Little Wolf released a heavy sigh as he pondered what this day would hold for them. As Sweet Medicine Chief, they belonged to him; they were his responsibility to care for and protect—a daunting task on most days, a heartbreaking impossibility of late.

But they were in more familiar country now. It was here where Little Wolf began to feel his first real sense of reassurance. As vulnerable as they were, the people could move quickly here and easily scatter out into the uncountable creeks and ridges surrounding them to avoid conflict.

As if to remind him, the snowy crests of the ridges above the creeks south of camp brightened in the growing light, resembling gnarled, skeletal fingers that extended into the broad shadow across the earth and pointing out each pathway for a swift escape.

Comforted, Little Wolf whispered, "*Nea'eše*," and began to prepare the pipe, singing a song of gratitude as he did. With his light still diffused behind the veil of clouds, *Eše'he* finally appeared over the horizon, just as the chief lit the pipe and offered it to the four directions, the sky, and the earth. He sang softly between puffs until the tobacco was spent. As he leaned down to tap the ashes onto a stone, he heard a muffled cry coming from the darkness below him.

"*Nehne'ėstosemėstse!* Pull me out!"

The chief paused to make sure that the voice had come from the bottom of the hill and not inside it. A few more angry grunts and growls assured him that it had. He remounted and started toward the cries, allowing the mare to carefully pick her way down the slick hillside as he continued to listen.

Other panicked voices soon joined the first, and Little Wolf realized the commotion came from the direction of Wolf Tooth's fire. When he reached the bottom of the hill, he rode to the edge of the trees and peered between them to see what was taking place at the camp across the creek.

In the dim light, it appeared that Wolf Tooth's wives and father-in-law were trying to stand a large log on its end. Time and again though, the log proved too heavy, and they dropped it to the ground, only to quickly try to raise it again.

*Where is Wolf Tooth?* the chief wondered, *and why don't they just roll that log to the fire?*

He watched them struggle for a while before he decided to ride over and help. As he drew near, it occurred to him that he had not seen a log that large anywhere near their camp the night before.

The desperate family again had the log about halfway up when Little Wolf coughed loudly to let them know he was approaching their fire. Everyone turned in surprise to see who was coming, and the log fell again. Little Wolf was close enough now that when it hit the ground, he heard the log give a loud grunt then growl in anger. Looking closer, he saw the log had large tufts of hair showing at both ends. Buffalo hair.

Little Wolf slid off his horse and, trying not to laugh, grabbed a handful of hair on one of the ends with his good arm. With the help of the others, he heaved the hide-encased Wolf Tooth to his feet.

"This is frozen around you," the chief said.

He was amazed at how the robe had stiffened during the cold night. Wolf Tooth had pinned the robe closed around him with two small branches and had lain down to sleep. During the night the hide froze solid, trapping him inside and gripping the man as firmly and tightly as wet rawhide held an arrowhead in the shaft when it dried. One side of the robe had a flat edge where it had lain against the ground. The other had conformed to the contours of the man's body, locking his left arm and leg in the positions they had been in while he slept.

The young man's face was visible through the opening at the top of the robe. It contorted as he strained to push his left leg down so he could stand on two feet instead of one. His foot reached the ground after much effort, and he finally stood on his own. The anger and panic in his eyes lessened now and were quickly replaced by a look of amusement.

"*Shaa!*" He laughed at himself and tried to shake his head in the tight confines, which made him wobble precariously. Little Wolf reached out to steady him, and as their eyes met, they both laughed so hard tears came, and Little Wolf's chest wound began to hurt.

With one hand on Wolf Tooth and the other across his chest, Little Wolf studied the robe, trying to figure out how to free his friend. He used a stone to knock the pins from their positions and tried to pry the robe open without success. He wedged one of the pins under the fringe of the robe and tried to leverage it open, but he only managed to break the pin and knock the bound man down again.

Wolf Tooth's wives rolled him over on his side as he groaned in pain and frustration. The pain of falling had taken some of the humor from the situation. Little Wolf knelt down in front of him.

"Friend, the robe is holding you in there too strong. All I can think of is to try to cut you out."

"Ahhh! No!" Wolf Tooth growled. "This is a good robe."

"It is, but we must leave soon, and you cannot travel with it holding you the way it is. We need to take it off of you."

Wolf Tooth lay silent for a moment, staring at the ground and trying to think of another solution that didn't involve hacking his new robe to pieces. "My legs," he said finally. "Just free my legs. I can walk then, and later, I might find a way to open it enough to take it off."

Little Wolf examined how the robe sheathed the man's body. "That can be done. It would be hard to do any cutting up higher anyway. We could end up gutting you like the last owner of this robe if we tried."

The young man's wives went to work, carefully wedging their knives into and against the hide as Little Wolf and their parents watched. After a few close calls that had Wolf Tooth barking at the women to use more caution, Little Wolf decided that the situation had been resolved and that his help was no longer needed. He stepped quietly to his horse and led the animal back toward his own fire.

# Finding Friends

"THEY SAY THEY ARE CHEYENNE." WILD HOG READ THE BROAD gestures called wolf sign that had been flashed by one of the riders descending a hill downstream.

Little Wolf and the other Cheyenne leaders nodded to each other as signals were given to those behind them, letting them know that it was safe to come out from the trees that lined the frozen Tongue River.

They had first noticed the small party of *xamaevo'ėstaneo'o*, who had been watching them from a ridge to the north, just beyond gunshot range. The sighting sent many among them racing for the safety of the trees, fearing another attack. It was only when the smaller group drew closer that one of them held out his left arm and motioned as if he were cutting it three times with his right arm, indicating their tribal affiliation.

It would not have mattered whether the group had been more Wolf People out scouting for the soldiers. If it meant finding food and shelter for the many weak and wounded among them, and as long as the newcomers were not shooting, the Cheyenne would have allowed anyone to draw near without giving them a fight.

Little Wolf recognized two of the men, Black Hawk and Yellow Weasel, as they approached. These men had left the larger group before it entered the mountains about a moon earlier. They had left to go in search of a small Crow village to steal horses. Both of their faces went slack as they rode closer. Their eyes flicked back and forth, surveying the line of impoverished people in front of them until they realized their gawking had become impolite.

Each man in the small band lowered his gaze as they arrived in front of the chiefs and their destitute entourage. Little Wolf was glad to see that Morning Star, Old Bear, and the others made no move to dismount. This would have meant they intended to begin a formal conference by preparing a talking area, similar to that which they had prepared for the wolves who reported on the soldiers before the attack.

Desperation demanded they press forward with their search for the Lakota. The chiefs were eager to keep moving, and those in the war party were anxious to find their families, so the discussion took place on horseback and progressed quickly.

Black Hawk and Yellow Weasel described an uneventful trip to the west where they had revisited the scene of the fight on the Little Sheep River. They had picked through the bones and debris still lying about, looking mostly for bullets, with little success. They then sat in stunned silence as Wild Hog described to them the soldiers' early-morning assault on the village and the desperate dash into and through the mountains.

A chill wind blustered up the river valley. It pushed Morning Star's unbraided hair off his shoulders and prompted him to ask the one question on everyone's minds.

"Have you heard where our Lakota friends might be camped? We have many among us who need robes and a seat by a lodge fire."

Black Hawk nodded. "We met a party of Oglala hunters who told us they were camping at Beaver Creek, but game has been scarce this winter. They may not have stayed there long."

"We might at least pick up their trail there." Wild Hog's eyes brightened with this new hope. He glanced back and forth at the other leaders, unable to contain his excitement.

"It is good that you are all back with us again." Little Wolf spoke up as he rode over alongside Morning Star. "Your people need every brave man they have left. Most of you have family with us; you should go now and be with them. *Nea'eše*."

The men rode on through the crowd that had gathered around them. A couple of them slid off their horses right away and embraced their relatives, while the others continued up the valley looking for theirs. The youngest among them, Wooden Leg, moved slowly through the crowd. Little Wolf knew the young man's parents were both alive, and they would be glad to see their son—and would appreciate the extra robe that was tied to his saddle.

Like the others in his group, Wooden Leg's eyes barely contained his tears upon seeing the devastation wrought upon his friends and relatives. A look of bewilderment came over him, however, and he stopped and stared off to his left. Little Wolf followed the young man's gaze to the now-familiar form of Wolf Tooth waddling along in his still-frozen buffalo robe. It had been trimmed back more, allowing him to walk safely, but his arm still jutted out at an awkward angle. His wives walked nearby just in case.

"*Hoovehe!* My friend! It is good to have you back with us again." Wolf Tooth wiggled his extended arm at Wooden Leg.

Wooden Leg paused as if he needed time to absorb the man's hearty greeting. His expression showed his conflicted emotions. He finally responded with a short nod—and a hesitant smile.

"*Haaahe!* Nice robe."

Wolf Tooth smiled and nodded as much as the stiff hide would allow him to then resumed his measured walk.

Little Wolf turned back to Morning Star, who had also watched the odd exchange, and gave a suggestion. "I think that when we find a warm lodge for everyone else, he should still be kept outside, just to keep that robe on him a while longer."

Morning Star chuckled as he turned his horse and urged it forward.

Otter Creek soon lay just beyond the range of hills to the east. It joined with Tongue River about a half day's ride downstream. The chiefs decided that it would be quicker to cross over the hills that separated the two waterways now and head north for Beaver Creek. They could make it there in about two days if the weather held.

Two days later the sweet scent of lodge smoke slipped over a low ridge ahead, telling them they were close. They crossed over the wooded crest from the southeast, and Lakota lodges could be seen between the trees below them.

The Lakota camp was almost four times the size that the Cheyenne's had been before the attack. Many bands and family groups the Lakota called *Thiyóšpaye* had decided to winter together for their mutual protection after the turbulent summer.

The exhausted Cheyenne emerged from the timber and descended the ridge. Little Wolf scanned the wide crescent of lodges sprawled across the valley floor in front of him and quickly picked out the several shorter and wider Cheyenne lodges mixed in among them.

Morning Star rode beside the Sweet Medicine Chief. He leaned toward him and spoke quietly so only his friend would hear. "This will not be an easy time for you, but it is good that we have found them."

Little Wolf agreed. He was relieved the Lakota had been found, but what his friend said was true—his problems with both Crazy Horse and the Cheyenne medicine man, Ice, would make his time at this camp a difficult one.

The camp dogs greeted them first, as usual, running toward them in noisy, barking packs. Typically, they would scatter when they reached the warriors, who would race forward, circle around the camp perimeter, and fire their guns into the air in the traditional manner of greeting a friendly camp. The dogs would circle around the charge only to be met by the arriving party's dogs, and loud, snarling fights would break out.

But these visitors did not charge the camp, and there were no dogs left among them for the Lakota dogs to fight with. The four-legged welcoming committee came to a confused standstill and watched with puzzled looks as the weary and wounded people trudged past them.

The Cheyenne moved without ceremony to an open flat near the village and began setting up their meager lodges. At first, the Lakota were unsure who these poor strangers were and whether they posed any danger. They milled about nervously until they recognized the Cheyenne, then people streamed out of camp carrying food and clothing for their devastated friends.

A steady wail rose from the Lakota as they began to realize the level of loss suffered by their friends. This was the second time since last spring the Cheyenne had come to them after a great loss. This time was by far the worst. Tears came to all but the most stolid eyes.

It was as if an exploding ball from a white man's wagon gun had landed in their midst, spreading grief to all.

Little Wolf waited on a nearby rise with Morning Star and a few of the other headmen while their families were welcomed by their concerned friends. As the initial rush of aid flowed into the Cheyenne camp, several mounted men appeared at the edge of the Lakota camp and rode toward the Cheyenne leaders.

Crazy Horse did not stand out from those who rode alongside him. He was an average-sized man who did not often wear ceremonial regalia. Had Little Wolf not been as familiar as he was with the Lakota leader, he might not have been able to single him out from the group.

He Dog and Touch the Clouds, Crazy Horse's two closest friends and confidants, rode to his right, while Black Moccasin, the fourth and final Old Man Chief of the Cheyenne, and Two Moons, a well-respected Kit Fox man, were on his left. Two Moons was an uncle to Young Two Moons and had given the younger man his own name. Behind everyone, but making his way hurriedly toward the front, was Ice, Black Moccasin's adopted son and noted Cheyenne medicine man.

Keeping his eyes trained on the approaching men, Little Wolf leaned toward Morning Star. "I should stay out of any talk here. It would not be good for me to speak what is in my heart today."

Morning Star nodded and intoned a simple "Mmmm," acknowledging his friend's concern. After a moment he tipped his head toward their families, most of whom were now being led back to Lakota lodges, where warm fires and food awaited them.

"Try to look at the others over there," Morning Star said. "Let them be in your heart today."

Little Wolf quickly found the pregnant form of Inside Woman being tended to by several women from the Lakota camp. She and the rest of his family were being ushered toward the protective circle of the lodges. Day Woman was now wrapped in a wool blanket instead of the hastily halved buffalo robe.

After a quick sigh of relief, the Cheyenne leader turned back to the approaching party of men, and the stern and steady gaze of Crazy Horse.

# A Hunger for Home

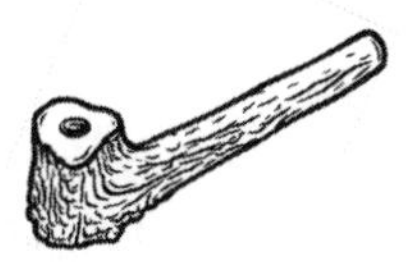

WE RODE OUT OF CAMP THE NEXT MORNING IN A TIGHT COLUMN of fours, though we all knew the military order would come undone as soon as we were out of sight of military eyes. Once beyond the first ridge, the scouts would string out, single file, to finish the trip to Camp Robinson and the Red Cloud Agency, Indin style.

I lifted my collar against the sharp wind pushing against our backs. I should have felt better, considering I was headed for home, but I didn't. I was in the front row with Old Crow on my right and Sharp Nose, the head man for the Arapaho, and Three Bears, the Lakota leader, to my left. Billy rode his sorrel in the second row behind Three Bears. I felt his eyes on me every now and again as we started away from camp.

Some of the Lakota at the rear of the procession were singing celebratory songs as we departed. Along with their scout pay, they had each received a few horses taken from the Cheyenne camp as compensation for their service. Several had forged friendships with many of the soldiers and some of the Pawnee scouts. For them, the trip had been a great success and very profitable.

I could tell that Billy wanted to fall back and sing along with the others, but he couldn't, at least for now. We hadn't talked since just before the battle, which was fine with me, but I figured he likely heard talk around camp that I was upset with him and he'd been avoiding me.

I knew this big slope country well. We rode southeast, up a long rise toward Box Elder Creek. That drainage would take us along the old Indian trail that skirted the western edge of the Black Hills. We would cross the Cheyenne River near the southern end of the hills and continue south up Hat Creek, eventually crossing over the

Hat Creek ridge, a rugged, pine-covered divide standing just to the north of the agency. The trip would take five or six days if all went well—three to ride the length of the hills, and two to travel up Hat Creek, cross over the ridge, then head down Soldier Creek to where Camp Robinson and the Red Cloud Agency waited alongside the White River.

The Black Hills were the spiritual center of the world for both the Cheyenne and Lakota. These days, it seemed that they had become the center of all the trouble in the world for them. Gold had been discovered there a couple years back, and since then a lot of folks, Indian and white man alike, had been killed over it.

A dark line of tree-covered ridges peeked over the horizon at the end of the rolling, tan prairie to the east. A hard day's ride northeast from our location would take us to the foot of a huge stone tower that rose several hundred feet straight into the sky. The Cheyenne called this place Bear's Lodge and considered it to be sacred. I'd been to many a sun dance at its base. The soldiers and miners who had invaded the area over the last couple of years had taken to calling the place the Devil's Tower.

A couple days' ride due east was the holiest of Cheyenne sites, *Novavose*, or Bear Butte as the white man called it. Cheyenne legend says that it was there, in a secluded cave, where the Sacred Ones presented Sweet Medicine with the four Sacred Arrows, along with instructions for how the Cheyenne should organize their tribe and their lives. He carried this all out with him and shared it with his people, who have tried to follow what he told them ever since.

The promise of gold had once again called the greediest and most ruthless of my race from every rathole shanty and ivory tower in the east. They streamed across the land looking to claim and rename every mountain, stream, and animal that they came across just so they could leave some kind of mark on the place. The US government was no better. Just three months earlier, another so-called treaty commission came out from Washington and told the Indians they could either sell all that land to the government or starve to death.

"The Great Father does not wish to throw a blanket over your eyes and ask you to do anything without first looking at it." Black-coat Henry Whipple used his best come-to-Jesus voice when he addressed the bad-tempered crowd of Indians that day.

The preacher spoke under a large canopy that had been raised a few miles downstream from the agency, on the north side of the White River. A few hundred Lakota sat in the shade of the surrounding ash trees that had just started to show their first yellow splotches of fall.

Most of these men had made a choice to stay at the agency and not to join the northern bands that summer. Others had snuck back after the big fight on the Little Bighorn, hoping to avoid punishment. The agency leaders, Red Cloud and Spotted Tail, sat in the inner circle under the canvas.

I sat with Billy Garnett and few other Lakota interpreters that day translating the Episcopalian bishop's words and those of the other five commissioners who had come to explain the terms of the new so-called treaty the government had put together. Directly in front of me were the few Northern Cheyenne headmen who remained at the agency: Living Bear, Broken Dish, Turkey Legs, Spotted Elk, Standing Elk, and Black Bear. In the government's eyes—and conveniently serving their purpose, with nearly all the rest of the tribe off to the north—this small handful represented the entire Cheyenne Council of Forty-Four.

George Manypenny, a past director of the Bureau of Indian Affairs, was the commission leader. After Bishop Whipple's opening remarks, Mannypenny read the treaty out loud to the crowd. Like any government document, it was long-winded and far too complicated. I struggled to keep up with the words that tumbled from the man's mouth.

"The western boundaries shall commence at the intersection of the one hundred and third meridian of longitude with the northern border of the State of Nebraska; thence north along said meridian to its intersection with the South Fork of the Cheyenne River; thence down said stream to its junction with the North Fork; thence up the North Fork of said Cheyenne River to the said one hundred and third meridian along said meridian to the South Branch of Cannon Ball River . . ."

"Bill, what's a meridian?" Billy had leaned over, his eyes clouded with confusion.

I had to reach way back to my time with Captain Stansbury's survey crew. "It's a line on a map that goes north and south. Just tell 'em it's a white man's medicine line, like the Canadian border."

We all gave it our best to keep up through the rest of the reading, but most of it came so fast I doubt that most caught more than the gist of it.

When Manypenny was finished, the Indians tried to absorb what they had just been told. Puzzled looks were traded, and a buzz of questions started among the leaders in the inner ring.

Billy translated their concern. "They want to know what that all means."

A third commissioner, Augustine Gaylord, a recent assistant attorney general for the government, stood up. "I'll tell you what that means," The man with the heavy beard shouted above the grumbling crowd. "We are here to offer you the most effective solution to the problems that have been taking place. There has been much killing, much blood on the ground, because we cannot get along. The Great Father in Washington has asked me to give you his words. He said that if you sign this paper, you will all keep your guns and horses, but you must stop attacking the miners in the hills north of us. There is much good land far south from here, which has been set aside for you. The Great Father would like you to send a few men down to look at it and consider going there to live. If you decide not to go there, you must still leave these lands and move to the east, closer to the Missouri River, where it is easier for him to send you gifts so your people can be happy."

Another wave of grumbling started when the change of reservations was mentioned.

"Remember this! Remember this!" The commissioner shouted down the resistance. "Everything that the Great Father gives your families today—food, blankets, medicine—is all from his good heart. Your first agreement with him is finished, and he does not have to keep giving it to you in this way. His heart will not be good if you do not sign his paper. He only wants to make it so that we can all be happy without any more fighting."

The mere mention of losing their annuities pissed the Indians off pretty good. They figured that was their reward for staying at the agency and not going to war against the whites. Now it was being used to force their hand to sign another paper that gave away even more land and required them to move yet again.

It was at that point that I understood why there was recent build-up of troops at Camp Robinson. Colonel Mackenzie and six companies of the 4th Cavalry had arrived there just a short time before the commission showed up. They knew the Indians would be pissed.

One Lakota man rose from the crowd and shouted at Gaylord, "Your words are like a man hitting me in the head with a stick. What you have spoken has put great fear upon us. Whatever we do, wherever we go, we are expected to say, 'Yes! Yes! Yes!' And when we don't agree at once to what you ask of us in Council, you always say, You won't get anything to eat! You won't get anything to eat!"

Dead silence followed. Mannypenny, ignoring the complaint, nodded to his assistants and told us interpreters, "Tell them to line up and sign."

The grumbling continued then, but one by one, and then in small groups, they came forward. Most Lakota did little more than give their names and lightly touch the pen that was held out to them. One man pulled his blanket over his eyes, so he wouldn't have to watch himself do it, and held out his finger. The clerk touched it with the pen.

The Cheyenne didn't put on quite the same show and actually tried to curry favor from the commissioners instead. Living Bear came up smiling and reminded Mannypenny that they had met during our trip to Washington back in seventy-three. I noticed, though, that Standing Elk got up and quietly left when the call to come up and sign was given. *Well, good for him*, I thought. It weren't long after that when he lit out to join the northern camps.

That was it, though. The Hills now belonged to the white man, and I truly doubt that most of the Indians even realized it.

We made camp that night several miles west of a peak the Lakota called *Inyan Kara*, or Rock Gatherer. It's more sacred to the Lakota than it is to the Cheyenne, but the boys cheered and sang songs along with the larger group of scouts as the departing sun honored the high granite summit by bathing it in a bright amber glow. Old Crow and the others circulated around the Lakota fires, but I crawled into my bedroll early.

We figured we'd meet the replacement scouts at any time along this route. They were supposed to number about five hundred, so I didn't expect to have any problem locating them, and I was right. They showed up late the following morning, trailing out of a creek several miles to the east. The line stretched well over a mile out onto the prairie before the last rider came into view. As they came closer, I recognized the wiry figure of Charlie Tackett, a friend from the agency, and White Thunder, a Lakota headman, riding at the front of the new recruits.

Three Bears greeted White Thunder as the two men drew near each other. "*Hau tȟaŋhaŋsi , Lila tanyan wacin yanke.* Hello, cousin, it is very good to see you."

White Thunder's reply surprised everyone. "*Hau tȟaŋhaŋsi, Unsimala.* Hello, cousin, I have a bad problem and I need your help."

I knew enough Lakota to understand the man's plea and shot Tackett a questioning look.

"We ran out of grub yesterday morning," the middle-aged man explained. "We're all pretty damned hungry about now. Sure was glad to see you coming down the crick."

By the time the last of their party arrived, we had made a good start on getting them all fed from our own limited supply. As soon as the last meal was handed over, our company, now four times its original size, immediately struck south. We had no time to waste. With the extra mouths to feed, we now faced three or four days of trail with barely enough food for everyone to have a couple small meals.

We put a long day in the saddle then pitched camp on the east side of a pine-covered ridge, out of the wind. After nibbling on some hardtack, several of us gathered around a large fire to discuss our plans. Three Bears had just suggested that the Hat Creek stage and telegraph station might have some extra stores available, and it was on our way.

"We will all survive a few days without food if it comes to that," he explained, "but the clouds I saw in the sky today tell me that there is a big cold time coming. Without food, it is going to be dangerous. We will need to be very careful these next few days."

The man's warning was well taken. When he finished, Tackett, who was sitting next to me, gave me a nudge. I tracked his gaze to see Billy approaching the fire with a couple other young men: Louis Shangreau, and Louis Richard, the scouts Crook had sent to collect these fresh recruits while we were still out on the Powder. They were both French-Lakota half-breeds in their late twenties. Their families were rough-living clans who had lived around the Fort Laramie area for many years. I had plenty of dealings with their elders back in the day but didn't know these boys too well, other than that they were part of the group who had been such a bad influence on Billy when he was growing up. It was disappointing to see the boy practically pounce on them when they arrived.

Charlie leaned over closer as they approached. "We were moving slower than we shoulda been, and that's likely why we run outta grub. Truth be told, there's some who weren't real happy about leaving warm robes and agency fires to head out to look for another fight in all this cold."

I called to the boys as they found spots by the fire. "Shangreau, Richard, General Crook sent orders for the two of you to head out first chance you got to meet up with him and the others."

The two men looked dumbfounded.

"Aw, bullshit. Quit funning us!" Shangreau piped back.

I smiled and turned to Three Bears and signed for him to tell them what Crook had told us about these two before we left. Three Bears repeated the general's orders in Lakota to the stone-faced young men.

I continued where Three Bears left off. "They're making their way back down the Belle Fourche, and if you leave in the morning, you'll most likely find them around the Pumpkin Buttes. Good news is, we'll make sure you have plenty of grub to make it there."

"Dammit to hell," Richard grumped.

A moment passed, then Billy spoke to his friend. "I'll go with you."

Now, I'd rather have seen him head off with those boys, but I knew there'd be trouble if he did, so I had to put a stop to the idea. "No, Billy, you're staying on with us."

The boy stiffened up like I had poked him with a hot brand.

"Your orders are to return to the agency with us. These boys are heading out by themselves tomorrow."

Billy eyed me for a bit until a smirk curled his lip, and he turned back to his friends. I could tell he was figuring to go anyway, so I thought I'd help him think his plan through a little better.

"What do you think Crook and Mackenzie are gonna do when they see you coming over the hill after telling you to go home? You got away with not listening up in them mountains, boy, but try it again, and they'll beat you back home like a heart-broke dog."

The smirk fell from Billy's face as he realized what I said was true. There was a lot more I wanted to say, but I had already embarrassed him in front of the others. A chilly silence settled over the fire, until Tackett stood up and forced a yawn. He placed his left hand palm up in front of his heart. He followed with his right hand, palm up in front of his left, then extended it in a small outward arc. "I'm hitting the bedroll," he said.

A blanket of frigid air descended over us during the night, just as Three Bears had predicted. The silver plate in my head throbbed like I had been kicked by a mule. I rolled and twisted for a while, trying to find any small corner of warmth that might remain in my robes, but eventually, I abandoned hope and grabbed a stick to stir the fire. The flames rekindled, and Old Crow sat up, clutching his robe close around him. He growled then puffed out his words into the clear sky above us.

"*Oh! Eve'ōhketoneto*. Oh, it's bitter cold."

I left him to roust the others while I went to make sure Shangreau and Richard were ready to leave—by themselves.

When I got to their fire, Billy was busy packing his gear. Shangreau and Richard were already gone.

"So, they left already?"

"Looks that way, don't it?" The boy continued tying down his gear without so much as a glance my way. I figured it was about time that he was brought to book.

"Don't get pissy with me, son, not after the shit you been pulling."

"I ain't done nothing different than anybody else here, Bill."

"That's bullshit, Billy, and you know it."

"What you got stuck in your craw, Bill? Just spit it out."

I had no call to hesitate and gave him what for. "You pulled down on that fella and bellered for everbody else to start shooting. You opened the whole goddamned ball up there, Billy."

"Hell, Bill, Scraper was all bent on getting in there, and Bat was already claiming horses along the way. I just went along with 'em is all."

"Other people getting the jump on you ain't no excuse. There's a lot of good people dead now, all on account a you getting worked up about a man beating you to a horse."

Billy finally turned to face me. "So, you're saying all those people are dead 'cause of me?"

I waited to see if the boy's conscience would find the answer to that question, but he decided to test mine instead.

"And what was your part, Bill?"

I tried not to react, but I had been asking myself that damned question for the entire last month. I paused, and Billy took advantage of my silence, his breath coming at me in small white puffs.

"You rode in there just the same as everyone else, Bill. You did what you had to do, and we all did what we had to do. You got no call judging anyone for how things turned out."

Billy climbed onto the small sorrel mare and informed me as he turned her toward the darkness, "I ain't leaving with them boys, Bill, but I sure as hell ain't leaving with you either. I'll see you back at the agency."

I couldn't move. It wasn't the cold but his words that froze me where I stood. None of us had any excuse for what happened in those mountains.

# An Angry Alliance

A THICK CLOUD OF SMOKE ROLLED THROUGH THE VENT HOLE OF the noisy Lakota Council Lodge and disappeared into the night sky. Standing Elk had been speaking to the gathering for some time now. His voice droned on above the murmurs and muted discussions taking place among the large circle of men sitting three rows deep around the fire. The Cheyenne Council chief was elaborating on his reasons why the Cheyenne and Lakota should stay together.

The arrival of the battered and impoverished Cheyenne had disturbed the Lakota. Once the immediate needs of the wounded were addressed, a Council was called to consider a course of action. Many in the lodge had already spoken on the matter, with opinions ranging from a full assault on each of the soldier forts to flat-out surrender. The majority favored surrender, but the opposition to it was fierce.

Despite the abject poverty of the other Cheyenne, Standing Elk was clad in his finest beaded buckskin. He had somehow managed to keep what was important to him despite the attack. As usual, the man's words came from a safe middle ground, where he could appear to be on everyone's side. It was just his way. He rarely suggested anything that would place him in a position where he would meet strong opposition, unless he knew he had even stronger backing.

Little Wolf sat next to Morning Star in the front row. Bored with Standing Elk's monologue, he had been scanning the crowd to see who all was in camp. When he finished, he busied himself with an inspection of his left forearm where shrapnel from Red Pipe's gun had sliced into him. The jagged line of dried scabs had just begun to peel off, revealing a fresh pink scar. The chief traced his finger along the itchy gash. The wound under his left hip ached, so he shifted his weight. Settling on his right hip, he returned his gaze to Standing Elk.

"*Hoovehasėstse*, my friends." The experienced Council chief raised his arm and his voice, trying to win back the attention he knew he had lost. "Friends, let us decide together what we should do today. It is not good for us to argue on this matter like we have been. It is better that we should listen to each other and make a decision that we can all agree on." Standing Elk signed his words for those Lakota who didn't understand the Cheyenne tongue. "Each side must listen to the other if there is to be any hope for us. Let us talk without fighting and find a path that we can all walk together."

A Lakota stood up on the far side of the circle and interrupted the long-winded Cheyenne. "This man speaks the truth. My ears hear his words, and what he has said is wise and comes from a good heart."

Little Wolf smiled. He knew the surprised look on the Standing Elk's face came as much from being told he was right as it did from being politely interrupted.

The Lakota, a prominent leader called Carries the Drum, kept talking, which gave Standing Elk the unspoken message that his time was finished. Both men knew that it would be improper for him to interrupt a man who lavished such praise on him.

Carries the Drum was a large man with a round, friendly face. He was liked by everyone, whether they were Indian or white, and Little Wolf had long believed that he could play a significant role in making peace between the two cultures.

"My Cheyenne friend has spoken the truth about what must be done here." The Lakota took a step forward into the circle. "We should try to get along with each other and decide what we must do about these white soldiers who are now always looking for a fight, these Amare-cans." He practiced the word the white men used for themselves. "I say, let us go to them to see if they wish to stop this fighting and talk peace. We went hard on them this summer at Greasy Grass, and now, " he gestured toward the Cheyenne side of the circle, "now our friends have lost all their homes and many loved ones. I say that each side has seen enough of their own blood spilled on the ground."

Heads nodded throughout the lodge; some were tentative while others bobbed more vigorously. Many in the crowd agreed with their kinsman, but there were those who kept one eye on the group at the back of the lodge. Crazy Horse and a cadre of Lakota headmen sat there, surrounded by a larger group called *Akicita*, the camp guard.

Crazy Horse knew people waited on his reaction. He nonchalantly played with the fringe on his plain buckskin shirt, allowing the speaker to flesh out his plan. Carries the Drum did just that.

"Here is what I think," he said. "Not too long ago, some of our young men returned with several horses they took from the new soldier fort on Elk River. I say, let us send a few of our brave men to return these horses to the soldiers to show we wish to talk for peace. I am told that there is one important man there, a man who wears a bear coat and decides for the rest. This man might decide to talk peace if we give these horses back. I will take any brave man who will ride with me to see if this is true."

"*Hou! Hou!*" A chorus of agreement rose from the crowd, and many drummed their chest with a fist to signal their approval.

Little Wolf struggled to his feet. His legs were stiff, and he had to place a hand on Wild Hog's shoulder as he rose. Once erect, he straightened his blanket and cleared his throat. Carries the Drum sat down, ceding the floor to the Cheyenne leader.

"Friends, there was a time when I would have stood to tell you that our friend Carries the Drum spoke the words of a fool. When I would have carried the pipe to each of you and said we should come together and fight these soldiers wherever they are. But I have been across the big river to the place they come from in the east. I have seen how many more will come behind these who already have no fear of attacking us in our camps.

"Every man here knows that I am not afraid to ride out to fight any enemy who comes against us. I would fight for our families, for our elders, our women and children—all those who cannot fight for themselves. In this attack in the mountains, we tried, but it was not a fight. These soldiers brought Wolf People, and Snakes, even Lakota and Cheyenne, with them. We did our best, but we could only hold them off long enough to let our loved ones escape." The chief gave a brief glance down at Morning Star's unbraided hair. "Even so, we have lost many."

He paused briefly out of respect for those no longer with them. "When they come into our camp again, maybe we will not hold them back, and we will all be killed. Even if we could kill some, like at the fight last summer, they will keep coming, like the leaves that always grow back on trees.

"I agree with my friend Carries the Drum. Let us send those horses back to the soldiers, and let him and a few others smoke the pipe with them. We must go to them before they come into our camp again. *Hena'haanehe*, I am done talking now."

Little Wolf knelt down and rolled carefully over onto one hip. Wild Hog tucked his arm behind the chief, lest he roll too far backward as he settled into his place. The murmur from the crowd sounded generally agreeable but quieted when Crazy Horse rose to speak.

The light-haired man with the scar on his cheek took time to adjust the blanket wrapped around his waist, then cleared his throat.

"*Mitakuye oyasin*, all my relations, I have not been to the land where the sun rises as some here have. I have not seen all the *Wasichu*, the white men who wait to come here. I have not seen them, so I am not afraid of them." He glanced over at Little Wolf as he spoke these last words. "Even if they come here, I will not be afraid of them."

Little Wolf knew he was being baited, but he let the man finish.

"If it will end all the fighting and we can go back to hunting, then I am for talking with this Bear Coat. But hear me—I think he will only want to fight more because we killed so many of his kind last summer. He will not forget how we embarrassed them.

"We can talk again when these peace talkers return, and you will see that I speak the truth."

The Lakota leader sat back down, and Carries the Drum rose to begin choosing who would go with him.

It was late when Little Wolf and Morning Star finally left the lodge with a small group of Cheyenne. They walked slowly among the Lakota lodges that glowed amber against the soft-pink blush growing in the eastern sky. Most in the group were looking forward to their first comfortable sleep in a warm lodge with a decent robe after many nights without either.

Two Moons, Ice, and Black Moccasin, the three Cheyenne leaders who had ridden out to greet them when they first arrived, walked with the group. The party was discussing plans for a Cheyenne-only Council later that day after everyone had slept.

"Crazy Horse should not agree to any talk of peace with these *ve'ho'e*, these white men," Ice grumbled while peering into the shadows that crossed the ground in front of him. "How can we talk peace with an enemy who continues to attack our camps?"

"It is a strong enemy who can climb into the mountains and take our homes from us," Little Wolf replied. "When *Eše'he* climbs into the sky today, look around you. It has been a hard winter. Crazy Horse's camp is large but not much stronger than ours was before the attack. His horses are thin and eat mostly tree bark, and we have brought more mouths to feed. Now is not the time to talk war."

"Do not talk to me about making peace with your white friends," Ice spat back. "You would have us all killed if we let you walk us in front of their guns."

Morning Star intervened. "Let us talk about this in Council. Now is not the time."

Ice wanted the last word. "I only say it is foolish to ride down to the soldier fort. Crazy Horse is right to worry that these soldiers want to keep fighting. They want their revenge—and our land."

Little Wolf let Ice's last words hang in the air. He knew it made no sense for him to try to discuss even the color of the sky with the short, stocky medicine man. He would let Morning Star deal with him if he continued.

Having said his piece, Ice stomped away to his lodge. The rest of the party disbanded as each man left to enter the lodge where he had been invited to stay. The arrangements were a temporary but welcome respite to the makeshift war lodges they had been living in since the attack.

Little Wolf, Morning Star, and Two Moons soon walked by themselves. Two Moons had invited Little Wolf and his family to stay in his lodge, and Morning Star would stay in the lodge of one of his Lakota relatives that was on their way. Now that the others were gone, the Sweet Medicine Chief spoke to his friends in a low voice.

"From what I see, there is only one man who decides in this camp, just like at the soldier fort."

Two Moons peered into the shadows around them, making sure they were alone. "Crazy Horse has become very suspicious of everyone these days. People are sneaking away and returning to the agencies. He is afraid of losing his fighting men and worried they will help the soldiers fight against him next summer."

Morning Star nodded. "He tries to control this camp, the same way Last Bull did with ours in the mountains. If the soldiers come here this winter . . ." The older man could not complete his thought.

Little Wolf finished it for him. "We have many who need to stay here until their wounds heal. If this soldier chief who wears the bear coat does not want peace, and Crazy Horse gets the fight he is looking for, many of our weak ones may not be able to get out of the way this time."

Morning Star expressed their common hope before he stepped into his relatives' lodge. "Maybe Carries the Drum and the others will return with something good to tell us,"

Little Wolf and Two Moons stepped into the latter's lodge, which was crowded with the prone forms of their sleeping families.

Little Wolf shared his concern. "Even though we were warned, the attack in the mountains was a big surprise. If our own people are helping them, then I think these white soldiers will find us wherever we are and attack again."

Two Moons nodded in the dim glow of the fire as he placed a couple of small pieces of wood on it. At thirty winters, he was a well-respected man, thickly built, and brave. Many in the tribe thought he would one day be an Old Man Chief. He nudged the logs together with a stick and considered Little Wolf's words.

"I believe what you say is true, my friend," he began. "Crazy Horse and Ice say you are afraid to fight, but I was beside you when the soldiers attacked our camp on the Powder River last spring. You have been a brave man of our people since I was a young boy. I remember that it was you who bought my father's body home when he was killed at the fight on Turkey Creek in the south many years ago. I was told that you went back to get him even though the soldiers with the long knives were very close. You care about our people more than you do prideful things, and I know that is why you want them to go to the agency." He tapped the stick in his hand for a moment, as if drumming up the courage for his next words. "But I think as Crazy Horse and Ice do. I think we can still whip these white soldiers and push them off of our land. Sitting Bull has promised to return to meet with us soon. If he and his Hunkpapa stay with us in this country, then the soldiers will be afraid to come. They know we would treat them as badly as we did those who came last summer. I've been told he will come back to Powder River very soon." He pointed to the east with the stick then chuckled. "There is talk that when he gets here, we might even go looking for some soldiers to fight. Ho! Maybe we will find those soldiers that attacked your camp and take all your things back."

Little Wolf appreciated his friend's humor but knew that the large gathering last summer had disbanded for a reason. There was simply not enough game left to support a camp of that size. Maybe in years past, further south, and during the sun dance moon, but they were in the north now, and it was winter.

Little Wolf looked over the forms of his sleeping wives and family before he laid back among them. He would not disagree with their host in his own lodge. Both men stretched out in their robes as best they could in the crowded space.

The tired chief studied a star through the smoke hole and asked, "I have heard the one who led the soldiers at Little Sheep last summer was Long Hair, the one who killed Black Kettle at Washita?"

"*Hau*, it was."

"*Epeva'e*."

# A Line along the White

Camp Robinson appeared to rise from the ground at the far end of the flat in front of us as we rode down Soldier Creek, the final leg of our long journey home. As each adobe and log building came more into view, an uneasy feeling rose along with it.

The military outpost had been built shortly after Doc Saville's nephew Frank was killed by an angry Lakota at the Red Cloud Agency two years earlier. Doc had sent me the eighty or so miles to Fort Laramie to fetch military help. That was another tough ride—nine hours in the dark, after sneaking my way past the camps of all the northern bands that had come south and were harassing everyone at the agency.

We all figured that after things had settled down, the soldiers would return to Fort Laramie. Instead, they stayed and built the post a mile and a half west of the agency at the spot where a shallow creek flowed into the White River from the north. The Lakota and Cheyenne took to calling the stream Soldier Creek.

Ulysses sniffed the air as he walked, catching the first faint smells that drifted up from the post. There were many to choose from: fresh-hewn lumber from the post sawmill, dinner being cooked at the mess hall, lye soap being boiled down at the laundry. His nostrils flared as he took each odor in then exhaled it only to grab another, then another. With our destination now in sight, my mind was doing the same thing with all the questions I had tried to ignore during the campaign, rolling from one to the other in rapid succession. It wouldn't be long now, and I'd have to answer them.

*What was my part in it all? How the hell do I tell Sis about all the dead—about how we chased the rest into the mountains? How could they survive that storm? Where were they now? What the hell was*

*I even doing up there?* Each question nagged at me for a moment then went away unanswered as another rose to take its place.

Huge sandstone buttes jutted high above the pine-covered hills on either side of the creek. To me, they resembled tall rows of gigantic, broken, yellow teeth cropping up from the earth. They were easily the most prominent features in the area.

A mile and a half east and downstream from the post, the log bastion of the Red Cloud Agency showed above the bare branches of the ash trees on the south side of the frozen White River. It was there, just a few hundred yards from the agency, where Sis and the kids were waiting for me. The agency had been our home since its beginning in seventy-three when Doc Saville asked me to hire on to help him.

I figured everyone here had heard of the attack by now. Shangreau and Richard had made it back afterward, and they were not known for having tight lips. Even so, Major Mason, the post commander, kept Tackett and me longer than the others to question us about our thoughts on the trip. I told him about Billy, who hadn't been seen yet. I told him it was likely the boy had first gone to a relative's lodge and would show up in a day or so.

Once we were finally dismissed, I stepped out onto the porch of the major's quarters and was surprised to find my second-oldest son, James, waiting for me.

"Howdy." The young man had a one-word greeting.

"James," I replied.

Neither one of us was much for chitchat.

James was tall and lanky, like most of my boys. His darker skin showed his mixed heritage at a glance. A light mustache was just beginning to show on his upper lip. The eighteen-year-old handed me Ulysses's reins then swung up on his large bay and waited for me to mount. We rode off toward home, and our conversation expanded a bit.

"You need a shave."

"I need more'n that."

The road to the agency led east out of camp and down into a large bend of the river created by the wide seasonal sweeps it often took back and forth along its flood plain. We forded the river and turned left off the road before it climbed up onto a low bench on the other side. We stayed low, moving along the southern edge of the flood plain for about a half-mile, heading toward a thick maze of barren ash downstream. We were nearly across the meadow and approaching the first stand of trees when James's curiosity got the better of him.

"Heard there was a fight," he said.

A vision of Walking Whirlwind's dirt-filled eyes came out of nowhere, then one of Red Pipe lying in a heap. Then came the butchered man at the top of the draw, then Walks Different pitching backward into the ditch behind her. I couldn't push them away.

"There was," I said.

I filled him in as we entered the thicket of gnarled trees.

"Weren't good."

Alice Jane held her youngest brother, one-year-old Edward, on her hip while she helped Zach, the seven-year-old, button the strap on his overalls. She looked up when she caught our shadows swaying among those that stretched from the trees behind our lodge. She released the boy's strap and raised her hand against the late afternoon glare. She peered into the gray shadow below the sunlight and caught a glimpse of Ulysses's buckskin coat.

"Daddy!" Her shriek pierced the crisp afternoon air.

"Daddy, Daddy!" the chorus of a half-dozen young voices soon echoed her cry as children came tumbling from the lodge and bushes surrounding the teepee that stood by itself in the small clearing.

Sis rose up from the meal she had been fixing at the fire and turned to watch our arrival. Despite her forty years and nine children, she was still a slender, good-looking woman. The only real signs of her age were the deepening rows of wrinkles on the exposed areas of her dark skin. It was there where the weathering of a hard life had taken its toll on her. She held out her left hand, palm down, and barked, "*Neve'nėheševe!* Stop doing that!" The children obeyed and quietly gathered between the lodge and the fire until James and I had left the trees and were safely dismounted.

She watched me step down from the saddle. It had been two

months since I had climbed into it on my way to Fort Fetterman to see about "making some good money."

"You're skinny," she said as I slid the saddle off of Ulysses and handed his reins to James.

"And tired," I sighed.

I turned toward her, and her eyes lingered on me for a moment, glassy with emotion. I tried to push a tight-lipped smile through the mat of hair on my chin then stepped toward the fidgeting children.

"Nope, nope. Line up now, you know the deal." I drew an imaginary line in the air in front of me.

The youngsters shuffled past and around each other, trading small pushes and shoves, getting themselves in position, oldest to youngest, so we could say our howdys one at a time instead of having me be swarmed.

Six-year-old Jack stood farthest to the right. Next to him was Zach, with his britches still undone, then Ben, age ten, and Willis, thirteen. Patrick, the four-year-old, who cared nothing of lines, had wedged himself between Willis and fifteen-year-old Alice Jane, who still held Edward on her hip.

I knelt with a groan in front of the first youngster. "So, Jack, you been a good boy for your mama while I been gone?"

"Yeah. You smell bad, Daddy."

I laughed. "You're right, I do. So, how about just a handshake fer now until I've had my bath?"

I reached my hand to the boy, who grabbed it and gave it a couple hard pumps, the way he had seen the white people at the agency do.

"And, how 'bout you, Zach? Will a handshake do till I get spruced up a bit?"

"Yeah. You missed Crissy-mas, Daddy."

I shook his hand and counted back through the number of days I had been gone. It had been a good two months. I gave a cluck and tousled the boy's mop of short black hair.

"And I'm sure sorry 'bout that, but I'll tell ya what. I'm going back over to see the major tomorrow, and he's gonna give me a piece of paper that says we can all head over to the trading post afterward and have ourselves a sorta late Crissy-mas this year. How's that?"

Zach nodded hard as he pushed his hair back in place.

I turned to Ben, but the youngster surprised me with a quick hug before I could extend my hand for a shake.

"Ugh! Jack's right. You smell bad," he said, giving me a quick shove away.

"Well, you brought that on yourself then, didn't you?" I laughed and patted Ben's shoulder.

Dipping to my left, I swooped and picked up young Patrick, holding him at arm's length and giving him a playful shake.

"And, how 'bout you, little man? You think your daddy stinks too? Hmm?" I pushed my face into the child's neck and growled, "Well, that's just too bad, cause I'm getting me some sonny-boy snuggles anyway."

The four-year-old squealed and pushed himself away from me trying to escape both the tickle of my beard and the smell that came from it. When his feet found the ground, he turned to Willis, who did nothing to protect him, so he took refuge behind his brother's leg. His eyes danced with the thrill that had just grabbed him.

Willis extended his hand. "Welcome home, Papa."

I nodded at the son who was more like me than any of the others then reached for his hand. Quiet, like I was at that age. He was slender, with fine brown hair instead of the coarse black that his siblings got from their mother. He had outgrown the bibs, now worn by the younger boys, and wore a plain muslin shirt instead. The shirt was tucked into a worn pair of gray canvas pants; both were hand-me-downs from his older brothers, William Jr. and James.

"Willis. Good to see you, son. You been helping out around here while I been gone?" I knew I needn't ask.

"Yes, sir, been trying."

"I'm sure a that. Seen Junior lately?"

"He's up working for Mr. Yates at the trading post today. They had a shipment come in."

At twenty-three, Junior was Sis's and my oldest boy. He found occasional work with Frank Yates, who ran one of the two trading posts at the agency.

"That's good. You know if Yates has settled down any 'bout

his brother getting killed out there with Custer this summer?"

"Not really."

"Mmm, too bad. Hope Junior don't catch too much hell from him on that account."

"He still likes it there."

"That's good."

I gave the boy a nod then turned to Alice Jane, who was waiting patiently with Edward perched on her hip.

"Welcome home, Daddy."

"*Nea' eše, katse'e.* How goes things in camp?"

"We make do." The girl smiled. She liked it when I spoke to her in Cheyenne. For me, it was to respect how hard she worked helping her mother around camp.

Sis told me that she had explained it to Alice Jane once. "Your place in this family is not an easy one," she had said. "A Cheyenne woman has many responsibilities. Your father knows this and speaks to you in this way to let you know that he sees you as a good Cheyenne woman, even though, to him, you will always be *katse'e,* his little girl."

I made a show of looking around the area, paying no mind to the scorched square of ground behind us, where our cabin had once stood before my run-in with Water Walker a little over a year back.

"*Navenòtse epėhevenono'e.* My home looks nice."

"*Nea'eše,* Daddy." Alice Jane's eyes twinkled as she emphasized the English word for me.

Sis stood near the fire a few feet to the left of the children. Neither of us said a word at first, but we each tried to read the other's eyes. I fought to keep a smile, but I was bone-tired, and she had such a troubled look on her face.

"So, how much you heard?" I asked.

Sis turned to the children and shooed them away in her heavily accented English. "*Shaa!* Y'all go play now. G'wan."

The children disappeared quickly, heading back up the creek or into the lodge and leaving us to a more private reunion. After Alice Jane handed Edward through the door to Willis and stepped in herself, Sis leaned against me, and I pulled her close.

"Pah! You do need a bath." She groaned without moving.

I smiled and eased her away to arm's length. "So, I heard. Now, how much do you know?"

Sis glanced toward the fire then stepped quickly toward it to adjust pots and wood, trying to keep the meal from getting over-cooked. "I heard there was a big fight." She put the largest pot on the ground and turned to face me again. "They said it was the big Cheyenne camp, and that many were killed. They said Little Wolf was killed." Her throat closed, and she looked to the ground as she spoke the name of her brother-in-law.

"I seen a lot of them get away." I tried to ease the blow. I stepped closer to reassure her—and so I could speak quietly. "Couple different fellas claim they shot him, but far as I can tell, your sister and the kids got away."

Sis stifled a small cry as she stepped into my arms again. Her knees gave out, and I eased her to a sitting position near the fire. I swallowed hard as she sobbed in my arms.

"Oh, what did you do? What did you do?"

I had asked myself that very question so many times since that day, but none had cut my heart open and found the answer the way hers did.

# Another Attack

A Lakota boy appeared among the branch-and-willow lodges above the slope where Day Woman and her friends were sledding. She saw another to the left walking slowly out from the trees upstream. Spinning and glancing downstream along the same slope that ran from the flat to the creek, she saw a third. He crossed the creek and began moving up the far side of the stream toward them.

Her lips parted in an open smile. She looked back to the first boy, who had casually edged closer while pretending to be interested in something to his left. She knew what was happening. This band of Lakota boys were setting up a surround and were about to rush in to spring the game called Capturing Prisoners on her and her playmates. She needed to warn the others.

"*Otahe! Otahe!*" She ran toward her friends Wallowing Woman and Red Earth Woman, who were dragging their buffalo rib sleds back up the hill while helping the younger girls wade through the knee-deep drifts at the crest. "*Nanehama'oene!* They sneak up on us!"

She ran into the center of the girls, grabbing and shaking them to get their attention. The game had begun. Any of the girls who were caught would be marched around the camp on display as the boy's prisoners until their captors decided to release them.

It took a few moments before the girls realized what was happening. The boys, aware they had been discovered, raced to use what advantage remained in the girls' panic and confusion. Several more youths raced from behind the trees and lodges. The girls finally saw them and screamed. They erupted from the snow bank like a covey of frightened quail, flying in every direction trying to escape.

Day Woman squealed with excitement as she dashed straight away for the creek. Her plan was to cross it and escape behind the lodges on the other side. She made it to the frozen stream and turned to see if the boy downstream had come any closer. She collided hard with another girl trying to cross the slick ice at the same spot she had chosen. Both tumbled to the hard ground on the far side.

In her scramble to get up, the other girl stepped on Day Woman's dangling shawl, pulling it from her shoulders. Day Woman made a grab for the garment, and a flash of memory slammed into her, stopping her in mid-reach.

She saw herself and White Voice tumbling on the ground after their horse was shot the day the village had been attacked. Her robe had been pulled off of her, and she was crawling around in a daze trying to locate it as White Voice screamed in her ear, "*Amaxėstse!* Run away! Keep running!"

The red dust blinded her as pain from the fall throbbed in her shoulder. Screams echoed around her, giving voice to the terror that sliced through her stomach. Bullets, sounding like angry bees, zipped into the dirt around them. One slammed into a woman who was running past, flipping her into the creek where she landed face-down. Day Woman couldn't tell who it was but recalled the woman's blood flowing from her head out into the stream, dark red at first then swirling into a pink fan that grew lighter until it was finally washed downstream toward their attackers. White Voice grabbed her then, just as her fear grabbed her now, and she had gone blank.

She was gasping as she fought back her tears. Her extended hand hovered over her shawl, and it began to tremble. She pulled it slowly to her chest, held it with her other hand, then sank to the ground and began to sob.

A Lakota boy, about twelve winters old, raced up and cried, "*Thǒka kte!*" intending to count coup on the Cheyenne girl cringing on her knees in front of him.

Before the youth could deliver his symbolic blow, another boy, about his same age, tackled him from the side and slammed him to the ground.

It was Gathering His Medicine. It was he who Day Woman had

seen walking farther down the creek. She had been mistaken. The Cheyenne youth punched the Lakota, then stood him up and shoved him away from the sobbing girl.

"Do you not have eyes?" he asked the confused boy in Cheyenne. Shooting two fingers away from his eyes and down toward the girl, he demanded the Lakota take a better look at how frightened Day Woman had become. It was clear that this was no longer a game to her.

The Lakota boy stared for a moment. Confusion clouded his face until he heard the squeals of the other girls running between the lodges on the other side of the creek. He shook off the uncertainty and, saying nothing, raced away after them.

Gathering His Medicine knelt next to his young friend with his hand resting gently on her back. "Day Woman, what is wrong? Why do you cry? Are you hurt?"

The young girl gave no answer other than to quiet her sobs. The boy noticed that despite the cold, small beads of perspiration had formed on her brow. He gathered her shawl, gave it a shake to get the snow off of it, then wrapped it around her and helped her carefully to her feet.

The girl clutched her friend and buried her head into his shoulder. It took a moment to catch her breath and steady her legs as she slowly came back to the present day. When he felt her standing better, the boy turned and walked her carefully back across the creek and toward her family's lodge.

The fire in front of the round-topped willow lodge crackled for a moment as Wooden Thigh adjusted the long log that fed into it. The frame of the low shelter sagged a bit under the weight of a pair of untanned elk hides thrown over the top to keep snow off of the meager furnishings inside. He then sat down next to his father. He had returned the night before from another hunt and hoped to catch up on news of what had happened while he had been away.

Little Wolf took a series of short draws as he lit an undecorated pipe, a gift he had received from his friend Two Moons. He offered the smoke to the four directions then handed it to his son and pulled the older robe he wore—another gift, this one from a Lakota friend—tighter around his shoulders. They would talk after their smoke.

The devastating cold of a few days ago had passed, and though it was still chilly, people had become more active outside. Lightning, Two Woman, and Chopping Woman were busy working a couple of cold-stiffened buffalo hides in a clearing nearby. Wooden Thigh and Pawnee had brought these and the two elk hides back from the hunt.

White Voice was away again, helping Starving Elk's parents, and Day Woman was off playing with friends near the creek. Were it not for the large number of branch-and-willow lodges around them, it appeared to be a typical winter day in camp.

The large camp was preparing to move south, back toward the foothills of the Shining Mountains where they could gather the long and straight lodge poles used for the frame of a respectable Cheyenne home. The women were busy working hides in order to have enough to cover them. Their wolves had told them the soldiers had left the mountains long ago and traveled east, so it was safe to return. Word had also come that Sitting Bull and his Hunkpapa were indeed moving south along Powder River and intended to camp with them soon.

Little Wolf was handing the pipe to his son when the lodge behind them suddenly shifted, and a light covering of snow slipped to the ground like a shrugged-off robe. A large appaloosa horse, a generous gift from the Lakota Carries the Drum, had somehow slipped its picket and was now scratching its head on the backside of the lodge.

"*Neve'nėhševe!* Don't do that!" Two Woman barked as she left the hide work and stomped toward the animal. She led the animal back to its picket near Wooden Thigh's horse and the buckskin mare he had given to his father.

Wooden Thigh turned back from watching his mother and smiled. His father had sat perfectly still the whole time, holding the pipe out toward him, waiting patiently for him to accept it, a true example of the chief's way of not reacting to such trivial matters. The young man took the pipe and felt calmer himself as he exhaled a long plume of smoke into the air. He waited for his father to settle back before he handed him the pipe, but he saw Little Wolf was distracted. Following his father's gaze over the bowl of the pipe, he saw that Gathering His

Medicine had appeared a couple lodges away. The boy was walking toward them with his arm around his youngest sister. Uncertain of what he was seeing, Wooden Thigh made a joke.

"She is too young to be courted."

After a few steps, Day Woman stumbled, and it was clear something was wrong.

Little Wolf labored to stand up as he called to his wives. Wooden Thigh took the pipe from his father and raised an arm to steady him as he teetered. Once he found his balance, the chief limped toward the approaching children.

Lightning reached the children first. She took Day Woman from Gathering His Medicine's embrace and into her own. She spoke softly to the trembling girl and checked her for injuries. Little Wolf arrived and took the boy aside.

"What happened? Why is she like this?"

Gathering His Medicine shook his head. "I was walking back to my mother's lodge and saw some Lakota boys chasing her and her friends. She and another girl ran into each other, and she fell. She was not hurt too bad, but she still started to shake and cry."

The boy turned to Lightning, who was still trying to get her daughter to respond. "She has said nothing since then," he told her.

Little Wolf studied his daughter's condition for a moment then said to no one in particular, "I have seen this happen with young men after their first big fight. They do well during the fight and are fine afterward, but when they are home with their family and their lives became quiet again, they are visited by bad spirits." He raised his voice. "She must see Bridge. He has medicine for this kind of thing."

He placed his hand on Gathering His Medicine's shoulder. "Now friend, you must run to his lodge, down where this stream joins with the bigger one. Tell him that I am asking for him to come and that he should be ready to chase bad spirits from someone when he gets here."

Gathering His Medicine nodded and started off through the snow without saying a word.

Little Wolf raised his voice so everyone, including Day Woman, would hear. "She will be well soon. Bridge's medicine is strong with this kind of thing."

"*Heehe'e*," Lightning agreed as she helped the dazed girl through the door of the lodge. She gave directions over her shoulder before she entered. "We will be in here when he comes. Two Woman, you should put away those hides for now. *Nahtse*, daughter, make us a smudge and some yellow medicine to drink."

Two Woman returned to the hides while Chopping Woman sorted through a burlap sack that the women were using to collect herbs and dried flowers. Once carefully organized in a pair of parfleche containers, their stores of medicines and cooking supplies were now jumbled loosely together in this one bag.

The pregnant woman's chopped hair fell across her face as she rummaged through the bag. She gave the ragged locks a toss backward and pulled a small bundle of green-gray plant stems out of the sack. The yellow flowers that once identified the plant for its healing properties were long gone, but the stems still held the medicine needed for both a soothing smudge and tea. She rolled a few of them between her palms and dropped them into a partially filled buffalo bladder that hung on a tripod near the fire. She used forked sticks to pull a couple of hot stones from the fire and carefully slipped them inside the bladder to start the drink steeping. She placed a few more of the stems and leaves onto a shard of a porcelain plate and dropped a hot coal on them. She carried the smoldering dish to the lodge to be used for the smudge. She returned to the fire and carefully slipped another hot stone into her sister's drink.

Little Wolf spoke quietly to Wooden Thigh as he watched as his eldest daughter tended to the needs of his youngest.

"Our little ones should not hurt like this. We do not even have cooking tools to care for them." The chief sighed, shook his head, and continued his lament. "I have seen much war, and I know most of our young men are still hungry for it, but we cannot keep fighting against an enemy who can do this to our children."

"Have the peace talkers come back yet? Carries the Drum might still bring us good news," Wooden Thigh said.

Little Wolf looked surprised. "You have not heard?" he asked.

"No, I have heard nothing about them. Are they back?"

Little Wolf motioned his son back toward the fire. This time they sat facing the lodge, watching Lightning console Day Woman.

"When they reached the soldier camp, a few of them rode down from the hills with Carries the Drum. He had a white cloth tied to his lance. They were met by a group of Crow soldier wolves. At first they were given handshakes, but then the Crow attacked. All of the peace talkers were chased down and killed. Those who stayed on the hill could only watch as Carries the Drum and the others were shot down like buffalo. They were too far away to do anything."

Wooden Thigh's mouth fell open. When his father finished, he asked, "Do you think the soldiers told the Crow to kill them?"

"I don't know, but Crazy Horse believes they did. The soldiers later captured a handful of Cheyenne women who had become separated from the camp. There was a skirmish afterward, but we couldn't get them back. Wool Woman, Twin Woman, and Crooked Nose were among them.

"Crazy Horse has decided that no one can leave our camp because of it all. He has grown fearful that more will be captured, or killed, or even turned against him like those who helped the soldiers attack us in the mountains."

"No one can leave?" Wooden Thigh could not believe his ears.

"We have had messengers from the White River Agency come and tell us that Three Stars, the new soldier chief there, told them we can all come in and he will not fight with us, but Crazy Horse sends his *Akicita* to chase down anyone who leaves." The chief explained, "He has his men shoot their horses and destroy their belongings."

"He is doing what you said Last Bull did, back in the mountains before the attack," said Wooden Thigh.

Little Wolf nodded. "I hope it does not end the same."

The younger man looked down at the pipe in his hand. "Let us finish our smoke," he said. "Bridge will come soon, and my young sister will be better then."

"Until the next time the soldiers come," Little Wolf said. "With all the fights in this last year, I have seen too many of our children become quiet like this. If it were only me, I would fight these white men until they either killed me or I wiped them out. But when I see my daughter like this, walking in her own camp with her heart on the ground, I know we must try another way. For them."

The two men continued to smoke.

"We no longer meet these white soldiers to fight out on the prairie, away from our women and children," Little Wolf went on. "They attack us in our camps now. We cannot keep our people safe, even this far from their forts."

Wooden Thigh nodded. "Your words are true. Even when we have fought them on the prairie, it has gone hard on us. Everyone has lost loved ones over the years."

A silence followed as each man reflected on the tremendous toll the people had suffered. Little Wolf watched Lightning continue to tend to Day Woman while his son watched for Bridge to come trudging through the shin-deep snow along the creek.

Wooden Thigh gave an approving grunt when the old medicine man finally appeared. Gathering His Medicine was at his side, helping him waddle past slippery spots where the snow had been packed down by many moccasin-clad feet. The two visited as they walked, and Little Wolf could hear the elder explaining some of his medicine to the youth when they came closer.

"I do not always chase bad spirits away. Many times I call a person's own spirit back to them, to give them courage to keep the bad spirits away themselves."

The boy's eyes appeared tethered to the healer's gentle eyes, but he glanced ahead occasionally, watching out for slick areas on the path ahead. Bridge looked up and smiled as they approached the fire.

"This boy was given the right name," he puffed. The effort of walking up the slippery trail had winded him. "He has not stopped asking questions since he came to my lodge. He is very worried about his friend."

Gathering His Medicine looked embarrassed until Bridge reached over and gave his shoulder a light shake with his small hand, letting him know he had done well.

Little Wolf looked from the boy back to Bridge then pointed with his chin toward his wife and daughter in the lodge. The effeminate man reached for the small pack that Gathering His Medicine had been carrying for him.

"*Nea'eše*, now you should finish your walk back to your mother's lodge. She is waiting for you. I will tell your friend to come see you when she is better."

"*Haaahe*." The boy was slow to agree, but he nodded his goodbyes to each of the men and headed back in the direction that he and Day Woman had come from earlier.

Bridge walked to the lodge and groaned as he knelt to enter. Little Wolf and Wooden Thigh watched Gathering His Medicine begin a careful trot through the snow. He moved up the draw at a steady pace.

"He is growing up well," Wooden Thigh said.

Oddly, the sound of the boy's footsteps seemed to grow louder the further away he ran. Little Wolf listened closely before he realized that the sound was actually coming from behind them. He turned to see Wild Hog running toward them. The big man slipped on the slick snow and went sprawling to the ground.

Father and son laughed as snow flew into the air when the large man rolled several times before he could stop his ungainly tumble. Wild Hog sprang to his feet with an urgency that showed he was desperate to get to them.

"Wagons!" he cried. "Wagons and soldiers are coming!"

# A Bow is Unstrung

THE WAGONS WILD HOG HAD WARNED ABOUT TURNED OUT TO BE the Red River carts of a northern people called Metis, who often traded with the Hunkpapa. Sitting Bull had finally arrived. Instead of facing another fight with the enemy, the Cheyenne welcomed allies, and the large camp that had repelled two soldier attacks last summer was reunited. There was great reason to celebrate.

For two days, a circle of young men stomped, shot, and stabbed unseen enemies, all to the frenzied rhythm of the Lakota drum. They all danced around the large fire, each giving the watching crowd a spectacular reenactment of his heroic deeds during one of the recent battles.

Wild Hog stood on the perimeter of the thick ring of observers, flexing his knees in time to the driving beat that pushed the dancers inside the circle to even more dramatic gestures.

"Get in there," Little Wolf's voice sounded in his ear. "You have more scalps and have counted more coups than anyone in there. You should show them how to do it."

Wild Hog grinned and continued his light step as he turned toward the chief. "I could, but I will be kind to them today and stay out here."

Both men knew that Wild Hog's reserved step would be all the dancing that either of them would do this night. It was the day after Sitting Bull's arrival, and the first Council of all the tribe's leaders had been called.

The men left the dance and walked through camp. Their voices softened as distance and lodges muffled the sounds of revelry behind them.

"Have you heard about Last Bull and the Kit Fox?" Wild Hog asked.

Little Wolf sighed. "Now what?"

"They have put him out."

"What? Out?"

Wild Hog nodded. "Young Two Moons told me this. He said that he and the others were tired of being embarrassed by his actions and told him so. His treatment of Two Twists after the fight was what caused many of them to finally come forward."

"Did they all agree to this?" Little Wolf was amazed.

"Not all. There were some who sided with Last Bull, but most are done with him."

"So, who have they chosen to replace him?" Little Wolf asked.

"They had a Kit Fox council earlier today. They should be finished, so we will know soon."

Wild Hog stepped closer to Little Wolf and gave a friendly nod to a group from Sitting Bull's band that was walking by on their way to the dance. He waited until they were out of hearing range and expressed concern.

"I have had a chance to walk through Sitting Bull's camp. They should have more lodges, and many of them look almost as poor as the rest of us. What happened?"

Little Wolf explained what he knew. "I was told the soldiers found their camp too, north of Elk River, and told them to go in to the agency. They refused, and the soldiers fired their wagon guns in among the lodges. Everyone had to run, like we did."

Wild Hog's heavy brow pressed lower as his friend continued the far-too-familiar story.

"They abandoned their lodges to get away as fast as they could. Some had good luck, though, and were able to save their belongings and many of their horses. Still, they lost much. Many families live together in one lodge, as we do."

"Where are the others, though? They should have more than double the people that are here."

"They went in to the agencies. Almost four hundred lodges, I was told."

"Wuh!" Wild Hog was surprised at the number.

Little Wolf leaned toward his friend. "That means that it is even more important that we go in now." He motioned toward the lodges around them and explained. "This camp is not even half of what was at Little Sheep River. We do not have as many fighting men, but we still have too many to feed while we wait for the soldiers to come again. What makes it worse is, since Sitting Bull has arrived, people are feasting like we are all doing well. This camp cannot stay together for very long. We must separate, but still, the soldiers will come."

Wild Hog took in the pleasant scene about them with some trepidation. The slender arc the new moon had risen in the eastern sky. Its faint white light complemented the amber glow of the lodges crowded together in the broad valley beside the river.

"It is strange to see these many lodges together with so much snow on the ground," he said. "I keep reminding myself it is a long time until the sun dance."

Standing Elk had invited the Cheyenne leaders to meet at his fire so they could walk as a group to the large Lakota Council Lodge. The Council chief had somehow obtained a fine-looking lodge from his Lakota friends. Had Little Wolf not known different, he would have thought the man had been with the Lakota all winter. Morning Star, Two Moons, and several other Cheyenne headmen were already sitting at the fire.

Wild Hog had a final question for his friend as they approached the circle. "Instead of waiting for the soldiers to come here, do you think that Sitting Bull and Crazy Horse will want to attack their fort on Elk River? I heard that the Hunkpapa wagons carry many bullets."

Little Wolf stopped and shrugged. "They might. Sitting Bull's blood is not as hot as Crazy Horse's, and he has always tried to avoid any dealing with the white man. He has now lost much to them, though, and he might want to see some of their blood spilled on the ground to settle things."

A hard voice interrupted their conversation. "If he does, I will join him in the fight."

Ice stepped out of the darkness and moved past them toward an open seat at the fire. He turned and spoke louder so everyone at the fire could hear him. "I think that if Sitting Bull and the Hunkpapa are with us, we will wipe out any soldiers who come after us, just like we did last summer."

The broad-chested man with the round face looked around him to see who agreed. A few at the fire watched him closely. Two Moons did not. Sensing his friend's resolve might be waning, Ice spoke directly to the man.

"Why should we just give our land and our women over to them? I am not afraid to fight them. I say let us join with our Lakota friends and hurt these soldiers again. Let us make them fear fighting with us. Why should we be afraid of them when we are here in our own land?"

Two Moons finally glanced up at the heavyset medicine man, which seemed to satisfy Ice, who gave one last exhortation before taking his seat. "We must stay together and fight these *ve'ho'e*, these white men."

Some nodded in approval, while others remained quiet. Other Cheyenne leaders arrived, and everyone began arranging themselves for the walk to the Council.

Coal Bear chose to stay in the new Sacred Hat Lodge the Cheyenne had built, so Little Wolf, Morning Star, Old Bear, and Black Moccasin—all four Old Man Chiefs—walked together at the front. Council chiefs occupied the next several rows, walking four abreast. The society headmen came next, and it was there, next to Wild Hog, where Two Moons made his first appearance as the new headman of the Kit Fox Society.

Ice assumed his position behind the society headmen, clearly upset that he was so far back in the procession. He held more sway in camp, but tradition dictated the order, and he could not change that.

With the exception of Standing Elk, it was easy to see who had been involved in the fight in the mountains. Most wore little to no regalia. Regardless, each man walked proudly, for he knew he represented a proud people and was ashamed of nothing.

They arrived at the Council lodge and were seated as a group. The four Old Man Chiefs were in the front row, and Ice was allowed to sit in the second row, simply because he had the favor of many of the Oglala headmen. Pipes were passed, and preliminary words of welcome were shared. It would be some time before any serious discussion began. Little Wolf had no plans to speak tonight, but he did intend to listen very closely to everyone else.

Much was discussed by lesser chiefs, but Crazy Horse eventually rose to his feet, cleared his throat, and addressed the gathering.

"*Mitakuye oyasin*, all my relations, I am grateful to everyone here with us in this camp. We are always seen as one by *Wakan Tanka*, the Great Mystery, and it is good that we can all be with each other tonight."

The light-haired Lakota was more eloquent than usual. He signed his words while he spoke; the long fringe on his painted shirt danced and swayed like an eagle's wings as it landed on its prey.

The Lakota leader's eyes flashed as he described the united force this camp had become with the arrival of Sitting Bull, and how they would now be able to meet the white soldiers on any field of battle and once again rule the day. They would not only defend their land from the greedy *Wasichu*, but they would also drive them off of it and live as freely as they ever had.

Little Wolf felt his blood stir as Crazy Horse spoke. The Lakota described his vision of a return to the old ways of traveling freely across their own land without fear of attack. It was enticing, even thrilling, and for a moment, the Cheyenne chief was taken back to his youth, when all the people's northern bands would travel south together across the Moon Shell River to join their southern relatives for great hunts and the sun dance. He sighed as a bittersweet ache reminded him that those days, and those times, were gone.

Crazy Horse finished with a flourish, inspiring those around him to cry out as they thumped their chests, shook rattles, and raised war clubs in support of his ambitious plans.

A respectful silence fell over the crowd as they waited for the next man to speak. They all knew it would be Sitting Bull, and they knew that he would also inspire them, perhaps sharing another vision that told of yet another great victory soon to be theirs. Their anticipation grew.

The Hunkpapa *wicasa wakan*, or medicine man, studied the ground in front of him for a moment then slowly stood, favoring an old wound. He received no help, but hands were ready if needed. Once erect, he carefully adjusted the blanket wrapped around his waist. He was a stocky man, but his legs were unusually short, and the blanket bunched at his feet. He adjusted it as best he could then raised his eyes. He had the attention of every man in the lodge.

"My friends, my relations, it is good to see you all here tonight," the somber-faced man began. "*Wakan Tanka* has been kind to make it so we can all come together again in this way. These times have been hard on all of us, and like my friend has said, it is good that we can be with each other. It reminds me how strong we can be when we are in one camp. It is always good when we can see each other and eat well together."

He paused for a moment then took a short stutter-step as if dancing to the throb of the distant drum. His change of stance proved to be more than just a physical one.

"When I was a boy, back when the old ones were still with us, we always came together like this. But times have changed, and those good gatherings have come to an end. That is the way of things. When each new moon comes, it tells us it is time for us to end certain things, to change our ways and do things differently to prepare for the times that are coming."

The Hunkpapa prophet raised his eagle fan toward the smoke hole.

"A new moon is above this lodge now, this moon of popping trees. We know when it comes that we should stay close to camp. Deep snows and a big cold can come quickly at this time. If we have food, and we do not need to fight, it is our way to unstring our bows during this time and go somewhere safe, where our enemies will not bother us. But this too has changed. Our enemy now comes to our safe places and fights us in the snow and cold."

Sitting Bull lowered his fan and studied the faces of the men around him as if he would never see them again. He handed the fan to a man on his right, who replaced it with a bow. The *wicasa wakan* held the curved piece of unadorned ash forward to the approving cheers of many around him.

"My friends, I told you when we left each other last summer that I would come back here to be with you again, and I have kept my promise. I know there are many here who want to go after these *Wasichu* and spill more of their blood on the ground, just as they have spilled much of ours. You know that I am not afraid of them, that I will not go to their agency, even when they come looking for a fight. But I have always only wanted to be left alone, and now is not the time for me to go looking for enemies to fight. So, I tell you now: I will not go with you to fight them. I will unstring my bow and go north across their medicine line, where they will not come after me and bother me anymore."

Surprised gasps and shouts followed as Sitting Bull quickly slipped the taut sinew bowstring off of the upper nock, and the bow straightened.

Little Wolf kept Crazy Horse in the corner of his eye throughout the tumult that followed. The slight Oglala sat stone-still, staring at the lodge fire with a set jaw, all while his advisors, He Dog and Little Hawk, appeared to be arguing with each other through his ears.

Sitting Bull traded the bow back for his fan and raised it once more, this time to quiet the crowd.

"Those who wish to come with me are welcome. *Tatanka*, the buffalo, are still many in the north. Hunting is good for all of us there. I will leave after two more sleeps to give everyone a chance to get ready and to say goodbye. That is what I have to say. *Mitakuye oyasin*."

# Escaping Rescue

Little Wolf reached for the breast strap that held the travois on the back of the buckskin mare then realized that Two Woman had already adjusted it. He looked behind the horse and beyond the travois to where his wives and daughters were helping each other shoulder their packs.

"*Nonotoveohtse!* Hurry up!" he urged.

Lightning shot him a scowl, but Little Wolf was already talking to Pawnee, who waited on horseback. She turned back to adjust Day Woman's pack and gave her some parting instructions.

"There, you are ready. Now you go with the others, and listen to what they say."

The girl nodded and left to join her sisters.

Wooden Thigh approached on horseback as *Eše'he* glared over his shoulders. Little Wolf had to shade his eyes as the young man addressed him.

"The herders took our horses north last night, and Starving Elk and Wild Hog are waiting for their sign. Morning Star and the others have already gone up along the river."

It was time to go. Lightning took the mare's lead rope from him before Little Wolf could turn to tell her to. He stepped back and looked everything over one last time before he mounted.

"*Nomonėhe'še.* All right, let us go ahead."

He turned his horse and started for the southern end of camp.

A day had passed since the Hunkpapa left for the north country. They left behind a camp both disheartened and divided. Little Wolf and the others had decided that they would leave as well, but they knew that Crazy Horse would not allow them to go as freely as he did the Hunkpapa.

The Lakota leader resented their presence in camp, but he would still oppose their leaving because he would lose more fighting men. He couldn't prevent Sitting Bull and his large camp from doing as they wished, but he would certainly try to stop the Cheyenne, who he easily outnumbered. The women had started packing under the cover of early-morning darkness, and everything was ready when *Eše'he* walked above the eastern hills.

The chief, with his wives and two sons, rode south through camp, moving slowly so everyone had a good chance to notice they were packed to leave. Their departure was noticed, and the clatter of hoofbeats racing off in different directions behind the lodges assured them that the news would spread quickly.

They had just moved beyond the lodges on the southern edge of camp when the sound of many riders hastily approaching rumbled behind them. Little Wolf looked over his shoulder to see the Akicita as they raced out of camp and separated to approach his party from opposite sides.

Wooden Thigh reached for his rifle.

"*Neve'nėheševe*. Stop doing that," Little Wolf advised his son as he turned to face their pursuers.

The riders approached slowly.

"I thought you were the Cheyenne's brave man." Crazy Horse appeared out of the crowd that had gathered. The Oglala chief rode forward with his rifle butt resting on his right leg, the muzzle pointed to the sky. Little Wolf knew what was coming. He opened his hands, slid off of his horse, and spoke to his sons in a calm voice.

"*Homevonehnėstse*. Get down from your horses."

Wooden Thigh and Pawnee both slipped to the ground, and Little Wolf took a step toward Crazy Horse.

"Friend, why is it that you stop us? We have only decided to leave, just the same as our friend Sitting Bull." The Cheyenne chief signed his words to be better understood.

"This is not the same. He told us in Council that he was going away. You sneak away like a coward."

Little Wolf heard Wooden Thigh take a couple steps forward. He turned and shook his head, stopping him.

"I am no coward," Little Wolf said. "You know that. I said nothing because I knew there would only be hard words between us."

"We have treated you well, given you many gifts since you have been with us. So, you just take them and leave? We are having hard times like everyone else. Do you think we have so much that we do not care if you take from us and leave?"

Little Wolf kept his eye on the rifle resting in the hand of the angry Lakota who continued to chastise him.

"You act like the white soldiers. You come and take all our things, then leave. The only thing is, you do it without any shooting." The angry man spoke to the semicircle of armed Lakota. "I say, for it to be done right, there must be shooting."

With that, he lowered the muzzle of his rifle and shot the appaloosa in the head. The animal fell in a heap behind Little Wolf, and the air exploded around them as the *Akicita* shot the rest of the group's horses, killing each where it stood.

Lightning and Two Woman clutched each other and screamed. Little Wolf and Wooden Thigh did their best to stand still, but both flinched instinctively as the loud barrage shook them. Pawnee grabbed his ears and dropped to a knee.

Despite the loud ringing in his ears, Little Wolf heard the echo roll through the hills on either side of the river. He turned to make sure his wives and sons were not injured. He then took a quick glance to see which rifles were still pointed at them and noticed Two Moons standing in the crowd behind Crazy Horse. His mouth was open and his face drained of blood. Ice had the same look on his face.

Crazy Horse returned the rifle to his thigh. A satisfied smirk now curled his lips.

"There! Now we have had shooting." The smug Lakota's voice sounded small and trivial following the thunderous explosions. "I can see your friends are waiting for you." He gave a nod behind the now horseless family to where a small group of men watched from the brush, upstream along the river. "Take your belongings and go to them. Tell them what a lucky man you are to have everything that we have given you. But tell them also that you can no longer come to us to stay in our lodges, to eat our food and take our horses, then leave while we are sleeping. No more!"

Little Wolf did not like being called a coward and a thief in front of his family, especially in such a public way, but he knew that he was doing the right thing by not defending himself. He gave a small nod to the others, which signaled them to begin stripping the horses of their gear and preparing the travois to be drawn by hand.

He turned back to Crazy Horse and raised his voice so everyone could hear him, and signed with broad gestures. "The Lakota people have been good to us, and we are grateful. We say *Nea'ěšemeno*, thank you all for all the kindness you showed us when we came to you in such a pitiful way."

Crazy Horse tilted his head as the Cheyenne chief continued his curious show of gratitude.

"We are going on our own way today, but only so that we will no longer hunt the same buffalo or burn your wood in our fires. You have given us much, and we know you would continue to be kind to us, but we must go now. We will come back when we can be as generous to you as you have been to us."

Wooden Thigh stepped behind his father and whispered. "Morning Star gives the sign. The others are safely away, and we are ready."

Without acknowledging his son, Little Wolf glanced quickly at the hills across the river, behind Crazy Horse on the north end of camp, where the last of a long line of Cheyenne were just disappearing over the ridge top. He raised both arms and addressed the crowd one last time.

"*Nea'ěšemeno, Nea'ěšemeno*. Thank you all, thank you all. You have been good friends. *Hena'haanehe*. That is all I have to say."

He turned to meet the suspicious eyes of the Oglala headman. Each man stared at the other for a moment before Little Wolf turned and walked to the travois near the body of the buckskin mare. He leaned and patted the neck of the bloodied animal, then picked up his end of a pole that Wooden Thigh had slid through the tethered point of the improvised drag. He leaned into the pole, and his son did the same.

Once they were beyond hearing distance of the crowd, Little Wolf addressed his son. "That mare was a good horse."

Wooden Thigh glanced over at his father to see how he was holding up under the strain of the load. "It was, but you were right. We could not have had strange horses, or he would not feel he had hurt us enough. It is too bad to lose that appaloosa, though. He is a fool to shoot a good horse like that."

The chief stared straight ahead and replied. "No, I liked that little mare better. It had a smooth ride and was well trained. That big horse was *etavahe*, dumb. I have no time to try to train a horse like that."

Wooden Thigh always marveled at how his father could go from a life or death matter to joking so quickly.

Morning Star's oldest son, Hump, waited near the thickets along the river with a bay horse. The travois was quickly loaded on the animal, and they stepped into the brush, moving straight for the river where Morning Star and a few others waited.

"It happened just as you said it would," the old chief greeted his friend. "Everyone was watching you and Crazy Horse, and no one looked back to see Wild Hog and Starving Elk take the others into the hills. They have all gone over the ridge now and are on their way to where the herders will have our horses waiting."

"*Noxa'e, noxa'e!* Wait, wait!" Day Woman laughed as she ran to keep up with White Voice, who was determined to be the first to climb the timbered hillside south of the new camp to gather firewood.

Lightning helped Two Woman pull a stand of willow over with a rope to make a temporary shelter for the night. She paused to watch her youngest daughter running after her older sister.

"It was good that she went with the others when we left," Lightning said. "She would have been so afraid when the horses were shot."

Little Wolf watched from the back of a rangy black horse that Hump had given him. He gave an absentminded nod as the girls darted around in the shadow of the trees. He puzzled at how children could recover so quickly after such difficult times and find their spirit again.

"I think the bad spirits have left her. She runs like a little girl again," he replied.

Two Woman groaned as she finished tying the rope to the base of a willow then stood up. "Unnh, I don't see how anyone can still run after a day like this one. I will sleep hard tonight."

After the people had crossed over the wide ridge west of Tongue River, they descended into a draw that emptied into the valley of the Little Sheep River. They were a day's ride south of where the big fight had been the summer before. The steep canyon was a difficult passage and a path they normally would not have taken, but it was the most direct route away from the Lakota camp. They knew Crazy Horse might easily decide to come after them.

A few older boys had climbed up the hill under the guise of guarding the girls who were gathering wood. Little Wolf tried to remember which boy Day Woman had said had been coming around looking for White Voice. *Was it Looking Back?* It didn't take him long to spot the youth standing by a rock outcropping near the top of the hill. The boy's eyes tracked White Voice closely as she casually made her way up the hill toward him.

The chief smiled as he turned the champing black horse to leave. *The soldiers may try to kill us all, but I think there will always be Cheyenne in this world.*

"I am going to find Morning Star and will be back before dark," he told his wives.

He passed Chopping Woman on her way back from picketing the bay horse, another gift from Hump.

"Now, you cannot have my grandchild until I get back here," he teased.

The very round and tired young woman puffed back. "You should not stay away for too long then."

Little Wolf smiled and started across camp. He had not gone far when a cry came from the wood gatherers.

"*Tàhoohto'àheotse! Enèxhooheama'haso'hestove!* Run home! Riders are coming."

The chief twisted in the saddle and searched the hillside to see where the cry had come from. Looking Back was pointing toward the last high ridge they had crossed before descending to where they were now camped. The tall lances and single file formation told Little Wolf immediately that the riders were not soldiers. *Crazy Horse must have changed his mind when he found out everyone had left. Does he come here to tell us to return? Or maybe to fight us?*

He urged the fidgety black horse up the bare hill behind him to get a better view. The approaching party had sent out a single rider, who raced to a point in front of them and started spinning his horse around in one spot. After several turns, the man stopped and dismounted.

"*Enėhevoone, "Namȧhehevesenehe'tovȧhtseme.* They say they are friends," Little Wolf shouted down to the others as he raised his right hand with his first two fingers extended together, up and away from his face.

The riders continued down the ridge. Little Wolf guessed that about eight or nine lodges traveled with the procession. As it drew closer, he recognized the two men who rode at the front.

It was Two Moons and Ice.

# Each Their Own Way

*HAA'HAVĖHANE*, WIND, HAD SCOURED THE NORTH-FACING SLOPES above Rotten Grass Creek, and *Ešė'he* had warmed the southern exposures. Between them, only twisted snakes of crusted snow remained in their protected, shady swales.

The exposed foothills held good grass, and there were many streams, most of which were frozen. A few were fed by warm springs, which made for open—though bad-tasting—watering holes. Willows, in quantities plentiful enough for both lodges and fuel, graced the bends of all the surrounding creeks.

This was a good place, far enough removed from the white man's forts to lessen the chance of being attacked. However, it meant the Cheyenne were closer to the lands of their enemies, the Crow and the Snakes, but neither of them had wagon guns, nor did they often attack in winter. The people could rest here. They were close enough to the mountains to gather good lodge poles and would be able to hunt the elk and mountain sheep that fed on the exposed slopes.

Halfway up the hillside, Little Wolf raised his pipe to his mouth and began his predawn ritual of prayer. The new Sacred Hat Lodge glowed brightly in the center of the camp below him. It was midwinter, and the strong light of the nearly full Hoop Moon illuminated the lodge. The newly sewn white hide cover was painted with a small, blue, double cross at each of the four sacred directions. The symbol represented the protective spiritual power of the dragonfly.

The fire inside the lodge combined with the moonlight gave the tall lodge a radiant appearance. Some had said that, with the addition of Black Moccasin, the fourth Old Man Chief, along with Ice and Two Moons, nearly the entire Northern Cheyenne tribe now encircled the sacred lodge, and the medicine of *Esevone* was stronger than usual. The ethereal scene below him made it difficult for Little Wolf to doubt the claim.

The door of the sacred lodge lifted, and Coal Bear emerged. The Keeper faced east and briefly prayed before he turned and walked reverently around the shelter, pausing to pray and tap each lodgepole with his staff as he gently woke the Hat to the new day. While the Keeper performed his morning ritual, Little Wolf puffed slowly on his pipe and reflected back to the day that Two Moons and his band had joined them, making the camp whole again.

"You put yourself in a bad place for our people," the Kit Fox headman explained the night he arrived. "I saw that you were not afraid as they surrounded you, and that your sons and wives stood beside you. At first, I thought you were all very foolish to bring this kind of treatment on yourselves. But when I went back to my lodge and saw that everyone else had also left, I realized what a brave thing you had done. I was embarrassed that I was staying there only for my own protection. So, I decided I should come here and be with you. I cannot think of only myself when our people are in such need."

The peaceful scene in the camp cheered the Sweet Medicine Chief. Coal Bear tapped the last pole just as *Eše'he* peeked over the horizon. After a short prayer of welcome, he turned and reentered the lodge. Little Wolf was content to stay on the hill a bit longer before he descended to help his people through another day.

A pair of hunting parties had gone out, and no Council was planned for the day. In years past, when the Cheyenne camped here, he would have been busy planning a war party to head west against the Crow or Snakes as soon as the grass was green and the horses were strong. He knew there would be none of that this spring.

He eventually descended to the black horse that was picketed at the bottom of the slope. It shied a bit as he approached.

"Maybe I will work with you today, my friend. You are a bit young to be asked to do too much, but much is asked of all our young these days."

He turned the horse so he could mount it from the high side of the hill. He lifted his new, unadorned pipe bag out of the way, slid his leg over its back, and coaxed his wide-eyed mount to turn and start toward his lodge.

Later that morning, the chief stood in a clearing along the creek south of camp. He was talking softly to the black horse while Pawnee approached them with a blanket that flapped in the steady breeze. "*He'kotomȧhtse, nėsema'haahe*. Be quiet, my friend." He held the animal's lead rope and tugged gently on its ear to try to keep its attention on him. Still, the young horse flared its nostrils and fixed its eyes on the approaching blanket. Little Wolf stepped slowly between the horse and the blanket to reassure the animal.

Gathering His Medicine made a sudden appearance, racing out from behind a nearby plum thicket. Father and son turned their heads toward him, and the young horse reared and lunged away from the surprise visitor, jerking Little Wolf off his feet.

A sharp, stabbing pain stung his right shoulder when he landed, and he lost his grip on the lead rope. The rest of his wounds all bit at him as he rolled on the ground. He came to a stop on his belly and immediately grabbed for the rope that lay nearby. The horse reared again, yanking the rope away then galloping up the creek. Pawnee dropped the blanket and raced after the frightened animal. Little Wolf rose to his knees and brushed the dirt from his clothes with his left arm. He held his throbbing right one close to his chest and turned to scold their surprise visitor.

"*Shaa!* Why did you come running up on us like that? You should know better."

The embarrassed boy lowered his head. He had been given an important task, and he had only caused trouble.

"I'm sorry; I should have looked around. But . . . but, Morning Star sent me to find you. A *ve'ho'e*, a white man, has come into the camp and waits at the Sacred Hat Lodge. He carries a message from the soldier chief at Elk River."

Little Wolf stopped mid-brush and placed his good hand on the youth's shoulder. "Go help Pawnee catch that horse. Have him take it back to my lodge, then come find me."

Eager to make amends for his disruption, Gathering His Medicine nodded and ran up the creek without a word. Little Wolf turned and limped toward the center of camp, brushing himself off as he lumbered along. People hurried past him in the same direction, no doubt having heard the same surprising news.

He approached the Sacred Hat Lodge and pushed his way through the crowd that had gathered. He was polite at first but was soon shouting for people to move so he could get through. "*No'hovehne.* Move out of the way." His right arm was useless for shoving, but when people saw who tugged on their shoulder, they stepped aside. Little Wolf emerged from the crowd of onlookers to find Starving Elk standing by the door of the lodge.

"They are waiting for you," his friend said.

"Why are they inside?" the chief asked.

"Coal Bear would not shake the man's hand when he first arrived, so he just ran past him and jumped inside."

Little Wolf glanced at the blue dragonfly symbol painted above the door. Every Cheyenne knew that no one could harm a man under the protective power of the lodge. Someone must have told the man this beforehand.

He pushed the door aside and stepped inside. The slender face of Wool Woman, sitting on the robes to his right, immediately caught his attention. She was the only female in the lodge and one of the women who had been recently captured by the soldiers. Next to her sat a young man he did not recognize, though he was clearly a mixed-blood with his honey-colored skin, short hair, and thin, dark mustache.

The chief moved around the lodge behind the others on his left to take his place beside Coal Bear. He greeted Morning Star, Old Bear, Black Moccasin, and each of the other headmen in attendance with a quick nod. Coal Bear cleared his throat and filled the chief in on what had been discussed to that point.

"This man is called Big Leggings. He was in Sitting Bull's camp last winter but now works for the soldier chief at the new fort on Tongue River. He just told us that Carries the Drum and the other Lakota peace talkers who went there were not supposed to be killed." The Hat Keeper turned back to the visitor and gestured toward the other headmen gathered in the lodge. "*Tse'tohe mȧhavoo'ešenano tseevėhetȯhoneto.* Show all of them what you are signing."

The breed resumed telling his story, his hands skillfully carving the air as the Cheyenne leaders looked on.

"Those Crow who shot Carries the Drum and the others were punished. They were bad Indians who did not listen to what they were told. Bear Coat shamed them and threw them away. He did not want anyone to be killed. He is sorry that these good men died, and he wants you to know that it will not happen again. He sends you many gifts to show you that he wants to be your friend and will not fight you if you come to see him." He motioned toward Wool Woman. "This woman will tell you that I speak the truth."

Wool Woman watched the man's signs, nodding as he made his points, then spoke when he referred to her.

"*Ehetometo.* It is true. This man, Zhon Brew Yer, speaks with a straight tongue." She did her best to pronounce the breed's white man name, John Brugier. "We have been treated well at the soldier fort. Their headman, Bear Coat, has told me that he wants to be your friend. He does not want to fight with you anymore and has sent you many gifts. We left many loaded wagons a little ways from here."

Clearly, she was the one who had told the man to jump past Coal Bear and claim safe refuge in the lodge. Little Wolf held his questions and allowed others to ask theirs first. Morning Star cleared his throat, indicating he wished to speak. He spoke Cheyenne and used sign talk so the visitor understood.

"It is good to hear friendly talk from the soldier-chief, Bear Coat. Messengers from Red Cloud's agency have also come to us, when we camped with Crazy Horse. They told us that the soldier chief there, the one called Three Stars, has said he is also not angry with us, and he promises no harm will come to anyone, even those who fought against them, if we go there. What does this Bear Coat say he will do with the ones who fought against the soldiers this summer?"

Big Leggings nodded that he understood and answered quickly. "Bear Coat said that if you come to him, you will belong to his Great Father, so he can make you no promises about what will be done with anyone who was his Great Father's enemy. But he said that if they come in and do not cause trouble, he will tell his Great Father that they are now his friend and that he thinks no harm should come to them."

Morning Star pressed the young man, continuing to use what little leverage he had. "Three Stars wants us to give him our horses and guns. What does this Bear Coat say about these things?"

"Anyone who comes to Bear Coat will be his friend. You will only have to give up your old horses and old guns. He does not want you to have many, but you can keep your good ones."

The leaders exchanged contented glances at the prospect of being able to keep these valuable belongings.

The breed kept signing. "He wants you to know that if you go in to Red Cloud's agency, Three Stars will not keep his promises, and you will not be treated well. It will be better for you if you come in to the fort on Elk River."

Little Wolf looked at the Morning Star and the others. It was surprising to hear one soldier-chief talk against another like that. He had not heard such a thing before.

The headmen began to discuss the competing offers among themselves.

"We must smoke on this!" Coal Bear spoke above the tangle of voices. "Let us have this man smoke with us before we trust his words."

The Hat Keeper produced his pipe, and the process to hold the messenger accountable began.

Big Leggings took four draws on the pipe and, by doing so, gave his solemn promise that his words were true. After being passed to the others, the spent pipe was handed back to Coal Bear. The young priest leaned forward and tapped the ashes onto the messenger's muddy moccasin, then explained why.

"Eight winters ago, a white soldier attacked and killed many of our people who were camped at a river called Washita in the far south. After some time, this same soldier returned and wanted to make peace with the Cheyenne. He smoked the pipe of peace with Stone Forehead, who was the Arrows Keeper then. He promised that he would never attack our people again, and Stone Forehead bound his promise with the ashes of the pipe they had smoked. Just as I have done with you. Stone Forehead told this man that he must keep his word, or he would die because of his lie. The Cheyenne called this soldier Long Hair, and it turned out that he had no ears for Stone Forehead's warning. He attacked our camp again, this last summer, only a day's ride downstream of where we now sit."

Coal Bear knew he needn't finish the story. Instead, he watched for the man's reaction. Big Leggings nodded, thought a moment, then signed his reply, along with a couple of Cheyenne words that Wool Woman had taught him.

"I have ears to hear these words. I know that I only carry Bear Coat's promise to you, but it is the same as if I give it to you myself. Still, I say that my words are *hetomestòtse*, the truth. I speak to the Arrows on this, and I speak to the Hat. I speak *hetomestòtse* to my good friends, *Tsitsistas*, the Cheyenne people."

The man's resolute pledge brought a sense of relief to Little Wolf's heart. *Maybe now my people will listen*, he thought. *Maybe now they will understand.* The Sweet Medicine Chief turned to his friends.

"We must call a full Council and decide what shall be done. We have had a hard year of fighting, and our families are suffering. We must decide now how we will take care of them."

A large crowd gathered around the fire in the center of camp. Only those too sick or feeble to attend stayed at home. The councilmen took their usual places sitting closest to the fire, and the society men stood closely behind in the second ring. Behind them sat elders who were generally not involved directly in politics or the decision-making process but were now eager to hear how things would be decided. Everyone else crowded in behind them. Mothers with young children stood at the edge of the crowd, jostling their babies and pinching their noses to keep them quiet. No one wanted to miss what the visitor had to say or miss out on their share of the gifts that he brought for them.

Big Leggings stood near the fire in the center of the crowd. He signed his story again, explaining Bear Coat's invitation to come to the post on Elk River. Wool Woman interpreted the breed's signs so that all who were unable to see past the ring of society men might hear the proposition. When the man finally rubbed his palms together, signaling that he had said all he had come to tell them, Little Wolf stood to address the tribe. He was unsure how what he was about to say would be received by many of those around him. His stomach turned a little as he raised his hand to gain everyone's attention.

"My friends, this man called Big Leggings carries the promise of a better way for us. I know there are some here who will hear only a demand for surrender in what he tells us. They will say it is a demand that we surrender our honor and give up our land, but I say, look at us. Look at us!"

The chief called for the attention of the men in the first two rows around him. "Brave men, look past the circle that you sit in today. Look out into the larger circle of those around you. These may sound like words of surrender to you, but to these people gathered around you, these are words of hope.

"We have all fought for land, horses, and honor, but what good are these things if those around us are starving and weak? If we have no one left to share them with? Look at our people here."

The chief's tone was stern as he motioned for Wild Hog and a few others to step aside so everyone could see the old ones and the wounded gathered behind them.

"They are sick and hurting. What honor is theirs now when you fight only to save your own? Look how they are living." The chief pointed to the first row of branch shelters behind them. "These are not homes; they are war lodges. You no longer ride off to war. The war road now leads to the pitiful doors that your women and children sleep behind.

"Look where we are. Can you not see that we camp here on the edge of the lands of our enemies, the Snakes and the Crow? In the past, we have come here to plan our raids against them. Today we are here hoping they don't attack us, while we watch behind us for the white soldiers. We cannot fight any of these enemies like we once could.

"My friends, it is time for us all to go in to the agency. Either to the Elk River fort, where our friend here has invited us to go to, or to Red Cloud's agency, to live with the Lakota as we have been promised by the white man's treaty.

"Look around you. The only thing we have to decide today is how our weak ones will leave this place: by the white man's promise, or by his bullets."

Without warning, Last Bull again pushed his way past those in the front row and spoke just as boldly as he did in the mountains before the attack. "Either choice you speak of means that we are defeated. If I am to be defeated, then I will die in the fight. I will never live as a defeated man. I will not go in."

It surprised Little Wolf to see the angry gleam still flashing in the big man's eyes. The deposed Kit Fox headman had been relatively quiet since he had been ousted. His stubborn way was better understood when he was joined in the circle by a smaller, more sinister, figure.

"I hear Last Bull's words, and my heart is the same as his." Black Coyote stepped beside the larger man, making his first foray into a tribal debate. "I am a free man. I will not let the soldiers, or any man here, decide how I will leave this place. I am afraid of no one, and I will stay out and live as a free man, the way I have lived all of my life. Any who wish to do the same can join with us. We will not go in."

Whetstone and Vanishing Wolf each gave a hearty "*Hau!*" from behind the two and were echoed by a few others, all young men from the northern bands.

Morning Star rose to stand beside Little Wolf and spoke to the small faction that had just formed. "Then you should do what pleases you. I say, let each man make the choice for himself about what he will do now. If you wish, stay out by yourselves—but remember, when you do fight and die, things will go hard on your women and children. They will be out here without any relatives around to take them in.

"I am taking my family to a safer place. I think that this is the right thing to do. They will not have to worry anymore about being hungry or being attacked. How is it that we would be defeated if our women and children are warm and happy and have full bellies? A nation is not defeated until the hearts of its women are on the ground. Then it is finished, no matter how brave its warriors or how strong their weapons."

Little Wolf smiled at Morning Star's ability to say in a few eloquent words what he had tried to express ever since returning from their long trip, three winters ago. The young men had been challenged by the old chief's words, but still remained free to do as they saw fit.

"It is decided then." Standing Elk rose and stood beside the two Old Man Chiefs. "Every man will choose for himself how he will go from here. Each will go his own way. For myself, I will take my family, and we will go to Red Cloud's Agency on White River."

# Too Poor to Tell

Little Wolf curled the front leg of the black horse to inspect its hoof. He held a small stub of pine branch in his teeth as he patted the shoulder of the uneasy animal with his free hand.

"*Shaa!* You should be used to this by now. Stop moving, my friend."

The horse continued its three-legged dance while Little Wolf grabbed the stick from his mouth and scraped the packed mud from the hollow of its hoof.

The chief dropped the cleaned hoof and moved around the front of the horse to check the other side. Wild Hog was tending to his own animal, as were several others in their group. The trail down into Soldier Creek would be slippery.

This ritual of stopping to clean their horses' hooves had been repeated many times since they left Rotten Grass creek a moon ago. The weather had warmed, and the ground was thawing. It's surface was now a slimy, sticky gumbo, which slowed their progress and made each hillside a dangerous undertaking. They typically would not be traveling at this time of year, but they could not wait for the soldiers to decide to come looking for them again. They had to strike out for their own safety.

Little Wolf reviewed the caravan of about forty people and sixty or so horses. They would not be making any grand entry to the agency, which waited at the other end of this creek, but he was glad that they were almost there. The end to their troublesome journey was near.

Turning back to Wild Hog, he dropped the stick on the ground and sighed. "I think that when we get to the agency, I will have the iron shoes put on this horse. Then I will not have to worry about him slipping all the time."

Wild Hog smiled. "Then you should wear the white man's shoes on your own feet too. That way you can both walk the new road together."

Little Wolf considered the feeling of pushing his feet into the hard leather clutches of an army boot. He reached down and retrieved the stick he had just dropped.

"Maybe I will keep this a little while longer."

The black horse gave a soft nicker.

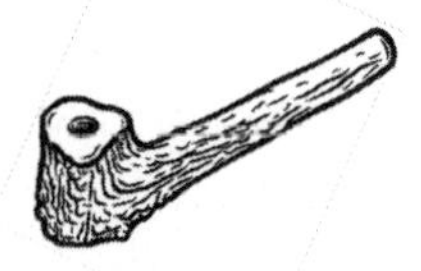

The late February afternoon was warmer than usual, which suited me just fine. I was on my way to another sign talk lesson with Lieutenant Clark at Camp Robinson. The lessons were not as frequent of late, as Clark had found others to practice with. He had picked the language up faster than anyone I had ever seen. What once had been a daily event out on the campaign now happened once a week at best, and it had become more of a visit than an actual lesson. I planned on telling Clark that today would be the last day I'd accept any pay for our talks.

Ulysses dropped his head and sniffed the large frozen clumps of earth on the edge of the gritty pathway of dirt thrown across the frozen White River. He was not at all convinced that it would be safe to step onto this strange surface with his freshly shod hooves.

"C'mon, now. Git-up. We need to be getting there before sundown." I pressed my knees against the horse's ribs.

Ulysses responded by tentatively placing one hoof, then another, and another, on the path, until he had gingerly walked across the narrow stretch of ice and started into a confident trot on the other side.

I could see a company of mounted cavalrymen assembled on the parade ground in the middle of the cluster of buildings on the flat above me. I heard the order "Dismissed" float through the air as the tired-looking group of horsemen broke ranks. A few of them dismounted, but most simply turned and rode between the cavalry barracks and the adjutant's office on the west side of the half-acre parade ground, on their way to the stables and corrals down by Soldier Creek.

By the time I reached the parade ground, it was empty. I rode north through the four-acre rectangle of grass with officer's row on my right. These six small adobe buildings were set apart from the other buildings by more than the width of the parade ground. Each officer's residence was made of adobe instead of the pine logs used for the rest of the buildings. Each was also neatly skirted by a white picket fence, giving them a real hoity-toity look. Lieutenant Clark's quarters were at the north end.

Each end of the parade ground was framed by a log infantry barracks, and four buildings lined the west side: the cavalry barracks, the adjutant's office, the guardhouse, and the commissary storehouse. This last building was having an addition put on its north end, part of a rush of construction that began after the Custer fight. The stables and corrals and several smaller buildings, including a bakery and a grain house, stood just west of the confluence of Soldier Creek and White River. The post sawmill stood across White River from the other structures and, with plans for several more buildings to be built, seemed to constantly be putting out new lumber. The place couldn't seem to stop growing.

It had been two months now since the expedition ended, and our spat over my not wanting to leave the column with Billy had been forgotten when the lieutenant arrived at Camp Robinson a few weeks back.

"No call to fret about that, Bill," he told me. "Things happen out on campaigns that don't happen anywhere else. One learns to not let it affect them afterward. You just get past it."

"You're right about that," I agreed. "That was for sure a heat of the moment deal."

We agreed to let bygones be bygones and shook hands. I knew, though, that there were still some things that happened out on that ride that would stay with me the rest of my days.

As I figured he had, Billy holed up with an uncle for a couple days before coming in to the post. He continued to crow about how he planned and organized the whole affair up in the Bighorns, but he stayed pretty quiet around me and kept his distance.

The lieutenant was waiting for me on his porch. I wrapped Ulysses's reins around the hitching post in front of his quarters and struggled with the latch on the gate.

"Goddammit! Begging your pardon, sir. I never been much for gates and such." I stopped and drew a circle around the entire camp with my finger. "Y'know, there used to be a cordwood barricade round this whole damn place a year or so ago. Things would be a lot easier round here if they had just left that up instead of putting all this fancy foofaraw in the way of a man who's trying to get somewhere."

Clark laughed as I finally gave up and stepped over the fence. "I feel the same way, Bill. These picket fences won't help much if we ever came under attack, although they do seem to slow you down."

I smiled and stepped up onto the porch. I extended my arms, palms facing each other, and pulled them back toward me a few times in quick succession, asking Clark to take pity on me.

Clark placed both his forefingers pointing up in front of his chest and pushed them out toward me. He dropped both, then swept his right hand, palm down, out in front of him, rolling it to the right and to a palm-up position, telling me that there would be no pity coming from him.

He did invite me to sit, though. "Let's visit on the porch this time, Bill. This sunshine feels quite nice today."

"Suits me just fine, sir."

"So, this barricade . . ." Clark paused to think of the sign for barricade. He started to make the sign for corral, but I waved it away and chopped the back of my left hand twice with my right, for chopped wood, then extended my arms wide to each side, before bringing my hands together to create a circle with my thumbs and forefingers, the sign for surround.

"Chopped wood surround." Clark repeated the words as he copied the signs, then finished his question, signing as he spoke. "I assume it was built as a temporary bulwark while the northern bands were threatening to cause problems here?"

"Yep, though things have changed a fair bit since back in them days. I recall when they wouldn't even let Doc Saville raise a flagpole over at the agency there. Said it was too much like he was raising his own sun dance medicine pole here in the middle of their land. It got real ugly there for a while. A Lakota, name of Carries the Drum—the fella we just heard got killed by them Crow scouts up there at the Tongue River Cantonment—he showed up with a bunch of his kin and ran them northern bands off, but it sure left a bad taste in their mouth."

"Caused a lot of dissension between the bands, I'll wager?"

"Sure did, but remember, there has never been just 'one way' with these tribes. Depending on which band or military society they belong to, they'll argue with each other about most anything. But they have a way of eventually getting it all worked out."

"I've noticed that tendency they have to fight among themselves, Bill. In fact, I'm trying to implement measures to take advantage of it."

"How's that?"

"Well, I've chosen a few Lakota men and sent them out as envoys to try to persuade anyone with the northern bands who might be having second thoughts about coming in. There's sure to be more of them who are inclined to do so, especially after word of our fight with the Cheyenne has gotten around. They're to meet with the headmen first, but if they have no luck there, I told them to try to help as many of the others as they can to slip away and come in. It seems to be having some effect. We've seen small groups of two or three lodges starting to trickle in lately."

I saw the sense in his plan, but it still bothered me. I reached for my pipe to buy some time and gather my thoughts.

Clark noticed I was stalling and became curious. "You seem troubled," he said.

I tamped my pipe, lit it, and exhaled a long cloud of smoke.

"What's on your mind?" Clark signed the words, pressing me for an answer.

"Well, here's the thing." I pointed with my pipe, like some invisible object had just appeared between us. "What you sent them fellas out to do is pretty risky business. It's one thing to invite the headmen to come in and talk; that's how things are usually done. But when you ask other people to go in and get folks to sneak themselves outta there, well, people can get killed, and pretty damned quick too."

Clark seemed unfazed by the warning. "I understand it has its risks, but if my emissaries can take advantage of any cracks in their alliances whatsoever—"

"I know how spies work, sir," I cut him off. "Standing Bear helped General Crook find them Cheyenne up in the Bighorns just fine. And he and the rest of us didn't like going up there with you, but we did, and I tell ya, we'll likely have hell to pay next time we meet up with those folks if we meet again. But these Lakota, they run by a whole different set of rules."

"What do you mcan?"

"Well, the Cheyenne tell of how Sweet Medicine instructed them that it ain't allowable for any of them to kill another Cheyenne, but the Lakota don't worry themselves too much about killing one of their own if he's standing in the way a something they want bad enough."

"Like power?"

"Specially that. How do you think old Red Cloud got hisself to a place where the US government had to parlay with him and give him his own agency?"

"Who did he kill?"

I caught sight of a plume of dust behind the lieutenant and up the creek a ways. A lone cavalryman appeared, galloping down Soldier Creek toward us as I answered.

"Man name a Bull Bear. It was before my time in these parts, but a whole lot of other Lakota have done the same since. If a Cheyenne killed one of their own, they'd get run off by the whole tribe. Tradition says they'd have to stay four rivers away for at least four years and have all their belongings taken or broke apart. All the Lakota need to do is keep an eye out for some pissed off relative coming to get even with 'em."

"So, what's your concern with all this, Bill?"

The rider was getting closer to camp and still riding hard.

"Well, the Lakota got enough blood feuds going on already, sir. If you start working them one against the other like this, it's liable to all blow up in your face. Things could get real ugly real fast if you ain't careful. Now, what's this about here?" I lifted my chin toward the oncoming rider.

Clark finally heard the hammering of hooves and turned to watch as the rider entered the compound.

"Indians coming in, sir!" The soldier reined his horse to a stop in front of the lieutenant's gate and fired off a salute. "Bout forty head or so, sir. They're coming down the west fork of the creek up there."

"Sioux or Cheyenne, Sergeant?" Clark rose to his feet and reached for his gun belt.

"Don't know, sir. They all look the same to me. I have a Lakota scout keeping an eye on them until we send troops."

"All right, then. Go inform Major Mason, then get down to the agency and round up Billy Garnett. Tell him to get up here on the jump if he knows what's good for him."

"Yes, sir." The soldier's horse was moving down officers' row before he finished his short reply.

"Bill, head across to the cavalry barracks and tell Lieutenant Cummings to have his men saddle back up. Tell him we need to take a short ride up the creek."

I had already tapped the ashes from my pipe and jammed it in my pocket. When I reached the gate, I put my hand atop the latch-post and just hopped over, then reached for Ulysses's reins.

Within twenty minutes we were riding up Soldier Creek at the head of the remounted cavalry unit. After a couple miles, a pair of riders came galloping up the creek behind us. Billy Garnett reined his winded horses to a trot on the other side of the lieutenant.

"Got here fast as possible, sir," Billy reported as he and his mount settled into the slower pace. "Heard there was a good-sized bunch coming in. Any idea who we might have?"

Clark shook his head. "Not at this point. We have a scout out ahead of us who should be returning soon."

At that, a uniformed Lakota topped a rise in front of us, riding quickly in our direction.

I was still not used to the sight of an Indian in a soldier's uniform and puzzled at the odd appearance of the man's braids bouncing off of the collar of his fatigue blouse as he galloped along. The wide-eyed scout reined to a hard stop in front of us. Clark saluted him then addressed him in both English and sign language.

"Private Woman's Dress, what is your report? Are these Indians looking for a fight? Are they Sioux or Cheyenne?"

"You will not have to fight these Indians. They are too poor to fight anyone. I rode here to tell you they are not far away. You will see them before you come to where this creek splits apart."

Clark repeated the last part of his question to the scout. "Sioux or Cheyenne?"

Woman's Dress paused, his mouth opening a bit as he tried to find the white man's words. "They are very pitiful, too poor to tell."

"What does he mean by that, too poor to tell?" Clark asked us.

"Don't know, sir." Billy shrugged.

We moved up the creek to where the west fork of Soldier Creek emptied itself into the main branch. It didn't take long before we spotted the small band about a half-mile ahead, moving slowly out of the west fork into the main branch. They stayed close to the hills on the west side in case they need to run.

The words *too poor to tell* made sense as soon as we laid eyes on them. They had no trappings of any kind, no colors displayed or regalia worn that would indicate their tribal affiliation. In fact, many had no blanket or robe at all, and those that did had only green, untanned hides resting stiffly on their shoulders.

A few of the horses pulled a small travois, which told me that these people had next to nothing in the way of camp supplies or other belongings. It finally hit me.

"I think this might be the first bunch of Cheyenne from the fight in the mountains to come in."

Lieutenant Clark leaned forward to study the destitute group, which had stopped, still about a half-mile across the creek from us. "I think you're right. They lost pretty much everything they had up there."

A large man rode forward from the group with his arm raised. In it he carried what might have been the only blanket they had. He dismounted on a small rise and waved his extended right hand over his head before using the blanket to make signs to the soldiers.

Clark turned toward me. "What's that about, Bill? I'm not versed on signals of that sort."

"It's called wolf sign. He's asking for us to come down there and parlay with him, sir—leaving the soldiers here, of course."

Clark urged his horse forward, speaking over his shoulder as he moved. "Lieutenant Cummings, stand at the ready. Garnett, you're with Bill and me."

We separated ourselves from the rest of the command, riding at a walk toward the tree-lined creek bottom. A second man joined the large Indian, and they both rode down the slope toward a small meadow where the creek made a sweeping bend.

We rode cautiously into the creek bottom, peering ahead through the leafless but densely clustered branches of the ash trees to see if the two Indians had already entered the clearing. They hadn't, so we waited at the meadow's edge until we saw glimpses of them and their horses as they came through the trees on the other side.

The large man entered the clearing first, and despite his gaunt appearance, I recognized Wild Hog right away.

"Cheyenne, sir. His name's Wild Hog. He's a friendly, a good man, but a handful if you piss him off."

Wild Hog recognized me and gave a slow nod as he waited for the second man to arrive. The skittish black horse the man rode danced sideways as he left the cover of the trees, giving me a good straight-on look at Little Wolf as he reined the horse in.

"And him?" Clark asked.

My mouth seemed stuck open, making it impossible for me to form words. The best I could do was turn and stare at the lieutenant and the blood-drained face of the young scout beside him.

# Red Cloud Reunion

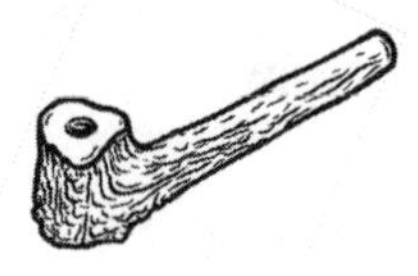

WILD HOG SLIPPED A THREADBARE AND STAINED FOUR-POINT trade blanket off the hindquarters of his horse. He spread it on the ground between us and gave it a hard flick to lay the far corner flat, then stepped back, inviting us to sit.

Lieutenant Clark's eyes shifted from the large warrior to me and back again. I stepped onto the worn wool and sat cross-legged on the left corner. Billy took the right, and Clark, following our lead, took the middle, status position.

Wild Hog sat in front of me. The big man took up a quarter of the blanket by himself. Little Wolf filled the other corner, leaning to his left while keeping his right leg stretched toward the center of the blanket. He looked pretty stiff and stove up.

An uneasy silence sat between us for a spell.

Clark tossed me a few nervous glances, like he was waiting for some sort of cue. I gave him a nod, and the officer cleared his throat.

"My name is Lieutenant William Clark, with the 2nd Cavalry of the United States Army, and I accept your surrender."

We had agreed that I would handle the initial translation to avoid risking any error, but I kept my hands still at my chest and said nothing. When his words weren't translated, Clark looked over at me.

"What, Bill?"

"Sir, we don't know if that's what they're here for yet. They ain't said."

"Oh." Clark turned back to the Cheyenne headmen.

"Just your regular pleasantries would be a good start, sir. Welcome and such."

A crimson flush climbed up Clark's neck as he launched into his best cordial greeting. "Welcome, Little Wolf and Wild Hog. It is good to sit with you and talk today. I am Lieutenant William Clark, with the 2nd Cavalry of the United States Army. I am called White Hat by your friends, both Cheyenne and Sioux. I know that you are both important men of the Cheyenne, and it is my honor to meet with you."

Clark watched as I went through the translation, nodding his head as he recognized the signs. I'd barely finished the last words before he resumed his opening comments.

"We have not met each other before, but I was at the big fight in the mountains three moons ago. I hope that today we can end the fighting, and that we can now speak of being friends."

I made the translation and watched the shoulders of both Cheyenne men lower when they heard the young soldier chief's words of peace.

Little Wolf cleared his throat. "I think it is a good thing that we talk before any fighting. It is what I tried to do that morning you found our camp in the mountains. I think if we had talked then, we would not have had the big fight and we could have smoked together instead."

Clark nodded as the chief spoke and signed, then he turned to listen to me to make sure he understood it right. Little Wolf continued when the lieutenant turned back toward him.

"I think if you have any fire makers, it would be good that we smoke now, so we will all have good hearts, and only good words will be spoken between us here."

Clark nodded again and looked at me. I figured he understood what Little Wolf said and was already reaching into my coat pocket. I gave my fixings to Wild Hog, who had already pulled his pipe from its bag.

It took no time for him to fill, tamp, and hand it to Little Wolf, who lit it and offered its first smoke to the four directions, the sky, and the earth.

I noticed how thin my friend was as he raised his arms to make the offering and how stiffly he moved. He leaned forward with some effort and handed the pipe to Clark, and I noticed the still-healing wound high on his right leg. I wanted to ask a thousand questions, but now was not the time. The lieutenant's questions would come first.

Once the pipe was spent, Wild Hog carefully returned it to its sheath. He gathered the tobacco and lucifers and started to hand them back to me. I looked him in the eye and nodded to let him know they were his now. The big man, who had always looked to me like he grew up nursing on a garden spade, nodded and gave me a smile that put his whole face to work.

The lieutenant resumed the conversation. "I know your people are waiting up there for us to finish our talk here. When they come down, we'll escort them to the post, where we can count them and write their names in our book. After that, those who need to can see our doctor, and you will all be fed."

"Our horses and guns?"

"You can each keep a horse, but I will take all your guns when we get there."

The chief gave a resigned nod.

Wild Hog spoke up. "The people with us are afraid of your soldiers. I should go now to let them know there will be no fighting and that it is safe to come down here."

Without waiting for Clark's consent, he got on his horse and rode out of the creek bottom where the rest could see him sign for them to come down.

The man's abrupt departure surprised the lieutenant, but it would have to be done anyway, so he said nothing.

I saw my chance in the quiet moment. "'Tenant, you mind if I visit with my friend a bit?"

"No, Bill, if you don't mind translating."

"Thank you, sir."

I looked at my hands, took a deep breath, and cleared my throat. I started in and immediately found myself struggling past watery eyes and a throat that was trying to close up on me.

"My friend, I thought you were killed. My eyes are glad to see you sitting here today. I also wanted there to be talking instead of shooting that day in the mountains. It hurt my heart to see the people lose so much. We buried as many of those who were killed as we could. Your daughter's husband was with them."

Little Wolf listened closely. When I finished, he looked down and studied the worn strands of the blanket as if the words he was about to say were woven into them.

"Many people were killed in that fight, and we have all suffered much since then. But you and I have always known that there might have to be a big fight before the others would listen. That has happened now, and I think all the people finally have ears to hear what we have been telling them since we returned from our talk with the great white father. They know that we need to come here to live and to learn to walk the white man's road."

I still felt a need to explain how the hell I ended up in those mountains and riding into his camp. "When the others and I left here last fall, we were told we were going to find Crazy Horse and his Oglala. I knew you were trying to get the Cheyenne to come here, and I thought it would be easier on you if Crazy Horse was brought in first. I did not know we would ride into your camp instead."

Little Wolf shrugged. "You are the soldier's wolf, so you fight who he tells you to fight. There are others who are more to blame for what happened than you."

I wasn't sure what he was talking about, but I figured the story would be told in due time.

"Maybe I will also become the soldier's wolf," the chief continued. "It would make my heart good to help them fight Crazy Horse. *Emomata'ehe*, He is very angry and mean these days."

Clark sat a little straighter when the chief signed the name of the Lakota leader.

"Does he know where he is?" he asked aloud

I translated, and Little Wolf nodded. "It took us a long time to get here. It is hard to travel through all the snow, and there is much mud on the warm days. On our way here, we met some from his band who said that he has gone off by himself on Little Powder River. They said many are now leaving his camp." The chief curled his lip in scorn. "First, he punished anyone who left to go into the agency, and now he abandons everyone and goes off by himself. He has always been odd, but now some say they are afraid his head is broken."

The lieutenant tapped a finger on his lips as he listened.

"So, he said his people have left him?" I asked, and Little Wolf clarified.

"It is more like he has left them, from what I am told. He camps alone."

Clark's finger drummed out the rhythm to a quick grass dance as he listened. "I have sent out Red Cloud himself as an emissary to persuade the northern bands to come in," he said excitedly. "What a ten-strike it would be if he could convince any of them to leave Crazy Horse."

I struggled with finding words for emissary and ten-strike and finally settled on wolf and coup.

"I think Crazy Horse will return to his people," Little Wolf replied right away. "He has a bad head now, but I know it is the worry in his heart for them that makes him that way. He cannot abandon them for long."

I had seen the lieutenant's concern for the soldiers under his command and knew he understood as well. "But still you will fight him?" Clark asked.

"I worry for my own people. The Lakota have been good to us. Crazy Horse has not."

The small group of Cheyenne had started down from their secure position, moving toward us with great caution. Clark kept his eyes trained on the slow-moving crowd.

"Where are the rest of them?" he asked.

I listened to the chief's reply and translated. "He says the rest are coming along later with Morning Star. Most of the wounded are with him, so it'll be a bit for he gets here. Little Wolf said that maybe some others will go to the Tongue River fort; they were thinking it over when he left."

Clark grew tired of the delay between question and answer and started signing for himself. His hands sliced through the air. "Where are they? How many sleeps before they arrive? How many are fighting men?"

Little Wolf looked surprised at how fluidly the young officer's hands moved as he rattled off the questions in rapid succession. He endured the inquisition then frowned and held both hands near his chest, each thumb and forefinger a small distance apart.

"In a little while." I read the sign, then added, "I think I'd let it go at that, sir. He don't appear to like being pinned down to an exact time. It's likely he ain't sure for himself exactly when, but if he says they're coming, they're coming."

Little Wolf watched as I advised the lieutenant.

Officer and chief each studied the other for a moment as if each were taking the measure of the man in front of him.

Little Wolf decided to expand on his answer. "We came ahead of the rest to let you know that they are coming. We wanted to tell you that you do not need to have another fight with them. It will take some time, maybe by the time the grass is green again, but they are coming. There are many among them who are too weak to move very fast."

Clark nodded his head to show he understood.

The small band had now moved across the flat and down the open incline on the west side of the creek. They continued at a slow pace with all eyes trained on the body of soldiers across the creek.

Clark stood up to see better. Billy and I followed suit.

"Who's the woman painted all red and walking out in front of everyone, Bill?"

"That would be Rabbit Woman, the wife of Coal Bear, Keeper of their Sacred Buffler Hat. Coal Bear's the feller riding behind her there. The hat's in that big bundle on her back. Whenever she travels, the Keeper's wife carries her. She stays out front with her like that and leads the way."

"Her? Interesting. You speak of it as if it's an entity."

"A whatitty?"

"An entity, a living being."

"Well," I thought a moment, "I reckon that's how they see her."

Behind Coal Bear came a ragged bunch of forty or so worn-out travelers. The slippery incline added to their cautious pace.

"And it appears she's about all that's keeping 'em going right now."

It amazed me that they could travel at all in their condition. Every horse in the party was gaunt. I could see the curved shadow of each of their ribs from where I sat. Most of the men, like Little Wolf, wore stiff, green or uncured hides that did little to cover them. Some of the women fared no better. The several children who rode with them did have better robes than the adults, but they were still in poor shape.

"Who else do we have here, Bill?

"Well, that's Old Bear up in front there. He's another of the Old Man Chiefs. Looks like American Horse there just behind him. There's Black Wolf back a ways. The rest of them, riding out on the edge there, are Crazy Dogs, and you got quite a few Elk Soldiers in there too. That's Tangle Hair way in back there; he's a Dog Soldier."

Clark leaned over and spoke under his breath. "Do you think there's any chance they might give us trouble?"

"Naw. You see the kids they're keeping in the middle there? They're likely more concerned about you going after them than anything else. They're in no shape to fight, and they know it."

Clark spoke the obvious. "They look like they're starving."

"I imagine so."

When the motley band neared the creek bottom, Little Wolf led his horse to a log and climbed on top. I reached down and started to shake out the blanket but stopped when I saw the black horse's eyes widen. I turned around, folded it, and returned it to Wild Hog when he rode up.

I suggested to Clark that the soldiers should take the flank and allow the Cheyenne lead the way in. I climbed on top of Ulysses and turned toward the formation with Billy and the lieutenant when Little Wolf called out to me.

"*To'ėsemotšėške!*"

I turned Ulysses around, and the chief spoke in halting English.

"You should ride with us to the soldier's camp."

I looked at Lieutenant Clark, who smiled and nodded his consent. "It appears that all is forgiven, Bill," he said

"Be nice if that was all it took, sir. I'm afraid there's plenty others who'll still hold a grudge."

Rabbit Woman crossed over to the east side of the creek and walked south across the flat. Coal Bear trailed behind her. I rode four abreast with Wild Hog, Little Wolf, and Old Bear. The rest of the band stayed clustered close together behind us.

Little Wolf had some questions for me as we rode along. "This soldier chief said he wants to put our names in his book. Why does he not just count how many we are, like the others have done in the past?"

"Things are different now. There was a new treaty signed since you left here last summer. He does not just count how many are in each lodge; now he wants to make sure he has everyone's name so he knows who belongs to the tribe."

"Standing Elk told us of this treaty. Who touched the pen to agree to it if we were all away?"

"There were a few who stayed on here at the agency: Living Bear, Turkey Leg, Broken Dish."

"They signed for all the Cheyenne?"

"There were a couple others who signed. They asked me to translate for them. There was plenty Lakota who signed off on it too."

My friend was in a tough spot. He, Morning Star, and a few others had signed the Fort Laramie Treaty back in sixty-eight. It was a good treaty for the Cheyenne because it forced the army to close some forts down that they shouldn't have built, including Fort Phil Kearny, the one Little Wolf later burned, and it assured the Cheyenne they could stay here in the north, near the Black Hills. Problem was, since it was just those few who signed it, there were many in the tribe who opposed it just for that reason. So, he couldn't argue against this new treaty now and not look like a hypocrite.

"Besides our names, what else do they take in this new treaty?"

"The Black Hills and all the land to the west."

Little Wolf and all the others looked at me in shock.

It was a tough spot, indeed.

We rode in silence for a ways. I could tell that my friend was struggling with the news about the Hills as well as his inability to speak against those who signed them away. The way of a chief is not to allow his emotions to cloud his judgment. After a bit he looked up and scanned the countryside in front of us. "Are you and your family's names in this soldier's book?"

"No, we are not listed there," I replied.

He kept his eyes forward and spoke in a matter-of-fact tone. "You must put them in there with ours then."

I felt my shoulders drop a bit. It was only one man's forgiveness, but I figured I could deal with what them others might have to say when that time came.

# The Talking Wire and Trickery

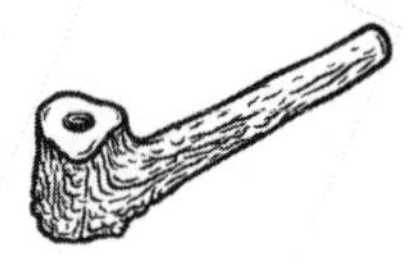

LIVING BEAR WAS A SKITTISH GENT, A SQUAT, THICK MAN WHO SEEMED always to be talking through an anxious grin. Today was no different, even as he scoured the gloomy interior of the quartermaster supply building, peering through the shadows trying to see where the redheaded private we had given the requisition had gone to.

"He is coming now. I think I see him," he whispered.

Taller, and a bit on the lanky side, Plenty Camps stepped up beside his more talkative friend, sharing in his anticipation.

Private O'Malley reappeared from the back storeroom with a stack of folded blue wool in his arms. He looked at the Cheyenne, then down at the requisition from Lieutenant Clark in his hand, then over at my boy James and me, and shook his head.

"Oi dannea see 'ow suiting injuns up in our own duds is any too good an idear," he groused.

The private draped a blue fatigue blouse and trousers over the extended arms of the two newest additions to Lieutenant Clark's growing company of Indian scouts at Camp Robinson. As they received their uniforms, Living Bear and Plenty Camps looked to me for help with understanding the soldier's words.

"He says you both look like you will be some good soldier wolves."

James looked away in a bad attempt to hide his grin.

The Cheyenne men smiled and thanked the soldier in unison for his compliment. "*Nea'eše.*"

I didn't worry too much about not giving them the right translation since the man's brogue-laden complaint wasn't typical of how the majority of soldiers at the post treated the Indians. Most of them had actually become so friendly with the Cheyenne during the two months since they had arrived that many of the Lakota at the agency had become jealous of them.

With his new uniform in hand, Living Bear was certain about what he wanted to do next. "Now, let us now go back to White Hat and show him we are ready to join the others and be soldier wolves for him."

Lieutenant Clark had started up a squad of Indian scouts and was bent on training them to act and look like any other group of soldiers, complete with uniforms. The tough part was getting them to understand the drill commands. James had come with me today so we could have another interpreter on hand to translate the orders that were being barked to the squad. We had just finished a run-through on the parade ground, and after we were done, Clark sent us over with his two newest hand-selected recruits to get them suited up.

We stepped from the storehouse to the sound of whoops and hollers. A group of soldiers and Cheyenne were all hunkered down together among the stacks of logs lying near the north end of the new addition to the building. It wasn't too far out of our way, so we went to see what the commotion was about.

From the edge of the noisy circle, I could see Tangle Hair kneeling in the center of the crowd. The small but scrappy Dog Soldier headman had a firm grasp on the rod at the top of what looked to be a telegraph battery with his left hand, while his right was poised above a bucket of water. A quick glance at the folding money in people's hands told me that wagers had been placed and everyone was waiting to see if the payoff was theirs.

A telegraph line had been strung up to Deadwood in the Black Hills over the last year, and a branch was now being split off of that at Hat Creek and brought down to Camp Robinson. The battery was supposed to be waiting in storage for the line to reach the post.

Tangle Hair thrust his hand into the bucket, and his whole body started writhing like he'd been kicked in the gut. He looked like he was trying to push his hand through a tabletop instead of water. He gave a loud grunt and yanked his hand from the bucket as he collapsed and rolled on the ground, holding his hand against his chest.

A cheer went up in the crowd, telling me who had won the bet. I leaned toward the closest soldier. "What's all this about? What's the bet?"

The soldier kept his eyes glued on the payoff that was being stuffed in his hand as he answered. "There's a few nickels at the bottom of that pail, and the Injuns want to see who can reach in and grab 'em while they hold onto the battery pole. Gives them a helluva shock. They think it's some kinda magic in it, but each one thinks they got enough magic of their own to beat it."

I cringed. I could still recall the odd surge of energy that shot through me when I had accidentally brushed against a similar battery when I was asked to carry a message to the telegraph station on Hat Creek last year. I learned the hard way that electricity was used to send each dispatch. I couldn't imagine sticking my hand into the water and feeling that same agony for a few nickels.

I turned to tell Living Bear and Plenty Camps we should get going but found the boys working their way around the crowd. Like moths at a campfire, their eyes were glued to the odd device in front of them, and they were looking for a way to get closer.

"*Otahe! Otahe!*" I called out, trying to get their attention. Lieutenant Clark and Little Wolf expected us all back at Clark's quarters right now.

Living Bear raised his hand to acknowledge that he heard me, but he kept his eyes trained on the scene around the battery and bucket. "Tell White Hat we will be there soon. We will not be long."

I knew Clark wouldn't like this, but I was an interpreter, not a nanny, so I nudged James and tipped my head toward officer's row.

"Good luck with that, boys," James threw over his shoulder as we left.

Neither man answered him.

We crossed in front of the infantry barracks at the north end of the parade ground. From there, I could see across to the other side, where Little Wolf, clad in his own scout uniform, was having a chat with the lieutenant on the officer's porch.

Clark had made it clear that he wanted Little Wolf to stay behind while we went to get the uniforms. He had been having a lot of these private discussions with people lately. Nothing on the sneak that I could tell, just little one-to-ones off to the side like this.

From his signs, I could see the lieutenant was telling the chief something about riding north into the hills. He noticed James and I coming back from the quartermasters and turned to greet us.

"I see you've lost our friends. Was there a problem getting their uniforms?" Clark had continued to sign as he spoke so Little Wolf could follow along.

"Naw, they're suited up just fine. Just got a bit sidetracked is all. There's a little wagering, on the other side of them logs there, about who's got the stronger medicine, them or a telegraph battery."

I fumbled with the latch to the lieutenant's gate for a moment then gave up and stepped over the whole contraption. I aimed myself toward the open chair next to Little Wolf when I heard the gate open and close behind me as James followed me to the porch.

Clark smiled. "I've heard that's been going on for a couple days now. But now that all the poles are in, the stringing crew should have the wire here to the post any day. I honestly don't know what will be had for entertainment once that battery is used for the purpose it was actually intended to serve."

"It'll be nice not to have to make those rides out to the Hat Creek station anymore. They been getting shorter the closer that line comes each day, but it's still a bother."

Little Wolf spoke up. "This talking wire," he tried his best to pronounce the white man's word for it, "this tul-a-graf, is strong medicine. I have not seen the gambling yet, but I would not bet against the white man's medicine. This noise that brings words from far away tells me only that we cannot win against the soldiers. I think it is good that we can now join with you to fight against your enemies. When Morning Star and the others get here, there will be even more soldier wolves to go against Crazy Horse if you fight with him."

Clark turned toward me but kept signing for Little Wolf to see. "I just informed Little Wolf that we have received word from Hat Creek station that Morning Star and his band passed by late yesterday afternoon. We will be riding out with a supply train tomorrow to meet them and help them come the rest of the way in. I was about to tell him that Crazy Horse and his band were also spotted, north of the Cheyenne River, and that he's on his way in as well. Moving slowly though."

Clark turned back to Little Wolf. "It will be good to have you and the Cheyenne on our side if we need you, but I was also told that Crazy Horse is coming here to surrender. People are saying that he is done fighting too. That is why . . ." Clark paused and looked at me. "Its Three Stars and Bad Hand, right?" He checked the names that the Indians used for General Crook and Colonel Mackenzie.

I nodded.

"That is why Three Stars and Bad Hand both came back here last week. To make sure Crazy Horse comes to surrender and not to fight."

Little Wolf was glad to hear the soldier chiefs had their doubts about the Lakota leader. "It is good that they watch out for him. He has a bad heart these days. You cannot trust what he says from one time to the next. He may talk peace then change his mind and talk war. Even if he does smoke the peace pipe with the soldiers, it would be good to give him a reservation far away from the rest of us. Let us stay here, by Novavose, our medicine hill, and send him to that place in the south."

As soon as Indian territory was mentioned, Clark gave the conversation a hard turn in that direction. "Living Bear has told me that he and Spotted Elk traveled to see your relatives, the Southern Cheyenne, in Indian Territory last fall. He said that he thinks it is a good land for your people."

Clark's quick change of subject caught us both off guard. The officer had a clear interest in working Living Bear into all the doings of late, and it for sure sounded like there was some sort of plan afoot.

Little Wolf had plenty else on his mind already and was clearly frustrated by the politicking of the agency men to gain power. He let the lieutenant know where he stood on that whole deal right off.

"Living Bear and those few others do not speak for all the Cheyenne. They cannot decide for the rest of us to give away our sacred mountain and to leave our land to go live somewhere else. When Morning Star and the others arrive, we will ask for a Council with Three Stars and Bad Hand. We will tell them, as we have told all the others who have tried to get us to go to the south, that we do not want to go live there. We belong here.

"I must go now and tell my men that we will need to be ready to go with you to meet our relatives tomorrow. I have two daughters who are with them who I am anxious to see again. One was close to giving birth when we separated, so we left them with family."

Clark listened quietly to what some might have called insubordination had it come from any other sergeant under his command. "Very well then, let's get you going," he said almost cheerfully. "Just be sure you tell Living Bear about our plans as well. What's that saying for ending a talk, Bill?"

"*Hena'haanehe.* That's the end."

"*Henna Hawnahay.*" Clark lilted the word to Little Wolf as they stood.

Little Wolf gave an uncertain nod and turned to leave.

"*Otahe,*" the lieutenant called for the chief's attention. "We are good friends, but when you wear that uniform, you must remember that you are a soldier now. A soldier must always salute his superior officers whenever he comes or goes."

Little Wolf thought a moment then slowly raised his hand as he had been taught to do. Clark snapped off a sharp salute in response.

"Dismissed." Clark released the chief with great ceremony.

"*Epeva'e.*" Little Wolf seemed amused.

My friend left the porch and stepped over the fence, careful not to raise his leg too high on his way to his horse. He mounted the black with some effort, keeping his leg close as he slid it across the horse's back. His healing had gone well in the couple months he'd been at the agency, but he had stiffened up while sitting after the drill.

He turned the black and headed straight for the quartermaster's building to find Living Bear and relay their orders to him—and no doubt to ask the man a few questions.

Clark watched the chief ride back along the same route that James and I had taken when we arrived. He let him get a ways off then commented, "You know, he carries on a pretty decent conversation for a dead man."

"Yes sir," I replied, "and a pretty lively one at that."

James gave a small groan.

Clark did a quick turn and got right down to business. "I'd like to leave just after adjutant's call at nine o'clock tomorrow, Bill.

I'll leave it to yourself and Little Wolf to have the Indian scouts ready to depart at that time."

"We'll be ready, sir."

"Very good. We'll likely be out a day, maybe two, depending on their ability to travel when we find them."

"Yes, sir."

Clark paused and gave me the once over. "You seem quiet, Bill. Something on your mind?"

The man had a way of reading folks that was pretty uncanny.

"Well, sir, got a question or two, if you don't mind."

"Absolutely not. Go ahead."

I turned to James. "Why don't you go on home? Tell your mother I'll be along."

James gave me a wide-eyed look but nodded. He left the porch and walked to the gate, quickly flipped the latch open, and closed it back behind him. He swung up on his horse and nodded again before he turned toward the agency and started off at a trot.

"What's on your mind, Bill? Speak freely."

I stared at the latch on the gate for a spell, considering my approach. I decided to just go right at it. "What's with all the palaver about Living Bear, sir?"

The corners of Clark's mouth turned up. "Perhaps I was more transparent than I thought." he laughed as he returned to his seat. "Well, you see, Bill, now that the Indians are coming in, it is important that we seek out those who want to work with us as we implement our plans for them."

He sat down on the edge of his chair and leaned forward to finish his point. "And, as you know, some time ago, the general appointed Living Bear as the chief for the agency Cheyenne. He has served well in that capacity, and while we understand and respect the traditional position of others—like Little Wolf, and Morning Star when he gets here—we intend to maintain our existing relationship with Living Bear and the others who have stayed at the agency and who have proven themselves to be reliable and trustworthy allies."

"You did say speak freely, sir?" I asked.

"I did."

"Well then, that sounds like a bunch of horse shit to me."

Clark's smile showed his teeth this time. He settled back in the chair and brought the fingertips of each hand together with the index fingers resting on his lips. "Care to expand on that, Bill?"

"Well, I think it's pretty plain what's going on. You're working them the same way that you did the Lakota. You want to get them fighting with each other to the point they don't notice that you're getting them to do everything you want."

"How did we work the Lakota, Bill?" There was an unusual smugness in his tone.

I stood up to try to get some of the antsy out of me. The lieutenant knew what I was about to say, but I was going to tell him anyway, if only to get it off of my chest.

"All right then, here's the whole load of hay. After the treaty was signed last fall, Red Cloud got pissed off and took all his folk away and moved 'em down river. After Mackenzie and you all went and rounded him back up, General Crook made a big deal about appointing that Brule, Spotted Tail, as the big chief of all the Lakota.

"So, Red Cloud didn't like that, but after pouting a bit, he came back around to Crook's way of seeing things again, all on account of he didn't want to lose that title of being big chief. Don't get me wrong—he's an important man all right, but there ain't never been anything like one big chief of all the Lakota. That is, 'till Crook made him the first one. Now, it's clear you're trying the same thing with Living Bear and the Cheyenne."

"What's wrong with that, Bill? In the long run, it's all about creating lasting peace."

"Well, it's like I told you that night before we headed up into the mountains. There ain't never been just one big toad in that puddle, never has been, and there's good reason for that. Little Wolf and Morning Star are both highly respected though, and if you set Living Bear up over them, if you go messing with how they decide to arrange things themselves, I think you're asking for a whole shitload of problems."

"I understand your point, Bill." Clark finally started to get serious. "But we need a single point of contact who we can go to in order to address the matters we need to resolve. We simply don't have the time to sit down and have a lengthy Council over every little issue that comes up and then have to wait while forty or fifty differing opinions get sorted through. That's not how things get done in the army."

"Well, you see, that's where I think you're headed back-asswards."

Clark's brow pinched together on that one. I couldn't tell if he was getting pissed or if he was just confused about my point. I figured I probably should explain it.

"You said yourself that the army has an odd way of pulling themselves apart and putting themselves back together again at the drop of a hat. By my count, there's been about eight or nine commanding officers here at Camp Robinson since it started just two years ago and probably just as many agents at Red Cloud, and the last five of those was army issue."

"What's your point?"

"Stay with me here. I'm getting to it. Now, we also just got ourselves a brand-new president in this country when President Hayes got sworn in a month ago, in March, right?"

"Yes?"

"Well, that whole mess around getting him elected started clear back last fall, before we even rode up into them mountains, right? So why couldn't they just decide and plunk him right in there like they put Colonel Mackenzie in as the new camp commander soon as he got here last week?"

"That's simple, Bill. Being elected the leader of a nation is quite a bit different than being appointed camp commander. There's a whole different process involved."

"Exactly! So, you see, you're trying to treat them like they was all in the army, but they ain't. Naming Little Wolf sergeant of your scouts is one thing. Just like they've had three different headmen for the Elk Horn Scrapers since the fighting started last year. They can get by with doing that sort of thing, but making Living Bear chief of all the Cheyenne? That's a whole different process, just like the Hayes deal. And on top of it all, when you don't involve the Cheyenne in the decision? Well, I'm afraid you're backing a badger into a bucket on that one."

Clark gave a dry smile like he had better things to do than argue with me over this. "Bill, using those tactics has brought about a significant turning point in this conflict. I cannot see how it can do anything but help our cause if we continue."

"Sir, they've had their land taken from them, you've beat them up hard from the outside, and now you're working on tearing them apart from the inside. And when you're done with that, you'll be trying to ship them all off to somewhere they don't want to go. All I'm saying is, sooner or later, the badger stops backing up."

"Bill, the general said that he's working on getting them a reservation here in the north, and I've also heard that President Hayes is very sympathetic to their cause."

"Oh, bullshit. We both know that William T. Sherman is the Commanding General of the US Army, and if he wants them all in the south, then that's where they're god damn going."

Considering that the lieutenant and I were each leaning forward in our chairs by now, our voices were a lot louder than they really needed to be. We eyed each other hard, and my last comment seemed to hang in the air between us with runnels of disrespect dripping off of it and falling to the porch floor.

"I think that's enough, Bill."

"That's all I was looking to say."

"I'll see you here tomorrow after adjutant's call."

"We'll be there."

I stomped off the porch, stepped over the fence, and climbed up on Ulysses. I turned the buckskin toward home as a raucous cheer erupted from the gamblers on the other side of the parade ground.

# Hearts on the Ground

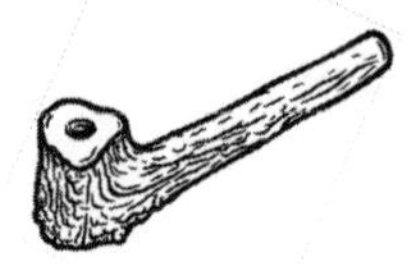

Just as Little Wolf told us he would, Morning Star brought over five hundred tired, hungry, and beat-up Cheyenne to the Red Cloud Agency by the time the grass was green.

The sun was shining, and the meadowlarks were sending their own bright, cheerful messages back and forth along the new telegraph line we followed on our way out. It took about a half-day to cover the eight miles up Soldier Creek, eight more along the Hat Creek ridge, then a couple more down a winding gulch on the north side to the start of Hat Creek itself. Here the ridge met with the long expanse of prairie that stretched some forty miles north to the Black Hills, the same piece of ground that we traveled when we returned from the expedition in January.

They were camped there, waiting, as if they knew we would come. We saw a few outriders at first, so we assembled on a rise where they could see us. It wasn't long before more started to come up from the protective cover of the dry creek bed and appear on the flat below us. Each looked more pitiful than the one before them. The men appeared first with no guns showing or any sign of hostile intent. After a bit a few women and children joined them, then the rest came, staying all bunched together.

I leaned toward the lieutenant. "They're presenting themselves to us so we can see they ain't no threat."

Most of the children all had some sort of a wrap, leggings, and rough-made moccasins, same as it was with Little Wolf's bunch, while the majority of the adults had little or nothing. Some wore a stiff animal hide bent around them, while others had only torn remnants of blankets, barely enough to discreetly cover themselves. Many had their hair either hanging loose or cropped short in mourning, and the majority of the women had half-healed, self-inflicted gashes that showed their grief to the world. Frostbite blackened the faces and limbs of almost all of them. I near cried when I first seen 'em. Clark didn't hold up so well.

At first, the lieutenant was excited to see a group this large coming into the agency, but as they continued to assemble, his smile faded to a somber, then shocked, expression. As their sad condition became more apparent, the officer's eyes welled with water. Those who couldn't keep up with the others continued to emerge out of the creek bottom, most on a travois, too injured or feeble to walk on their own. I had never seen any group of Indians this bad off.

I recognized Morning Star and Standing Elk when they rode out of the crowd with a couple others. Standing Elk was toting a white flag as all four lined up and headed our way. Little Wolf and Wild Hog moved closer to the lieutenant and me so we could ride out to meet them. As we prepared to start, I leaned toward the lieutenant and, keeping my eyes to the front, waved my hand like I was shooing an early spring blowfly from my face.

"Sir, we don't want to embarrass them."

Clark threw a quick glance my way. It took him a moment to realize I was talking about the tears that had trickled down his cheeks. He quickly turned and brushed them away with the back of his gloved hand and set his jaw, like he was mad at himself for showing that much concern.

The sight of a white man crying over the troubles of an Indian was foreign, but I couldn't gawk. I also had to keep my eyes off the shabby condition of the bunch coming across the flat. I was glad when a jackrabbit broke from a clump of sage he'd been holed up in and raced away toward the creek, no doubt cussing those of us who were intruding on his peaceful dinner.

We met in the middle of the flat, where Standing Elk did the talking. It was no surprise, since he had always had a gift for gab. While everyone else was in rags and green hides, he had managed to keep some pretty nice duds on his back, including a hair pipe chest plate that he often brought out for special occasions. He presented himself pretty damned well, and I could tell Clark was impressed.

Morning Star was a sight. The old chief was gaunt, his hair was undone, and he had a thin, wore-out trade blanket wrapped around his shoulders. He clearly wasn't in any mood to talk.

They were all exhausted, but they wanted to head right on into the agency since it was so close. There would be a half-moon in the sky later, enough light for us to travel safely, even if we were just poking along. First things first though—we had to get them all fed. The trail down through the creek was pretty well-traveled, so getting the chuck wagons down to where we waited weren't no problem. Indians aren't real fond of hardtack and bacon, but they were happy to get their hands on any grub we had for 'em at that point.

As they ate, Clark struck up a conversation with Standing Elk, who was only too glad to talk. The officer was soon peppering him with questions. By now he could have held his own with sign talk, but he asked me to help out so Standing Elk and the others might feel more comfortable.

"Is this all that is left of your people, or are there any more?"

"There are some that have gone to the new fort where Tongue River meets Elk River."

"How many went there?"

"About three hundred. They are with Two Moon, Black Moccasin, and Ice. Box Elder also went with them."

"Are there any others still out?"

"There is a band of young men who still do not want to live at any agency. Just a few, though. It will be hard on them to stay out long by themselves."

"What about the Sioux? Do you know anything of Crazy Horse? There are rumors he might be coming in."

"He comes behind us. We passed his camp near Red Paint River. He has many people with him, so he moves slowly. I think, too, that it is hard for him to come in."

Clark had been watching Standing Elk, but his head snapped in my direction. "He's coming? Red Paint River, where is that, Bill? How far away? Wait, how big is his camp? Who is with him?" The officer had more lather on his lips than a finish hog at feeding time.

"Red Paint is what the whites call the south Cheyenne River, sir, south side of the Hills." I asked Standing Elk the rest of the questions and gave Clark the answers. "He has twice as many as we have with us. The only ones not with him are Lame Deer and his band. They are somewhere on the other side of Tongue River."

"My God, Bill, this is news!" Clark was beside himself. "Do you know what this means? Save for Sitting Bull, we've about got them all."

"Yes, sir, I believe that's the case."

Clark plunked down in front of Standing Elk and began signing his own questions. The Council chief held the same puzzled expression that Little Wolf had when he first saw how fluent the soldier chief was.

I looked around for Little Wolf, but he had slipped away, somewhere beyond the growing line of Indians at the chuck wagons.

"*Memeehe, Nanehove Memeehe.* Grandpa, I am your Grandpa." Little Wolf's words were meant as much for himself as they were for the infant he held close to his face or, for that matter, anyone else who might be listening.

With her child due sometime during the next moon, Inside Woman had stayed behind in Starving Elk's lodge. She would have caused Little Wolf's group to travel slower, and they needed to get to the agency as soon as possible. White Voice had stayed to help her.

The baby boy was already two moons old and not as chubby as Little Wolf thought he should be. His mother was also thin and had clearly not been eating well herself. Cheyenne tradition dictated that the men would be fed first for defensive reasons, so his daughters had not been to the wagons yet. Still, Chopping Woman and White Voice stood next to him busily chewing on the dried meat that Lightning has sent along for them.

"You have no belly, little man." The chief cooed to his grandson as his daughters continued their feasting. "We will have to fatten your mother so she can give you more to eat. You are skinny as a blade of grass, and you must be strong."

Born with a full head of hair, the child trained his still-developing eyes on the strange man with the deep voice and smiled. Little Wolf pulled him closer to his face again, pressed his lips against the baby's ear and whispered, "You are why we have all taken this walk, little man. You need to live and grow strong so you can care for us when we're old and for the new ones who come after you. You are part of this circle now. We need you here."

He settled the child back against the crook of his arm and continued talking so his daughters could hear. Your young aunt, Day Woman, is waiting for you. I thought she might crawl in my saddlebags with the dried meat so she could come with me, but she sent you this instead." Little Wolf reached into his soldier coat and pulled out the small doll that had been passed on to Day Woman by White Voice. "I think she will have to hold on to it for a little longer. What do you think, eh? We will get you a good bow instead." Little Wolf sucked air through his teeth, making a few bird chirps, and the child startled.

Before he could cry, White Voice reached over with her free hand and lightly pinched his nose, making it hard for him to gather enough air to release even a whimper. The girl left the remainder of the meat for her older sister and reached for the now fussing infant.

"Come here, No Belly," she said, using the name her father had just bestowed on the child. She took him from Little Wolf and slipped a finger into the child's mouth to pacify him. "*Etonėstao'o, nahko'eehe naa tsehevasemeto?* How are my mothers and my little sister?" she asked. White Voice practiced the steps to the sweetheart's dance as she bounced the infant.

Little Wolf recognized the step. *She is too young for that*, he thought, but he answered her question.

"They are well. They worry about you, but we have plenty to eat, and there is no concern about fighting. The soldier chiefs say if we stay, they will stop attacking us."

Chopping Woman slowed her eating. "We should have come back sooner than this." The young mother had said all she wanted and returned to quietly chewing her food. Had it been anyone other than his daughter, Little Wolf would have defended his efforts to sway the Council during their recent travels. As it was, he knew there was no defense he could give that might ease her pain.

"*Ehetometo*, that is true," was all he said.

The black horse began pawing at the ground, and Little Wolf realized he had been gone too long from his responsibilities.

"We will be leaving soon, so I must go be with the soldier chief, White Hat, and the others. You have enough dried meat to last until you get to the agency. The soldier food will make your stomach bad for traveling."

He reached into another saddlebag and pulled out two pair of newly made moccasins and a small blanket. "Two Woman sent these along for each of you. You have only a short way left, but they will help."

"*Nea'eše*." Each daughter took a pair, and White Voice wrapped the blanket around the baby.

The chief placed his hand on his grandson and gave his daughters a nod then climbed on top of the black horse and turned him back toward the front.

We took it slow coming down into Soldier Creek. People were tired and stumbling, but we managed to get everybody onto the flat above Camp Robinson without harm. Clark had sent a rider ahead so they knew we'd get there about daybreak.

This was the main body of the tribe, so it would be common to have a traditional show of numbers as they approached. Each warrior society split off by themselves and took turns singing their society's songs as we got closer to the post.

After a bit I leaned over to the lieutenant. "You familiar with all the traditional foofaraw that goes on when a camp is approached?"

"I believe so. I've seen how other tribes posture and pretend to attack."

"So, you know there's likely to be some shooting?"

"I've seen it before, yes."

What would normally happen was the different societies would start high-tailing around each other, yelling and firing their guns into the air, staging a mock attack as they announced their arrival. As we approached, a few shots were touched off, but everybody pretty much stayed put. There wasn't even a fake fight left in them boys.

Soldiers had gathered around and in front of the different buildings at the post, all gawking and trying to get a peek at the largest group of Indians to come in that spring. I was a little nervous one of them might spook and send a couple rounds our way. About that time Clark eased my fear when he filled me in on the rest of the plan.

"Bill, this is where I leave you for a while. Take them over to the flat beyond the agency and have them set up camp there. I'll collect General Crook, Colonel Mackenzie, and a few others, and we'll meet with all the men on the parade ground at noon."

Clark rode off toward the post at a canter, and we moved on across the river. After everyone had settled in, the Council and society men headed back to the parade ground to meet with the soldier chiefs. I rode up front with Little Wolf, Morning Star, Old Bear, and Standing Elk.

Before Standing Elk had left the agency last fall, he had a fair relationship with some of the officers, so it was decided that he would be the main speaker for the Cheyenne. Little Wolf was a bit unsure of this, but he went along with the others.

The guard was doubled around all the buildings as we entered the large rectangle between them. We dismounted and stood facing east, toward officers' row.

Lieutenant Clark and a few junior officers were mounted and facing us, while a squad of enlisted men flanked us on each end of the parade ground. We all waited for Crook and the others to join the party. There were several large piles of blankets covered by tarps behind the officers, which would be handed out at some point. Before long the door to the general's quarters opened, and Crook, Mackenzie, Major Mason, and a visiting officer, General Forsyth, appeared and walked down to the front. It was time for me to go to work.

As the headmen from each side came together, I made a quick introduction. "General Crook, I'd like to present to you Standing Elk, a Council member of the Northern Cheyenne."

Standing Elk stepped forward and shook the general's hand. He looked a bit nervous, and when he spoke, he kept repeating himself.

"I want to give you my gun. I want to shake hands and give you my gun." He turned and made a sweep toward the men behind him with his arm. "All my young men here want to give you their guns. We want to give you our guns today. We want to shake hands and bury the hatchet."

With that, he made a big show of levering open the breech of a nice-looking Henry rifle and pushed it toward the general. Crook joined in the ceremony, using both hands to receive the weapon. With the show was over, a man named Fire Crow stepped forward and handed Major Mason his Sharps. I suspect he was the one who hit Frank North's coffee cup that night up in the mountains. After that several others followed suit, and Lieutenant Clark and the other officers stepped forward to receive their weapons. They built up quite a pile behind the stacks of blankets. There was everything from simple bows and arrows to muzzleloaders, as well as quite a few of the newer trapdoor Springfields that were most likely picked up at the Custer fight.

Crook waited until everything was handed over before he began his talk. "It is good to see my friends the Cheyenne coming to make peace with me today. I agree with my friend Standing Elk that it is time that we bury the hatchet and end the fighting between us. You have given me many guns today, but I know there are many more. I will tell you now that any man who does not give me his gun is not my friend, and I will treat him badly. If you bring your gun to me now, you will still be my friend."

Crook stopped for a minute and, sure enough, a couple fellas slunk forward and each handed over a pistol they had tucked away. Crook let them get back to their places before he started up again.

"My friends, when we are done here, I will send a message to the Great Father in Washington through the talking wire that you can now see coming down the hill over there. I will tell him that the

Cheyenne have decided to come in and want to be his friends, and he will be very happy with you.

"I will tell the Great Father that you want to live in peace now and learn the white man's ways. He will want to make it so you will not be bothered by greedy white men and can hunt freely and your children can go to the white man's school to learn this new way.

"I must tell you that you need to decide where you want to live. You can move south to live with your southern relatives at their agency, or you can go to the Shoshone and Arapahoe agency over beyond the Bighorns. I know you want to stay here with the Sioux, but I cannot say that you will be allowed to do so. I will let you stay for one year, and we will see where you go after that."

Crook was better than most about talking slowly and allowing me time to translate without getting in too big a rush. He kept his words short but let them know there would be more talk later.

"My soldiers will come to take your horses. I will allow each man to keep one to ride, but that is all. When you return to your lodges, I will have my man come to put your name in our book and count how many are in your lodge so we can make sure you get enough food. Tomorrow we will have your leaders come back here, and I will let them know what your white father has to say to them. I will also have many gifts to give you then. I know you did not come here so I could just take things from you. I have some small gifts for each of you today just to show you that my heart is good and that I am happy to see my friends today. Come up and take these, and then go back to your families, and we will begin to get everyone fed."

The tarps were pulled off, and the blankets were handed out pretty quickly. Some of the boys seemed pretty content about what the general had to say, while others were clearly upset, mostly over losing what few horses they had left. I also knew that there were plenty of guns still unaccounted for.

I watched Standing Elk say his goodbyes and climb back on his horse to head toward camp. But before he left the parade ground, Living Bear caught up with him and struck up a conversation. They weren't sign-talking, so I had no clue what it was they were saying, but it looked damned serious.

# *Epevo'eha* (Broken to Pieces)

EVERY SPRING, THUNDER, THE MAN IN THE SOUTH, FIGHTS HIS WAY back into the sky above the northern plains and makes his annual return. He battles against Winter Man, who reluctantly releases his grip on the world and retreats to his home in the far, far north. Green grass starts to show beneath the dry husk of last year's offerings, and the four-legged seek it out. When the four-legged start to move again, the people begin the hunt, and when the hunt is complete, they work to preserve their bounty and prepare for the inevitable return of Winter Man. This is the circle of renewal that the Cheyenne have been a part of since the old times when they first left their home inside the earth and began to live on top of it. In April of 1877, that circle was broken.

A spring squall blew in overnight, and the day was raw and miserable. The meeting between the Cheyenne leaders and the soldiers was changed to the Council building in the southwest corner of the Red Cloud Agency because there was no room large enough at the military post. The three stoves inside the low log structure were fired up, and the structure was plenty warm by the time everyone arrived.

When the Indians came through the gate, I saw that the agency men, Living Bear and Spotted Elk, walked on either side of Standing Elk. It was clear they had been tugging on his ear since the meeting yesterday, and they weren't about to let go of it this morning. What had me a tad bit concerned was that they had him nodding his head.

Little Wolf was not in uniform today; instead, he wore a red muslin shirt and black pants that the lieutenant had given him shortly after his arrival. He had a blue trade blanket wrapped around his waist. Morning Star was dressed in similar fashion with a new green blanket presented to him personally by General Crook the day before. It was good to see the old fella wearing more than the rags he came in with.

The younger officers milled around, looking nervous and talking quietly to each another. I figured they didn't welcome the idea of entering a closed room with this many Indians even if they had handed over a whole pile of weapons just the day before. Lieutenant Clark seemed especially preoccupied. Ever since he heard that Crazy Horse was coming in, he and Billy Garnett had been spending quite a bit of time together. They were deep in conversation when Crook called out to get things started.

The Cheyenne had pared their numbers down to about a dozen and were matched by about as many officers. A squad of forty or so soldiers remained outside, though, a few on guard detail with the rest milling about in the yard, close enough to respond quickly if any trouble were to break out. There was a time when the Indians would have violently objected to such a strong military presence at their agency, but those days were gone now.

The Cheyenne all sat on the floor as was their custom during any Council. Crook, Mackenzie, and Forsyth sat on chairs in front of them, and the rest of the officers stood in an arc behind them. There was also a pair of correspondents from a couple newspapers back east who had wedged themselves into the back of the room. Word had gotten out that Crazy Horse might be coming in, so they came to get the scoop. They likely needed to write about something while they waited for their big story to arrive.

I took my place across from the door and in the middle of the two groups crowded into opposite ends of the narrow building. I joined in the preliminary smoke and other social niceties that started things off. When those were done, Crook and Mackenzie both wasted no time in getting down to business. Crook was the first to speak.

"My friends, I hope you have all have had a chance to rest and plenty to eat. We have much to talk about today. I have told the Great Father that you have come here and that you want to live in peace and take up the white man's ways. He is very happy to hear this good news, and he has a plan to help you do these things."

The Cheyenne kept all eyes on me as I finished translating Crook's opening remarks. A few heads began to nod as I finished up, but the general spoke again.

"My friends, the Great Father has decided that the best place for you to be is with your relatives in the south. He has asked me to tell you that you should get ready to move there. He will send food and supplies right away so you can get started."

The protests started before I could finish my translation, so I had to raise my voice to be heard above them.

Morning Star was supposed to do most of the talking today, but Little Wolf clambered to his feet, using Wild Hog's shoulder like a ladder and pulling himself up. He skipped the usual pleasantries and got right after it, reminding me of when he was younger and often took command of any conversation he had a stake in.

"You told us yesterday that we could stay here for a year. Today you tell us that we must go now. Most of our people are still tired from their long walk here. You cannot expect us to pick up and leave right away. We did not come here only to be sent away."

Crook tried to quiet the man. "You will not have to leave tomorrow. It will take some time for enough supplies to arrive to take with you on the trip. By the time they get here, your people will be rested and your ponies will have their bellies full of green grass and they will be stronger."

Little Wolf would have none of it. "Every promise that is made to us is pulled away almost as soon as it is made now. How do we know that tomorrow you will not come to us and say, you must go now, hurry grab your families and go? How can we go from here and tell our families that we know anything about what will happen if each day you tell us something different?"

The chief saw his friend Morning Star was waiting to speak, so he sat down, his face still dark with resentment. Morning Star rose slowly. He arranged his blanket in the traditional manner that Cheyenne men do at Council, tucking the green cloth a bit tighter around his thin frame lest it slip to the floor. He cleared his throat before offering his thoughts.

"We have all come together in a good way this morning to try to do what is best for our people. We have many sick and wounded here who have suffered for many moons as we traveled across very hard land to get here. These words you give us now are just as hard to hear as that ground was to cross. I agree with my friend—we must move slowly and be careful.

"We came here instead of the new fort on Elk River to live near our Lakota friends Red Cloud and Spotted Elk. That is what we were told we could do, even just yesterday and many times before then. When we touched the pen for the treaty that gave up the forts and allowed us to stay in this land, it said on that paper that we could live here, and we reminded the Great Father of that when we went on our long trip to visit him four winters ago.

"We do not want to go to the south. Our place is here in this place where we were all born and where bones of those who came before lay in the hills around us. There are some who have gone down there to live and like it, but we do not. We want to stay here."

Mackenzie leaned over to Crook and asked permission to speak. Crook nodded.

"That agreement was long ago, and there have been new ones that have been made since then, but there are many other reasons why you should want to go there. It may come to be that even the Sioux will have to go south. Your relatives the Southern Cheyenne live down there, and they will give you a good welcome when you get there. They have been treated very well there, and the beef issues they receive do not have to travel so far, so the animals are in much better shape than the ones given here. I have been down there and know that the winters are not so cold and there is plenty of game to hunt. There is also much good land for you to learn how to farm on. It is the best place for you to be. You must go. You have no choice." The colonel bounced what was left of his mangled right hand in the palm of his left as he emphasized his last few words.

I wasn't sure if the part about having no choice was all that true, but my job was just to give them his words, not judge them, so I did what was expected of me.

Morning Star politely heard the man out then gave him a proposition of his own. "I did not sign any other paper since that one, though I have heard that a few here may have done so. Even so, the rest of us do not want to go. After you destroyed our camp, we struggled through much cold and were very hungry for a long time. When we came to the camp of Crazy Horse, most of his people treated us well, but Crazy Horse and some others were very stingy and mean to us. There are many of our men who would be willing to join with your soldier wolves and go out to fight against Crazy Horse and any others who decide to fight with him. If we stay, you will see how we can help you to whip these bad Indians."

After these words the old chief again arranged his blanket and sat back down.

A condescending smile crossed Mackenzie's face before I finished the translation.

"That is a kind offer you make," Mackenzie said, "but I am told that Crazy Horse is already on his way here. He should arrive in a few days, and I don't expect there to be any fighting when he arrives."

As I started into my translation to the Cheyenne, the colonel leaned over and had a quiet talk with Crook. It was still going on after I got done, and we had to wait on the two officers to finish. Mackenzie started nodding and soon rose back up and turned to face the Indians.

"I told you before that the land in the south is very good and that I know you will be happy once you go down there. Two of your own men, Living Bear and Spotted Elk, have even gone down there and come back to say it is so." The colonel gestured with his good hand toward the two agency men, who nodded in return.

"Here is something for you to consider," he continued. "You can all go down there to see this land, and you will see what we are all saying is true. If it is not what we claim it to be and you do not like the place and still want to come back after a year, we will make it so that can happen."

As if to seal the offer, Mackenzie looked over at Crook, who nodded his agreement.

The boys got busy after Mackenzie's offer. A serious discussion rolled from side to side and front to back as the chiefs considered the deal. From what I could see, most of them still disagreed and wanted to stay put.

Standing Elk rose to talk next. As usual he was decked out in some nice duds and had the part in his hair painted red, the sign of a man of high bearing. He too adjusted a fine blanket, looking every part a chief as he did so.

"We are all friends today," he began. "We no longer fight with each other, and that is good. Many people on both sides have been killed over the years, but today I know there will be no blood on the ground when we are done. This makes me happy."

The Council chief reached for Mackenzie's good hand to shake it. "You were the one I was afraid of when you came here last summer," he went on. "When you brought Red Cloud and Red Leaf's people back to the agency and took away their horses, I thought you would come for my lodge next. That is why I left. Today I have eyes to see that you only want to be my friend and that you will not mistreat me if I stay where you want me to stay. You are good to my people when we listen, and you give us what we need. Today we smoke the pipe of peace and shake each other's hand."

Mackenzie allowed Standing Elk to shake his hand the whole time he spoke. The kowtowing chief finally released it and turned toward the agency men who had been at his side since he arrived.

"I have talked this over with my friends Living Bear and Spotted Elk. They have both been down to see our relatives in the south, and they tell me it is a good place for us to go. The hunting is good there, so we will have enough to eat, and the white man will give us wagons and oxen and teach us how to follow his road." As he testified, Standing Elk slowly turned and addressed the rest of the Cheyenne, eventually making a complete circle and finishing his address again facing the officers. "You have told me that we can go down there, and if we do not like it after a year, we can come back here. That is fair."

He paused and gave the agency men one more look, then looked Mackenzie straight in the eye and declared, "We will do as you want. We will go there."

I couldn't start my translation without first giving Little Wolf and Morning Star a quick look. They exchanged a quick look between themselves as if each was checking with the other to see if what they heard was right. They were as shocked as I was that Standing Elk would be so bold as to speak for the entire tribe. Living Bear and Spotted Elk, on the other hand, sat there with eyes glistening, like a couple young-uns who had each been promised a piece of hard candy.

Now, if there had been only Cheyenne sitting in that room, I'm sure there would have been some cross words shared, but with the officers all right there on top of them like that, it would have been just as disrespectful for Little Wolf and the others to confront Standing Elk as it was for him to make such a self-serving commitment. Perhaps if there had maybe been a bit more time, someone might have raised an argument, but the jarring sound of gunfire brought our proceedings to a quick end.

The door was right in front of me, so I was the first to make it out of the cabin and into the yard. The soldiers who had been idling there were now in an all-out run through the gate with rifles at the ready. I fell in behind the flow of blue uniforms, stretching my neck to see beyond the entrance what all the fuss was about.

A skirmish line had been established just outside the gate, with every rifle aimed at a group of twenty or so mounted and armed Indians about a hundred feet away. The Indians sat wide-eyed and stock-still, obviously flat-out surprised to see that many soldiers come pouring out of the nonmilitary agency stockade. Lieutenant Clark, who was right on my heels, raced by hollering, "Hold your fire! Hold your fire! Nobody shoot, dammit!"

One by one, I recognized the whole bunch of them. Last Bull, Black Coyote, and Whetstone were there among several other young men who usually ran with the northern bands. Little Wolf had told me they had all decided not to go to a fort with either group when they split up. It must have been a little tougher than they figured to stay out by themselves, and they had decided to come in after all. They had staged a mock attack when they approached, unaware that the agency stockade was chock-full of soldiers.

Last Bull raised his empty hand slowly, letting us know he wanted to say something, so I moved up on the left side of the skirmish line, opposite from Clark.

"We are not here to fight. We come to join the camp."

The soldiers didn't move a muscle, even after I translated Last Bull's words. Clark peered at me as if he wanted me to vouch for the man. I gave the small band another look-over. Some of them had run with Water Walker, the fella I shot and killed a couple years earlier. The small and wiry Black Coyote was one of them, and he was giving me a real sour look.

"I believe I'd get their guns before you tell your boys here to stand down," I told the lieutenant.

"I'd say that's a good idea, Bill," Clark replied. "Sullivan, Fink, Ware, at the ready."

"Hold up!" I warned. "No quick moves till I explain what's going on to them."

Clark showed the three soldiers the palm of his hand, and they held still while I spoke to Last Bull.

"This soldier chief says you can join the camp here, but you must first give him your guns and bows. Everyone else here has already done this." I gestured toward the unarmed Council members who now stood watching the standoff from the open gate.

Last Bull had a few words with his boys. They all dismounted and prepared to hand over their weapons. All, that is, except Black Coyote, who urged his horse to take a couple steps toward me.

The sound of all the soldiers turning their rifles toward him stopped him from getting too close. He gave all the weapons a dismissive glance, then turned and looked toward the west, to where my lodge stood in a clearing by the river, about three hundred yards away. He turned to me with a smirk.

"*To'ėsemotšėške*, Long Knife, I see that you did not rebuild your cabin after I burned it down two winters ago. If you had not run to the soldiers like a coward that day, I would have killed you and let you burn with it. You are a white man, and you killed my friend Water Walker. That means I can kill you anytime I want now."

"He has given gifts to make things right." Little Wolf raised his voice to be heard from the gate. "He has settled the debt." The chief referred to the Cheyenne custom of giving gifts for compensation of one's wrongdoing to another. Doc Saville had helped me out by providing Water Walker's relatives with a half-wagon full of dry goods, but some from the northern bunch still thought I ought to be held more accountable.

"I have received no gifts," Black Coyote snapped back. "Water Walker was like my brother, and I have seen nothing but his body lying in the rocks up there." He thrust his chin toward the sandstone bluffs to the north. "And I saw this man riding with these soldiers against our camp in the mountains."

He continued to glare at me. I kept my eyes glued to his but heard the two distinctive clicks that told me he had cocked the hammer on the Springfield that he held across his saddle.

"Nothing is settled," he snarled.

It was only then that I realized I was standing in the middle of this whole fracas without a weapon of any kind.

Last Bull eased his horse up alongside his angry friend, and I thought, *Oh, shit, here we go now.* The deposed Kit Fox headman surprised everyone when he placed his hand on the stock of Black Coyote's gun and gave him a simple command.

"*Nėhe'še.* Stop."

He stared Black Coyote down for a bit, then just shook his head and said, "Now is not the time to fight. This will only make it harder on the others."

Black Coyote gave him an angry look, then me, then the soldiers who still had him in their sights. He let Last Bull slowly pull the rifle from his grasp and give a defiant holler. Then he turned and galloped off toward the Cheyenne camp.

"Let him go," Crook hollered from where he stood near the gate. "We have bigger matters at hand. One more hungry Indian won't be that much of a bother." Crook waved his hand as if he were shooing away a fly.

"Mr. Rowland," he called to me. "Come here and help me finish with these men before you assist the lieutenant with those."

For a moment I watched Last Bull ease the hammer forward and hold the rifle out to the closest soldier. I felt myself start to breathe again and coughed out a hoarse, "Yes, sir."

Crook started right back in, like nothing at all had happened. "My friends," he began. "It is good that we have come to an agreement and that you are willing to go to your relatives in the south. We will begin making arrangements for you to leave as soon as possible. You must go now and tell your families to ready themselves. I will let you know how soon you will be leaving."

I'd never seen a snake oil salesman shuck his marks any faster than the general got rid of those Indians that day. Of course, Last Bull, Black Coyote, and their bunch gave him the perfect distraction to turn their heads while he pushed them out the door and left them wondering what the hell had just happened.

The confused councilmen walked toward their horses at the hitching posts outside the stockade wall. Little Wolf, Morning Star, and the rest moved slowly with stunned expressions. Living Bear and his bunch once again circled Standing Elk and escorted him away. Each of them was grinning and eager to spread the news.

It wasn't until I turned back to help Clark disarm the new arrivals that it occurred to me—I had never seen the Cheyenne tribe so torn apart.

# A Journey Begins

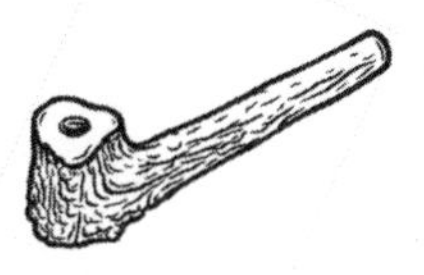

A COOL WAFT OF AIR STILL TUCKED IN THE MORNING SHADOW OF Lieutenant Clark's quarters slipped inside my shirt as I stepped from the saddle and headed for the officer's porch. I savored the brisk feel of it knowing that I'd be spending the rest of my day out in the sun and dust once we started our long ride south. The lieutenant had asked me to come see him one last time, and while I generally avoided saying goodbyes, I felt obliged.

Much had happened since that day at the agency when Standing Elk committed the tribe to going south. The telegraph line reached Camp Robinson that same day, and the noisy, click-clacking contraption at the end of the wire started giving us news of events happening around the region and the country—sometimes even the same day they happened.

One of the first messages to arrive told us that Two Moons and Ice had brought their band into the Elk River fort; more recently, we received word that Ice and a few others helped General Miles corner Lame Deer's bunch on a creek up near the Rosebud in Montana Territory. It sounded like they all but wiped them out, killing Lame Deer and several others.

This news hit Little Wolf and Morning Star hard. It was clear they had chosen the wrong agency. Those who went to the Elk River fort were doing exactly what his people had hoped to do by coming here to Camp Robinson. Instead, they were being sent away to the south.

The news that really got the talk going was when the Hat Creek telegraph station rattled off that Crazy Horse and his bunch were riding past the station on their way to surrender. The message said there was nearly a thousand of them. I imagined the agent there hiding under his desk as they filed by and reaching up with his hand to tap out the news.

Food was sent out right away as a sign of goodwill, and Billy went along as interpreter. They were moving very slow, so messengers rode back and forth for about a week as plans were made for their eventual arrival at the agency.

The day came when we headed up Soldier Creek to meet them. Clark took a squad of twenty Lakota scouts, and I rode with Little Wolf and about the same number of Cheyenne. Word was this was going to be a peaceful affair, but Little Wolf and the boys were champing at the bit to jump in if any fighting kicked up. They were still pretty pissed at Crazy Horse for the little bon voyage party he threw for them when they left his camp a few months earlier. Clark knew how Little Wolf felt and figured it would be best if we waited off to the side while he and the Lakota scouts went on ahead.

We watched the doings from behind a nearby rise while Clark and Billy sat on blankets with Crazy Horse and a few others talking peace. I was glad things went as planned. Even though the Cheyenne can hold their own in a fight, that creek bottom was swarming with edgy Lakota. They had quite a talk, and I could see a few gifts changing hands. By the time the lieutenant got up from the blanket to lead them in, he was wearing a war shirt and a headdress. He looked as odd in them as a Lakota private in an army uniform. I didn't dare crack a smile though, on account of Little Wolf and the boys was all in a sour mood watching Crazy Horse enter the agency like he owned the place.

Prepared to say my goodbyes, I stepped over the gate and climbed the steps to Lieutenant Clark's porch. Clark opened the door before I could knock, and I could see Billy and his friend, the Shangreau boy, sitting at a table inside. Neither of us acknowledged the other.

"Good morning, Bill. Thank you for coming." Clark's cheer seemed at odds with the dark feel of the room behind him. He turned to the boys and said, "I'll be right back," then stepped out onto the porch with me and closed the door.

"Well, so this is it, eh?" The lieutenant smiled up at me as we stepped to the porch rail and looked out over the parade ground.

"I do believe so," I replied.

"Bill," Clark paused as his smile broadened and his eyes glistened just a bit, "I . . . Thank you. You have been such an asset to me these last several months. Your insight and advice, all the hard work, not to mention the sign lessons—everything has been so helpful. We are where we are with these Indians due in large part to the services you've rendered. I can't say enough about how valuable you've been in all of this."

The lieutenant had been obsessed and distracted since Crazy Horse had come in, so it was nice to see him set all that fuss aside for just a moment. It wasn't his words but how he said them that told me the man I had learned to call friend was standing in front of me once again.

"Well, thank you, sir. I for sure appreciate hearing all that. It's been quite a ride since we left here last fall. I been thinking, before I go, I always figured I'd show you this one last sign someday. It's a bit easier than the one I showed you that morning up in the mountains."

I put the first two fingers of my right hand in front of my throat and raised them up and away from my forehead.

Clark's smile grew even broader. "Oh, I've known that one for some time, my friend, and I figured you'd show it to me sooner or later. I understand why you showed me the two-handed version first." Clark repeated the sign for friend that I had shown him the morning before the fight.

"And one last bit of advice, if you don't mind," I added.

"What's that?"

"Well, I seen Billy and the Shangreau boy in there, and I know you're all trying to figure out how to get one over on Crazy Horse. I've seen how you've been working them Lakota in the last few weeks—even harder than you worked the Cheyenne when they first come in. I see that you set Crazy Horse up as your sergeant, just like you did Little Wolf, to try to make the agency men uneasy. And I know that you're getting some of Crazy Horse's own friends to go against him. I gotta tell you, sir, that's all going to make for some bad medicine on down the road."

Clark's warm smile faded, and a cynical grin snapped back in place. "You know, Billy said he didn't like Crazy Horse and his friends being scouts either, but like I told him, nothing will make an Indian more pliable than the fear of losing a position of status. I swear, Bill, they aren't afraid of bullets, but tell them they'll no longer be a big chief and they come around to seeing things your way, just like that." Clark snapped his fingers as if he had just fired his pistol.

He was using Billy and his friend Shangreau just like he was using everyone else. Them two had grown pretty damned cocky in the time since Crazy Horse had come in, and Clark had leaned on them heavily to carry out his wishes. They were completely blind to how they were being finagled by the young officer.

I knew there was nothing I could say or do to get him to change his ways, so I just tried my best to smile and shook his hand. "Be careful, friend."

Clark's eyes softened for just a moment, like the part of him that knew better was trying to come back, but it was gone quick as it came.

I didn't look back until I'd stepped over the gate and had climbed up on Ulysses. I touched my hat in a weak salute, and the lieutenant did the same. I turned and headed for the river with a bad feeling crawling up my back.

I passed by Mackenzie's quarters and nodded at the two newspaper reporters who were waiting for the colonel to make his first outing of the day so they could pepper him with questions about what was going on with Crazy Horse.

"Morning, gentlemen," I said.

The gents looked me over like I was some old, crow-bait mule that some chiseler was trying to sell them.

"You know there's about a thousand Cheyenne fixing to leave the agency just across the river there."

"So?" one of them asked.

"Just thought you'd be interested is all. Morning, Colonel!"

The two easterners nearly fell over each other trying to get turned around to look at the colonel's still-closed door.

"That's not funny!" one barked at the back of my head as I rode past.

"I sure as hell thought it was," I said to Ulysses, who clearly didn't want to get involved.

It was late May, and the leaves on the ash trees along the river were dark green now and hardening out for the coming summer heat. I crossed the narrow but rising stream, turned east toward the agency, and eyeballed the sandstone bluffs on the north side. As it often did, the image of a gigantic, broken, and decayed jawbone came to mind. I imagined some great beast that had once dominated the countryside died in that spot centuries ago and had laid there to be picked over by scavengers and to bleach in the sun ever since.

The life the Cheyenne once knew was as gone as that great beast, and as gone as the buffalo. The Hills were crawling with gold miners now, and the new town of Deadwood had established a firm foothold there that would allow more and more of them to come. I'd seen the same thing happen with Denver City years back. It wouldn't be long now before that damned Man-infest Destiny overran another part of Indian country. I couldn't help but think that maybe it's a good thing we were all going south.

I rode from the shade of the ash trees to what was left of our camp. Junior and James had just finished loading the wagon with all our worldly belongings and now heaved the lodge canvas into the back of the buckboard to spread it out as a cover for everything. Willis helped Alice Jane climb up on top and handed his younger brothers up to her. Sis hovered over all of them, like a mama prairie hen, directing the show.

Lieutenant Lawton had been assigned to escort the Cheyenne down to Indian Territory, and I could see him waiting near the gate of the agency stockade with a couple squads of soldiers and about a dozen wagonloads of provisions. I told Junior that I had to go speak with the officer and that he should get everyone up to the camp on the other side of the stockade.

When he wasn't drinking, Lawton was as steady a hand as you'd want to handle a chore like this. He was sitting horseback as I rode up and looking off to the southeast, intently watching the goings-on in the Cheyenne camp about three-quarters of a mile away on the flat. The camp was being struck, and the people were packing their belongings in preparation for the long trip ahead of them. The few tall, traditional lodges had been taken down, and the lower willow-and-wall tent lodges were slowly being stripped of their covers. It was hard from this distance to see more than that.

Lawton was so focused on the camp that the private next to him had to announce me. "Squaw man's here, sir."

Lawton turned to me and smiled. "Morning, Rowland. Looks like great weather for a ride, eh? We're just giving the camp some time to muster, and we should be on our way here soon."

"Morning, 'Tenant. It is a pretty day to get started for sure," I replied.

Junior led the family past us and kept them moving on toward the Cheyenne camp. He and James rode horseback at the front while Willis drove the two-mule team pulling the wagon. Alice Jane watched over the five younger boys in the back of the wagon, and Sis brought up the rear of the short procession on foot, leading a third mule with a loaded travois.

The officer coaxed his horse a few steps closer to where I had stopped, away from the rest of the soldiers. We'd gotten to know each other a little better since that night in the cabin when he was drunk, and Lieutenant Clark was right—Lawton was actually a pretty kind and caring fella.

"That's quite a sizeable brood you've got there, my friend," the tall man said. "I don't think I've seen them all together at once like this."

"Yes, sir," I replied. "Figgered I might decide to become a cattle baron while I'm down south, and I'd have me a whole outfit of ready-made drovers to push 'em north when the time come."

Lawton chuckled at my grand scheme and watched my family move into the open space between the camp and the agency stockade. When they reached the midway point, he turned to me with a more serious tone in his voice. "They ever have trouble living between the cultures like they do?"

The officer's question was unexpected. Most white folks didn't generally inquire about half-breed offspring, other than to use them as interpreters or labor of some sort. I puzzled a bit then tried to answer.

"Oh, they have their days. I recall a time, back at Fort Laramie, I s'pose it was, when James was eight or nine. He come home pretty roughed up and crying. Said some of his friends had taken to calling him ve'ho'keso 'little white boy.' Weren't long after that, I seen him and a couple of his friends get shooed off a stoop by a commissary clerk who called 'em some 'thieving, little redskin, good-for-nuthins.'"

"They get it from both sides then?"

"Mhmm. Though, over time, and after a few scrapes, James became pretty good friends with most of them boys. Hell, he's related to them all anyway."

"And the commissary clerk?"

I traced the ragged curve of an old scar on the knuckles of my right hand. "Well, he found out who the boy belonged to and stopped. I'll just leave it there."

Lawton gave a small smile and a nod.

"Speaking of belonging," he said. "I must say I appreciate you making this ride with us. Being a white man yourself, we both know you don't have to go down there with us if you don't want to."

"Well, these are my wife's folk," I answered. "And after all these years, they've become my kin as well. I'd be a fish out of water if I weren't around them for any stretch of time."

"I imagine so," the officer said. "Lieutenant Clark tells me that you're originally from Missouri, though. Rather than riding off to Indian Territory, have you ever given any thought to going back there?"

"Not really. After near thirty years out here on the prairie, I got no call to go back there other'n to pay respects."

"It's been that long?"

"Yes, sir. Naw, I belong here with these folks, just as much as my young'uns do."

The lieutenant considered my words and nodded. "Well then, it'll be good for you all to have this chance to reunite with your southern relatives."

Lawton, like Clark, had no idea of the effect that this forced removal was having—and would continue to have—on these people. I decided I'd ask a question or two to see if the young officer might catch on.

"So, where you from, 'Tenant?"

"Hmm? Oh, I was born in Maumee, Ohio, but I suppose I'd have to claim Fort Wayne, Indiana. That's where I was raised for the most part. We moved around a bit, but I made a point of moving back first chance I got. I guess you could say that's where I belong."

"Always good to have a place you can say that about—'that's where I belong.'"

"S'pose you're right."

"A place like that becomes a part of who you are, how you see yourself, y'know?"

"Yes, I can see that."

"You plan on getting back again sometime soon?"

"Indiana? Oh, of course, Rowland. It's my home."

# Holding Hope

"All get ready to move. The soldiers are coming to take us from here." Standing Elk's deep voice faded as he rode around what remained of the ramshackle collection of wall tents, tepees, and lean-tos scattered across the prairie. Typically, a society crier would have been sent out to spread this news, but Standing Elk wanted to perform the duty himself. He had ridden the same circle the night before, letting people know that the time was drawing near when they would have to prepare their belongings for their long journey south.

Little Wolf watched from horseback on a small rise to the west as the council chief rousted the camp. Morning Star, Wild Hog, and Old Crow sat on their own mounts next to him. The chief had climbed the small rise before sunrise for his morning prayer, and when Morning Star noticed his friend had remained on the rise for longer than normal, he rode out to join him. The other two followed suit soon after. They all knew Standing Elk would make this ride and the effect it could have on the traditional leadership of the tribe.

"Standing Elk wants everyone to think that he decides for everyone now and that we all must listen to him," Wild Hog complained. "He has learned, like Living Bear, that the soldiers and agents favor those who say yes the most. The soldiers say, 'Move to this place, give us your land, give up your ways,' and they say, 'Yes, yes, yes.' He no longer looks for what is the best way for us all to live together; he only looks to find the best way to live for himself."

Old Crow replied as if he were trying to convince himself. "He wants to be the white man's chief, but the people will not agree to it. The council will not recognize him."

Wild Hog and Old Crow gave words to the frustration that Little

Wolf felt, but was not free to express. When the sound of the rifles had drawn everyone outside on the day when Standing Elk committed the entire tribe to go south, the chief sat still for several moments struggling with the fact that the man had spoken for all of the Cheyenne, and he had said nothing to refute him.

But had he not done that very thing when he, Morning Star, and a few others signed the treaty nine winters ago that allowed them to stay here with the Lakota? They did not come together with the entire council to make that decision, but he knew it was the right one to make and had steadfastly defended it nearly every day since. Now another man had made an agreement, supported by just a few others, saying that everyone should be sent away. How could he argue they had no right to do so, but he did? That arrogance was not fitting for a Cheyenne chief. Even if he felt he must express his disapproval, a chief's dissent in tribal concerns was better expressed by his silence on the matter, not through outspoken opposition.

It also made no sense to oppose Standing Elk in front of the soldiers when the man was giving them exactly what they wanted. He knew he would only appear weak and ineffective when they ignored his argument and still reached out to shake the councilman's hand. No, the best he could do was to show that he held no anger in his heart and was willing to let the people decide for themselves whether the man spoke for them or to express their own disapproval.

"Maybe they will agree with him, maybe they won't," Little Wolf said. "But if the white man wants to use him to get what they want, then we cannot change that. The council cannot change it either."

Wild Hog both admired and wondered at the chief's seemingly calm acceptance of the threat to his leadership. Morning Star added his thoughts.

"I am not the trusting child the new white father wants me to be, and I do not want to leave our home. Standing Elk should not have agreed to have us all go to the south, but he did, and it is done. Now I say, let us try what the white man asks of us. Let us go down there and see if it is a better place. I have been told it is a place where our children can go to the white man's schools and learn his ways, and where our women won't cry themselves to sleep over their dead husbands and starving children. If it is as they say, then I will go there and stay. If it is not, then I will come back here."

A thoughtful silence followed the older man's words while his friends considered the sound reason they held. Standing Elk was still visible in the distance, but his voice could no longer be heard. Behind him the canvas coverings were being stripped from the lodges, and the camp appeared to be dissolving before their eyes.

Little Wolf brought their attention back to the inevitable. "The soldiers will be coming for us soon, and I must see that my family is ready to leave. Let us all go now and do the same before we gather together at the front."

Wild Hog nodded. "I'm sure Standing Elk will already be there waiting for us."

Little Wolf rode away with Morning Star, each headed for where their lodges once stood and where their families waited for them. Though he had put on a calm front with the others, Little Wolf took advantage of his time alone with his old friend to talk freely.

"Your words were true. I am also not the child of the white man's new great father, or even of the old one, Grant. They both push us out of the way of those who want to come and take our land. A father does not treat his children so badly."

Morning Star nodded as the two approached what was left of Little Wolf's campsite. Lightning, Two Woman, Inside Woman, and White Voice were busy bundling what few belongings they had and loading them on a pair of travois. The soldiers had returned some of the horses so they could be used during the trip. The plan was that they would be sold when they reached Indian Territory and the money used to buy livestock.

"If these horses are sold when we reach the south, we will have no horses to return with. I do not trust their promise." Little Wolf raised his biggest concern. "You and I both touched the pen on the treaty that said this agency would be made and that we could stay here. That promise has been broken, like every other one we have been given, yet they still want us always to trust them like children? Why do we continue to hope that these promises will be kept?"

Morning Star paused before he continued on to his own family.

He was searching for words to answer when Day Woman walked through the sage nearby. In her arms rested a tightly wrapped No Belly. She had assumed the role of babysitter while her older sisters and mothers struck camp and prepared the family's belongings for the long trip ahead.

The young girl walked slowly, giving the appearance that she was simply wandering about, trying to keep the baby entertained. She bounced the infant with each step and sang softly as she edged closer to a travois at the next camp where Gathering His Medicine was helping his mother prepare to depart.

The boy fumbled with securing the family's belongings to the simple framework. His frustration was clear as he admonished himself for not remembering the knots he needed to use to tie the load. His father, Red Pipe, had always completed this task before each move, and the youth now wished he had paid better attention.

Little Wolf followed Morning Star's gaze to where his youngest daughter had drawn near the young hero who had saved her from the inconsiderate Lakota youth. She would never be so bold as to walk directly toward him, yet placing herself in his general vicinity as she had sent a subtle message of childish affection. Gathering His Medicine gave her a quick side glance and redoubled his efforts to cinch the ropes tighter around the bundle.

It was not a traditional courting practice, but Little Wolf and Morning Star both recognized that the two children, despite all the trauma and upheaval around them, had managed to develop their first childhood infatuation.

The older man smiled.

"There. They are why we hope."

# Acknowledgments

I AM CERTAIN THAT MY ANCESTORS WOULD WANT ME TO FIRST recognize our homeland. So many of them "threw away their lives" (using the Cheyenne vernacular of the time) to protect it, and so many died trying to return after they had been taken from it. As much as this is a story about people, it is also a story about place. Ultimately, it is a story about their dogged defense of the right of every individual to say, "This is who I am, and this is where I belong."

I owe many thanks for the information and help used in the telling of this story. I will acknowledge everyone as best I can over the course of all three volumes, but for this first, I would like to recognize those who I consider as being instrumental in the process of getting this very first one finished. I certainly apologize to anyone who feels wrongfully omitted.

I am grateful to my family, both immediate and extended, who knew me growing up but loved me anyway. That is not an attempt at humor. I came to writing late in life, due mostly to my personal inability to act in any way other than in my own self-interest. The old adage "write what you know," explains the ease with which certain less-than-prudent characters in this story were written.

The rest of the writing, at least that of any merit, is the direct result of a synchronistic anomaly called Windhover: a writing group whose members allowed a complete novice into their midst and nurtured whatever glimmer of potential they may have seen in him. Barbara Fifer, Bill and Betty Lovelady, Anne Bauer, Theresa Boyar, Chelsia Rice, Georgia Lovelady, Kerri Kumasaka, and all the others who filtered in and out of that room, thank you all for your honesty, your encouragement, and your trust.

My cousin, the late David Spang, and my sister Sandra Spang

both deserve recognition and thanks for their intense passion and ground-breaking work on Cheyenne genealogy. They provided me a tremendous amount of information and help in understanding not only who I am, where I'm from, but volumes more of the same information about all my relations.

I owe a special thanks to my brother-in-law, Francis Limpy, who is a respected elder and member of the Kit Fox Society, for his gentle explanations and guidance concerning matters of Cheyenne tradition, language and culture.

Ken and Cheri Graves have done an exceptional job in their stewardship and sharing of the land and the history of the Red Fork Battleground. They have welcomed and educated visitors and descendants alike at their family ranch outside Kaycee, Wyoming for years. Those interested in touring the battlefield are always warmly welcomed and treated like good friends.

The late Tom Buecker of the Nebraska Historical Society and the Fort Robinson State Park was a tremendous resource in the early days of my research, prior to his unfortunate passing. To say that his knowledge of the people and places of this era was prodigious would be an understatement. I never had the opportunity to meet him face to face, but every communication with him left me feeling like I had a good friend who wanted to help. He went above and beyond every time I reached out to him.

With regard to the actual production of this book, Kristen Hall-Geisler, of Indigo Editing, was an instant friend and champion of this book. I could not ask for better collaboration or professional expertise than what she provided in her effort to help this story be told in a good way. A big thanks also to Jonathan Brazee with edityourbook.com for his thoroughness, encouragement, and insight. Erin Greb, of Erin Greb Cartography, also expressed great personal enthusiasm and professional skill in bringing the face of Grandmother Earth alive via her detailed maps. Kathy Springmeyer and her team at Sweetgrass Books took me by the hand and walked me through the daunting process of designing, formatting and publishing in order that my words ended up in your hands.

I would like to extend a special thank-you to the Mari Sandoz

Heritage Society who first honored me with a very generous research endowment then helped with the publishing expenses for this volume. *Cheyenne Autumn* by Mari Sandoz was the first book on Cheyenne history that I ever read. It was clear from the day I opened the book that the author was a woman who cared deeply for the Northern Cheyenne and their plight. Her dedication to writing about all things related to her beloved plains is clearly exhibited at the foundation that bears her name. The directors and staff there reflect that dedication through their encouragement and support, for not only for this author, but for all who hold a love of the plains in their hearts and who strive to share it with their words.

I grew up hearing the Cheyenne language spoken around me on a regular basis, but have never been a fluent speaker. My ability to use Cheyenne words and phrases in this book comes as a direct result of years of hard work and research by those involved in the Cheyenne Studies Program at Chief Dull Knife College in Lame Deer and, in particular, those involved in the development of the Cheyenne-English Dictionary. For those interested in learning more about the Cheyenne language visit: http://cdkc.edu/cheyennedictionary/index.html.

Finally, but most importantly, were it not for the loving support and constant encouragement of my wife, Connie, I likely would not have come to write at all. Thank you, sweetie, for helping me to discover this passion. It is exceeded only by my passion for you. Who knew that all it would take was 493 clumsy attempts and every ounce of your patience? You are my sunshine.

# The Cheyenne Story Glossary

In his initial trip to the Northern Cheyenne reservation in 1954, noted anthropologist, educator, and author, Verne Dusenberry, observed that the Cheyenne language was the primary language spoken there. In 2007 when the Northern Cheyenne enrollment was estimated to be 9,496, the average age of the youngest speakers of the language was approximately 50. Currently, in 2019, with an estimated 11,266 enrolled members, it has been calculated that far less than 400 members speak the language fluently. I, personally, am part of the third generation of my family to have attended an Indian boarding school where speaking any native language was prohibited.

Things are changing. As I mentioned in the preface, the Cheyenne are a resilient people. Today, many tribes, including the Northern Cheyenne, are making heroic efforts to save their language by teaching it from K to 12 classes, immersion camps for youth, writing lesson materials in the Cheyenne language, etc.

I have long felt that any book that attempts to tell an accurate story of a culture should include their language in some way. Below is a list of the Cheyenne terms and phrases used in the writing of this story. Anyone interested in learning more about the Cheyenne language can visit: http://cdkc.edu/cheyennedictionary/index.html

- *Amaxėstse!* Run away!
- *Ea'o'tseo'o.* They are dancing the Scalp Dance.
- *Ehetometo.* It is true. (Something inanimate is showing truth.)
- *Ehoometatsesta.* He felt guilty about it.
- *Emanėstsenovo.* They made it. (They are safe.)
- *Emomata'ehe.* He/She is very angry and mean.
  (Singular. Very angry and mean.

- *Enėhevoone, "Namȧhehevesenehe'tovȧhtseme."* They said "We are all friends."
- *Epeva'e.* It's good. (More accurately, *Epėheva'e.*)
- *Epevo'eha.* Broken to pieces.
- *Esaahova'ėhevėheo'o.* They are nothing.
- *Eše'he.* Sun.
- *Esevone.* The Sacred Buffalo Hat.
- *Etavahe.* Dumb.
- *Etonėstao'o, nahko'eehe, naa tsehevasemeto?* How are my mothers and my little sister? (Literally younger sibling.)
- *Eve'ȯhketoneto.* It is bitter cold.
- *Haaahe!* General greeting or term of agreement, used only by males.
- *Haa'havėhane.* Personification of wind as a spiritual entity.
- *Haahpe'e'hahe!* Holler loudly!
- *Hahkota.* Grasshopper.
- *Heehe'e.* Yes. (Used only by women.)
- *He'emane'e.* One who walks as both man and woman.
- *He'konetanȯhtse.* Be strong.
- *He'kotomȧhtse, nėsema'haahe.* Be quiet, my friend.
- *He'kotoo'estse.* Sit still, calm down.
- *Hena'haanehe.* I am done talking, or, that is all there is.
- *He'nevo'ȧheotse!* Spread out! (More specifically, Scatter!)
- *Henova'e?* What is it?
- *Hestaneha.* Take him.
- *Hetomestȯtse.* The truth.
- *Homevonehnėstse.* Get down from your horse.
- *Ho'neheso.* Little Wolf.
- *Hoovehasėstse.* My friends.
- *Hoovehe.* Friend. (Male to male.)
- *Hosovo'ne'eohtse!* Step back!
- *Ho-tashko.* War lodges.
- *Hova'ȧhane.* No.
- *Katse'e.* Little girl.
- *Maahotse.* The Sacred Arrows.
- *Maešehe.* Brother-in-law.

- *Ma'haokohtše.* Old Crow.
- *Ma'heono.* Sacred Powers.
- *Ma'heo'o.* The Holy One.
- *Mahta'sóomah.* A living spirit that is divided into four parts, two of them good and two of them "crazy."
- *Mo'ehno'hame.* Horses.
- *Motse'eoeve hėstaneheono.* Sweet Medicine's People.
- *Naešena'so'enohe.* I am full already.
- *Nȧhtanėheševe.* I will do that.
- *Nahtse.* Daughter.
- *Naměšeme.* Grandfather.
- *Nanehama'oene!* They sneak up on us!
- *Nanehöve Memeehe.* I am your Grandpa.
- *Navenötse epėhevenono'e.* My home looks nice.
- *Nea'eše.* Thank you (said to one person.)
- *Nea'ěšemeno.* Thank you (from more than one person to more than one person.)
- *Ne'anöhevonehnėstse.* Climb down from there.
- *Ne'ěšehosotomoo'ėstse.* You rest now.
- *Nėhe'še!* Stop!
- *Nehne'ėstosemėstse!* Pull me out!
- *Neho'e.* Father.
- *Neneeva'eve?* Who are you?
- *Nenomahtse'heoneve.* You are a thief.
- *Nepėhevehetaneve.* You are a good man.
- *Nestsėhe'ooestse!* Come here quickly!
- *Nėstseve'ponenene!"* Do not shoot!
- *Nėstsevovohponeexoveestsehena.* You must wear a warm coat.
- *Netaexo'asenȧhnemane.* Let us build a fire.
- *Netoněšenohtovetsėhesenestse?* How do you know how to talk Cheyenne?
- *Nevaahe tseneveohtaoo'ėstse?* Who is on the scaffold?
- *Neve'ea'xaame.* Don't cry.
- *Neve'nėheševe!* Stop doing that!
- *Nexhaahepe'e'haestse!* Holler loudly!
- *Noheto.* Let's go.

- *No'hovaoohe'tome!* Run to the hills!
- *No'hovehne.* Move out of the way.
- *Noma'keso.* Little Fish.
- *Nomonėhe'še.* Alright, let us go ahead.
- *Nonotoveohtsėstse!* Hurry! (*Nonotoveohtse!* - if said to more than one person.)
- *Noohe!* Expression of surprise (used only by women.)
- *Novavose.* Bear Butte.
- *Noxa'e, hetsėheohe nėšeešėhoo'e.* Wait, stay here.
- *O'komoxhaahketa.* Little Coyote.
- *Onetȧhevo'ha'ehnėstse.* Walks Different.
- *Otahe!* Listen!
- *Oxėse tsėhetoo'ȯhtse.* Look away.
- *Shaa!* Expression of surprise, wonder, or exasperation.
- *Sṓ'taesėstse.* A separate tribe that was absorbed by, yet remains distinct from, the Tsitsistsas. Called "the Left Behind People" by some, "the Ridge People" by others.
- *Taesetove e'evo'ȧxeha!* Cut it in half." (Literally, "Cut him in half" because a robe is animate in Cheyenne.)
- *Tahoohto'aheotse! Enėxhooheama'haso'hestove!* Run home! The riders are coming!
- *To'ėsemotšėške.* Long Knife.
- *To'ha'ovenano!* Stop them!
- *Tsehehamooneto.* Uncle.
- *Tse'tohe mȧhavoo'ėšenano tseevėhetȯhoneto.* Show all of them what you are signing.
- *Tsitsistas.* We who are Cheyenne. (The technically correct spelling is *Tsetsėhestahėse* which is difficult to read.
- *Tsitsistats.* Those who are Cheyenne.
- *Ve'ho'e.* White men.
- *Vo'aa'e.* Antelope.
- *Vo'keme.* Winter Man.
- *Vooheheve.* Morning Star.
- *Xamaevo'ėstaneo'o.* Native people.

# End Notes

*The Cheyenne Story* is anchored in historical fact. Because of this I feel a responsibility to indicate as best I can those areas where I present situations and events that are contrary to commonly accepted historical accounts. I also need to discuss those places where I take creative license and explain why.

Along with the different names for members of Little Wolf's immediate family, I present other facts that some folks might take issue with. I'll begin with what I consider to be the most benign. John G. Bourke, General Crook's aide-de-camp, made an erroneous assumption in his diary that the battery used in the Camp Robinson gambling scene came from the camp hospital. Electricity was only used in cutting-edge medical procedures during that time and, given that Camp Robinson was one of the most remote army outposts with medical capabilities at the time described as being little better than first aid, it is very doubtful that such a modern innovation would be available there. The post was, however, awaiting the imminent arrival of a telegraph line, which utilized such a battery for transmission.

Another deviation from a commonly held belief is when Standing Elk tells Colonel Mackenzie that he left Camp Robinson because he was afraid of him. Many history books attribute this statement to Morning Star, who actually left Camp Robinson in July of 1876, a full month prior to Mackenzie's arrival there in August. It is also well documented that Standing Elk slipped away from Camp Robinson to join the "roamers" at about the same time that Mackenzie made surrounds on Red Cloud and Red Leaf's camps. The claim that it was Morning Star can be traced to a column for the *New York Tribune* dated April 23, 1877. Given the well-documented whereabouts of both Cheyenne leaders the prior year, it's clear that the correspondent likely suffered from a case of "they-all-look-alike-itis."

A third point I make draws upon recently made observations by James Leiker and Ramon Powers, as well as John H. Monnett, who present clear reasoning as to why it was more likely that Little Wolf's younger brother, Big Nose, was the primary agitator of Captain Fetterman and his troops at Fort Phil Kearny in 1866 and not Crazy Horse, as popular history likes to claim.

Finally, a misconception that is entrenched in popular history is that it was Dull Knife's camp that Mackenzie attacked in the Bighorns. Frank North recognized in his diary that it was, in fact, Little Wolf's camp, as did Bill Garnett in the Eli Ricker interviews. Also, in his first monthly report as an agent of the Red Cloud Agency in November of 1873, John J. Saville noted that

> *On the 4th of November, after the departure of "Dull Knife" and his party, the Cheyenne met in council and deposed "Dull Knife," and appointed "Little Wolf" to be chief in his place.*

To leave no doubt, Morning Star (aka Dull Knife) himself stated in an 1879 interview with a Dakota correspondent from the *New York Herald*, while convalescing on the Pine Ridge reservation, that he had "resigned his chieftainship in favor of Little Wolf," and that at the fight in the Bighorns, Little Wolf was then "in command as chief." There are several reasons why Dull Knife was, and still is, consistently recognized as the principal chief, all of which would make for a great journal article someday.

My greatest deviation from historical fact involves the two youths, Day Woman and Gathering His Medicine. As I mentioned in the preface, not much is written about the children of the Cheyenne during this time period other than that they were terrified, they were taken, or they died. Day Woman was actually about five years old at the time, and I elevated her to age eleven. Gathering His Medicine was actually twenty-one, and I reduced his age to twelve. By doing this I feel they are better able to provide a voice for a very important and pivotal age group. They are the ones who would have been involved in the normal course of learning who they and their people were and how they all fit into the world. Instead, they watch everything they've known get destroyed and witness the deaths of friends and family alike.

For brevity I have used Chopping Woman's son No Belly (a fictional name) to represent three younger children who, according to census rolls, were in Little Wolf's household at that time. That said, I do not apologize about the large number of Cheyenne names used in this story. The fact is, many more could have been included. This is the story of a tribe, and limiting the narrative to only a few is disrespectful to the many others who struggled or died during this time.

While I did exclude the details of the Battle at Belly Butte, I respectfully acknowledge the Cheyenne, Big Beaver, and Lakota men who gave their lives there.

According to Kingsley Bray in *Crazy Horse: A Lakota Life*, Little Wolf had eleven horses shot by the Akacita when he left Crazy Horse's camp. However, the manner in which the rest of the tribe left camp is fictional.

The burial detail in the story did not actually take place. It occurred to me as I was writing, and I'm sure it was heavy on the hearts of those who I portray as having taken part, that such an action should have been taken.

For readability and to avoid confusion, I have made several difficult but necessary decisions. I refined some character's names. Crow Split Nose and Crow Necklace were changed to simply Split Nose and Necklace for obvious reasons, and Sitting Bear was changed to Bear Sitting Down to avoid readers confusing him with Sitting Bull.

I must acknowledge my omission of the highly respected allies and relatives of the Cheyenne, the Northern Arapaho or Sage People. My goal was to keep a clear focus on the Cheyenne to avoid confusion, and no disrespect was intended.

As for the Cheyenne themselves, I make no mention in the story of the ten separate and distinct tribal bands of the tribe, nor the important distinction between the *Só'taeseѐstse* and the *Tsitsistas*, two historically unique segments of the tribal body. I also intentionally do not mention familial relationships that might cloud the water throughout the story. By that I mean such relationships as the character Bull Head being the half-brother of Little Wolf, or Iron Tooth Woman's relationship to Sis Frog and Lightning, or some claims that Morning Star and Little Wolf were second cousins. There were many other such involved and intricate relationships that I chose not to mention.

I have modified the families of Morning Star, Wild Hog and Red Pipe, partly to aid the telling of the story and partly due to incomplete or conflicting records. I invite the reader to do their own research to ascertain for themselves the most accurate understanding of these families.

Just as families of any nationality do, when the Cheyenne come together, there is often much connecting to one another through our common ancestors. It is vitally important to understanding who we are and how we're related. I ask the forgiveness of anyone who feels their ancestor was neglected or slighted in any way through the writing of this story. My intent was to portray a more emotionally complex picture of the Indian Wars as well as a more complex view of all of those involved. In the Cheyenne Journey of Life, it is believed that we all possess *mahta'sóomah*, a living spirit that is divided into four parts, two of them good and two of them "crazy." Please be patient and allow the story and the spirit of each character to evolve.

And lest it be forgotten, whether we are Cheyenne, Lakota, Arapaho, Irish, English, French, Iranian, Ethiopian, four-legged, winged, or grown from Grandmother Earth . . . we are all related.

*Hena'haanehe*